Silhouette

is pro...

Together for
Christmas

Will new love make this a Christmas to remember?

LYNNETTE KENT

is a child of the North Carolina mountains but seems destined to find herself living anywhere *but* the mountains. Her family moved to Florida when she was nine, inspiring her with a lifelong love of the ocean.

Contrary to her husband's preference for nice hotels, Lynnette would rather sleep in a tent than a bed, and would rather rake leaves than vacuum a carpet. And she'd rather spend more time writing romance than raking or vacuuming. Or, for that matter, sleeping!

SHERRY LEWIS

learned to read at the age of four by listening to her parents read aloud. Since Sherry learned to read so easily, it's not really surprising that books would become her first love. As a child, she dreamed of writing Nancy Drew mysteries. As she grew older, her dreams changed only a little and her dream of writing novels never diminished in spite of detours along the way.

She lives at the base of Utah's Wasatch Mountains with her youngest daughter, who keeps life fresh and interesting. Her oldest daughter lives nearby and attends a local university. Sherry also lives with three cats who love to "help" crochet and jockey for position on the arm of her writing chair every morning.

Together for
Christmas

by

Lynnette Kent

&

Sherry Lewis

*Silhouette and Colophon are registered trademarks of
Harlequin Books S.A., used under licence.*

*First published in Great Britain 2005
Silhouette Books, Eton House, 18-24 Paradise Road,
Richmond, Surrey TW9 1SR*

TOGETHER FOR CHRISTMAS © Harlequin Books S.A. 2005

The publisher acknowledges the copyright holders of the
individual works as follows:

Shenandoah Christmas © Cheryl B Bacon 2001
The Christmas Wife © Sherry Lewis 2003

ISBN 0 373 60393 2

161-1105

*Printed and bound in Spain
by Litografia Rosés S.A., Barcelona*

Shenandoah Christmas

by

Lynnette Kent

For my friends who meet on Sundays
at the corner of Ann and Bow Streets,
especially all the children
who share the laughter and the songs.

And for the women who have taught me so much
about music and about sisterhood—
Charlyne, Sharon, Linda and Maryann.

PROLOGUE

Eighteen years ago

"WE NEED more feathers." Ten-year-old Cait Gregory sat back on her heels and surveyed the project on the floor in front of her. "We've still got half a wing to cover."

Her sister, Anna, bent over and pressed a feather into the tiny bit of glue she'd squeezed out of the bottle she held. "We don't have another pillow."

"Daddy has pillows."

"Are you crazy?" Anna pushed back her curly red bangs and stared at Cait in horror. "He wouldn't let us use his pillows. He's gonna be mad enough that we used our own."

"He's a minister—he has to do what's good for Christmas."

"You only say that because you're the angel in the Christmas Eve pageant this year." Anna tried to be the boss, just because she was two years older than Cait. "There's lots more important stuff about Christmas than that."

"No, there's not." On her feet now, Cait propped her hands on her hips. "The whole point of Christmas is the story the pageant tells. And the main part of the story is when the angel announces the birth of the baby to the shepherds. I've already got the words learned. 'Fear not, for I bring you good tidings of great joy....Ye shall find the babe wrapped in swaddling clothes, lying in a manger.' See?''

Her sister shook her head and glued another feather onto the shapes she'd drawn and cut out of white poster board. Anna was an artist, for sure. The wings—wider than Cait's shoulders and as long as she was tall—curved just like the pictures of angels she'd seen in books. Covered with millions of tiny white feathers, they would be the best wings any announcing angel ever had.

As soon as she found one more pillow.

Prowling the house, she tested every cushion she came across, but only the pillows on her dad's bed had feathers. Cait stood gazing at them for a long time. Did she dare?

Later that night, lying flat on her bed in the dark room she and Anna shared, with tears drying on her cheeks and her stomach growling because she hadn't gotten dinner, she wasn't sorry she'd taken her dad's pillow. Nothing mattered more than making the pageant the best it could possibly be. This was Christmas, after all.

And for Cait, Christmas would always be the most wonderful day of the year!

CHAPTER ONE

The present

WITH HIS CHISEL poised to make a delicate cut, Ben Tremaine looked up as footsteps crunched through the fallen leaves outside the open door. "Maddie? Shep? That you?"

He had just enough time to put down the tool before two small cyclones whirled into the workshop, bringing with them the crisp scent of autumn. "Daddy!" Maddie dropped her book bag and threw herself into his arms. "We're home!"

When Shep wiggled in beside her, Ben closed his arms tight around his children, kissing first Shep's smooth blond head, then Maddie's tight dark curls. This was his favorite part of the day. "Good to see you guys. How was school?"

"I got a hundred on my math test." Maddie settled in on his knee. "We had a handwriting quiz—Miss Everett said mine was the prettiest in the class. We played hopscotch at recess and I won. And during story time Miss Everett read what I asked her to—'How the Leopard Got His Spots' from *Just So Stories*. You remember that one, Daddy?"

"I sure do. Sounds like you had a great day. How about you, Shep?" Without answering, the little boy slipped from his hold and moved to the workbench, running his fingers lightly over the fretwork veneer Ben had been working on. "How'd school go?"

His son shrugged one shoulder and gave a small nod. Knowing the futility of pushing any harder—Shep hadn't said a single word to anyone in the eighteen months since his mother died—Ben stifled a sigh of frustration and looked at Maddie again. "This is Wednesday, so you went to choir right after school, didn't you?"

"Brenna's mom took us." The little girl's face brightened with enthusiasm. "Miss Caitlyn played her guitar and sang us some of the songs she wrote. They're so beautiful, I can't believe it."

This wasn't the first time Ben had heard about the wonders of Caitlyn Gregory. "I bet you'll be glad when Miss Anna can come back, though. I know how much you like her as your regular choir teacher."

"Miss Anna's really nice." Maddie nodded. "But Miss Caitlyn kinda…sparkles." She gave a worshipful sigh.

"I'm sure she's fun to sing with. Just remember—" He debated the warning for a second, then decided to go with it. "Remember she won't be here for very long. She's pretty famous and she has lots of work to do in other places. It's nice of her to come and help out, but once Miss Anna's baby is born and the doctor says she can get back to normal, Miss Caitlyn will be gone."

"I know." Maddie's smile dimmed. "Brenna said Miss Caitlyn's some kind of big rock star or something." She slid off his lap and started toward the door, then turned back, her face shining again. "But Christmas is only nine weeks away. Maybe she'll be here at least until Christmas. Wouldn't that be neat, Daddy? I bet she sings carols like an angel!"

Ben called up a halfhearted grin. "I wouldn't be surprised. You and Shep go into the house and get started on your homework. I'll close up and be right there.'' He turned to straighten his tools and clean up the workshop while the kids streaked across the backyard in the gathering dusk.

As he swept cherrywood shavings into a corner, he realized with surprise that more than two-thirds of October had come and gone. Having accustomed himself to the slow pace of life in the country, Ben rarely looked very far ahead anymore. He hadn't realized how soon the holidays would arrive.

Another Christmas, he thought, deliberately relaxing the set of his jaw and the tight grip of his hands on the broomstick. *I can hardly wait.*

THE THIRD TIME her brother-in-law David commented on the number of meals they were eating out of cans, Cait's redheaded temper caught fire. She spent Friday morning studying Anna's cookbooks and making a grocery list. Just after lunch, while her sister napped, Cait headed for the only grocery store in Goodwill, Virginia.

Driving through the little town, Cait rolled down the car windows to catch the breeze. In the past ten years she hadn't had time to notice the seasons much, and she was realizing what she'd missed. Old trees lined the narrow streets, their leaves turning gold and maroon and brilliant orange with the arrival of chilly fall nights. The forested mountains to the west blazed in the early afternoon sunshine, an impressionist collage of all the reds and yellows imaginable. Eastward stretched the rolling pastures and fields of the Shenandoah Valley, their gentle summer greens fading now to tawny. Under a wide blue sky, the ancient hills imparted a sense of time to spare. Cait hadn't felt so free of obligations in years.

Time had, in face, been kind to Goodwill. Set on lush lawns among the colorful trees, many of the houses in the area dated back a century or more; the town had been settled before the American Revolution and had escaped most of the ravages of the Civil War. Windows paned with antique wavy glass looked out over a brick-paved main street called, simply, the Avenue. Old buildings of brick and stone and painted wood siding had aged gracefully, adapting to changed circumstances and purposes with dignity. What had once been the schoolhouse was now a computer software business. The one-time blacksmith's stable had become a bookstore, and a dress boutique occupied the shoemaker's shop.

Yet the bakery still used wood-fired ovens built two hundred years ago; descendants of the first attorney in town still practiced in his original building and the physician's office still housed a pediatrician. Modern intrusions were few and carefully designed, including Food Depot, one block east of the Avenue. Old brick with white wood trim disguised a very modern grocery, while the mature trees standing between the parking spaces out front created an arbor on what would have been a bare asphalt plain.

Inside the store, Cait pulled out her list and prepared to concentrate on shopping. Her dinner preparation usually consisted of making reservations or ordering take-out food. But she didn't expect to have much trouble cooking a real meal. How hard could pot roast be?

Potatoes were the first problem. Idaho? Golden? Red? New? Cait tried to visualize the last pot roast she'd eaten, but ten years on the road, staying in a different town every night, had buried the memory too deep. She decided she liked the look of the small red ones, and moved on to carrots. Organic versus…what? Did organic change the taste? Would David notice? And should she peel them herself, or be lazy and get the ones already peeled?

The vegetables were easy, however, compared to the meat department. All the plastic-wrapped roasts looked the same. The recipe called for rump roast or shoulder roast or round roast. Which was the best? How was she supposed to choose?

She flipped her braid over her shoulder. "Why isn't beef just beef?"

"I beg your pardon?" A baritone voice, soft southern vowels, obviously startled.

With her cheeks heating up, Cait glanced at the man standing beside her. "I...um...was talking to myself. Sorry." He flashed a half smile and returned to studying packs of hamburger.

She took advantage of his preoccupation to steal another look. This was a man to write songs about. Dark-blue eyes, wheat-gold hair in short curls that reminded her of an ancient Roman statue, impressive shoulders under a cinnamon-colored sweater. He reached down to pick up a package of meat, giving her a view of lean hips and long legs in faded jeans.

Wow. Cait mentally fanned herself. She'd shared the stage with several of Hollywood's biggest heartthrobs at an awards ceremony a few months back, but none of them had left her breathless like this. Who knew Anna's tiny town could offer such interesting options?

"Excuse me." Following her impulse, she tugged on the elbow of his sweater.

Her reward was another chance to gaze into those deep, deep eyes. "Yes, ma'am?"

A gentleman all the way. Better and better. "Do you know anything about pot roast?"

His brows, slightly darker than his hair, drew together. "Pot roast?"

Cait gestured at the meat case. "Which one works the best?"

That small smile of his broke again. "Oh. No, I don't do the fancy stuff. But I think my mother-in-law uses chuck roast." Leaning across her, he lifted a huge hunk of meat out of the cooler one-handed. "Like this."

"Ah." Cait held out her hands and he eased the roast into her grasp. Mother-in-law. So much for options. "Thanks for the help."

He nodded. "Anytime."

Don't I wish. Feeling like a kid denied her lollipop, Cait pushed her cart toward the dairy section. Anna needed to drink milk every day. Two percent? Whole? Skim?

And why were all the really great men already married, anyway?

The ultimate torture was standing behind that same guy in the checkout line—her chance to pick up all the details she'd missed before. An easy stance, a strong jawline, square, long-fingered hands which saw their share of physical labor, if a few healing cuts were anything to go by. Not to mention all the kid groceries in his cart—small juice cartons, boxes of animal crackers, fruit roll snacks and cereal with marshmallow shapes. The guy not only had a mother-in-law. He had children.

A tune from a few years back came to mind, a daughter singing about the strength and love in her daddy's hands. This man had that kind of caring, working hands. Lucky kids.

Lucky wife.

Cait shook her head and fixed her gaze on the tabloids in the rack beside her cart. After ten exhausting years, her music career was about to break into the big time. She had a New Year's Eve slot on a major network show and an album scheduled to start production in the spring. Who needed a husband and kids? Or a house to keep?

Anna was the domestic sister, the homemaker, the mom-to-be. Cait knew herself for the wanderer, seldom happy for more than a little while in one place. She hadn't seen a town she couldn't leave. Hadn't met anyone she wanted more than she wanted the smiles and the tears, the sighs and the applause, of a live audience.

But she had to admit, watching the guy in the cinnamon sweater reach for his wallet, that an available man who looked as good as this one might tempt her into changing her mind.

BEN FELT the presence of the woman behind him in the checkout line as if the air around them stirred slightly every time she took a breath. That minute by the meat case had left him with fleeting impressions. Hair in every shade from gold to copper, tamed into a thick braid over her shoulder. Eyes the color of spring leaves, fringed by dark lashes. Skin as smooth as a little girl's, sprinkled with freckles. A cigarettes-and-whiskey kind of voice which, along with the fact that she looked very much like her sister, told him who she must be. Cait Gregory, superstar, was shopping for pot roast at the Food Depot in Goodwill, Virginia.

He could see what Maddie meant about "sparkle." Ms. Gregory possessed the kind of charisma he'd noticed in movie stars and politicians during his years with the Secret Service in Washington. If what he'd heard about her recent concert tour was true, she could reduce a rowdy crowd to absolute, focused silence with the sound of her voice. Even "pot roast" sounded sexy when Cait Gregory said it.

Unloading his sacks of groceries into the back of the Suburban, Ben sat behind the wheel with the motor running and faced the fact that he should have introduced himself to his kids' choir director, if only to be neighborly. They would meet at church eventually. She would wonder why he'd kept quiet, especially since she'd obviously been willing to give him more than just the time of day.

Maybe that was why he hadn't said more. Cait Gregory demanded acknowledgment as an attractive, sensual member of the very opposite sex. The soft green sweater that molded the curves of her breasts, the snug jeans that emphasized the flare of her hips...

Ben shook his head and jerked the truck into reverse. He'd noticed a hell of a lot more about Cait Gregory than he was comfortable with. He hadn't thought about a woman as *female* since Valerie's death, and he didn't want to start now.

Especially not with this particular woman. One look at her red hair, at the hint of temper in the arch of her eyebrows and the tilt of her lips, foretold every kind of emotional experience but peace. And peace was all Ben really wanted.

So she could just take her tempest somewhere, and to someone, else. He did not intend to pursue more than the slightest, most temporary acquaintance with the famous Ms. Gregory. His life worked okay these days; he gave everything he had to taking care of Shep and Maddie and to building his custom furniture business. That was the way he liked it and nobody was going to make him change his mind.

Ben dared them even to try.

ON FRIDAY AFTERNOON, Harry Shepherd got home from work an hour later than he'd planned. He usually finished early at the office on Fridays, but today's meeting had run long, there had been a report to generate afterward, and some new figures faxed in just as he was getting ready to leave. As vice president of one of the country's leading furniture manufacturers, he never walked out the door until the week's work was done.

But the grandkids were due for supper any minute. He and Peg took them on Friday nights to give Ben a little privacy and a chance to get out, if he wanted, without worrying about Maddie and Shep. As far as Harry could tell, though, all his son-in-law did with his free time was go back to work. Harry wished that would change. Harry had been the one to suggest Ben set up his own custom-made furniture business and he knew that getting a new enterprise off the ground required a great deal of focused effort. But some time off now and again brought a fresh attitude and increased energy to the job. Besides, Ben needed a social life. A man shouldn't spend all his days and nights with his kids.

Headlights flashed on the trees at the end of the driveway as Ben's Suburban pulled in. Within seconds, Maddie jumped out and grabbed Harry around the waist. "Hi, Grandpa! We're here!"

"I can see that, Magpie." He rubbed his hand over her curls, so like her mother's had been at that age. Shep trailed behind her, his head down as he studied the toy plane in his hands. "Very nice," Harry said. "Is that the one that broke the sound barrier?" The little boy glanced up out of the sides of his eyes and nodded, but didn't volunteer any more contact. Would they ever see him smile again, or hear his voice?

"Hey, Harry." Ben joined them and they walked as a

group up the steps onto the porch. "You sure you feel up to dealing with these characters tonight?"

Peggy had opened the front door. "Of course we do. Come in, Maddie, darling. Oh, Shep, how did you get that tear in your sweater?"

"That's what little boys are designed for, Peg." Harry put a hand on her shoulder, leaned in for his welcome-home kiss. Her cheeks were still rose-petal smooth, although she and Harry had both hit sixty this year. "The apparel industry counts on him to make sure his clothes don't last too long."

Unlike *Harry's* company, which made furniture that lasted for generations. He took a lot of pride in having helped to build a reputation for quality.

Peggy clucked her tongue, examining Shep's sleeve. The boy pulled away, leaving the sweater hanging in her hands. "Shameful waste, if you ask me." She sighed, but only in part, Harry knew, because of the garment. Shep's withdrawal worried her deeply. "I'll mend it later. Meanwhile, all of you come in. I've got some cheese and crackers set out. What would you like to drink, Maddie?"

Kneeling at the coffee table, Maddie stacked cheese slices and crackers into a tower. "Can I have a soda?"

"No." Ben still stood near the front door. "You can have juice. Or milk."

Maddie stuck out her lower lip. "Apple juice, I guess, Grandma."

"Excuse me?" Her father's voice was stern.

The little girl got the message. "Please could I have apple juice, Grandma?" She glanced at her brother, who nodded without looking up. "And for Shep, too."

"Right away. Ben, what can I get you?"

"Nothing, thanks. I need to get back to the house."

"Oh, but—" To her husband's surprise, Peggy actually

blushed. "I thought you might stay for dinner tonight. I made a big pot roast and...invited some extra people."

That was a surprise. Friday nights were supposed to be just for the grandkids.

Ben evidently had similar ideas. "Thanks, Peggy, but some other time." Backing up, he reached for the door handle. As he touched it, the bell rang. He gave his usual half grin. "I'll get it."

The grin widened when he glanced outside. "Hi, Anna. How are you? You're looking great, as usual." He drew Anna Remington into the house with his left hand and extended his right to her husband. "Hey, Pastor Dave. What's going on?"

In the midst of giving Anna a kiss on the cheek, Harry saw Ben's jaw drop for a second, saw him swallow hard. "Come in. Please."

Harry understood Ben's shock when Caitlyn Gregory stepped across the threshold. Anna was a sweet and pretty woman, but her sister...*well*. Caitlyn wasn't wearing anything fancy, just a gold sweater and a long, narrow black skirt. But she lit up the room like a Roman candle.

He cleared his throat. "Ms. Gregory, I don't think we've met. I'm Harry Shepherd."

"I'm pleased to meet you, Mr. Shepherd." She crossed the front hall to shake his hand. That voice alone would scramble a man's brains. Which might be why Ben was still standing by the open door, letting in the October chill.

"Cait, this is Peggy." Anna brought her sister farther into the living room. "And I think you know Maddie and Shep."

"I certainly do. Two of my favorite choir members." She smiled at Peggy. "Thanks for inviting me, Mrs. Shepherd."

Peg waved away the formality, as she always did.

"Harry and Peggy will do just fine, Caitlyn. And this is Ben Tremaine. Our son-in-law."

The singer turned back toward Ben with what looked like reluctance. She put out a hand. "How do you do?"

Ben barely brushed her palm with his. "Good to meet you. I've heard a lot about you." Their eyes locked for a second, then each looked away. Ben finally shut the front door.

Harry stared at his wife, a suspicion forming in his brain. Was there more to this dinner than just friends getting together?

But Peg was immersed in her hostess role, not open to receiving unspoken messages. "Harry will take your coats. Anna, you sit yourself down on the sofa. I'll bring some juice for you and the children. David, Caitlyn, will you have something? A glass of wine, perhaps?"

The younger woman smiled. "Wine, please."

The minister took a seat next to his wife. "That would be great, Peggy."

She looked at Ben. "You'll be staying, of course. What can I get you?"

Taking Ben's jacket as he shrugged it off, Harry heard him sigh. Then he said, "A glass of wine sounds good. Can I help?"

"No, no. Y'all just sit and talk. I'll be right back." Peg disappeared toward the kitchen. Harry shut the front door, then went to lay the coats on the bed in the guest room. When he returned to the living room, only Maddie was attempting conversation. Shep was busy landing his supersonic aircraft under the coffee table.

"My friend Brenna says you're a big star." The little girl bit into a cracker and chewed for a second, staring seriously at Caitlyn Gregory, then swallowed. "Do you like singing for people?"

"All I wanted to be—when I grew up—was a singer." Cait sat in the armchair closest to the children, leaning forward with her elbows on her knees. She wore a column of thin gold bracelets on each wrist, which drew attention to her pretty hands.

"Our dad used to say Cait sang before she could talk," Anna told Maddie.

Harry, watching closely, saw the singer's mouth tighten, then relax. "That might be true. I sang at church a lot, when I was young."

"I like to sing," Maddie confided, as a cracker crumbled through her fingers onto the carpet.

Caitlyn nodded, which set her long gold earrings to swaying. "And you have a very good voice. You help the other children learn the songs."

"My daddy sings, too."

"I'm sure he does." Caitlyn lifted her chin, almost defiantly, and gazed at Ben. "I could tell when we talked that he would have a nice singing voice."

"You've already met?" Peg returned with a tray of drinks. "I didn't know that." She looked a little put out.

Oh, Peg, Harry groaned silently. *What are you trying to pull off this time?*

"We ran into each other only this afternoon, as a matter of fact," Ben drawled, his voice dry. "In the meat department at Food Depot. Over pot roast."

HE COULD HAVE introduced himself. Cait took the glass of white wine Peggy offered and held the cool bowl between her palms. Her face felt hot, which probably meant she was blushing.

Why had Ben Tremaine pretended not to recognize her? She'd been teaching his children in choir for three weeks. Maybe he'd never heard a single one of her recordings, but she and Anna looked enough alike that he would have known right away whom he was talking to. This was a small town. So far, Cait hadn't met a single person who didn't already know who she was and why she was here.

But Ben Tremaine hadn't even bothered to make her acquaintance through a simple exchange of names. If he'd been married, that would have been a reason, she supposed, for him to steer clear of a single woman who'd made it clear she found him attractive.

That was not quite the case, however. Anna had explained the situation during the drive to the Shepherds' house tonight. Ben's wife—Harry and Peggy's daughter—had been killed in a car wreck. Shep had been in the car with her, and though his physical injuries were minor, he hadn't spoken a word since. That accounted for why he was attentive, but completely silent, during choir practice. As for Maddie—losing her mother's love and attention in such a tragic way had caused the little girl to hoard every bit of affection or praise she received.

And Ben must still be in deep mourning for his wife. Did that absolve him from simple friendliness?

Evidently. "Dinner's ready," Peggy Shepherd announced, waving through a wide doorway toward the table. Anna had mentioned that this house was one of the town's oldest, dating back to the early 1800s; beautiful wainscoting and woodwork in the dining room and entry hall testified to the craftsmanship of long ago. "Caitlyn, you sit here on Harry's left and Ben, you can…" Her voice trailed off, and her eyes widened as Ben took the chair diagonally opposite Cait, as far away as he could manage. "That's…that's fine. David and Anna, would you like to sit next to Ben?"

That seated Shep beside Cait, then Maddie next to her

grandmother. Harry handed over a platter heaped with carrots and potatoes…and pot roast. "Help yourself."

"Thanks." Cait took a healthy portion of the succulent meat and vegetables, then hesitated. Should she serve Shep? Her area of expertise these days was music. What she knew about children she'd learned at choir practice, and that wasn't much.

"Shep?" When she said his name, the little boy lifted his long-lashed brown gaze to her face. "Would you like some meat and vegetables?"

He looked away again, but nodded. Cait took a deep breath and forked over a piece of roast. "Potatoes?" Another nod. "Carrots?" The little boy shook his head.

"Have some carrots, son," his dad instructed from across the table. Obviously, Ben Tremaine was keeping an eye on them.

Shep's pout, as Cait ladled a few of the smaller slices onto his plate, conveyed quite clearly what he thought about carrots. She looked at that full lower lip, stuck way out, and had a strong urge to hug him. Such an adorable little boy.

His grandfather made the same impression. Harry Shepherd was handsome, young-looking, with brown hair that showed only a few strands of gray, and brown eyes like Shep's that twinkled when he smiled. His wife was simply amazing. Peggy had orchestrated a dinner for eight people, yet looked completely relaxed. Her silver-white hair remained smoothly drawn into a ponytail, her pale blue sweater and slacks didn't exhibit a single spot of food. So far, Cait couldn't seem to cook for three without making a mess of herself and the kitchen, a fact Anna's husband pointed out as often as possible.

But then, her sister's attraction to this particular man had always been a puzzle to Cait. Thin and balding, though he wasn't yet thirty-five, David Remington lacked the easy social skills Cait remembered in her father and the other ministers she'd met as a child. David's eyes were round, as if constantly surprised. He always seemed to be in a hurry, always anxious, always thinking ahead.

Like now. "Are you tired?" he asked Anna, before she'd even sampled her food. "Should we be getting home?"

Anna gave him her sweet smile and shook her head. "I'm fine. I took an extra-long nap after Peggy called to invite us this afternoon, so I could feel good tonight."

"How many weeks do you have left?" Peggy brought a second basket of biscuits to the table.

"Eleven, if everything goes perfectly." Anna put down her fork and sighed. "The due date should be January 10. But the doctor doesn't think I'll get that far. He's hoping for the middle of December. The longer, the better, as far as the baby's concerned."

The older woman looked at Cait. "Will you be able to stay until then?"

Cait noticed Ben glance up from his plate at Peggy's question, though his gaze came nowhere near hers. "That's what I'm planning. After Christmas, my schedule gets hectic, but for now, I'm here to help Anna…and David," she added belatedly, "any way I can."

"Oh, boy!" Maddie clapped her hands. "That means you'll be here for the holidays. Won't that be cool, Daddy? Miss Cait is going to help us with the Christmas pageant!"

With a roaring in her ears, Cait stared at the little girl. *Christmas pageant? I don't do Christmas.*
Not for the last ten years. Not this year…
Not ever again!

CHAPTER TWO

OH, DEAR. Anna saw resistance dawn on her sister's face at the mention of Christmas. She'd planned to present the idea gradually, easing Cait into the role of directing the annual holiday program. When the doctor had ordered Anna to stay home and take things easy, she'd known she would have to find someone to take over her responsibility for the pageant. Cait had seemed like the perfect answer—for both their sakes.

But not if she got stubborn. "I hadn't mentioned that to you," she said, catching Cait's eye across the table. "We usually start preparing around the beginning of November."

"It's lots of fun," Maddie said. "We have angels and shepherds and wise men and a procession on Christmas Eve."

Cait made a visible effort to relax. "We used to have a Christmas pageant when I was growing up. I remember how exciting it was. But—"

"The pageant has been a Goodwill tradition since I was a girl," Peggy said. "Most of the children in town participate. When I was ten, I got to be the announcing angel." She smiled at her granddaughter.

Maddie nodded. "That's what I want to be. I already started learning the part. 'Fear not...'"

Cait pressed her lips together and lifted her chin, a sure sign she was on the defensive. Anna sat up straighter, trying to think of a distraction. This was not going well at all.

"First, we have to get through Halloween." Ben Tremaine's calm voice came as an answer to prayer. "Have you decided on your costume yet, Maddie?"

The little girl nodded. "If we got a angel outfit, then I'd be all set for the Christmas pageant. That's a good idea, isn't it?"

There was a second of silence, during which Anna imagined all the adults—herself included—grappling for a way to deal with that question. The very existence of the pageant was in doubt this year. And there would be other children wanting the angel's role. If she counted too much on getting the part, Maddie might be severely disappointed.

"My favorite Halloween costume of all time was the year I dressed as Zorro," Cait said.

"You had Zorro when you were growing up?" Maddie's eyes widened. "I love that movie."

Cait grinned. "Zorro's been around a long, long time."

"But can a girl be Zorro?"

"Why not? Black cape, mask, sword...poof! It's Zorro."

"Yeah." The little girl was obviously taken with the idea. Anna chuckled. Leave it to Cait to come up with the solution nobody else could see.

"And I'll tell you a secret." Cait leaned over Shep, pretending to whisper to Maddie. "I taped a crayon to the end of my sword, so I could slash real *Z*'s everywhere I went. It was incredibly cool." She imitated the motion with a few flicks of her wrist.

"Wow..."

"And what should we think up for Shep?" Cait's hand rested lightly on his blond head for a second.

"He likes that guy in *X-Men*." Maddie served as her brother's voice most of the time. "The one who's sorta like a wolf."

"Wolverine? I met him at a party once. He's really cool." Cait looked down into Shep's upturned face. "That would be an excellent costume."

Shep nodded decisively, as if the issue were settled.

"Amazing," Ben commented, leaning back in his chair with his arms crossed, "how an outside perspective can simplify the most complicated problem." His emphasis on *outside* was slight, but noticeable, nonetheless.

Another silence fell. "Dessert?" Peggy said at last, a little too brightly.

As the rest of them tried to restore some semblance of civility over brownies and ice cream, Cait stayed quiet, her smile stiff, her cheeks flushed with temper and, Anna knew, hurt pride. Tonight was her first real social venture since she'd arrived in town, and persuading her to come hadn't been easy. In her frequent phone calls and e-mails, she'd rarely mentioned friends, or even casual acquaintances. The guys in her band—all of them married—were the people Cait spent most of her time with. This visit to a stranger's house for dinner was an effort on her part.

But then, she wasn't the only one acting out of character. In the three years she and David had lived in Goodwill, Anna had never known Ben Tremaine to be anything but kind and caring. Even right after Valerie's death, when he was nearly paralyzed by grief, he'd reached out to express his concern over Anna's first miscarriage.

Judging by their interaction so far, though, he and Cait seemed to bring out the worst in each other.

And Anna had hoped for something very, very different between them.

She sighed, and David's hand immediately covered

hers. "I really think it's time for us to go. You should be in bed."

"I'm fine."

But David wasn't listening. "Peggy, Harry, it's been a great meal." He was standing behind her, waiting to pull out her chair as she got to her feet. "But I do think Anna's had enough excitement for one day. Will you forgive us if we don't stay to help with the dishes?"

Peggy shook her head. "I wouldn't have that, even if you stayed all night. We've been delighted to share your company. And to meet Caitlyn." She smiled. "Please feel free to drop by any time for a cup of coffee and a chat."

"Thank you for everything. I've enjoyed meeting you." Now Caitlyn had turned on her "professional" smile—a little too bright, rather unfocused. She turned to Maddie and Shep. "I'll look forward to seeing you on Sunday at church and at choir next week." Then she moved away from the table, without a word or a glance in Ben Tremaine's direction.

"I'll get your coats." Harry led them to the front hall, with Peggy and the children following. Anna looked back to see Ben standing just inside the opening between the living and dining rooms.

He lifted his wineglass in a silent toast and gave her a warm smile. "Take care of yourself."

She didn't return the smile. "I don't understand—"

David wrapped her coat around her from behind. "Here we go, sweetheart. Night, Ben." And then her husband was easing her down the porch steps and into the car like an ancient statue that might break if he set it down too hard.

"We can't be careful enough," he said later, in their bedroom, when she told him how she felt.

"The doctor didn't say—"

"The doctor said you should have as little stress as possible." He came out of the bathroom wearing a clean white T-shirt and soft flannel pajama bottoms. Brushing her hair, Anna watched her husband moving around the bedroom, getting ready for sleep. David wasn't handsome, and he wasn't a big man, or obviously muscular, but he had a lean strength that had always excited her. She loved the smell of the fresh cotton T-shirt combined with David's own, unique scent. Just the thought was enough to raise her pulse rate.

"Having dinner with Harry and Peggy is not stressful." Which wasn't exactly true, considering the way Ben and Cait had behaved, but she wanted David to think so. If he thought she was feeling really well, maybe they could make love. The last time had been before her most recent doctor's appointment, two weeks ago. Much too long.

She left her hair down around her shoulders, rather than braiding it for sleep, and instead of going to her side of the bed, she went to sit on the edge beside David. Putting her hand over his ribs, she rubbed gently. "Neither is being with you." With her other hand braced on the pillow beside his head, she leaned close to brush her lips over his.

David's reaction was everything she hoped for—a quickly drawn breath, an immediate claiming of her mouth with his own. His hands claimed her as well, and she felt the surge of his passion in the grip of his fingers on her shoulders. With a sigh of pleasure and surrender, Anna lowered herself more fully onto his chest.

But instead of drawing her even closer, instead of taking them deeper, David softened his mouth, shortened the kisses.

"You're so sweet," he murmured against her temple. "I love you." Without her cooperation, he sat her up and away from him. "Come to bed." He put his glasses on the table and pulled the blankets up to his chin.

As she turned off the lamp on the dresser and the light in the bathroom, Anna tried to believe that what she'd heard was an invitation. In the darkened room, though, she slipped into bed to find David on his side, facing away from her. Had he fallen asleep so quickly? Or did he just want her to think so?

She sat up to braid her hair, then eased under the covers again. David was tired, of course. All the responsibilities of running the church fell onto his shoulders, now that she couldn't work. Typing, answering the phone and handling all the paperwork, plus his normal pastoral duties, kept him working late these days. With a sermon to preach on Sunday, he certainly needed to get a good rest on Friday night.

Still wide-awake, Anna sighed and turned her back on her husband...and on the memory of all the nights she'd fallen asleep in his strong, loving arms.

BEN LEFT the Shepherds' house as soon as he could get away. Maddie and Shep enjoyed spending the night with their grandparents, so there wasn't a problem with goodbyes. They knew he'd be back for them around lunchtime tomorrow.

At home again, he headed for the shop without even going into the house first, shivering a little in the frosty darkness. Ever since he was a boy, he'd found a kind of peace in his carpentry. The sweet smell of shaved wood, the physical effort of planing and sanding, the concentration on delicate cutting and carving—his work absorbed him, absolved him of the need to think.

Usually. Tonight, he couldn't get Cait Gregory's face out of his mind. Not because she was beautiful, but because she'd been hurt. By him. He'd gone out of his way to insult her, several times over. He might be forgiven for not introducing himself at the grocery store, but his comment to her at dinner had been totally out of line. That the remark had been his only means of defense didn't matter. He shouldn't need a defense.

But something about Cait Gregory set off all his alarms. There was an…aliveness…in her eyes that grabbed him and urged him near her. Adventure, challenge, emotion—somehow he knew he could find all of that and more with this redheaded woman.

Adventure had played a big part in his past—the Secret Service provided plenty of action, even on assignments that didn't involve the White House. He'd cornered counterfeiters and tax evaders during those years, taken out a would-be assassin. Challenge had come his way with the births of his children, with the decision a year ago to build a new life and a new business based on the work of his hands.

And he'd experienced a lifetime's share of emotion, though he was only thirty-seven years old. Valerie had been his partner, his lover, his best friend, since their second year in college together. They'd established their careers side by side—hers as a lobbyist for a consumer affairs agency, his with the government. They'd planned for their children, prepared for them, rejoiced in their presence. Their family had been a walking advertisement for the American dream.

In a matter of seconds, the dream became a nightmare, one Ben was still trying to escape. From the perfect life, he'd descended into a hell of pain and loss. Eighteen months later, he'd thought he'd climbed out of the pit, at least far enough to find a purpose in living, a willingness to keep trying. For a long time, he'd only functioned to take care of the kids. Nowadays, finally, he took care of himself, too.

But maintaining this equilibrium demanded all his strength. He had nothing left to give to a new relationship. Especially one with a woman like Cait Gregory. A man could lose his soul in her shining green eyes. Ben knew he needed to hold on to what soul he had left.

Still, he shouldn't flay other people because of his own inadequacies. Cait Gregory didn't deserve the way he'd treated her. And the injustice bothered him.

So he put down the sandpaper and chair leg he'd been smoothing, dusted his hands and picked up the phone. Dave Remington's number was on his autodial list—had been since he'd arrived in town after Valerie's accident. Taking a deep breath, Ben punched the button.

"Hello?" Not Dave's Virginia accent, or Anna's clear tone, but a siren's voice. "Hello?"

He straddled a chair and braced his head on his hand. "Cait? This is Ben Tremaine."

Immediate frost. "David and Anna have gone to bed. But if it's an emergency—"

"No. No, I called to…talk to you."

"Really?" As brittle as breaking icicles. "Was there some aspersion you forgot to cast?"

Strangely, he almost laughed. "I want to apologize. I acted like a jerk, in the grocery and at dinner. No excuses. But I am sorry. You didn't deserve it."

"Oh." Cait sat speechless as she held the phone to her ear, trying to think of the right response. Part of her wanted to punish him, to keep Ben Tremaine groveling for a long time. Part of her wanted to spare him any further embarrassment.

And part of her just wanted to keep him talking.

"That's…that's okay. No harm done. I've had my share of tough reviews over the years. I'll recover."

"I'm glad to hear it. I imagine there are legions of fans out there who'd be after me if I slighted their legend." His voice held a smile.

Cait found herself smiling in response. "Probably not legions. Or a legend. Janis Joplin is a legend. I'm just a singer."

"I bet you do a good version of 'Bobby McGee,' though."

"I've never covered that song."

"Why not? Your voice would be perfect."

Her chest went hollow at the idea that *he'd* noticed her voice. "Um…I don't know." Almost without her intent, the melody came to mind, and then the words about being free and being alone. The music possessed her, as a good song always did, and she sang it through, experimenting with intervals and timing. At the end, she was still hearing the possibilities, thinking about variations…until she realized how long the silence had lasted.

Talk about embarrassed. "I—I'm sorry." She felt her face and neck flush with heat. "I—"

"Don't apologize." He cleared his throat. "I was right—you're dynamite with that song. What do you have to do to get the rights to sing it?"

"Pay big bucks, probably. I'll get my agent to investigate."

"Good." He paused, and Cait could tell he was ready to say goodbye. "Well, I guess I'll let you go. I hope you know I really am sorry for…everything."

"Forget it." She wanted to keep him on the line but, really, what did they have to talk about?

"If you will."

"Then it's done." She took a deep breath and made the break herself. "Good night, Ben."

"Night…Cait."

She set down the phone and rolled to her side on the bed, breathing in the lavender scent of Anna's pillowcases. Flowered wallpaper and crisp, frilly curtains, lace-trimmed pillows and old-fashioned furniture…the guest room reflected Anna's careful, caring personality, her love of beautiful, comfortable surroundings. After two solid months on the road, sleeping in anonymous motel rooms, Cait reveled in the luxury. If only she could sing her songs, and then come home every night to something like this….

She drifted off to sleep, into dreams she sensed but couldn't remember, and woke to the smell of coffee. That meant she'd overslept and left Anna and David to get their own breakfast. Of course, ten-thirty was very early on a Saturday morning for most musicians she knew to be out of bed. Cait considered this just one more example of the way she would never fit in with the normal, everyday routine her sister lived. Not to mention Ben Tremaine.

Why bring him up, anyway?

She found Anna alone at the table in the cozy kitchen, looking as if she hadn't slept very well.

"Everything okay?" Cait poured herself a mug of coffee. "Are you feeling alright?"

"Why wouldn't I be?"

Cait blinked at the unusual sharpness in Anna's tone. "You look tired, is all."

Her sister took a deep breath and closed her eyes. "Sorry. I didn't mean to snap at you. I guess you're right—I am tired."

"Maybe we should have stayed home last night."

"I'm as tired of staying home as anything else." Again, the harshness in her usually gentle voice.

"Well, okay. I'll send you out on my next concert tour. You can ride all day and sleep in two or three hour snatches and eat lousy food two meals out of every three. I'll stay here and—"

Anna laughed, as Cait had hoped she would. "I get the message. The grass is always greener." She stared into her orange juice for a minute, then looked up as Cait sat down with her coffee and a sweet roll. "So what do you think about the Christmas pageant?"

After talking with Ben, she hadn't given the pageant any thought at all. But she didn't need to. "I'm not the person to be in charge of a program like that. And you know it."

"I know *you* think so. I'm not convinced you're right."

"You need somebody who believes in—what's the phrase?—'the reason for the season.'"

Anna lifted her eyebrows. "Are you an atheist now?"

"N-no." Cait crumbled a corner of her roll. "But that's theology. Your program should have a director who likes Christmas."

"Sweetie, it's been ten years. Don't you think you could start to forgive him?"

The unmentionable had just been mentioned. "Has he forgiven me?"

Now her sister avoided her gaze. "We…don't talk about you."

Cait nodded. "Because I ceased to exist for him the second I refused to do what he told me to. What kind of father treats a child that way?"

"He wanted so much for you—"

"Without ever bothering to find out what I wanted for

myself. And then he chose Christmas—of all times—to force a showdown.''

''I'm sure he's sorry.''

''I'm not sure of that. But I'm not sorry, either. He handed me the career I wanted by making it impossible for me to do anything else. If he can't live with my choice, can't connect with me in spite of our differences, then—'' she shrugged ''—that's *his* choice.''

Anna sighed. ''Okay, forget about Dad. The Goodwill Christmas pageant would be a one-time commitment for you. Is that too much to ask?''

''I wouldn't be any good at it, Anna. I could go through the motions, but that wouldn't produce the results you want.''

''You won't even try?''

''I can't just *try* something like this. I either do it, or I don't. And I really would rather not.'' She took a fortifying sip of coffee. ''There are other churches in town. One of their choir directors could organize the pageant.''

''Mrs. Boringer at the Methodist Church is sixty-five and has really bad arthritis.'' Anna ticked off one finger. ''John Clay, the Catholic priest, leads their singing, but he won't take on a project like this. And Lou Miller just accepted a job in a big church in Dallas, leaving the Baptists without a choir director at all. Our church is the only hope for this season. If we don't do it, Goodwill won't have a pageant…for the first time in forty-eight years.''

''So let David—''

''David doesn't sing. You know that. We have to have somebody who sings.''

Cait saw the anxiety in Anna's face, the tension in her hands wrapped around the mug of tea. This kind of stress couldn't be good for the baby. And it would kill Anna to lose another baby.

But…just the thought of involving herself in a Christmas pageant was enough to make her head pound and her stomach cramp. Cait closed her eyes for a second, swallowed back bile, then wiped her sweaty palms on her pajama pants.

"Look, let's do this." A deep breath. "I'll get them started on Christmas songs. The story's still the same, right?" She watched Anna summon up a small smile. "Meanwhile, you can ask around, find a mom or a dad who's willing to do the actual staging and directing. And, who knows, maybe by the middle of December your baby will be here and you can direct the pageant yourself."

Anna shook her head. "This isn't something we can put together in two weeks. Costumes, scenery, everybody learning their lines…"

The details made Cait shudder. "First things first. We'll start with the music."

And if I'm lucky, she thought, *the music is as far as I'll have to go.*

THE ADULT CHOIR sang for the first time under Cait's direction in church on Sunday. Three sopranos, two altos and four men was not a very large group, but they all had pleasant voices, strong enough for the old familiar hymn she'd arranged and rehearsed with them.

After the service, it seemed that every member of the small church stopped at the organ to compliment her. "What a pleasure," Karen Patterson said. "I'm so glad you're here to help us all out." She had her arm around her daughter Brenna, Maddie Tremaine's friend. "Brenna loves what you're doing with her choir."

"I have a good time with them, too." Cait smiled at Brenna. "They sing very well for such a young group."

Gray-eyed Brenna ducked her head, hiding a pleased smile.

"That was just lovely." Peggy Shepherd put her arm around Cait's waist. "I almost called out 'Encore!' But I thought David might be insulted."

Cait grinned. "The sermon is supposed to be the main point, I think." Her father had always delivered powerful, intelligent—and often intimidating—messages. As far as she knew, he was still preaching, still cautioning his parishioners against the dangers of stray thoughts and wayward deeds.

"A fine song," Harry Shepherd added. "One of my favorites."

"That was beautiful, Miss Caitlyn!" Maddie appeared suddenly in the midst of the gathering. "Can we sing that song in our choir?"

"Maybe you could. The melody, anyway." Cait felt, rather than saw, Ben Tremaine come to the edge of the group. He stood to her right, just out of her line of sight. She wanted to turn to greet him, but couldn't get up the nerve.

Maddie swung on her arm. "Guess what we're doing this afternoon, Miss Caitlyn."

"Um...going swimming?"

"Of course not. It's too cold to swim. Guess again."

"Building a snowman?"

"There's no snow." She said it chidingly, as if Cait should know better. "We're having a Halloween party. It's at Brenna's house, and we get to wear our costumes."

"That sounds like so much fun. What did you decide to wear?"

"Zorro, of course. I got a hat and a sword and everything. And Shep's going to be Wolverine."

"Wow...that's great. What are you going to be, Brenna?"

"An Olympic champion," the little blonde said softly.

"Brenna has horses," Maddie confided. "She's got all the fancy clothes, so she just made a gold medal on a ribbon and she's all set."

"What a great idea. Maybe you'll be an Olympic champion for real someday."

"I hope so," Brenna said, with the intensity Cait remembered feeling at that age in her desire for a singing career.

"I wish I could see all your costumes." She was beginning to wonder if Maddie would swing her arm right out of its socket. "Will you come trick-or-treating to Miss Anna's house?"

The swinging stopped. "Why don't you come to the party," Maddie asked. "I'm sure it's okay with Brenna's mom. Isn't it?"

Karen Patterson recovered quickly from her surprise. "O-of course. We'd be delighted to have you come by, Cait. As long as you can stand the noise twelve ten-year-olds will make."

There was no graceful way out. "I think I can stop by for a few minutes, at least. Where do you live, Mrs. Patterson?"

"Karen, please. We're kind of far out of town, but it's not hard to find. If you drive—"

Maddie tugged on her arm again. "You don't need to drive, Miss Caitlyn. My daddy can bring you with us."

As she turned to look at the man in question, Cait knew she only imagined that the entire group went completely quiet.

His smile waited for her, rueful, a little embarrassed,

maybe slightly annoyed. "Sure," he said, in that soft, deep drawl. "We'd be glad to take you to the party."

How she wanted to refuse. But Maddie was staring up at her with wide brown eyes, silently—for once!—pleading. Shep stood just behind Ben, peeking around his dad's hip like a little mouse out of a hole. Cait thought she saw an expression of hope on his face, as well.

She could brush off a grown man—had done it plenty of times over the past ten years. But disappointing a child was simply beyond Cait's strength.

"That sounds great." She grinned at the children, avoiding even a brief glance at their dad. "What time should I be ready?"

CHAPTER THREE

BEN RANG the Remingtons' bell that afternoon just before four o'clock. One glance at the woman who opened the door drove all good sense out of his head and all his blood…south.

Cait had dressed as a gypsy—her curling copper hair hanging loose under a bright gold scarf, gold bracelets jingling on her wrists and huge hoops in her earlobes, a flowing white shirt and a long skirt in gold and black and red that seemed to glow with a light of its own. Intense makeup darkened her eyes and lips, increased her air of mystery and adventure.

Just what he didn't need. Ben cleared his throat, fought for the right thing to say. "You look ready for a party."

Cait smiled—an expression of promise, of invitation. "I love Halloween."

At the Patterson farm, her presence quickly turned a normal, noisy Halloween party for children into an exceptional event. The kids swamped her as soon as she stepped into the game room, showing off their own costumes, exhibiting their painted pumpkin faces, begging for songs and stories. Shep, as usual, hung back from the crowd, all the while keeping close watch on what was happening. Though Cait tried to defer to Karen's plan of activities, the tide of popular opinion carried the day.

So the gypsy woman sat beside the fire, telling ghost stories from Ireland, teaching folk songs about fierce battles and dangerous voyages and lost loves. When Karen called the kids to the table for tacos and juice, Cait served food, wiped up several spills, and then led the children in a wild dance through the cold, crisp air, the last rays of the sun and the crackling leaves on the ground.

"I'm sorry," she said to Karen as the kids began to leave. "I certainly didn't intend to take over your party."

"Are you kidding? This is a Halloween they'll remember forever, and it happened at our house. Brenna is thrilled." Karen grinned. "Not to mention that in five years you'll have all the teenagers in Goodwill, Virginia buying your recordings."

Cait laughed. "You uncovered my real motive—increasing sales."

Standing nearby, Ben watched the remaining kids playing in the leaves and listened to the two women get to know each other. He hadn't participated in this kind of…easy…relationship, he realized, since moving to Goodwill. Although he knew most of the folks here by face and name, he didn't mix much with anyone but Harry and Peggy and, sometimes, Dave Remington. Valerie had been the social secretary in their partnership, keeping up with friends and family on his behalf. With her gone, he hadn't had the heart to continue the effort.

Cait Gregory made socializing look like a pleasure…one he might want to share.

She's a professional, he reminded himself. *The woman makes her living charming crowds of faceless fans. Do you want to be just another starstruck fool?*

For a minute, watching her laugh, Ben was tempted to answer yes. His life had been so somber for so long, now….

"Daddy." Maddie tugged on the sleeve of his sweater. "Shep's not feeling good."

He turned to see his little boy standing pale-faced and heavy-eyed behind him. Going down on one knee, he put a hand on Shep's forehead. "You do feel hot. Guess we'd better get you home and into bed with some medicine inside you."

This was something else he hadn't done much of until Valerie's death. Sick kids terrified him. What if he missed the difference between a simple cold and pneumonia? Or fell asleep when their fever went too high?

On a deep breath, he stood up again. He hadn't made a serious mistake so far, right? No reason to think this would be any different. There was always Peggy for backup, or Dr. Hall.

Scooping Shep up against his shoulder, he joined Karen and Cait. "Wolverine here's a little under the weather. We need to be getting home."

With four kids of her own, Karen reacted like the typical experienced mom—feeling Shep's forehead, thinking of practicalities. "There's a flu going around at school— three kids weren't able to come today because they're sick. Some fever medicine and a couple of days' rest, then you'll be back to fighting evil, you superhero, you."

But Cait's face mirrored some of Ben's uncertainty. "I'm so sorry," she murmured, almost crooned. She laid a hand along Shep's cheek. "It's no fun being sick, is it?"

Lower lip stuck out in a pout, Shep shook his head. Then he sat up in Ben's arms, reached over, and practically threw himself into Cait's embrace.

"Shep…" Ben felt his own face heat up. The woman didn't need a sick kid clinging to her. "What are you doing, son? Come back here."

But Shep, who rarely gave adults much notice these days, stuck to Cait like a sand burr. Chuckling, looking panicked and pleased at the same time, she shook her head. "It's okay. I'll carry him to the car. Thanks, Karen—it was a great party."

"Thank *you,* Cait. Come over and visit sometime this week."

"Sure."

In the Suburban, Shep wouldn't let go of Cait until she agreed to sit in the back seat right beside him. Exasperated, Ben made sure Maddie had buckled herself in on Cait's other side before climbing into the front all alone.

"Now I know how the president's driver feels," he commented, more to himself than anyone else, "waiting for the SAIC to get in beside him." They passed through the dark farm country like a shadow—the only movement or light to be seen for miles around.

"SAIC?" Cait said.

Ben mentally kicked himself in the butt. Was he showing off for her deliberately? "Sorry. Special Agent in Charge. The agent heading up any maneuver in which the president leaves the White House."

"Anna said you were with the Secret Service. Quite a glamorous job."

"Not unless something bad happens. Mostly it's planning, and more planning, then standing around waiting for the unplanned to occur."

"There are some radically unbalanced people out there, though, desperate to get noticed any way they can."

"No kidding. Have you had problems?" He glanced in the rearview mirror, saw her stroking Shep's head as the boy leaned against her shoulder. On her other side, Maddie had fallen asleep holding the singer's hand. The sight caught at his throat.

Cait shook her head. "Most people have been very good. A couple of guys stepped over the line, one in

Texas and one in California. The police were able to handle them.''

"So you don't have your own security?"

"My agent pushes for it every time we talk. But music isn't something I do *up here,*" she put her hand up high, "while people listen *down there* behind a barrier. The songs are—to borrow an overused word—organic. They depend on the different needs and desires of everybody involved. If I separate myself from the audience, the music sort of…well, freezes. Solidifies." Now she met his gaze through the mirror. "I guess that sounds pretty weird."

"No." He was surprised to realize he understood. "No, I see what you mean. Wood is like that. Not something dead I impose my will on, but something alive that I work with to reveal what's inside."

"Exactly." Her smile glinted at him in the dark car. "Anna loves the chair you built for her and David. It's beautiful. Their grandchildren will sit in it, and the generations after them."

"Hope so." Driving into Goodwill itself, along the straight streets with lighted houses on either side, Ben let the conversation—confessions?—lapse. He and Cait Gregory didn't need to understand too much about each other. That would only lead to trouble.

In the driveway of the Remingtons' house, he got out and opened the rear door. Shep woke up crying when the light hit him in the eyes. His cheeks were now flushed a bright red.

Maddie stirred. "Daddy? What's happening?"

"Just dropping Miss Caitlyn off, that's all." Ben avoided Cait's smiling gaze. "Can you slide out for a minute?"

Groggily, Maddie got out of the car. But when Cait

started to move over, Shep's sobs escalated to screams. Obviously he was able to make sounds. He just chose not to. Holding his arms out, he pleaded without words for Cait to stay.

She glanced over at Ben. "I hate to upset him when he's sick." Turning to Shep again, she brushed back his damp hair, wiped the tears off his cheeks. "Don't you want to go home now? Get into your pajamas and listen to your dad read a story? I bet he reads really good stories."

Shep nodded.

Cait leaned over and kissed the boy's forehead. "Well, darlin', to do that, you have to let me say goodbye."

In her smoky voice, that one word—*darlin'*—was a punch to the gut. Ben took a deep breath.

So did Shep. And then the tears came back, along with the huge, gulping sobs.

"Maybe we should take Shep home and get him settled first." Cait's voice was concerned, not angry. "I can call David to come pick me up there."

Ashamed in the face of her generosity, Ben nevertheless knew he didn't want to take Cait Gregory to his house. Didn't want a single memory of her inside the home he shared with his children.

But for his son's sake, he would risk letting her in. He just hoped he could avoid the consequences.

"Sounds like a plan." He helped Maddie get into the car and buckled her up again. In the driver's seat once more, he backed down the Remingtons' short drive. "We'll be home in about five seconds flat."

CAIT CARRIED Shep up the stone steps to the wide front porch and waited while his dad unlocked the door. She felt breathless from the unaccustomed weight of the child in her arms...and from the anticipation of going into Ben Tremaine's house.

Which was ridiculous. They'd only known each other three days. She'd be leaving town within two months at the outside. What difference did his decorating scheme make?

Still, a feeling of belonging hit her full in the face as she stepped inside. *Home.* She hadn't had one for ten years. Before that, she'd been a part of her father's house, living in his style and according to his rules.

But Ben's place was a real home. High ceilings, exposed wood beams, windows of different shapes, sizes, angles. Wood floors and cabinets finished with a light stain and a high gloss. Thick, dark-blue rugs under comfortable-looking red leather couches and chairs. A day's worth of clutter made the room looked lived-in—children's books stacked on the table and beside a chair, the rolled-up newspaper still waiting to be read, two stuffed dogs confronting each other on one arm of the sofa.

She glimpsed the details as she followed Ben up a freestanding staircase and along the hallway to Shep's room. Here, the style was Boy—blue walls and gray carpet, *X-Men* paraphernalia everywhere, Lego, toy cars and Pokémon pieces scattered on the floor, a rumpled bed on which a single teddy bear, nearly as large as the boy himself, lay waiting.

His face flushed, Ben bent to straighten the blue blanket and sheets. "I didn't get a chance to make beds before we left for church this morning."

"But now it's all nice and neat, just waiting for you," she told Shep as she lowered him to the floor. "Want your dad to help you into pajamas?"

The little boy shook his head violently and grabbed her around the thighs. Cait looked at Ben in dismay. "I—"

"It's okay." He pulled a set of colorful pj's from a drawer in the nearby chest. "I'll get the medicine while you help him change."

There was a question in his last words and in his eyes, as if he weren't sure she could or would help Shep out of his clothes.

"Okay." She gave him a confident, in-charge smile. "I baby-sat when I was a teenager—I think I remember the process."

Ben nodded and disappeared. Cait sat down on the bed with Shep between her knees. "Let's see what we can do here, okay? Ooh…Wolverine pajamas. Are these your favorites?"

He nodded solemnly, his eyes too dull, his cheeks too red. Humming softly, Cait eased him out of his *X-Men* jumpsuit costume and the long-sleeved T-shirt underneath, putting on the Wolverine pj top. She took off his shoes and socks, pushed his jeans down to his knees…and that was as far as she got. "Ben? Ben, can you come here?"

She sounded more panicked than she'd intended. He appeared immediately at the doorway. "What?"

Cait took a calming breath. "I thought you might want to get a look at Shep's legs before I cover him up again."

He knelt on the floor beside them, gazing at the huge red blotches on his son's legs. "Yeah, he gets a rash like this when he has a cold or the flu. I'll get some antihistamine. You go ahead and put him to bed."

She did as she was told and Shep went peacefully enough, holding his bear close to his chest.

"That's Bumbles," Maddie said from the doorway. She'd changed into a sweet nightgown with red and blue flowers all over. "Shep let me name him."

"I like that—Bumbles the Bear. Sounds like a song."

Cait pulled a waltz tune out of her memory and gave it words. "Bumbles the Bear hasn't a care. He stumbles and fumbles and tumbles along...." Maddie giggled, and even Shep smiled, so they were all pretty cheerful when Ben returned.

"Well, this doesn't look much like anybody's sick." He put bottles and cups and spoons on the top of the chest of drawers.

"Miss Caitlyn made up a song about Bumbles, Daddy." Maddie sang it through perfectly, after only one hearing. "Isn't that funny? Is there another verse, Miss Caitlyn?"

Cait moved out of the way and watched as Ben gently but firmly gave Shep the medicine he needed. The little boy struggled, frowning at the taste, but a Popsicle at the end of the ordeal got him smiling again. "I guess we'll have to make up another verse. Let's see... Bumbles the Bear, he's always there, he mumbles and grumbles but never for long...."

They finished three verses of the Bumbles song before Shep drifted into sleep. Cait got to her feet, with a stiffness in her shoulders and neck that testified to the tension she'd felt during this last hour. What kind of responsibility would it be to have the care of these children all day, every day? And all alone, as Ben did?

More than she could imagine. Which was why she was happy to stay single.

"Can you sing to me, Miss Caitlyn?" Maddie had hold of her hand again.

"Are you ready for bed?" Cait glanced at her watch and saw with surprise that it was after eight.

"Daddy lets me read before I go to sleep."

"Well, if he doesn't mind..."

Ben stepped out of Shep's room and pulled the door

partway shut. "Sounds great to me. I'll come up a little later and kiss you good-night, Maddie."

"Okay." Maddie's room was the complete opposite of her brother's—yellow and white, ruffles and gingham checks and eyelet lace, as neatly kept as Anna's half of their room had always been.

"This is wonderful, Maddie. You must love having such a special bedroom." Two dormered windows overlooked the yard, now hidden by the dark.

"Daddy and Grandma and I picked everything out." The little girl climbed on her bed. "My mommy couldn't help when we moved here. She went to sleep after the car wreck, and she couldn't wake up even in the hospital."

Cait forced words through her closed throat. "I'm so sorry." They stared at each other for a minute, until she found the control to say, "What shall we sing?"

Maddie asked for some of her favorite hymns from choir, and the theme song of a popular TV show. Her eyelids started to droop and she snuggled down into her bed, holding a beautiful doll with long dark curls in the crook of her arm. "This is Valerie," she said sleepily. "I named her for my mommy, 'cause they both have curly brown hair. Like me."

With her fingers trembling, Cait stroked Maddie's hair. "And you're as beautiful as she is. One more song?"

Maddie nodded, her eyes closed. Cait sang an Irish lullaby, using the Gaelic in which she'd learned it first. Then she sat, elbows propped on her knees and her chin resting on her fists, just watching the little girl sleep.

"Cait." Ben's whisper came from the doorway.

She stood reluctantly, but then pulled herself together and crossed the room. This wasn't her family, after all, or her house. She was just helping out.

Ben looked in on Shep, then led her to the first floor.

At the bottom of the stairs he turned, heading away from the front door. Cait followed, confused, until she remembered she'd said she would call David to come get her. Ben couldn't leave once the children were asleep.

But in the kitchen, she found the table set with bowls, a plate of bread, and glasses of tea. Ben turned from the stove with a pot in one hand and ladled soup into the bowls. "It's tomato, from a can. Not very impressive, but it'll fill you up until you can get back to Anna and David's house."

Cait could only stare at him in shock.

"Go on," he said, putting the pan back on the stove. "Sit down and have something to eat. It's the least I can do after letting my children abuse you and ruin your Sunday afternoon."

She sank into a chair because her knees really weren't too steady. "They didn't ruin my Sunday. Or abuse me. I had a good time at the party."

"I'm pretty sure being held hostage by a sick little boy isn't part of your usual weekend schedule." He took the seat across the table and picked up his spoon.

"Why are you so convinced you know all about me?" Cait kept her hands folded in her lap. "And why are you so positive you don't like what you know?"

He put down his spoon. "I—" His cheeks reddened. "I guess that's pretty much the way I've been treating you."

She nodded. "Pretty much."

Leaning back in his chair, he rubbed his hands over his face. "Sorry. Just call it a protective instinct."

"I'm not a threat to you, or anyone else that I know of."

His hands dropped and he gave her a wry smile. "Looked in the mirror lately?"

Cait felt her cheeks heat. "I saw lots of freckles, a snub nose and bags under my eyes from too many late nights."

Ben considered her, his head cocked to one side. "Well, yeah. But add to that a great mouth and eyes a man could drown in, plus a voice that sounds like pure sex. Now *there's* a threat." As if he hadn't just knocked the breath out of her, he took up a spoonful of tomato soup.

Cait finally recovered that voice he'd mentioned. "Sounds like *sex?*"

He nodded and pushed the plate of bread slices closer to her side of the table.

At a loss, Cait finally tasted what just happened to be her favorite soup. "Nobody's ever said it like that before."

"Hard to believe. Maybe you missed a review."

"My agent uses a press-clipping service. No article is too small." When her bowl was half-empty, she looked up again. "But that doesn't explain why I threaten you."

Under a sweater as blue as his eyes, Ben's shoulders lifted on a deep breath. He put his hands flat on the table on either side of his bowl. "For someone who writes loves songs, you're not using much imagination. I find you attractive, Cait Gregory." His eyes darkened as he stared at her. "Very attractive."

She opened her mouth, though she wasn't sure what she would say.

He stopped her with a shake of his head. "But even if I felt the need to date or have some kind of relationship, which I don't, I'm not into short-term affairs. And I can't imagine that you, with your career and your schedule, would be into anything else. That leaves me defending myself against—" he made a gesture that seemed to encompass her from head to toe "—you."

Cait allowed anger to override the embarrassment flooding through her. "You arrogant SOB." She got to her feet. "You're still making assumptions. About my morality, my taste in men, my—my lifestyle."

Ben stood up, crossed his arms over his chest, and stared her down. "Tell me I'm wrong."

"I don't have to tell you the time of day." Dropping her napkin on the table, she turned on her heel and stalked back through the house.

His footsteps pounded after her. "Where do you think you're going?"

"Somewhere else." She wrenched open the front door.

He caught her by the arm, shut the door again with the other hand. "You can't walk home in the dark."

Cait jerked back, trying to break his hold. "Let go of me. I can walk anywhere I damn well please whenever I damn well please. That's what makes me an adult." She struggled against his grip. "Let go!"

His free hand came to her other shoulder, not harsh or hurtful, but not to be argued with, either. He stared at her, his blue gaze angry, his mouth a straight, hard line. Cait, gazing up at him, caught the flicker in his eyes as that anger evolved, first to regret, then into desire. She would have continued to fight him, but the softening of his lips provoked a similar reaction within her. Instead of pushing away, her palms rested against his chest, absorbing his heat and the hammering beat of his heart. He was tall enough that she had to lean her head back to see his face; she felt exposed, vulnerable. Available.

Ben closed his eyes, wrinkled his brow as if he were in pain. When he looked at her again, need and passion had replaced all other emotions in his face. He dipped his head and Cait parted her lips, even leaned a little closer to hasten the kiss.

From the stairway behind them, a cry drifted down—small and soft, but they could hear energy gathering behind it to produce a full-blown wail.

Ben tightened his grip for an instant, then released her and backed toward the steps. "Look—I can't let you walk home by yourself in the dark, not even in this little town. If you insist, I'll put both the kids in the car and drive you myself. Or you can call David. I'll go upstairs and stay there until he gets here. I promise. Whichever way you want to do this is fine. Just don't leave alone."

Cait blew out a sharp breath. "I'll call David. And I'll wait for him to pick me up," she added, in response to the question in Ben's eyes. "You go up and make sure Shep is okay."

"Thanks." He turned and climbed the stairs with a heavy tread. She heard the murmur of his voice in Shep's room, the gradual easing of the little boy's cry. Drained, frustrated, insulted and sorry, Cait went back to the kitchen and called her brother-in-law to come take her home.

WITH ONE LOOK at her sister's face, Anna judged that the afternoon and evening hadn't been much of a success. "How was the party?"

Cait began to braid her tangled hair without combing it first. "I don't honestly know. Karen Patterson was nice, but I'm afraid I got in the way of her plans. The kids just kept asking for songs and stories."

Anna nodded. "You've always been a magnet for children. That's why—" She stopped herself just in time. Mentioning what their dad had planned for Cait's future—a career as a church musician working with children—was exactly the wrong thing to say. "You're later than I'd realized you would be. Did something else come up?"

"Shep started feeling sick. He wanted me to sit with him on the way home. Then he wouldn't let me out of the car. His father managed to control his disgust of me long enough to get the children to sleep and feed me a bowl of soup." Cait shrugged. "That's all."

That was far from all, Anna knew. "He's had a rough time," she said gently. "His whole life was shattered with his wife's death."

"And what am I supposed to do about that?" Her temper truly lost now, Cait paced the living room. "I'm not moving in on him. I don't even want to talk to him. And he doesn't have to talk to me. With the least bit of luck, we can avoid each other for the rest of the time I'm here. Which will suit me just fine." She stomped out as David came in from the kitchen.

He took off his glasses and rubbed his eyes, then looked at Anna. "What was that all about?"

"Cait and Ben seem to strike sparks off each other whenever they're together."

"That's not a signal for you to start matchmaking, Anna." He sat in the wing chair across the room and let his head fall back, his hands hanging loosely over the arms. "Your sister doesn't need a boyfriend."

"I think he would be good for her, give her roots. And she would bring him back to life."

"I think they would make each other miserable." He rolled his head from side to side, closed his eyes. "Man, what a day."

She hadn't seen him since their lunch with Cait after the church service. "What have you been doing all afternoon and evening?"

"I met with Timothy for a couple of hours, going over the books. The end of the year will be here before we know it. And with everything there is to do at Christmas, I thought I should get ahead.''

Guilt twisted her stomach. ''I'm sorry. If you brought some of the work home, I could help out here. I hate having left with you with so much to do.''

''Don't worry about it,'' he said gently, though his smile was a little forced. ''I'm just in a bad mood tonight, I guess. It's not all that big a deal. But I am tired. Ready for bed?''

He followed her into the bedroom, took his clothes out of the drawer and went into the bathroom, only returning when he was completely changed. Anna was already in bed, waiting. Hoping.

''Don't worry about Cait,'' he said as he turned off the light. ''She can take care of herself. No doubt about that.'' With a pat on his wife's hip, he shifted to his side and pulled up the covers. ''You just take care of yourself.''

Anna rolled carefully to face in the opposite direction, closing her eyes against tears. David was right, of course—she only had one responsibility right now, to do whatever was necessary to give this baby a chance. And though his…indifference…hurt her, he was simply doing everything he could to help her make the right choices. The doctor hadn't forbidden sex, though he'd suggested they keep it gentle. By eliminating their lovemaking, Anna was sure her husband thought he was helping her to keep their son alive.

The baby moved inside her—a little hand or foot pushing gently against her flesh—and she put a hand over the place, hoping he felt her love, her yearning for him to arrive safely.

Don't be in a hurry, she warned him. *I'll wait, for as long as you need.*

We'll all wait.

ON MONDAY EVENING, Harry sat at his desk long after everyone else in the office had gone for the day. For what was probably the fiftieth time, he picked up the letter he'd received that morning and read it through. The words still hadn't sunk in.

"New owner." "Efficiency expert." "Downsizing." "Restructuring." "Early retirement."

He understood the bottom line—he'd been fired. After thirty-five years of service, he had one week to clear out his desk, hand over his work and get out of the building. There would be a dinner to honor all the retirees at some future date.

Some honor. *We'll eliminate your job and give you a free dinner, maybe a gold watch.*

Oh, the benefits were good enough. He'd keep his health insurance, his investment plans, his retirement savings. This so-called efficiency expert simply thought Harry would cost the company less money sitting on his duff at home rather than working. Who was he to argue?

But how was he going to tell Peggy he didn't have a job anymore?

And what the hell would he do with the rest of his life?

CHAPTER FOUR

NEITHER MADDIE nor Shep came to choir practice on Wednesday afternoon. Cait started the children singing Christmas carols, but without Maddie's strong voice, the sound just wasn't the same. Brenna, looking rather wan herself, said Maddie hadn't been to school all week.

Karen Patterson confirmed the news. "I know Ben's had his hands full—two sick kids is a lot for one adult to manage." She put a hand over Brenna's forehead. "I think I'm about to get my own case to deal with. Come on, honey." She put an arm around her daughter. "Let's take you home to bed."

Brenna looked up in horror. "Mama, it's Halloween!"

Karen winced. "Oh, yeah. Let's get some medicine, then, see if you feel well enough to go out tonight." She looked at Cait. "School might be optional, but trick-or-treating is a mandatory commitment."

Nodding, Cait kept her face straight. "Makes perfect sense to me." Then she smiled. "I hope you feel better, Brenna."

She wondered if Maddie and Shep were still too sick to enjoy Halloween. What a shame, after all the time and thought invested in their costumes. And poor Ben, having to be the one to say no.

Later that night, after the trick-or-treaters had stopped coming and Anna and David had gone to bed, Cait sat in the living room with her guitar, playing with chords she eventually realized had segued into "Bobby McGee." She might as well go ahead and call, she decided. Then she could get them all off her mind.

"Hello?" Even the one word sounded tired.

"Hi, Ben, This is…Cait. I, um, hear you've got two patients to nurse this week."

"Yeah." He gave a rough cough. "Which was bad enough before I got sick, too."

She squeezed her eyes shut. "That's awful. Have you got someone to help you? Did you call the Shepherds?"

"Nah. They don't need to come over here and catch this bug. Besides, I'm the parent—I can take care of my kids."

"But—"

"And we're doing okay. We sleep a lot. Take our medicines at the same time, read a story or two, doze off in front of a movie. We'll get through."

It was hard to argue with such stubborn independence. "Is there anything I can do? Do you need groceries? Drinks? More medicine?"

There was a long pause. "I—I think we're covered, thanks." He sounded stunned. "I appreciate the thought, though."

"Please call if you need something." He wouldn't, of course. Why should he think about counting on somebody who was only passing through?

Why was she making trouble for herself by wishing he would?

"I guess you started on the Christmas pageant in choir today," he said. "Maddie'll be sorry to have missed that."

If he wanted to talk… "We sang a few songs. She'll catch up."

"I think she knows most of the popular carols by heart already."

That sounded all too familiar. "You must really enjoy Christmas, having two children to share the season with you."

He cleared his throat. "To be honest, Christmas is the one time of year I almost wish I'd never had kids. As far as I'm concerned, it's just another day."

Now it was Cait's turn to pause. "Really?"

"And it takes everything I've got to get through the damn month of December without exploding—or simply walking away and never, ever coming back." The bitterness in his voice was barely suppressed.

Shock held her silent. Ben Tremaine, the ultimate dad, didn't like Christmas, either?

"Sorry," he said, when she didn't respond for a minute. "Chalk that insanity up to the fever and forget about it. And thanks for checking in."

"Don't cut me off." Cait sat up straight, clutched the phone tighter, to keep him with her. "You can't say something like that and just hang up."

"Sure I can. And should."

"What happened at Christmas that makes you hate it so much?"

"I can't just be a grinch on principle?"

"It takes one to know one." She grinned. "And I know that even grinches have history."

He drew a rasping breath. "Okay. It's not too complicated. When I was six years old, the woman who called herself my mother walked out of the house on Christmas Eve and didn't come back. My dad celebrated the next twenty-two anniversaries of her departure—until he died, that is—by getting drunk and staying that way until the new year. I just never got into the Christmas spirit, some-how.''

Cait was quiet for a long time. Finally, she took the risk. ''I know what it's like to—to dread Christmas.''

''I guess the holidays are a tough time to be traveling from one show to the next.''

Though he couldn't see her, she shook her head. ''No, what's tough is just watching. From the outside. Knowing you can't get in.''

''Why can't you get in?''

The hard part. ''I was kicked out, more or less. By my father.''

After a few seconds, he said, ''Your turn to explain.''

She sighed. ''My senior year in high school, he and I had major disagreements over what I would do after grad-uation. He was thinking about college, a music education degree, a job as a church choir director and organist.''

''While you wanted the career you've got.''

''Exactly. The sooner, the better. And it all came to a head on Christmas Eve, about an hour before the pageant I'd been working on for three months. My dad found the college applications he assumed I'd submitted, hidden where I thought he'd never find them.'' She gave a wry laugh. ''Just my luck, that was the year he decided to wear his plaid vest, the one packed away in a cedar chest. In the attic. Right underneath all those application papers.''

Ben's laugh turned into a cough. ''I guess he raised holy hell.''

''There wasn't much holy about it, in my opinion, any-way. He threw me out of the house and forbade me to darken the doors of 'his' church that night and at any time in the future.''

''What about your mom?'' A gentle question.

''She died when I was four, during a miscarriage.'' Cait

took a deep breath. "It's not just the baby we're worried about with Anna. The ultrasound her doctor did at her six-month checkup showed the same condition my mom had—the placenta is too low in the womb, which could cause serious bleeding. So...we have to be really careful."

"I didn't know."

"Yeah. Anyway, I haven't given Christmas much thought since the showdown with my dad. I mean, I believe the basic story, but the human applications..."

"Leave a lot to be desired."

How strange, to be understood. Even Anna didn't quite comprehend why Cait avoided Christmas. "Definitely."

"So we're a couple of Scrooges in the middle of a whole town of Tiny Tims."

That made her laugh. "I guess so. At least I can hole up in a hotel somewhere until it's over. You still have to make the holiday for Maddie and Shep, don't you?"

"My wife—Valerie—pretty much handled Christmas for the family, and let me kind of hang around the edges. But since she was killed...I'm the main source of holiday happenings. Peggy and Harry help, but they're not here every day for the countdown."

"It must be tough."

"I'm always really glad to see that ball fall in Times Square on New Year's Eve."

In the pause, a new voice came through the line. "Daddy? My head hurts." Cait heard the rustle of clothes, a grunt from Ben, then somebody's sigh. "Is that Maddie?"

"Yeah. The fever's coming back. For all of us, I think."

"I'll let you go, then, and hope the three of you feel better tomorrow morning. Call if you need anything."

"Sure."

Ben punched off the phone and sat for a minute, cradling Maddie in his arms and thinking about the woman he was reluctantly coming to know. Caitlyn Gregory, singer and sexy, talented rising star, was someone he could easily keep at a distance.

He wasn't so sure he'd be able to resist the simpler Cait's innate charm and warmth, her willingness to give of herself.

Maddie stirred against him and he felt her forehead. "Time for more grape medicine," he murmured against her curls. As he staggered to his feet, Shep made a small noise upstairs. The reminder brought him back to reality.

Attractive as getting involved with Cait might seem, this situation wasn't about *his* wants, *his* choices. He had a responsibility to keep his children safe from any more pain, any more loss, than was absolutely necessary.

And he'd do whatever he had to in order to protect his kids. Even from a woman as agreeable as Cait Gregory was turning out to be.

"So, CAIT, what are your plans for the Christmas pageant?" Soprano Ellen Morrow settled into her spot on the pew for Thursday night adult choir rehearsal. "We're all anxious to get started—costumes take a few weeks, you know."

Cait flipped the switch to turn on the electric organ. "Um…I don't think—"

"My boys are bugging me to lend you some ewes for the stable," Timothy Bellows added. Tall and thin, Timothy sang with a rich baritone voice on Sundays and ran a very successful farming operation during the week. "I'm thinking that would be a good idea. We never had live animals before."

"Jimmy Martin's got a donkey. And there are cows all over the place." Ellen brushed back her long brown hair. "All we would need is a camel. Anybody have a camel?"

"Hugh Jones has a zebra. Will that do?" The banter continued, while Cait tried to decide how to redirect the rehearsal to music. Quickly, before someone asked a question she didn't want to answer.

"Wait a minute, folks." Timothy held up a hand and the choir quieted. "We're getting ahead of ourselves here. We haven't heard what Cait's got to say."

"I thought we'd start on some Christmas music," Cait said. "But that's as far as I've gone."

Ellen nodded. "Music is good, but these kids need to learn their parts. Who have you picked for Mary and Joseph? And the announcing angel?"

"I haven't chosen."

"You had better get busy." Regina Thorne, alto, gave her a stern look. "Anna always has these things worked out by now."

"Anna lives here," Timothy pointed out, with a grin at Cait. "Caitlyn isn't quite so settled. But she'll get into the swing of things. I'm sure her pageant will turn out just fine."

The tension in the air relaxed, and the singers settled back into their chairs. Now they were all staring at her expectantly, waiting for some grand pronouncement.

"I don't know that I'll be directing the program," Cait said, as confidently as she could manage. "I think the person who does should choose the parts and the costumes and—and all the rest."

A stunned silence fell across the small choir.

"Why wouldn't you?" Ellen said, finally.

"I—I expect Anna will have had her baby by then. So I'll have to get back to work."

Another lull in the conversation. "But she won't be ready for all the work the pageant involves. Not with a new baby." Regina shook her head. "You'll just have to stay."

Every member of the choir nodded, as if the issue were settled. Cait couldn't fight them all, so she simply ignored the issue. "Open your hymn books to page 153. We'll warm up with a few verses of 'Silent Night.'"

The rehearsal proceeded smoothly after that, except for the suggestions that popped up with every new Christmas song—ideas about staging and casting and props, until Cait thought she would start pounding out a Bach fugue on the organ, just to keep everyone quiet.

Once they'd finished singing, Timothy joined Cait at the organ. "We've got money set aside in the church budget for the pageant, you know. You don't have to put something together on a shoestring." He winked at her. "As church treasurer, I might even be able to pad the expense account a little. Just tell me what you need to spend and I'll see that the money's there."

"That's good to hear," she told him. "But—"

"No buts." Timothy squeezed her shoulder and headed for the door. "You just leave it to me."

Ellen was the last one to leave, standing by while Cait straightened her music. "You're not really planning to leave Anna stranded on this pageant, are you?"

Cait slapped her notebook closed. "No, I don't plan to leave her stranded. I plan to be sure there's someone else to take on this project. You, for instance." She gazed at the soprano as the obvious finally hit her. "You'd be perfect, and you already have some great ideas."

"Oh, no. Not me." Ellen backed away, shaking her head. She was a tall, heavy woman with an incredibly pure voice. "I'm no good at telling people what to do."

"This won't be like ordering them to—to clean up their rooms or take out the garbage. They'll be glad to do whatever will make the pageant work."

Again, Ellen shook her head. "I've got three kids under eight. My husband works up at the furniture factory and he's not about to baby-sit when he comes home after a ten-hour day. My mama keeps the kids on Thursdays so I can come to choir, but she'd never stand for me putting in the kind of time this program will take. I just can't." Walking backward, she reached the door. "You're the one to do it, Cait. You know that." And then she was gone.

"No, I'm not," Cait said to the empty church. Ben Tremaine would understand. Strange, how they were so completely different, and yet they shared this—this *phobia,* she supposed they should call it, about the holiday most people loved.

"Yulephobia," she said aloud, walking to Anna's car through the cold November night. She would have to remember to mention the word to Ben when she had a chance. With pleasure, she could imagine the slow widening of his grin, the dawning laugh in his eyes. She liked making Ben laugh.

Anna didn't laugh the next morning when Cait recounted the conversation at choir practice. "I could have told you Ellen wouldn't be able to take on the pageant. She's got all the responsibility she can handle at home."

"That's what she said." Cait studied her sister, noticing the lack of light in Anna's brown eyes, the absence of color in her cheeks. "Are you feeling okay?"

"Kinda achy," Anna admitted. "Tired. The baby moved around a lot last night, and I couldn't sleep."

"You should go back to bed. There's nothing going on that I can't handle—a few dishes, a little laundry." She got up and closed her hands around Anna's shoulders, easing her to her feet. "Go on. Git. I'll wake you up for lunch."

With a sigh, Anna headed for the bedroom. "Give me enough time to take a shower first. Peggy Shepherd's coming by this afternoon. I ought to look halfway decent." She glanced at the mirror in the hallway. "As if that's really possible anymore." Her slow, scuffing footsteps faded as she moved down the hall.

Cait got the chores done, then sat down with her guitar in the living room, still playing around with an arrangement for "Bobby McGee." Why did the sweet, stirring words automatically bring Ben to mind?

Not much of challenge there—the man was seriously, fatally attractive. And off-limits to a rootless player like herself. One reason his assumptions had made her so angry on Sunday was that he was pretty much correct. The few close relationships she'd experienced hadn't lasted long. Working in the entertainment industry pulled people apart, no matter how much they cared about each other. And in the end, she'd always chosen the job over the man. So she would just have to put these Ben Tremaine fantasies completely out of her head.

Determined, she strummed up a loud and rowdy version of "Hit the Road, Jack."

Midmorning, David bolted into the house at his usual double-time speed. "Where's Anna?"

Cait ran through an arpeggio. "She was tired this morning, so I sent her back to bed."

He stopped dead in the center of the room. "Is she okay?"

"I think so. Just tired." David always worried too much.

"Have you checked on her?"

His voice had taken on a harshness she'd never heard

before. Startled, Cait stared up at her brother-in-law. "I figured she'd call if she needed something." By the end of the sentence, she was talking to herself. David had stalked down the hallway to the bedroom, his heels like rocks pounding on the wood floor.

In a minute he was back. "She's asleep."

"That's what I figured." Cait smiled teasingly. But David didn't smile back and she let hers fade. "What's wrong? Why are you so tense?"

He dropped into the chair just behind him, put his bony elbows on his bony knees, then took off his glasses to rub his eyes. "I—I can't take too much more of this."

"Of what?"

"The worry. The waiting. Never knowing if the next hour, or the next minute, will bring on a full-scale emergency." Shaking his head, he let his hands fall between his knees. "I'm so tired."

She wasn't sure what to say. "You always have to wait on babies. It's the nature of the process, right?"

David didn't answer, just stared at the floor, his head hanging low.

"It will be okay, David. You know it will."

"Do I?" He looked up again, his eyes bleak. "It wasn't okay the last two times. We were careful, and we prayed, and…the babies died anyway. There's no more guarantee with this one. And she's far enough along that we could lose Anna *and* the baby."

"You have to believe that won't happen."

"You're right. I do." He laughed, but the sound was bitter. "I'm the minister. My faith's strong, steady, one-hundred percent reliable. 'Whatever my lot…it is well with my soul,'" he said, quoting an old hymn. Then he muttered a rude word, one Cait had never heard him use.

"Cait? Who's here?" Anna came into the living room.

"Oh, David—what are you doing home in the middle of the morning?" She looked a little more rested, but no less pale.

David cast a warning glance at Cait and got to his feet. "I needed a book I'd left at home to work on Sunday's sermon." He crossed to his wife and brushed a kiss over her forehead. "See you for lunch." Before Anna could say anything else, he left the room, and then the house.

Anna sank onto the couch across from Cait. "What were you two talking about?"

"You, of course. You're everybody's favorite topic of conversation." But Anna shouldn't have to worry about David's doubts, so Cait decided to gloss over those details. "I must get asked five times a day how you're doing, and how much longer it will be and is there something somebody can help you with. You've got a lot of friends in this town."

"They're good people." She lay back against the cushions. "That's why I hate to disappoint them with the Christmas pageant. Maybe I can do it," Anna said, sitting up again. "I don't really have to stand up to direct or to plan. I can sit and think—"

"No, you don't." Cait put a hand on her sister's knee. "You do not need the stress of trying to plan and worry. You have to stay calm and relaxed. I'll find somebody to handle the program for you. I swear. I can't do it myself, but I won't leave you in the lurch."

For the first time that day, Anna actually smiled.

Cait only hoped she could deliver on her promise.

MADDIE AND SHEP were much better on Friday, though they still didn't go back to school. Ben was on his feet again, although not feeling a hundred percent, and he spent hours clearing away three-days' worth of mess.

When Peggy called to ask about the kids coming for dinner, he was sorely tempted, just so he could flake out for a solid night's sleep.

But he owed his kids more than that. "I planned to call you and suggest we skip this week. The kids have had the flu—"

"What? Why didn't you call me? Are they getting better? Have you taken them to see Dr. Hall?"

He smiled a little at her fierce concern. "I didn't want you and Harry getting sick. And yes, they're much better—enough that they spent the day running around the house whenever I had my back turned. I'll probably let them outside tomorrow, or maybe Sunday."

"Ben, I wish you wouldn't be quite so independent. They're our grandkids. We *want* to help."

"I know. And when I really need help, you'll be the first people I ask. But this was just the flu. No big deal." Discounting his sleepless nights, his foggy, bumbling days. "Anyway, I don't think we'll go out tonight. But Sunday everything should be back to normal." He hoped.

"Well, then, y'all will come to lunch on Sunday so I can fatten you up again."

"That sounds great. How's your week been? This cold weather must've killed off the last of your garden."

"It did. We need to clean up all the dead stuff. And I guess there's going to be plenty of time for that now." Peggy hesitated. "Harry's been asked to take early retirement."

"Just out of the blue?"

"Pretty much. Today is his last day."

"Jeez…Harry loved his work. Is he okay?"

"He says so. He's been doing financial calculations every night this week, budgeting, projecting, showing me how our money will work and what we'll be living on. It's all very well set up."

"It would be. Harry's great with numbers—the IRS should keep records as good as his. So you think he'll make the transition without too much trouble?"

"I think he has projects lined up to keep him busy for a couple of years. He wants to enlarge the vegetable garden, spruce up the bathrooms—I've already bought the paint and paper—and at least a dozen other jobs."

"That sounds promising."

"I suppose." She sighed. "I would have thought he would be more upset—he's worked at that plant since he was sixteen, full-time since he left the army. But I won't borrow trouble. You take care of yourself, now. And please call if you need anything."

"I will. I promise."

Ben punched off the phone, wishing his mood could be improved with a few kind words. Unfortunately, the one person he'd like to hear those words from was a lady who wasn't going to be around for long. So it wouldn't do anyone any good for them to get too close.

Still, when she showed up at his door Saturday morning, he couldn't deny he was glad to see her.

"Chicken soup," Cait said, holding up a jar. "It's store-bought, but it ought to be good for something. Books," she gestured to her other arm, filled with a stack of colorful paperbacks. "Guaranteed to occupy ten- and six-year olds for at least a couple of hours while their dad grabs a nap."

"Cait." He shook his head, laughing. "You didn't have to do this. What about Anna?"

"David is with Anna. And your poor children need to see someone besides their haggard dad this week. Now, do I get to come in?" She wore a sweater the color of emeralds over black jeans, both snug enough to jump-start a man's fantasies.

Fortunately for Ben's imagination, Maddie dashed into the living room, followed by Shep. "Miss Caitlyn!" Ben caught her shoulders just before she grabbed Cait around the legs. "I'm so glad to see you!"

"I'm glad to see you so bright-eyed. And Shep's looking pretty tough for a guy who's had the flu. Didn't let it get you down, did you?"

To Ben's surprise, Shep shook his head. He rarely responded to direct questions from anyone other than his dad and, sometimes, Peggy.

"Is that soup?" Maddie stared at the jar.

"Chicken soup. Why don't we go into the kitchen and warm it up?"

The three of them swept through the house, leaving Ben to close the front door. Somehow the presence of another adult in the house made him realize suddenly how ill he really felt. Even though the other person was Cait, and there were at least five good reasons he shouldn't depend on her, he had an overwhelming desire to go to bed. Alone.

"Are you still down here?" Cait stood in the doorway to the kitchen. "Do I have to carry you up to bed myself?"

He managed a grin. "Do you think you could?"

She looked him up and down, and his pulse jumped. "No. I'd have to drag you. You'd be better off walking on your own two legs." Turning on her heel, she went away again.

Although the stairs seemed incredibly steep, Ben climbed to the second floor and even changed into clean sweatpants and a T-shirt before crawling into his bed. A few minutes—or it might have been a few hours—later, he felt a cool palm on his forehead. "Medicine, SuperDad."

He gobbled the pills and slurped the water she brought.

"Now go to sleep." That same hand stroked his hair back from his face, and he smiled at the gentleness of her touch. Then the door to his room closed, leaving him to blessed, irresponsible darkness and sleep.

"THIS IS NICE," Maddie said late in the afternoon, when the four of them were sitting around the kitchen table finishing their soup. "You should come over more often, Miss Caitlyn."

"I've enjoyed myself," Cait said, ignoring Ben as he choked on a spoonful of chicken and noodles. "I don't get to read many kids' stories these days. But we read a bunch of good books together, didn't we?"

"My favorite was the fairy-tale book. I 'specially liked the story about the swan princess."

Cait noticed that Shep stared at his sister and shook his head. Obviously he didn't agree with her choice, but he wasn't going to share his opinion.

When the children wandered off to play video games, she made Ben stay seated while she cleared the table. "You can go back to the macho act in an hour or so. For now, just put up with being taken care of."

"Thank you. I'm grateful. Really."

Cait met his serious gaze. "I know." Tension stretched between them, a tightness she could feel pulling deep inside her. Looking away, she broke the contact. "I'm probably being nosy, so you can tell me to shut up if you want to. Have you tried any kind of therapy for Shep?"

He shook his head. "I'm not sure there's one we haven't tried. The therapists all say the same thing. Elective mutism—that means he can talk, and will when he wants to. Until then, forcing him would be tantamount to torture.''

''I don't know how you'd compel him to speak, anyway. It's pretty easy to understand what he wants and pretty hard not simply to give it to him.''

''Yeah.'' Ben rubbed his face with his hands. ''So we stumble along the way things are. He goes to choir to be with the other kids, even though he doesn't sing. He can do all the paperwork he's assigned in school and his teacher doesn't mark him down because he doesn't talk. But I'd really like to hear him say 'Daddy' again.''

The longing in Ben's eyes hurt her heart. She wanted to put her arms around his shoulders, give him her comfort. But Cait didn't have a single doubt about where such an embrace would lead. And neither of them wanted or needed any more complications.

She finished wiping the counter, folded the dishcloth, and then turned back to the table. ''I guess I'd better get out of your way.''

The phone rang. Ben picked up the receiver, but didn't say anything beyond ''Hello'' for quite a while. ''You're sure?'' he said at last. ''Right. Let me know if there's anything at all I can do.''

Cait thought he would hang up. Instead, he extended the phone to her. ''It's Dave. Anna's in the hospital.''

''Oh, my God.'' She took the handset with a shaking hand. ''David? What's happened?''

''She started bleeding. Not really bad, but—'' he sounded totally exhausted ''—we called the doctor, and he met us at the emergency room.''

''Is Anna okay? Is…is the baby all right?''

''So far.'' He sighed. ''But she's confined to complete bed rest from this point on. No going anywhere, no sitting up. She's to lie on her left side for six weeks, at least.

Longer, if possible." His voice wobbled, and he cleared his throat. "I knew it, Cait. I knew we shouldn't get our hopes up."

"Oh, David." She didn't have the words to console him. "Are you with Anna? Is she—can I talk to her?"

He didn't answer. "Cait?" Anna's voice was thick with tears. "Oh, Cait, what are we going to do?"

"You are going to do just what they said—stay in bed. I'm going to take care of absolutely everything else."

"What about Christmas? What about the pageant? I can't possibly do anything to help. If we have to cancel—"

"You don't have to cancel." None of the people Cait had talked to in the past couple of days had agreed to direct the Christmas program. Almost all of them would help, but no one wanted to accept responsibility for the ultimate outcome. "Don't worry, Anna. There *will* be a Christmas pageant. Count on it."

She got her sister to stop crying before she said goodbye. Then she put the phone back in its cradle.

"I'm sorry," Ben said. "This is a really hard time for your family."

"It could be worse." She saw his eyes darken, knew he understood that her comment referred to his own hard times. "But now I'm really trapped. No way out of the Christmas pageant anymore."

"What about the Christmas pageant?" Maddie padded into the kitchen. "Are we ready to start practicing? Remember—" she held out her arms in an imitation of wings. "—I get to be the announcing angel."

Cait chuckled. "No, we're not quite ready to start practicing yet. But at least we know for sure there will be a pageant, and who will be directing it."

"Who? Who's the director?" Maddie asked.

Reaching out, Cait ruffled Maddie's curls. "You're looking at her," she said.

"Oh boy!"

"You can say that again." An idea struck so fast, came through so strongly, she had no choice but to announce it right away. "I *am* going to pull this pageant together."

She looked across at Ben, met his suddenly wary eyes with a serious stare of her own.

"And your dad, Maddie, is going to help me."

CHAPTER FIVE

"No. Absolutely not." Ben paced across the kitchen and back again, looking like a man being chased by the ghost of Christmas Past. "I am the last person in town you should be talking to about pageants."

Undaunted, Cait folded her arms over her chest and leaned back against the counter. "You're only the second to last. I was the last, and I just caved. If I'm going down on this, I'm taking you with me." Ben had sent Maddie and Shep to their rooms, but she kept her voice as quiet as his, in case they were listening.

"Why? What did I do to you?"

She could have written a couple of songs about what he did to her. But that wasn't his point. "We're a matched set," she told him instead. "This year, the grinches do Christmas."

"A guaranteed recipe for disaster."

"As far as I'm concerned, if nobody else in this town is willing to take over for Anna, then they deserve what they get."

He shook his head. "I have zero enthusiasm for this project."

"That makes two of us." She watched him for a moment. "You told David to let you know if there was something you could do." Ben looked at her, his eyes narrow, his mouth open to protest. "*This* is what you can do for them."

Ben braced his arms on the kitchen table and let his head hang loose from his shoulders. *This* was not fair. He had enough trouble making Christmas for his own kids. Why should he have to make Christmas for everybody in the whole damn town?

But there was nothing fair about life. He'd known that to be true even before he'd lost Valerie. Now David and Anna stood the risk of losing their baby, and that wasn't fair, either.

In the face of life's devastating tricks, friends and family were the anchor, the link to solid ground. How could he refuse to return in kind what the Remingtons had already done for him?

If Cait had continued to argue with him, he might have been able to talk himself out of the situation. But she stood quietly across the room, letting him reach the only possible conclusion all by himself.

"Okay, damn you." He straightened and turned to face her. "I'll do what I can. I'll get my revenge, though. Someday, somehow."

"Such a gracious concession." Her grin took the sting out of the words. "I know it'll be terrible, Ben. But Christmas comes and goes. We won't have to suffer long."

He laughed in spite of himself. "I don't think they'll be using us for any Christmas card slogans this year."

"No, they can just take pictures of the pageant and leave the inside of the cards blank. Do you have a pen and paper?"

When he brought her a notepad and pencil, she sat down at the table, staring at him expectantly until he took his own seat.

"If we organize this now, we won't have to think so much later," she said. "Let's divide the show into committees. There's the music and script committee—that would be me. Costumes. Staging and props—that's you.''

Ben put his head down in his arms and groaned.

She flicked his ear with the tip of the pencil. ''Sit up and concentrate. Somebody said something about a reception at the minister's house?''

He sat up. ''There's a procession from the church to the house, and everybody goes in for carols and desserts.''

''Mmm. So we need a refreshment committee. And a decorations committee—Anna won't be able to do her own this year.''

''Who gets to run all these committees?'' He had to admire her organized approach.

''That's where you come in. I need suggestions, and you know the people here.''

''You want me to volunteer other people to do all this work?''

Cait smiled sweetly. ''Do you want to do everything yourself?''

''Good point.''

For the next two hours they plotted and planned—filling in names of volunteers as they occurred to Ben, discussing and making notes on the stage setup and materials.

''Animals,'' Cait said suddenly. ''We need an animal department. People want live ones this year.''

''Why not just use drawings?''

Her stare was contemptuous. ''We're setting a standard here. No skimping.''

''Yes, ma'am. So you need a cleanup crew, too.''

She reconsidered. ''Maybe we'll cover the floor with a tarp.''

He grinned. ''Quick thinking.''

''Well.'' Paging through their lists, she nodded her

head. "I think we've made a good start. I'll call people tomorrow and tell them their assignments." She pushed back the chair and got to her feet.

Ben stood, too. "Not ask them?"

"Nope. They had their chance to volunteer. Now it's time for the draft."

"You're a hard woman, Cait Gregory." He followed her toward the front of the house.

"I know." She turned back before she reached the door and before he'd quite stopped, which brought them close together. He could see the flecks of gold in her green eyes, the freckles across her nose and cheeks. Just below his line of vision, her breasts rose and fell on a deep breath.

His own breathing seemed to stop altogether. He was touching her, Ben realized with surprise, his hand resting lightly on her shoulder, his thumb rubbing over the curve of her collarbone underneath the emerald sweater. Cait's lips were slightly parted, her eyes dark. The next moment would, obviously, bring a kiss. And they both knew it.

She put her hand on his chest. "Ben. Not a good idea."

"You're right." He forced air into his lungs and stepped back, putting a decent distance between them. "Sorry. Um…I'll start sketching out some of the stage plans we talked about. And I'll call some of the *volunteers.*"

Her smile was quiet, grateful. Intimate, instead of the high-watt expression he'd seen her use in the past. Did she know how dangerous she was with that smile?

He opened the door, let the north wind in to cool him off. "'Night, Cait. I'll be in touch."

"Good night. And thanks."

"Sure." He stood on the porch and watched until she got to her car, kept his eyes on it until her taillights disappeared around the corner. Only then did he feel the cold porch stones under his feet, the headache pulsing behind his eyes.

Inside and upstairs, he checked on the kids and, with relief, found them both asleep. He really didn't think he could handle any more chat about Christmas tonight. With the house locked up, he went to his own room and took some medicine for the headache, popped a couple of cough drops into his mouth. He couldn't afford to use the stuff that knocked him out all night—if Maddie or Shep woke up, he might not hear them.

Once asleep, he dreamed, as he'd known he would. Dreamed that Cait hadn't stopped him, that he'd kissed her the way he wanted to. And then she was pulling out of his arms, walking away without looking back, and he just stood there and let her go.

He woke up, turned-on and furious and spent the rest of the night dozing in front of the television in the den downstairs. It wasn't restful. But at least he didn't dream.

HARRY DRAGGED HIMSELF out of bed on Sunday morning about nine o'clock. He found Peggy in the kitchen, cooking. Not breakfast, though.

"Meat loaf?" He pulled out a mug and poured some coffee, added sugar and cream. "Lasagna? What's going on?"

"Ben called. Anna Remington went to the hospital with bleeding yesterday afternoon."

Thinking through the implications took him a minute. "She's not due, is she? Did she lose the baby?"

Peggy opened the oven and pulled out a chicken casserole. "No. But she's on complete bed rest until the baby's born. I thought I would make them some meals they could stick in the freezer. That way Cait won't have to do all the cooking. She's taken over the Christmas pageant, so she'll be busy."

"Oh." Not a very sympathetic response, as Peggy's puzzled stare indicated. He gathered his thoughts. "I hope Anna will be all right, and the baby. I'm not worried about the Christmas program. Cait Gregory is a young woman who knows how to get what she wants."

"Evidently," Peggy said in a dry tone. "She's got Ben helping her with the pageant."

Harry choked and sputtered coffee all over his robe. "Ben? Christmas?"

"That's what he said."

Before they married, Valerie had explained to her parents Ben's reasons for avoiding Christmas. She'd hoped, Harry knew, that their own family traditions and the children's love for the holiday would change her husband's perspective.

Then they'd lost her. These last two Christmases, Peggy had worked hard to give the grandkids a special time. And Ben had cooperated. Was the fact that he'd agreed to help with the pageant a sign that the change Valerie had hoped for was coming to pass?

Or just a tribute to Cait Gregory's good looks and talents of persuasion?

The latter, Harry guessed, helping himself to another mug of coffee. Ben wasn't blind, or deaf. Or a fool.

"You're not supposed to have cream in your coffee." Peggy was molding meat loaf into pans. "And you're only supposed to have one cup a morning."

He grunted, sipped his drink, and heard her sigh.

After a minute, she said, "What do you have planned for today? I can clear out the bathroom, if you want to start painting."

"I don't think so. Doesn't seem like the right time to start a project that big."

"Oh." She put the meat loaf pans in the oven. "Well, Ben and the children are coming for lunch. But we could drive into Washington late this afternoon, have a nice dinner in Georgetown, see a movie." On her way to the sink, she stopped beside him and laid a hand along his cheek. "We could spend the night," she whispered into his ear. "It's been a while since we've been away for even that long."

A movie, he could have managed. Dinner, okay—he would eat sometime, though he wasn't too hungry these days.

But a night in a hotel with Peggy...Harry shook his head. She would expect him to make love to her. He was a lucky man, to have a gorgeous wife who still wanted him. Many men his age would envy him.

And yet, the thought of sex left him cold. For the first time in thirty years of marriage, he just...didn't want to.

She was staring at him now, waiting for his answer, a confused frown in her eyes. Harry struggled for a reasonable excuse to offer.

"I—uh can't get away today. I've got a church property committee meeting, even if David's not there. I don't know how long it'll take."

"Oh." Peggy moved away to work on the dishes stacked in the sink. Her straight shoulders and back conveyed their own message. She wouldn't get mad. But she wasn't happy about being turned down, either.

Harry put his mug on the counter and started to leave the kitchen. Then he turned back and put his hand on Peggy's shoulder. "It was a nice idea," he said. "Someday soon we'll do just that."

"Of course. Someday." She didn't move, or even bend her head toward him when he kissed her temple.

Might be sleeping on the sofa tonight, he reflected as he went upstairs to dress for church. Sofa or bed, didn't matter. The way he felt, he wasn't much good to Peggy regardless of where he slept. Wasn't much good awake, either.

Picking up his hairbrush, Harry looked at the man in the mirror, the man with nowhere to go Monday morning, or any other day of the week. The man without a job.

He just plain wasn't much good anymore at all.

Cait met the Tremaine family outside the church building just before the service. Under the pale-blue sky, a bitter wind whipped the fallen leaves along the brick walk. Standing with Brenna and two other girls, Maddie wore the perfect little-girl outfit—a bright-blue wool coat with a black velvet collar and shiny black shoes over white tights.

Nearby, Shep chased through the grass and leaves with his friend Neil, one of the few children besides Maddie with whom he seemed to communicate. He looked like a typical six-year-old boy. And he was...except that he refused to speak.

Ben himself was almost too handsome this morning to be real. A starched white shirt deepened his tan, the blue of his eyes was echoed in a blue silk tie, and his gray suit had been tailored to make the most of those wide shoulders and long legs. It was a sight guaranteed to destroy a woman's ability to concentrate. Or even breathe easily.

He grinned as Cait approached him. "So have you started handing out assignments? Do folks know what they're getting into?"

She shook her head. "I'll make my calls after the service. They can have their morning to relax."

As she walked toward the church door, he fell in beside her. "How's Anna?"

"Doing pretty well, thank goodness. She convinced her doctor that she would stay in bed if he let her come home, so the ambulance will bring her back this afternoon."

"How about Dave? Is he here?"

"He stayed at the hospital all night, and I don't think he slept, but he got home about nine and he's planning to preach."

"The man drives himself too hard. As far as I know, he hasn't taken a vacation since he started at this church. Definitely not since we moved here." He looked back over his shoulder. "Shep, Maddie—time to go inside."

Maddie ran down the walk. "Can Brenna sit with us, Daddy? Can she?" She stopped pulling on his coat sleeve and smiled at Cait. "Hi, Miss Caitlyn. Have you figured out all the parts for the Christmas pageant yet? Brenna wants to be a shepherd. Right, Brenna?"

But Maddie's friend was too shy to express a preference, and simply shook her head, avoiding Cait's gaze.

"Can the two of you sit together and be quiet," Ben asked.

"I promise, Daddy. We won't make a sound."

"Okay. Shep! Come on, son."

Throwing a last handful of leaves at his friend, Shep ran toward them. Ben took a second to brush grass and twigs and pieces of leaves out of the boy's hair and off his sweater, with his son squirming and frowning during the process. Then he reached around Cait to grab the iron door handle on the heavy wooden door. The move put her inside the circle of his arm. She glanced up...Ben looked down at her, and something passed between them that was real and warm.

Cait gave him a shaky smile and scooted into the church, down the aisle to the organ, where she was safe. With her back to the congregation—to *him*—she arranged her music and started the prelude, a Bach fugue which required all of her attention.

Music was the answer, she thought later, letting her mind drift away from David's sermon. Keep the career, the work in mind. That was the surest way to keep Ben Tremaine at a distance.

ANNA WASN'T ALLOWED even to walk into her own house—the ambulance attendants carried her on a gurney to her bedroom, where Cait and David waited with the bed turned down.

Cait started to pull the covers up, then stopped. "Do you want a clean gown? Or a shower?" She looked anxious. "Are you allowed to take showers?"

Some other time, Anna might have laughed. But not today. "He said to give it a few days. Sponge baths until then. I had one at the hospital, so I'm fine." She held out her hand for the covers. "Just a little cold."

Cait tucked the blanket and sheet around her. "Something to eat? Our special is chicken soup—I bought some extra of the kind I took to Ben Tremaine and his kids yesterday. It was pretty good."

"Not right now. I think I might take a nap." Which was a lie, of course, but it got Cait and David to leave the room and stop staring at her as if she would explode any second.

If she closed her eyes, the inevitable tears would start, so Anna stared at the wedding invitation in a silver frame that she kept on her bedside table. Three years ago, she'd

been the happiest bride the world had ever seen. David
had been appointed to his post in the Goodwill church,
they'd seen the really adorable century-old house they
would get to live in, and she just knew that she'd have a
baby to hold before a year had passed. Cait had always
been the ambitious sister. Anna had only wanted to get
married and have kids and keep house for the husband
she loved.

But it took longer than a year to get pregnant, the first
time. Much of a minister's work happened after other people had left their jobs—meetings with church committees,
evening services, counseling. David worked hard during
the days, too, writing sermons, visiting hospitals and people sick at home, just getting to know the members of his
church.

So the year had been more stressful than either of them
had anticipated, and they hadn't had much free time. Finally, though, on Valentine's Day of their second year
together, she'd been able to tell him they were expecting.

A month later, she lost the baby.

Everyone was very kind, especially Peggy Shepherd,
who'd lost several babies of her own before her daughter
was born. Anna had depended a lot on the older woman.
When she got pregnant again, she told Peggy before she
let her father know.

She'd kept that baby four months. The doctor advised
waiting at least six months before trying again. Meanwhile, David's responsibilities increased. Sex became an
appointment scheduled for the time of the month she was
ovulating, otherwise to be forgotten or put off.

Anna started to roll onto her back, then remembered
she was supposed to stay on her left side to promote op-
timum blood flow to and from the baby. She might go
crazy, lying on her left side for…how long?

Yesterday, when the bleeding started, her first reaction had been not fear, but relief. If the baby was born, the doctors would take care of him, be responsible for him, and Anna's life would go back to normal. David would look at her as a woman again, not an incubator with mechanical malfunctions. Sex could be something they did because they loved each other....

She must have fallen asleep, because when she opened her eyes again, the room was dark.

"Anna?" Cait stuck her head through the partially opened door. "You awake?"

"Mmm." Again, she started to roll over and stopped herself. "Come in."

Cait opened the door all the way and stepped into the room. She turned on a small lamp in the far corner. "How are you feeling?"

Anna bit back the urge to growl. "Next question."

"Okay." She sat in the rocking chair they'd asked Ben to make when Anna was first pregnant. "David had a class to teach at six. He'll be back in about an hour. Do you want something to eat now, or do you want to wait for him?"

I don't care was the first thought that came to Anna's mind. "We can wait," she said. "I'm not hungry."

After a minute, Cait said, gently, "What's wrong, Annabelle? You don't sound like yourself."

The urge to pour out all her complaints to her sister was almost overpowering. But Cait had never been really sure about David as husband material, and any hint that there was trouble might set her solidly against him. Not to mention the fact that Anna couldn't bear for anyone to know how much she didn't want to be pregnant anymore.

So she searched for a change of subject. "I'm just...worried. And still tired. And wondering what you've decided to do about the pageant.'' That should be enough of a diversion.

Cait actually chuckled. "I have everything planned out. Committees set up, people to be in charge of them, the whole bit."

"Really? And a director? Somebody to pull it all together?"

"Two, actually. Me—"

"Oh, Cait."

"—and Ben Tremaine."

The shock held Anna speechless for a minute. "Ben? Ben's helping you?"

"He is. He's also in charge of the stage and backdrops."

"How amazing." She didn't know exactly why he felt as he did, but Ben's aversion to Christmas had always been easy to see.

Her sister chuckled. "He was pretty amazed, himself."

For the first time since September, Anna's concerns about the pageant faded. "I'm sure between you, you'll produce a wonderful program. Thank you so much." She sniffed back tears. "I love you, you know."

Cait came to the bed and bent to give her a kiss. "Back at ya, Annabelle. Now let me go see about some soup."

Even lying on her left side would be bearable, Anna thought, now that she knew the pageant would be a success. Cait never failed at anything she attempted. Especially when there was music involved.

EXCEPT FOR the visit from Ben and the grandkids, Sunday at the Shepherd house passed pretty much in silence. Peggy didn't volunteer conversation and Harry couldn't think of anything to say. The property committee meeting didn't start until four, but he couldn't hang around the house with nothing to do, so he stopped by Peggy's sewing room a little before three o'clock to say goodbye. "I'm going on down to the church."

She didn't look up. "I'll wait dinner for you."

"Sure." He started to cross the room to give her a kiss. But what kind of expectation would that create? "See you later, then."

David Remington had left a message saying he would miss the meeting to stay home with his wife, so Harry unlocked the church when he arrived and turned on the lights in the office, even made some coffee while he waited for the other committee members. With half an hour left to kill, he decided to check the balance in the property budget and draw up some preliminary figures for the repairs needed.

The church accounts were still kept the old-fashioned way, written with pencil and ink in cloth-bound ledgers. Harry pulled out the book for the current year and sat down at the church library table, glad to have some numbers to think about.

That satisfaction didn't last long. The property committee budget should have been healthy, thanks to a bequest from Kathleen Fogarty, a faithful widow who had recently passed away. Her ten thousand dollars would make getting the roof fixed, or the heating and air-conditioning replaced—whichever priority they chose— much more feasible. But though he checked the figures several times, he could only come to one conclusion.

Mrs. Fogarty's ten thousand dollars had never made it into the church account.

POPCORN, Cait thought. *They're like popcorn.*

The first official rehearsal for the Christmas pageant children's choir was not going as planned. Most of the kids in town, from preschool through eighth grade, were in attendance. That was about twenty kids more than she'd expected. Ideally, they'd all be seated on the steps leading up to the platform at the front of the church, quietly waiting to hear her instructions.

In reality, they were constantly moving. No sooner did she get one corner settled than the Tyson twins shot out from the other side of the group, chasing each other down the aisle, making growling noises. She couldn't tell them apart, either, which made calling them to the front again a real challenge.

Even as she brought the rambunctious twins back to the steps, a new commotion erupted on the last row. Shep and Neil went rolling across the platform, coming to rest against the foot of the pulpit, where they continued to wrestle.

Cait flipped her braid behind her shoulder. "Shep. Neil." No response beyond Neil's giggles. "Shep!" She used her stage voice, the one that would reach the back row of an auditorium, if it had to.

That got their attention. The boys looked around, still holding on to each other.

"Sit. Down. Now." They didn't move for a second. Then Neil tickled Shep, and the fight began again.

"Shepherd Eldridge Tremaine, stand up." Ben's voice came from the back of the church. His deliberate footsteps on the bare plank floors of the room were loud in the sudden silence. "When Miss Caitlyn tells you to do something, you do it. Right away. No questions, no protests. Do you understand me?"

On their feet now, Shep and Neil both nodded and sidled into their spots on the back row.

"The same goes for the rest of you," Ben said. "Anybody who can't cooperate doesn't deserve to have a part in the pageant. Got that?'' In unison, the kids nodded. ''Good. Now listen to what Miss Caitlyn has to say.'' He sat at the end of the first pew, arms crossed, evidently intending to play bailiff.

Struggling with embarrassment and temper, Cait didn't have anything to say for a minute. Finally, she calmed down enough to give Ben a brief nod. ''Thanks, Mr. Tremaine.'' Then she turned back to the choir.

''Everybody sit down.'' The kids, of course, sat. Who wouldn't, with a Secret Service agent watching their every move? Cait picked up the red folders she'd prepared and began handing them out. ''This booklet has a copy of some of the songs we're going to learn for the pageant. We'll add more as we go along. At the end of today's practice, each of you can put your name on your folder and leave it here with me, so you'll have them every week.''

Maddie raised her hand. ''Have you assigned the parts, Miss Caitlyn? Who gets to be the angel?''

''I'll have that worked out by next week,'' Cait said, and watched Maddie's face fall. ''Everybody will get to wear a costume—everybody will have some part to play. That way, the pageant will belong to everybody.'' That didn't mean, of course, that some kids wouldn't be disappointed. She hadn't figured out how to avoid the inevitable cries of ''Why not me?''

With Ben standing guard, the rest of the practice proceeded without much trouble. The kids didn't sing very strongly—they weren't confident enough to perform for an audience, even an audience of one. But Cait got an idea of their voices, where the strengths and weakness of the choir lay. By the time their parents started arriving to take them home, she had some ideas about which children would be good in which roles.

When she dismissed them, the group exploded like a firecracker, with parts shooting off in all directions. Darkness had fallen outside before the church regained its peace. In the welcome silence, she could hear a sharp wind rattling the windowpanes.

"The weatherman said it might snow." Maddie helped Cait stack the music folders in a box. "Wouldn't that be wonderful? And maybe it'll snow for our pageant on Christmas Eve and we can walk through the snow for the processional. Wouldn't that just be amazing, Miss Cait?"

Though still upset, she couldn't hold back a smile. "I'd love to see some snow this early in November. Maybe we'll have a white Thanksgiving."

"Oh, wow." Maddie looked at her dad as he came across the room. "A white Thanksgiving, Daddy. Can you imagine?"

"Just barely." He grinned. "You and Shep get your coats. We need to let Miss Caitlyn go home for supper."

Maddie caught her brother by the hand and ran to the back pew, where the coats had been piled. Cait finished stacking the folders and put the top on the storage box, unwilling to argue with Ben over his interference—especially with the children listening—but unable to say a word about anything else.

"Those kids are wild sometimes." Ben shook his head and picked up the box of folders just as she started to. "I hope they remember to listen next week."

Cait put her arms around the box and pulled it out of his hold, then walked away. "I can carry this." She knew the gesture was childish. So was sulking.

"I'm sure you can." He caught up with her halfway across the church. "But you don't have to."

Despite her good intentions, she spoke through gritted teeth. "I can control my own choir, too."

"Whoa." He put a hand on her arm and turned her to face him. "What does that mean?"

"That I don't need you to browbeat these children into submission. If I had needed—or wanted—help, I would have asked for it."

His eyes narrowed. "I did not browbeat anybody."

"You intimidated them. And made me look weak in the process."

"They were out of control."

"I would have settled them down."

"That's not what it looked like to me. Anyway, my son was causing part of the problem. I had every right to correct his behavior."

"Okay. But you lectured the rest of them. And they need to respect *me*."

"In other words, you want to be in charge."

"Is that so unreasonable? I am the music director."

"By all means." He stepped back and made a mocking bow in her direction. "You're obviously the expert when it comes to show business. I'm sorry I presumed on your authority. I won't make that mistake again." Stepping past her, he headed for the back of the church. "Come on, kids. Time to go home."

"Bye, Miss Caitlyn," Maddie called. Shep waved.

"See you later," Cait called weakly.

Ben didn't look back as he herded the children outside. He let the wind slam the front door closed behind him, leaving Cait alone in the empty church.

Clara, Debbie, and Perdita—he's not sitting anywhere
else. They'll save him every time...

...they will do everything they possibly can imagine
to get your attention... they're just like that. I think
you're an idiot...

...I can't do anything more. She's got to go...

...from Saturday morning, from the look you're...

CHAPTER SIX

BEN PUT the kids in the back seat and warmed up the
engine, but he didn't leave the parking lot until he saw
Cait lock the church door, start her car safely and drive
away. Then, feeling like a sucker and a jerk at the same
time, he turned his vehicle in the opposite direction and
headed home.

Blocking all thoughts of their argument, he threw dinner together while listening with half an ear to Maddie's
exhaustive commentary on her day...and then felt guilty
because he wasn't paying more attention. Trying to make
up for being distracted, he interfered too much with her
homework, until they ended up fighting over whether or
not her math paper was neat enough to turn in. When
Maddie stomped upstairs to take a bath, Ben checked
Shep's work. Obviously, the boy had already mastered
most first-grade skills.

"You're amazing, Shep." He gave his son a one-armed
hug. "You get everything right the first time. No spelling
mistakes, no problem with adding and subtracting, great
handwriting. And it's only November. You really know
how to use that brain of yours." Ben pressed a kiss to the
soft blond hair. "If only you'd decide to use your voice,
too," he said softly.

If the wish disturbed Shep, Ben couldn't tell. The little
boy stacked his papers neatly, put them in his notebook
and stowed the notebook in the bright-orange backpack

he'd chosen. Pulling on his dad's hand, he climbed up-stairs to the kids' bathroom, where Maddie had finished and gone to bed without even saying good-night. Ben ran Shep a bath and sat on the edge of the tub while the boy washed. Pajamas, a selection from Pooh, a kiss, and Shep was down for the night.

Totally wrung out, Ben started down the hallway to his own room. Maybe a carpentry magazine would put him to sleep early. But first, he stopped at Maddie's doorway and peeked through. From the quality of the silence, he could tell she wasn't asleep.

"Maddie." He sat down on the very end of her bed. She jerked her feet up and away. "C'mon, sweetheart. I just want you to do your best work."

"I do." She sniffed.

"I know you do. Maybe I'm just grumpy tonight."

After a silence, she said, "You had a fight with Miss Caitlyn."

"Um…well, a disagreement. Yes."

"She's nice."

And I'm not? "Yes, she is."

"So you have to say you're sorry."

His immediate impulse was to say something stupid like, "Why can't she apologize to me?" But that would assign more importance to the incident than it deserved. What difference did Cait Gregory's opinion make, one way or the other? They would pull off this stupid pageant, and then go their separate ways. Caring enough to invest pride and hurt feelings in the process, or the relationship, was a mistake he did not intend to make.

"You're right. I will apologize the next time I see her. Better?"

She sniffed, then nodded. Maddie took a little time to

forgive and forget, but she got there in the end. Ben bent to kiss her cheek. "Love you. Good night."

And then he lay down on his bed alone, with a journal about woodworking in his hands and the image of Cait's snapping green gaze on his mind.

GIVEN THE DELICATE state of Anna Remington's pregnancy, Harry waited until Thursday to contact her husband about the missing funds. As church treasurer, Timothy Bellows should have been present. But Timothy had pleaded an out-of-town appointment he couldn't miss. So Harry met with the pastor alone.

Sitting behind the desk in his dark, Victorian-era office at the church, David Remington stared for a minute, his eyes round, his jaw loose. "Ten thousand dollars? Are you sure?"

Harry fetched the ledger. "See for yourself. Kathleen Fogarty died in April and her will cleared probate in June. So the check should have come in sometime that month or the next. Did we even get the money? Maybe the lawyer's office didn't send it."

The minister took off his glasses, propped his elbows on the desk and rubbed his hands over his face. "We definitely received the check. I remember seeing it."

"When was that?"

"I have no idea." David started to shake his head, then put his glasses on again and looked up at Harry. "Wait. It had to be June because that's when Anna found out she was pregnant. She was opening the mail that morning and brought the check to me. We were talking about Mrs. Fogarty...and then the phone rang and it was the doctor's office, saying her pregnancy test was positive." He smiled briefly. "We both went a little crazy."

"But what did you do with the check?"

"I'm sure I put it in the bank bag, along with the receipts from Sunday."

"Did you make the deposit?"

The minister shrugged. "I might have. Or Anna, or Timothy. I can't remember."

Harry swallowed a caustic comment. He didn't tolerate such uncertainty and inefficiency in his department. His employees were accountable for their every action.

Make that past tense, Harry reminded himself. *You don't have employees nowadays. Because you don't have a job.*

He blew out a frustrated breath. "Maybe we'd better look at the bank statements, see if the deposit just wasn't recorded in the ledger."

The bequest didn't show up in the checking account record, either. A quick call to the lawyer's office garnered the information that the funds had been withdrawn from Mrs. Fogarty's estate account. But not how or by whom. The canceled check had been endorsed with the church's regular stamp.

"I don't know how this could have happened." As David got to his feet, his cheeks were even paler than usual. "Give me a couple of days to track this down, Harry. The money can't have simply disappeared. Nobody in the church would have stolen ten thousand dollars."

Harry looked at the young man, taking in the frayed edges of his collar, the worn elbows of his suit jacket, thinking about the two used cars David and Anna drove. They had a baby on the way. They could find a lot of uses for ten thousand dollars.

"I hope you're right, Pastor," he said heavily. "I really hope you're right."

CAIT WAS ALONE in the living room about nine on Friday night, playing her guitar—resolutely avoiding "Bobby

McGee''—when the doorbell rang. She went to answer, still humming the snatch of melody she'd just found. The music died when she opened the door.

Ben stood on the front porch, his snow-dusted shoulders hunched against the wind, his hands in the pockets of a heavy leather bomber jacket. "Hi." He didn't grin. "Can I talk to you for a few minutes?"

Speechless, she stepped back to allow him inside the entry hall.

"Maddie's finally getting her wish for snow." He blew into his cupped hands. "We're supposed to have three or four inches by morning."

"That's what I heard. Why are you here?" Maybe it wasn't hospitality at its most gracious, but when there was something to be said, Cait liked to be direct. "David's at a dinner meeting and Anna's asleep."

His hands dropped to his sides. "I want to apologize. Wednesday's…argument…shouldn't have gotten so far out of control."

She shrugged and led the way into the living room. "If something is worth arguing about, you might as well give it all you've got."

"But you shouldn't leave the issues unresolved." The zipper on his jacket rasped, and she turned to see him hanging the coat over a chair back. He wore a dark-green sweater over a yellow shirt and tan cords—nothing special—but just looking at him drove her pulse higher.

"I care about our friendship," he said, and Cait forced her attention back to what he'd come to say. "And I regret the things I said Wednesday night. You made me mad."

Her legs threatened to give way. "Sit down," she told him, retreating to her place on the couch. He took the nearest chair, then leaned forward with his elbows on his knees.

"So..." His smile was tentative. "Can we back up and forget the fight?"

She stared at him, torn between the desire to smile back and an urgent need to protect her heart. Her independence. Her...life. "Sure," she said, the decision made before she realized it. "I could have been a lot more tactful in asking you to back off."

Ben laughed. "Is there a tactful way to ask somebody to back off?"

She grinned. "I guess not. I'm sorry I was rude. I...I'm used to being in charge. No one's ever accused me of having too small an ego."

"Don't worry about it." He glanced at the guitar and the notes she'd been jotting down. "Composing something new?"

"I'm not sure. Incidental music, maybe, to get us from one scene to the other. This melody just came into my head, so I thought I'd write it out."

"What's it sound like?"

Cait wasn't sure he was serious, but when he stared at her, waiting, she decided to take the risk. Some people understood the growth of music, and some didn't. She had a feeling Ben was one of the perceptive kind.

The melody Cait played was sweet, a little plaintive. For Ben, even without words, the tune conjured a desert night, a black sky and bright stars, a sense of awe. When the music abruptly broke off, he almost protested.

"That's special," he told her. "You draw pictures with music."

She bent over the guitar and her hair fell forward, hiding her face. "There's a lot more to it...I can't quite hear..." Her fingers roamed the strings, sometimes strumming, sometimes plucking, with an occasional slap on the soundboard—in frustration or as a special effect, Ben wasn't sure. So he leaned back in his chair, crossed his ankle over the other knee and settled in to listen.

And to watch. Soft lamplight played over Cait's loose hair, striking sparks of gold, silver, copper. Sometimes she pushed the long curls back over her shoulder and then he could see her face—eyes half-closed in concentrated dreaming, the dark lashes lying like black stars on her cheeks. Eventually the hair would fall again, hiding her from view, leaving the music to weave its spell. Alone, either the woman or the music would have exerted a powerful force of attraction. Together, they were irresistible.

After a while she paused, fingertips suspended over the strings, with the last chord still hanging in the air. Ben held his breath, hoping she wouldn't stop.

In the back of the house, a door creaked, then slammed shut. Ben jumped. Cait gasped, and the guitar jangled.

Striding in with his coat still buttoned, Dave looked as startled as they were. "Ben? What's wrong? Why're you here?"

Ben cleared his throat. "Nothing's wrong. Cait and I are…working on the Christmas pageant. She was playing some of the music she's composing."

"Oh." The minister lifted his glasses with one hand and rubbed his eyes with the other. "That's…that's great. You've taken a load off Anna's mind by agreeing to handle this project." He glanced almost nervously toward the hallway into the back of the house. "Is she asleep?"

Cait nodded. "She was when I looked in about eight-thirty."

"Oh. Good." Dave blew out a deep breath, started unbuttoning his coat. "Then I think I'll spend a few minutes on Sunday's sermon before I turn in. Y'all have a good night.''

Ben waited until the door to David's study had shut firmly. Then he looked at Cait. ''Is it me, or was that weird?''

She put the guitar aside. ''Things are pretty strange around here these days. Anna mostly sleeps, or stares at the wall—she doesn't read, doesn't want a television in her room, doesn't talk much if I sit with her. More often than not, David comes home late and he spends most nights on the couch in his library. I don't know whether to stay out of it or interfere—and what would I say if I did get involved?''

''My gut instinct says leave it alone.''

She frowned at him. ''That's what a man's gut instinct always says. But Anna's my sister and she's unhappy.''

''Marriage is between the two people involved. They're the ones who ultimately have to solve the problem. Nobody can do it for them.''

Her frown dissolved into a rueful smile. ''I'm definitely at a disadvantage in this discussion. You've actually been married.'' Suddenly, the frown reappeared. ''That's probably not the most sensitive thing for me to say. I'm sorry—I guess I'm out of practice at talking to…to…real people.''

''Don't worry about it.'' He shrugged. ''It's much worse when someone just ignores the fact that Valerie ever existed. That feels like…like treason or something. She *was* here and we had thirteen happy years together. I work on being grateful, instead of bitter over what's lost. Most of the time these days, I handle things okay.''

''And you have two great kids.''

''I do.'' He pushed himself out of the deep armchair. ''The good thing about kids is that they force you to keep waking up each morning. You can't give up when you've got them to take care of.''

Picking up his jacket, he walked to the door. Cait un-curled from the sofa and followed, wishing she could ask him to stay longer. For what, though?

"I've got some guys coming over tomorrow afternoon to start on frames for the backgrounds,'' he said, zipping up his coat. "Next weekend, we can begin painting.''

"Sounds good.'' Leaning against the wall next to the door, she watched him pull on well-used leather gloves. "Drive carefully—I imagine the roads are pretty slick by now.''

"Four-wheel drive and snow tires ought to get me the five blocks between here and home.'' He grinned and stepped forward to put his hand on the doorknob. "Good night, Cait. Thanks for the music.''

"You're welcome.'' She gazed up at him, noting the angle of his jawline, the arch of his cheekbones, the neat curl of his ear. His eyes darkened as he caught her staring, and the air around them got hard to breathe. All Cait could think was, *Please...*

And she wasn't even sure if she was asking him to go, or to—

Ben bent his head, tilted her chin with one gloved finger, and touched his lips to hers. The brief kiss felt like an electric shock—sharp, exciting. He drew back and she sighed with disappointment. So soon?

Suddenly, the storm outside was indoors with them, around them, as he closed his hands on her arms and brought her body up against his. Warm and deep and wild, the kisses he gave, the kisses he demanded, swept Cait into a dark place where nothing mattered but the need between them. She closed her arms around his waist, pressed a hand against the leather on his back, and the softer fabric over his rear. Ben growled deep in his throat and pressed even closer, his weight stealing her breath, making her ache.

But just as abruptly as it had started, the storm ceased. In an instant, Ben stood the width of the entry hall away, his chest rising and falling with the force of his breathing, his face pale, his eyes glazed. He looked almost panicked.

"I'm...sorry. God..." Both hands covered his face for a moment, then raked through his hair. "I really didn't mean..." He gave a shaky chuckle. "No woman wants to hear that you didn't intend to kiss her. But I thought I could let it go with just—just—" Rubbing his eyes again, he shook his head. "Dumb. Really dumb."

Cait held herself together with her arms wrapped around her waist. "It's okay," she whispered. "Really. I understand." She stepped back out of the way of the door, hoping he would take the hint and leave. Quickly.

He did. But with the door open, he stopped and looked at her once again. "You understand, do you?" Another strained laugh. "Maybe someday you can explain it to me."

Then he strode into the snowy night.

INSTEAD OF THREE or four inches of snow, they got eight. With Shep's unmistakable support, Maddie begged to stay at the Shepherds' house on Saturday morning to take advantage of the perfect sledding hill in the field next door to her grandparents' house. Much as he dreaded being left alone with his thoughts any longer than necessary, Ben okayed the proposal. Then, needing to escape the what-ifs and shouldn't-t-haves tormenting him, he pulled on his heavy boots and a wool cap and walked to the village center.

Always picturesque, today Goodwill looked like a postcard advertisement for small-town U.S.A. The town owned one snowplow, which didn't always work, so this morning the Avenue was still buried deep. But farmers and mountain folk with their four-wheel drives and trucks never let a little snow get in the way of Saturday's chores, so the merchants wouldn't find their profits too badly affected by the weather.

In the center of town sat a grassy park, complete with stone fountain, wrought-iron benches and a gazebo trimmed with Victorian ruffles and flourishes. On his way to the coffee shop, Ben grinned as he passed parents and kids adding to the crowd of snow people already gathering on the square.

"Hey, Mr. Tremaine!"

"Hello, Blackwell clan." He detoured to chat with a family of five boys creating a family of five snowmen, then moved on after promising to bring Shep to play with his buddy Adam one afternoon before Christmas. As he made his way around the fountain to the other side of the park, Ben looked down the slope of the street, to see a sports car heading toward him, its bright-red paint almost painful in contrast to the fresh snow. Completely without traction on the slick street, the red car climbed about a third of the way to the top of the hill before gravity, a lack of friction and a build-up of snow under the chassis stopped it cold.

At that point, the driver gunned the engine, which only spun the wheels and dug them in deeper. Next he rocked the car from forward to reverse, in an attempt to climb out of the ruts under the wheels. The sporty model finally broke free and started backing up, in a straight line at first, but then sliding sideways...directly toward a blue pickup parked outside the barber shop.

The crash wasn't too violent, and did more damage to

the sports car than the sturdy old truck. By the time Ben
arrived at the scene, the driver was out of his red Miata,
staring at the collision and swearing. Loudly.

"How the hell is anybody supposed to drive in this
godforsaken place? Whose stupid idea was it to put a town
on top of a mountain, so you can't even get up the damn
street in the damn snow?"

Just listening to the voice, Ben decided he didn't like
the guy. Then he got a good look at him. Camel-hair
overcoat, double-breasted, worn belted, matching felt fe-
dora. Gold-rimmed, dark black shades that cost at least
five hundred bucks and a watch worth five times as much.
Beige boots of some exotic animal skin, with toes as sharp
as ice picks. And a walnut tan. In November.

Ben swallowed his antagonism. "Something I can do
to help?"

Mr. Shades turned toward him. "Where the hell do I
find a tow truck in this place?"

"A gas station would be your best bet."

"Duh. Does this burg have one?"

"Jack Mabry runs the station you passed about a half
mile back, coming into town."

"Thank God." He dived into the open door of the car
and came out with a cell phone. "What's the number?"

After a restless night, Ben didn't have complete control
of his temper. "Do I look like Directory Assistance?"

The guy stared at him for a second, then reached up
and pulled off the sunglasses. His eyes were dark, narrowed and unfriendly. "You playing games, country
boy?"

"Just trying to help." Ben shrugged. "But I guess
you've got things covered." He stepped off the curb,
heading for the coffee shop across the street.

"Hey, wait a minute. I'm trying to find somebody in this stupid little place. She's at…"

As Ben glanced back over his shoulder, the guy bent into the car again, but more information really wasn't necessary. The man's attitude screamed "show business." He was looking for Cait.

Mr. Shades came out again with a piece of paper. "She's at 300 Ridley Place. Cait Gregory. Know her?"

"We've met."

"Well, how do I get there?"

Ben looked at the Miata. "First, you get your car unstuck and see if the drivetrain still works."

"Smart-ass."

"Then you try to get up the hill. Snow tires and chains help. Go to the end of the street, take a right and then two lefts. You'll see a stone church with a green door. The house you're looking for is on the corner just past the churchyard."

Without waiting for the other guy to acknowledge the directions, Ben turned again and started across the street. This time, he didn't look back.

Which was a good operating principle for last night's scene with Cait, as well. *Don't look back.* Forget how she tasted, how her mouth softened, how her body strained against his. Forget the sudden surge of need. Need had no place in a responsible father's life.

No matter how good it felt.

CAIT OPENED the door and let her jaw drop. "Russell?"

The man outside stamped caked snow off his boots. "Hi, babe. Lousy weather. Hope you've got something to warm me up."

She stepped back as he came into the house. "What

are you doing here? I thought you were in Las Vegas. Or Palm Springs.''

"I damn well should be.'' He flung his coat over the same chair Ben had occupied last night, took off his hat and smoothed back his hair. "But I obviously wasn't getting through to you over the phone. So I decided to exert my considerable personal charm face-to-face.'' His wide grin showed perfect white teeth. "Got something to drink?''

"Milk? Water?''

"I was thinking about Long Island Iced Tea. We are on the East Coast. Or how about a mint julep?'' He dropped into Ben's chair.

"How about coffee?'' She brought him a mug. "What do we have to talk about, Russ? I told you—I'll be ready to work the day after Christmas.''

"That's well and good, but I got a couple of gigs you'd be perfect for before then. I checked with the band— they're all cooling their heels, growing beer bellies. No problem getting them back on the road.''

"I can't leave until Christmas. My sister's in bed trying to keep her baby, and I'm helping her out. What don't you understand?''

"Hick place like this probably has a grandmother on every corner. Let them take care of her.''

Cait stared at him. "How come I never realized you were such an insensitive bastard?''

He shrugged. "Makes me a good agent, doesn't it?''

"Maybe. Look—I *want* to take care of Anna. I've made commitments here I can't get out of. No gigs until December 26. Clear enough?''

"The money's great.'' He named a figure that made Cait blink. "And this is Vegas. The exposure would be fantastic. Do you know how many people come to Vegas in the winter?''

Cait walked to the window and looked out into the snowy afternoon. The trees wore white frosting on their branches, all the way to the tips of the smallest twigs. A white blanket softened the hills and the blue mountains beyond. This world was quiet and still, with a kind of peace she hadn't realized she needed.

Vegas would be loud and crowded and bright. The mountains there were bare gray rock, the desert a vast emptiness around a neon oasis. Anna would be here, and Maddie and Brenna and Shep.

She refused to let her mind go further than that. But she shook her head. ''You made a long trip for nothing, Russ. I've been touring for a solid year, including five gigs in Vegas. I need a real break. I'm not working until after Christmas.''

Russell put his head back against the chair and groaned. ''Why do you always make me get tough with you?'' Leaning forward, he braced his elbows on his knees. ''I can charge you with breach of contract, you know. Our deal says you'll play the dates I get you except in case of illness or injury. My reputation depends on providing acts to the venues. I can't provide, I lose my contacts. Got it?''

Her breath caught on a hitch of fear. Russell had been her agent for the past five—increasingly successful—years. She owed a good deal of her current status to his savvy and his contacts in the business. Losing him as an agent would slow her career down just when she was poised to take off.

Cait sighed. ''What are the dates of these gigs?''

She let him run through the details, explain exactly how great an opportunity he was offering *her* when he had other clients—big names—who would take the jobs with no hesitation.

"I'll have to think about it," she said, when he finished. "If Anna has her baby by the middle of December, I might make the date on the 20. But Thanksgiving week-end…I just don't know."

On his feet, Russ stretched to his full height, nearly six-four. "You want to be in the business, you take the work, Cait. Maybe you need to decide what you're willing to do to get to the top. I thought you had the real stuff. Could be I'm wrong."

"Russell—"

Shaking his head, he pulled on his coat and left the house, striding out to the silly-looking red sports car parked on the street. As he fishtailed away, she saw the dented rear end.

"Cait?" Anna called from the bedroom.

"Hey, girl." Schooling her face to calmness, Cait joined her sister. "Good nap?"

"Was somebody here?"

"Um, yeah. My agent came into town to talk about a couple of jobs. Nothing big."

Anna's dark eyes widened. "Soon?"

"Nope. End of November, December."

"But—" She shook her head. "I'm being incredibly selfish. You took time out from your career to be here, and I'm trying to make you stay even longer. If you need to go—"

"I told him I'd think about it. I'll see how you're doing, how the pageant's pulling together, figure out if I can take a couple of days to fly out to Vegas. If not, he'll find somebody else."

"Las Vegas? That's a real opportunity."

"So's this." She bent to give Anna a hug. "We've

hardly seen each other in the last few years. And I've got a nephew coming. I'd love to be here when he's born. We'll see how it all works out, okay?''

The tension eased out of Anna's shoulders. "Okay."

"What sounds good for dinner?"

She shook her head. "When you're not doing anything, you don't get very hungry. Whatever you and David would like."

A door closed in the kitchen. "That's him now." Cait straightened away from the bed. "I'll go ask him about the menu and then he can come in to talk with you while I cook."

Anna's smile was sweet…but not very glad.

And David's face, when Cait got to the kitchen, was somber, though his expression lightened as he turned to face her directly. "Hey, Cait. How's your day been?"

There was no way to explain the combination of despair—about Ben—and uncertainty she'd experienced today. "Fine. Anna's feeling pretty good. Tell me what you'd like to eat before you go in to see her."

He took off his glasses and rubbed his eyes. "I…ah…I don't care. Whatever sounds good to you." Grabbing up an armload of books, he left the kitchen and went straight across the hall to his library. With her back to the door, Cait waited to hear him head for the bedroom, but the footsteps didn't materialize.

What is wrong with that man? She didn't have an answer, didn't have a clue.

She didn't know what to make for dinner, either.

Or what to make of those kisses from Ben Tremaine.

SITTING IN THE late-night dark on Saturday night, Harry aimed the remote at the television screen framed by his slippered feet and clicked through the channels. He was tired of stale, cynical jokes and wisecracking hosts. Tired of infomercials and documentaries about the plight of the misunderstood shark, the persecuted rhino.

"Harry?" Peggy leaned around the door frame into the den. "Harry, are you awake?"

He was tempted to pretend. But he'd been behaving badly enough this past couple of weeks. No need to add lying to his list of sins.

"No, Peg. I'm awake."

"Oh." She stepped into the room, a slender, feminine figure in her soft flannel robe. Peg was always clean and pretty at bedtime, no matter how hard she'd worked during the day. And the sight of her had never failed to excite him, in more than thirty years of marriage.

Until recently. Until he retired.

Harry kept his thumb on the channel button, hoping for a distraction.

Peggy sat down on the arm of the recliner and put her hand on his chest. "Are you watching something special?"

"No." This wasn't going to work. He couldn't avoid her yet another night. Clicking off the television, he looked up at his wife in the dark. "Ready for bed?"

She bent to touch his lips with her own. "Something like that." Harry tasted the honey she put in her nighttime cup of tea, and the sweetness that had always been Peggy's alone. Lightly, she slipped into his lap, into his arms, deepening the kiss. He waited for his body's automatic response to kick in.

Nothing.

Consciously, he followed the well-loved script, stroking her back, tracing the litheness of her spine, the gentle curve of her hip. Peggy sighed and slipped her hand inside his robe, her palm warm against his bare skin. That flesh to flesh contact was usually enough to set him on fire.

But not tonight.

Tightening his hold, he drew her against him, sat up, then got to his feet. She laughed a little and pressed her mouth against the side of his neck, under his ear where a touch could drive him crazy.

Nothing.

"You okay?" she murmured against his temple. "Too tired?"

Without answering, he carried her down the hall to their room, knowing there must be millions of men his age who would give a fortune to have a wife as responsive, as loving as Peggy. All of their marriage, Harry had known how special she was, how lucky *he* was.

She put her arms around his neck as he lowered her to the bed and drew him down with her, over her. He took her kisses, stroked her skin, did all the wonderful things he knew drove her to the edge, and over. Just doing them usually drove him to the edge, too. Tonight…

Nothing. He couldn't perform. Not…as a lover.

With his hands and his mouth, he gave her every ounce of satisfaction he could draw forth. And then he cradled her, gentled her, smoothed her hair and pulled the blankets up to cover her lovely body.

"Harry?" She turned in his arms, leaned up on an elbow. "What's wrong?"

Stroking her shoulder, he eased her back to his side, pressed her head onto his chest.

"Nothing," he said. "Might be coming down with that flu the kids had. I'm a little achy, tired. I love you."

"Mmm. Me, too." She kissed his chest, settled against him.

She wasn't convinced, he knew. But Peggy didn't nag

and she didn't pry. They had always been open with each other, frank about their feelings. Harry had never before kept a secret more important than a birthday present from his wife.

And he wouldn't be able to keep this one for long.

CHAPTER SEVEN

ANNA HAD BEEN awake for what seemed like hours when David came into their bedroom on Monday morning to get dressed.

"You can use the light," she told him.

He jumped and turned toward her. "I didn't mean to wake you up."

"You didn't."

"That's good." He went to the closet and turned on that light, so she saw him as a silhouette.

"What's your schedule today?"

He shrugged into a starched shirt. Anna had once taken pride in doing those shirts herself—now he drove them to a laundry in Winchester every week. "I'm going over to the hospital, then the nursing home. The interfaith lunch is at noon, and then I—I have some paperwork at the office to take care of." Standing at the dresser, he finally turned on the lamp to check the knot in his tie. "Why?"

"I just wondered. I wish I could go with you. I miss visiting with the ladies at Elm Haven."

"I'll tell Miss Violet and Miss Harriet you were thinking about them." He bent quickly to kiss her cheek. On impulse, Anna clutched at his shoulder, preventing him from straightening up. He stiffened. "Anna? What's wrong?"

"That's what I want to ask you. Why do I see so little of you? Are you avoiding me?"

Easing to sit on the edge of the bed, David laughed, a little shakily, and pulled her hand from his shirt. "I'm not avoiding you. I just…have to go to work."

"And in the evenings?"

"I have a hard time writing at the church office during the day. The phone rings and people come by…."

"You're spending enough time on your sermons to have a book full by now. You're even sleeping in your library." Tears clogged her throat. "Instead of with me."

"Well…" He played with her hand as he had when they were dating, running his fingertips lightly along her palm and over her knuckles and wrist. The touch of his skin on hers was sweet. "I—I think you'll rest better if you don't have to share the bed, that's all. I want to give you and—and the baby—every chance in the world to be safe."

"I don't need better rest. I need you to be with me." She heard herself whining and winced. But the words were true.

David shook his head. "You know I'm here for you. Whatever you need, I'll make sure you and the baby have it. And I'm never more than a phone call away. I have my cell phone on all the time. Every minute." He grinned, as if to reassure her. Or was it simply to pacify her?

"You don't understand." Now she was being childish. No wonder David didn't want to be with her. "Never mind. You need to go."

"Anna—" His tone sounded as if he wanted to say more, but he got to his feet, clearly relieved to be dismissed. "I'll see you tonight, okay? I'll be home pretty early."

She mustered the strength to be gracious. "That's— that's fine. Have a good day. I—I love you."

"Me, too." He stood for a second in the doorway, looking at her, and she hoped he would relent, come back and talk. But then he was gone, his footsteps retreating toward the kitchen and the door to the driveway.

By the time Cait looked in, Anna had cried her tears dry.

"Morning, Annabelle. What can I make you for breakfast?"

The baby needed nourishment, even if Anna didn't care if she never ate again. "Um…oatmeal with raisins, and juice?"

"Coming right up."

Cait brought a tray in a little while later and joined her at breakfast. "I need to get parts assigned on the pageant before rehearsal this week. Do you feel like helping me with that? You know the kids better than I do."

"Of course." Anna put down her bowl, still half-full of cereal. Thinking about the pageant would be better than lying here.

Her sister handed her the bowl again. "First, you finish this."

"Cait—"

"Finish."

"Yes, ma'am."

When the bowl was empty, Cait took the dishes away and came back with a pad and pencil. "Now, how do we do this? Everybody wants the most important part—whatever that is."

"You have to assure them that every part is important. And it's true—the different players in the nativity were all there for a reason. It wasn't just an accident that there were shepherds and animals and an innkeeper."

Cait's lively face softened. "I haven't thought about it like that in a long time. In my business, it seems like there's always a star, and then everybody else."

"Well, there's a star in this story, too. But let's start with the shepherds."

They went through the list of children who'd signed up to participate and gave each one a role to play, based on age and ability. At the end, they came to the angels.

"Maddie Tremaine is dying to be the announcing angel," Cait commented, her eyes on the list she was making.

"Is that a problem? She's got a good voice and she's not shy—sort of like someone else I remember at that age."

"Poor Ben." She didn't elaborate. "Has she ever done a solo in front of the congregation?"

"No, though I suppose she could, with enough practice. But the announcing angel is a speaking part."

"Well, see, that's the problem. I have this song—"

"Oh, Cait. You wrote a song for our pageant?"

"You might not like it."

"And the roof might fall in. Go get your guitar. I want to hear what you've done."

For the first time in days, Anna felt hopeful, even cheerful. If Cait was involved enough with the pageant to write a song…what other kinds of miracles might happen this Christmas?

MONDAY EVENING, Cait rang the Tremaines' doorbell and stepped back. She'd tried to time her visit so she'd arrive after dinner, but not so late that Maddie and Shep would have started getting ready for bed. She didn't want to see Ben alone.

Not a problem. Maddie opened the door. "Miss Caitlyn! Hi!"

"Hi, Maddie? Are you busy?"

"We're just watching TV. School was closed today 'cause of the snow. Isn't that cool?"

"Very cool." The little girl pulled the door open wide and Cait stepped inside. "I saw all your snow people in the yard."

"Me and Shep played outside all morning. Daddy helped us this afternoon. We made snow angels in the backyard. Wanna see?"

"You're not dressed to go outside...."

"We can see from the family room." She took off running down the hallway, leaving Cait no choice but to follow.

She hadn't seen this room—a small, glassed-in porch on the back of the house that looked over the yard and the garage Ben had converted to his workshop. The furniture was the same comfortable mix found in the rest of the house, with the addition of a big-screen television and all the necessary components.

Ben and Shep both looked away from the screen as Cait stepped into the room. Shep's grin was wide and immediate; Ben's expression was wary, questioning.

He picked up the remote control and the TV sound vanished. "Cait?"

"Hi. I didn't intend to interrupt. Maddie wanted to show me your snow angels."

"See—there they are." Kneeling on one of the couches underneath the windows, the girl pointed through the window. "We made hundreds."

Cait joined her on the couch. "I see. That looks like so much fun. A whole flock of angels in your backyard." She turned to sit on the sofa, looking at Maddie. "In fact, I came to talk to you about angels."

Across the room, the TV clicked off. Shep looked at his father, outrage written on his face. "We'll turn it back on later," Ben promised. "Right now we want to hear what Miss Caitlyn has to say."

Still sulking, Shep went to a toy box in the corner and rummaged through with a clatter of plastic, finally pulling out a couple of airplanes which he proceeded to land on the coffee table.

Maddie sat up straight, her hands gripped together in her lap. "What did you want to talk about, Miss Caitlyn? I get the main angel part, right?"

Cait took a deep breath. "I wanted to ask—would you like to share that part with Brenna?"

"But—" Maddie's dark eyebrows drew together, and her mouth stayed open in surprise.

Cait looked at Ben, but he only stared back at her, with an expression she didn't find encouraging. Even Shep was gazing at her, his eyes wide. Clearly, he understood what she'd said and the implications.

"There's only one angel," Maddie said. "That's what the story says. That's the way the pageant goes."

"I thought we might do something a little different this year. I've written a song—"

"I want to be the angel." Standing, now, the little girl's dark eyes were stormy. "It's my turn."

"Madeline—" Ben's voice was stern.

"I thought you and Brenna could sing the part of the announcing angel together." When Maddie didn't immediately erupt, Cait hurried on. "Singing for the first time in front of people can be pretty scary. But you both have nice voices, and I thought it would be a good chance for you to get used to singing without the choir."

Maddie stood still for a minute, her face stiff, her fists clenched. "I'm the angel," she said finally, then turned and ran out of the room. Footsteps pounded on the staircase, then a door slammed upstairs.

Cait put a hand over her face. "I—" When she looked up, both Ben and Shep were still watching her. "I'm sorry. I didn't think she would be so upset."

"Go to your room, Shep." Ben glanced at his son. "I'll call you when I turn on the movie again." Without any protest, silent or otherwise, the little boy trotted down the hall.

Then Ben turned back to her. "You didn't think this out too well, did you?"

She choked back her resentment. "I talked it over with Anna. We both thought it was a good idea."

"You knew how much Maddie was counting on that part."

"She still has the part! What's wrong with sharing?"

"Nothing, in theory. When you're ten, everything." He shook his head. "You should have run the idea by me first. I could have told you it wouldn't fly."

"Again, I'm sorry." Cait stood up. "I hope you can change her mind. We would be really sad if Maddie didn't help us with the pageant." A sudden thought struck her. "And if she doesn't...I guess you would resign your job as well. Or maybe you're already planning to?"

"I didn't volunteer to begin with, so I didn't think I had the option of resigning."

Could the conversation get much more depressing? "Please, feel free. I'm committed, but I really don't intend to torture you or your family with an unpleasant situation." Turning on her heel, she walked as fast as she could toward the front door.

"We'll let you know," Ben said, somehow arriving there at the same time without appearing to hurry. "I don't like backing out on commitments, and I don't like my kids to do so, either."

"Great. Just give us a call." She waited impatiently for

him to turn the knob and let her out. He was too close, and he smelled like fresh air and snow.

But he didn't move. "I met a friend of yours the other day—guy in a red Miata. Did he find you?"

She could imagine what kind of impression Russell must have made on Ben Tremaine. "Yes, he did."

"He doesn't know much about driving in snow."

"They don't get much snow in Southern California."

"Ah. Hollywood. A friend in the business?"

Cait didn't flatter herself he really cared. "My agent, actually, with a couple of good job offers. Now, if you'll excuse me—"

"Did you take them?" Ben couldn't believe he was conducting an inquisition. What difference did it make to him whether Cait accepted a job offer or not?

She looked up at him, her face every bit as troubled as Maddie's had been earlier. "I haven't decided yet," she said. "I guess it depends on how things go here."

Meaning if she didn't get her way, she'd pull stakes and go back to the big city? Was she holding him and his daughter hostage—either they helped with the pageant or there wouldn't be one at all?

Ben flipped the knob and swung the door open. "It's always good to have options."

Cait opened her mouth, but in the end just stomped by him, across the porch and down the steps, without a word. He was glad he'd cleared the walk—at her speed, she would have fallen on the snow and ice for sure.

Her car started with a blare of lights and the roar of a gunned engine; she fishtailed a little on the slick street, but slowed down and got safely round the corner.

Ben let out a breath and shut the door. Rubbing the back of his neck, feeling a headache growing behind his eyes, he climbed the stairs, wondering how hard it would be to convince his little girl to do the right thing.

TUESDAY MORNING, Harry dropped by the church. One glance at the minister's face conveyed the results of his investigation.

"You didn't find the money?"

David shook his head. "Anna remembered getting the check, too, but not the deposit. I called Timothy and asked him. He said he hadn't seen the check at all."

Bad news. If David, Anna and Timothy were the only people to make the deposits, then one of them had stamped that check and taken it to the bank. Which meant one of them was lying.

Or, at best, criminally negligent. Losing ten thousand dollars was a real problem for a church this size.

"I didn't tell them that the money was missing," David said. "No sense alarming people until we know there's a real problem."

Eyes wide, Harry stared at him. "I think ten thousand missing dollars qualifies as a problem, Pastor."

"I'll keep looking," the younger man promised. He swiped his fingers over his forehead. "I'm su˗ ˑthere's a simple explanation."

Harry was sure of that, as well. He w˗   ˑugh, that the explanation would result in a   ˑa-vid and Anna had been taken int˗   community and the church—loo˗   and daughter by the older fol˗   set. Timothy was a popula˗   city council, a source o˗   gregation. A mistake˗   one or more of t˗   spirit of the e˗

How would anyone in town be able to celebrate Christmas with this crisis hanging over their heads?

THE CHILDREN behaved better at the next rehearsal. Partly, perhaps, because of Ben's warnings and partly because of the presence of several mothers in the pews. But mostly, Cait thought, because she stood in front of them holding a notebook labeled Casting Assignments.

"Okay," Cait said, opening the book. "I talked a long time with Miss Anna about past pageants and what we could do to make this year special. We think every part in this program is as important as every other part. So whether you're a shepherd or sheep, an angel or a wise man or a donkey, we need you all and count on you to do your very best."

She drew a deep breath and began to read through the list. The five older boys who would be shepherds gathered on her left, along with some of the youngest, who would be sheep. The innkeeper sat in the middle of the top step with more of the little ones—the cows and donkeys and doves. On her right, three of the boys who sang particularly well gathered as wise men, with a servant for each. Shep had been included as one of the servants.

"The rest of you are angels." As Cait looked at them, the group of girls on the bottom two steps giggled and squirmed. This was the point at which Maddie would have asked, "Who's going to be the main angel?"

But Maddie and Shep hadn't come to practice.

Swallowing her disappointment, Cait forged ahead. _____ written a song for the announcing angel, but right _____ learn it." If Maddie refused to participate, _____ have to sing with Brenna, who _____ to carry the part on her own.

Maybe they'd end up with three or four announcing angels.

The rest of the crowd buzzed with conversation as the kids started taking on their roles—the cows were butting heads, a couple of donkeys were kicking up their back heels and the shepherds were trying to drive the sheep under the communion table.

Cait held up her hands to quiet the chaos. "What we're going to do right now is have each group meet with the mom in charge of their costumes, to get sizes written down. Then we'll come back together to practice the music."

The mothers stepped in to take charge before any of the children could misbehave. Karen Patterson and another mother came over to talk to the angels about their robes and wings and halos.

Knowing what parts they were to play made the kids more cooperative in learning and practicing the different songs, and the rehearsal went smoothly. As the end of practice approached, Cait got out her guitar and sat on the steps in the middle of the choir. "This is the announcing angel song." She strummed the chords of the tune she'd played for Ben. "Let's all learn it."

O, fear not,
Be not afraid.
I bring good news to you this day.
At Bethlehem,
A child they've laid
In the manger.
Wrapped with a cloth,
He sleeps alone.
But all the world will praise his name.
For love and peace

He will be known
From the manger.

The last notes died away into silence. Surprised, Cait
looked around to find all the children staring at her, their
eyes wide and shining.

"Oh, Miss Caitlyn," Brenna said softly. "You wrote
that for us?"

Tears started in her eyes. Cait blinked. "Sure. Do you
want to sing it with me?"

Three times through taught them all the words and the
tune. They sang it twice more, along with the mothers
still waiting, just because everyone enjoyed it.

Then Cait stood up. "Time for dinner. And you guys
go back to school tomorrow. I'll see you on Sunday."

The departing process was loud, as usual, and it seemed
that everyone had to stop and talk with her about the
schedule, the costumes, the song. Cait was finally free to
put the music folders away in a blessed silence when she
heard a single set of footsteps approaching from the back
of the church. She turned quickly, hoping it might be Ben.

But David joined her. "That really is a great song.
You've got an amazing talent, Sister Cait."

"Thanks." She smiled and closed the top on the box
of folders. "What shall we eat tonight? Canned stew or
canned soup?"

He laughed and groaned at the same time. "Such
tempting choices." But he sobered again almost immediately. "How do you think Anna's doing?"

"She was okay when I left the house two hours ago."

David avoided her gaze. "No, I mean...emotionally."

"Well, she's worried, and I guess she's pretty frustrated, having to lie in bed all the time. But you're her
husband. How do *you* think she feels?"

Taking off his glasses, he rubbed his eyes with his fingers. "I—I don't know."

"Have you asked?"

"I—" He shook his head and turned away from Cait. "Never mind. I shouldn't involve you."

She grabbed his arm and held on against his resistance. "That's probably true. But you have. So what's wrong?"

"I just…" He cleared his throat. "She wants me to stay with her all the time. And I can't—I mean, I have responsibilities to the members of the church and sermons to write, and she was doing the secretarial work until she got…until the baby, so now I'm doing all of that, as well. There's just not time to sit and—and talk. But I don't think Anna understands. I hate to make her unhappy but— but I can't be everything to everybody."

Cait pushed aside the anger that was her first reaction to David's comments. She wouldn't have expected the man who loved her sister to be so self-absorbed. Anna was having *his* baby, for heaven's sake, under life-threatening circumstances. And he was worried about his job?

Because Anna would want it, though, she stifled her objections. "I think it's a tough time for both of you, David. When the baby comes, everyone will feel better. Until then, I think Anna knows you have responsibilities—she doesn't want all of your time. Just some reassurance that things will be okay. I know you can do that." She smiled at him, expecting a smile in return, and his agreement that he certainly could do that.

Instead, David stared at her in silence, his expression blank. "I'm not so sure," he said, finally. Then he turned on his heel and strode toward the church door.

"What are you talking about? Why not?" Cait started after him. "David? David!"

She reached the outside door just as his car screeched out of the parking lot.

"What's wrong with you?" she shouted after him. The windy, bitterly cold night didn't answer. Cait closed the door and leaned back against it, staring down the aisle to the front of the dim church and the arched window in the eastern wall.

Just outside that window, though she couldn't see it tonight in the dark, an old dogwood tree stood bare, its gray branches exposed and shivering, its remaining red berries easy picking for the birds. Not exactly a symbol of the joy, the *goodwill* of the coming season.

But then, with Maddie's disappointment and Ben's stern attitudes, with Anna's fears and David's erratic behavior, Christmas didn't look to be very jolly in Goodwill this year anyway.

In fact, Cait was beginning to believe that only a miracle could turn the next six weeks into a holiday worth remembering.

BEN FOUND HIMSELF stymied by Maddie's absolute refusal to consider sharing the angel part with Brenna. No matter what he said, she remained adamant that she alone should play the role. Karen Patterson had called when Brenna came home from school in tears because Maddie wouldn't talk to her; trying to explain Maddie's unjustifiable attitude stretched Ben's patience to the limit. Karen assured him she understood, but the reserve in her voice said otherwise. And Ben sympathized. Why shouldn't she have the chance to enjoy watching her daughter in the spotlight, too?

On Friday night, he decided to consult a greater source of wisdom. While the kids played Parcheesi with Harry, Ben wandered into the kitchen.

"Smells good." He straddled a kitchen chair. "Your chicken casserole is worth starving a whole day for."

Peggy smiled. "You haven't eaten today?"

"I had some cereal with the kids before school. Then I got busy." No need to explain that any time he took his mind off work, thoughts of Cait Gregory distracted him from any other meaningful topic. Even Maddie. "I wanted to ask your advice about a problem we're having."

"What's that?"

He described Cait's visit, and Maddie's reaction. "I can't convince her to share the part. And I can't order her not to participate. The whole situation is completely screwed up—I may not have much experience with the Christmas spirit, but I'm pretty sure it's not supposed to work like this."

"Life rarely works out like the storybooks. Or a Clement Moore poem." Ben had a feeling she was talking about more than Maddie's program. But Peggy was busy again—she checked a couple of pans, turned down the heat on both, and went to the refrigerator to take out vegetables for salad.

"Can I help?" Salad was one dish he knew he wouldn't ruin.

But she shook her head. "I think better with my hands occupied. What does Maddie say? Anything at all?"

Ben closed his eyes as he thought back to that one devastating sentence. "Last night, I tried to talk to her with the light off—maybe if she didn't have to face me she might let her guard down, you know?"

Peggy nodded.

"Just as she was falling asleep, she said, 'Brenna has a mommy.'"

"Oh, Ben." With her back to him, Peggy set down the lettuce and bowed her head.

He got up and crossed the room to put his hands on her shoulders. "I'm sorry. I shouldn't have bothered you with this."

"No. That's not true." She faced him, her blue eyes bright with tears. "I want to know what Maddie feels about losing her mother. Valerie would want us to take care of her, to comfort her."

"Yeah, but how can I do that at Brenna's expense?"

"Maddie also has to realize that she can't use the loss of her mother to get her way every time."

Ben couldn't reply for a minute. "True," he said when he had his voice under control. "So how do we manage this?"

Peggy sighed. "I'll see if I can think of something. Meanwhile," she said, making a visible effort to cheer up, "let's have a pleasant evening together."

Pleasant was a lukewarm word, and pretty well described the atmosphere in which they shared the meal. Harry said hardly anything at all, and Peggy spoke only to the children and Ben. Neither of the grandparents took much food to begin with, and didn't finish that. If it hadn't been for Maddie's standard play-by-play of the school day, dinner might have passed in total silence.

Afterward, Ben went back to the workshop to start on the drawer joints for the chest he was building. Careful carving, measuring and fitting kept his mind well occupied—except when he stopped to get a good breath or change tools, and his eyes fell on the phone…and he considered calling Cait. He managed to shake off the impulse every time. But he was glad when his eyes started to feel as rough as the sandpaper he was using, when his brain fogged up so all he could think about before he fell asleep was how good the pillow felt under his head.

In the morning he picked Maddie and Shep up at the

LYNNETTE KENT

Shepherds' and took them to the library, then to lunch at the Goodwill Diner, a fixture on the Avenue for more than fifty years. Back at the house, they threw a few slushy snowballs before rain drove them inside again. Shep settled down with an airplane book in the den. Ben pulled out the dust rag and vacuum, but before he could get too busy, Maddie followed him into the living room.

"Daddy?"

"Mmm?" He kept his back to her, lifting the framed photos on the mantel and dusting underneath them.

"Did you know Grandma has pictures of Mommy as a little girl?"

"I've seen them. You have, too, but you might not remember. You were about five, I guess."

"I look a lot like Mommy did."

Ben took a deep breath. "You do."

"There was a picture of her as the main angel in the pageant. She was really pretty."

"Yes." He started work on the bookshelves.

"Do you think Miss Caitlyn would still let me share the angel part in the program with Brenna?"

"I don't know. I thought you didn't want to."

"I didn't. But Grandma says Mommy would expect me to be a real friend. And that means sharing."

Thank you, Peg, Ben told his mother-in-law silently. "I believe she's right."

"I guess I kinda thought—"

After a couple of minutes, he glanced at her. "Thought what?"

She shrugged. "I don't know...maybe that if I was the angel, and Mommy's an angel now..."

Ben closed his eyes as a giant hand wrung his heart like a rag.

Maddie sighed. "But probably the best thing is for me

to share with Brenna. That way Mommy can be proud of me.''

It was his turn to take a deep breath. "I know I'm really proud of you." Leaving the bookshelves, he sat beside her on the couch and drew her into a hug. "You're a very wise and special girl, to realize all these grown-up things."

Her head dropped against his shoulder. "Being grown-up is hard."

"Sometimes." He held her for another minute, then stood up. "Want to help me dust?"

She took the cloth and started on the coffee table. "When can we ask Miss Caitlyn if she'll let me be one of the angels?"

"She's coming over tomorrow after church to help me paint scenery for the pageant. We'll ask her then, okay?"

Maddie had regained her carefree smile, and her supreme self-confidence. "Okay! Won't she be happy to hear I'll sing after all?"

CHAPTER EIGHT

"I'M REALLY GLAD Maddie decided to come back to choir." Cait flipped her braid back and dipped her brush into the black paint. "She adds so much to the sound, and to the good moods of the other kids."

"I'm pretty proud of her for making that choice." Ben deliberately kept his eyes focused on the stable stall he was painting, rather than the view he had of the woman working with him—the soles of her sneakers and her round rear end as she knelt beside another of the backdrops for the pageant, filling in the night sky above Bethlehem. "It was a more complicated issue than I realized at first."

Cait looked at him over her shoulder. "She's a very brave little girl, and she's been through a really hard time."

Ben wished she didn't understand his kids—and him—quite so well. She'd spent the whole afternoon with his family—taking time off from painting to build Lego airplanes with Shep and advise Maddie on doll clothes and hair arrangements. They'd ordered delivery pizza for dinner, then she'd helped the kids with their baths and read their bedtime stories.

Now Maddie and Shep were asleep, he was alone with Cait in his workshop, and keeping her at a distance was getting harder every hour. Those green eyes, that husky voice, lured his mind into fantasies he had no business indulging. Let alone acting out.

He cleared his throat. "She was hoping to…uh…connect with her mom by being an angel."

Cait nodded. "I remember how that feels. You just can't believe there's no way to keep the person you've lost with you. Anna and I played with a Ouija board a few years after my mom died. We thought she could talk to us that way."

"She didn't, I guess."

"Not before my father caught us." She smiled, a little sadly. "I'd like to believe he was so furious because he wished we had a good idea. I know he missed my mom. But I think it's more likely we offended his religious sensibilities."

"Some people are more open to alternatives than others."

"Yeah." She sat back on her heels, surveying her work. "He tends to be a my-way-or-the-highway kind of person. Or he was, anyway. I haven't seen him since I left home."

"I don't think he's come to see Anna recently." That was probably a nosy remark. But Cait didn't seem to mind.

"He's been at a church in Florida for more than twenty years now. When we were growing up, he rarely took vacations—said he couldn't leave his flock. I imagine he still uses that excuse."

"Do you have other brothers or sisters besides Anna?"

"Nope. Just us."

"Then I bet he'll be up here when Anna's baby is born. Most people are dying to see their first grandkid. And all the others."

"You're probably right." Again she flipped the braid over her shoulder. "I hope I'm long gone by then."

Time for a change of subject. "What are you and Anna and Dave doing for Thanksgiving?"

"I thought I'd cook."

"Seriously?"

She turned around to stare at him, her hands on her hips. "Yes, seriously. What's the problem?"

Ben backpedaled quickly. "Well, I just got the impression—when you didn't know about pot roast—maybe cooking wasn't your strongest suit."

"That was several weeks ago. I've been practicing."

"Well, good. I hope everything goes…right."

"But you don't think it will."

He shrugged. "It's usually a pretty big meal, with lots of different foods that are all supposed to be ready at the same time. I've watched Peggy for the last fifteen years, and I still don't understand how she gets it all done."

Cait glared at him, her chin lifted. "Well, maybe you should just come to dinner and find out if I can manage to do the same. You and Maddie and Shep."

"I'd like to," he said with real regret, "but I know the Shepherds will be expecting us."

"So I'll invite them, too. I'm sure Anna and David would love to have company for dinner on Thanksgiving."

"You're going to make Thanksgiving dinner for eight people?"

"Sure. Why not?"

It was hard to resist the challenge in her eyes. Ben decided not to try. "Then we'll be glad to come. Watching you prepare the annual feast is something I don't want to miss."

WEDNESDAY AFTERNOON before Thanksgiving Day found the children making steady progress with their pageant performance. Choir and wise men had the chorus of their song, "We Three Kings," memorized, but the verses needed a lot of work. The angels, mostly girls, had mastered "Joy to the World" easily. As for the shepherds, at least they had four more weeks to practice before Christmas Eve. Cait felt reasonably confident that the program would be ready.

And then she would be free again. Whatever that meant.

Maddie and Brenna were staying to practice their song tonight after the other children went home. They were talented enough to sing separate parts, but fitting them together was a new experience.

"Don't wait so long on that note for 'laid', Brenna. Just four beats, while Maddie sings her echo."

"Yes, ma'am."

"Let's do it again."

"Again?" Maddie was obviously impatient. "I sang it right. I'm tired of doing this part."

"A little more practice won't hurt." Cait didn't soften the words with a smile. Maddie wasn't making the rehearsal process any easier. When the little girl had said she wanted to sing with Brenna, Cait had thought that was the end of the problem.

Instead, Maddie exacted her revenge in a subtler way, by simply being difficult. The rift in her friendship with Brenna was plain to see. Cait didn't know how to repair the damage, so she could only regret ever having proposed the duet to begin with and persevere. Maybe they would all learn something before the end.

On the next run-through, Brenna did her part correctly and Maddie made the mistake. "Again," Cait said.

Brenna sniffed in unmistakable comment.

Cait sighed. "Second verse, girls."

By the time they had gotten through the verses without a glitch, Karen Patterson stood in the back of the church waiting. Cait got up from the organ bench. "This week, work on memorizing the words, so you don't need the music."

Both girls pulled on their coats without comment. Karen looked around. "Where's Shep?"

"He was doing homework in that front pew." Cait walked over to see the worksheets, papers and pencils scattered on the seat cushion, but no little boy. "All the doors are locked, so he hasn't gone far. Let me go find him—sometimes he plays in the robing room."

She went through the door beside the stage into the large closet where music, candles and David's robes were stored. The light was on, but she'd probably left it that way. At first glance the room appeared empty. Cait started to turn away to check the church office down the hall, but a small sound stopped her.

Not a sound, actually. A melody. The tune for "Silent Night." Hummed in a little boy's voice.

Listening, she heard a roughness in the tones, as if the voice weren't used much. But the pitch was accurate, the simple song sweetly nuanced.

Shep Tremaine could sing.

"Shep?" With her soft use of his name, the humming stopped. "Shep, Mrs. Patterson is here to take you home."

No response, no movement. Cait considered the cramped space in the room and decided the hanging robes would make good cover. She sat down on the floor beside the row of long black gowns and began to hum a tune of her own—"Row, Row, Row Your Boat."

When the song ended, she waited. After a minute of silence, she got a melody in reply. "Michael Rowed the Boat Ashore."

Cait grinned, then hummed "Three Blind Mice."

Shep answered with a verse of "Old MacDonald Had a Farm."

Aware that Karen was still waiting, Cait risked a couple of lines from the children's farewell song in *The Sound of Music*.

Under the robes, Shep heaved a sigh. Finally, he crawled out on his hands and knees to stare at her. Then Karen's voice came from outside. "Cait? Did you find him?"

Shep's gaze asked a very specific question. Cait nodded quickly. "I promise," she said without sound. Then she called out, "In the robing room, Karen." Getting to her feet, she held out her hand to Shep. He allowed her to pull him up, and they met Karen at the door. "Here we go."

Karen shook her head at the little boy. "Your dad would chop my head off if I told him I'd left you somewhere in the church to spend the night. You know how he counts on you to wash the dishes!" She smiled and put a hand on Shep's shoulder. Cait let go of him, stepped back and followed the pair into the sanctuary to collect the girls.

But for the rest of the night she thought about Shep's singing. Why would he make music and not words? Why hadn't he been humming along with the choir?

Wouldn't Ben be thrilled to know that his son was taking steps to communicate again?

She couldn't tell him right away, of course. Shep wasn't ready to have his secret revealed. Betraying his trust might send him back into his refuge of silence. First she would have to gain his confidence, ease him into using the words of the songs, not just the tunes, and then into talking.

As soon as possible, she would tell Ben what was happening. Cait could imagine his reaction when he discovered that Shep had been "talking" and he hadn't been told immediately. But the thrill of hearing his son's voice would surely mitigate his anger. Either way, Ben's displeasure was a small price to pay for getting Shep to talk again.

Okay, maybe not so small. He was a closer friend than she'd had in a long, long time…maybe the closest, except for Anna. Even if they couldn't be romantically involved, Cait wanted him to remember her kindly when she left again.

Which would be two days from now, at least temporarily. She'd told Russell she would do the short gig in Vegas—she'd fly out of Dulles Airport early Friday morning, perform two shows on each Friday, Saturday and Sunday nights, then catch some sleep and be back in Goodwill Tuesday morning. Peggy Shepherd had said she would look after Anna when David couldn't be home.

First, though, there was Thanksgiving dinner to get done. Anna had reminded her to thaw the turkey yesterday—wouldn't it have been just great to serve a frozen bird and watch Ben's face say *I told you so?* She'd bought the traditional pumpkin, pecan and mincemeat pies at a bakery up in Winchester. No way would she try to make pastry crust just to impress Ben Tremaine.

Though it would be fun to see him gulp if she had.

So tomorrow, she thought sleepily, tumbling into bed, *all I have to do is throw the turkey into the oven.* Cook the dressing and mashed potatoes and green beans. Cranberry sauce. Oh, and Anna had asked for deviled eggs. David wanted yeast rolls. Peggy had said she always made sweet potato casserole for her family, and had offered to bring it with her, but Cait had asked for the recipe, instead. This was going to be her shot at a real holiday dinner—maybe the only one she'd ever prepare from start to finish. She would make it a success, and she'd do it all on her own!

ANNA BLINKED back tears as she looked around her dining room. Cait had managed a miracle. The table glowed with candlelight and gold mums arranged in a green vase their mother had always used. On the dark-green cloth, her own cream-colored stoneware, gold goblets and silver place settings richly complimented the bounteous meal steaming on the sideboard. Every dish, from the crisply browned turkey to the fresh cranberry sauce, looked perfect.

"How wonderful," Peggy said. "Caitlyn, this is just fabulous."

"Thanks." Cait set fresh rolls on the table. "I had a really good time. But I couldn't have done it all without Anna's directions."

"If you ever decide to get out of music, you could go into the restaurant business." Harry Shepherd looked tired, and the effort he'd made to entertain since he and Peggy had arrived this afternoon was obvious.

Maddie tugged on her dad's sleeve. "Can we eat now?"

"I think Pastor Dave is going to say a prayer first." Ben hadn't said anything about the food, which Anna found strange. But then his behavior whenever Cait was around simply defied explanation.

Standing at the head of the table, David cleared his throat. "Good idea." Everyone bowed their heads.

Everyone except Anna. It was irreverent, maybe even rude. But instead of participating in the grace, she watched her husband. His hands gripped the back of his chair, and his knuckles were white with pressure. He'd lost weight—his slacks hung on his hips, his sweater was too big. And he was a man who didn't have any pounds to spare.

Mostly, it was his face that had changed. His eyes were heavy-lidded, red-rimmed, as if he didn't sleep enough. The lines across his high forehead and the creases around his mouth had become deep furrows. His voice carried a permanent rasp.

And why? What was wrong? Anna finally closed her eyes to keep the tears from falling. Was it her? Or the baby? Or the whole difficult situation that he'd realized he just couldn't bear, but didn't know how to escape?

"Amen." David lifted his head and grinned. "Now, I think it's time to sample this delicious food. Anna, I'll make your plate."

Anna smiled at him and clutched her hands together in her lap. She felt like she'd been released from prison, to be out of her bed, wearing clothes again. The doctor had given her permission to attend the dinner, as long as she sat down right away and didn't stay up for more than two hours.

So she should take advantage of this time with her friends and Cait and David. Who knew when—or if— there would ever be another celebration like this one?

David brought her a huge plate of food, then Harry sat down beside her. She turned to him with pleasure. "How have you been? I'm sure you're keeping busy, even if you aren't going to work anymore. I've never known someone with as many projects planned as you seem to have."

He didn't laugh. He barely smiled. "I...do what I can."

Under cover of the others getting their food and sitting

down, Anna put her hand on over his on the table. "Is something wrong? Are you feeling okay?"

"I'm fine, Anna." He held her gaze with his own somber brown stare. "How are you?"

"Pretty well, all things considering." She smiled at him, though he watched her almost suspiciously. "As soon as the baby comes, we'll all settle down and be fine." At least that's what she promised herself. "David worries too much right now. I'll be glad when I can take some of the responsibilities off his shoulders."

Harry looked at his plate and pushed the dressing around. "Are you all set up for the baby to arrive?"

"Oh, definitely. I spent the summer buying linens and wallpaper and baby furniture. It was so much fun."

After a second, he cleared his throat. "I remember those days."

"I'm sure you do." She'd met the Shepherds' daughter only when the Tremaine family visited Harry and Peggy, but had liked her very much. "Are you and Peggy planning to do some traveling, now that you have the time?"

Harry looked at her again, and she saw real pain in his eyes. "I don't know. I haven't thought that far ahead. Doesn't seem to matter much where I am, one way or the other." He sounded…beaten.

"Well, Peggy wouldn't go anywhere without you." Across the table, Cait was sitting between Maddie and Shep, talking to both of them, making them smile. "Imagine all the places you could show Maddie and Shep."

Now Harry covered her hand with his. "You're sweet to be thinking about me. But you take care of yourself and that baby of yours." He forked up a bite of Cait's mashed potatoes, clearly unwilling to continue the conversation.

Though Anna let him go and turned to her own meal,

Harry's attitude stayed on her mind. Was Peggy aware of his mood, so unlike his usual cheerfulness? It was easy enough not to understand your husband's thoughts, if he didn't want you to know.

Maybe she couldn't manage her own situation, but Anna felt compelled to at least try to improve Harry's. Peggy might not yet realize what Harry was going through.

But she would in the very near future.

ANNA WENT BACK to bed after the meal, and Maddie took Shep into the living room to watch a Christmas video. The rest of the adults helped Cait clear the table, put away leftovers and load the dishwasher.

"Enough," Cait said, laughing. "Enough, already. David, take everybody into the living room to sit down. I'll be in shortly with coffee and pie."

"Sounds good," he said, leading a protesting Peggy down the hallway.

"Sure we can't help finish up?" Harry asked.

Cait stretched out her arm and pointed to the front of the house. "Go!"

Smiling, shaking his head, he followed orders. Ben came through the same door just a minute later, carrying a pile of napkins and the empty breadbasket. He hadn't said much all evening, and he didn't say anything now as he put the napkins on top of Anna's washer, and set the breadbasket on the table beside other silver dishes that would need hand-washing.

"Thanks," Cait said, to be polite. If he didn't want to admit she'd done a decent job with the meal, that was okay. She would have thought he would be a better sport, but maybe not...

"You are incredible." His deep, soft-voweled voice

came from just beside her. She realized suddenly that he had leaned his hips back against the edge of the kitchen counter, just inches from where she was pouring cream and sugar into serving pitchers.

"Um…" She glanced at his face, caught the intensity of his gaze and looked away again, flushing. "I told you I'd make a decent dinner."

"And I should have believed you. There's not much you couldn't do if you set your mind to it. Obviously, the pot roast issue was just lack of focus."

"Thank you…I think."

He grinned. "But it's the whole package I'm talking about. You're about to break into the big time, yet you take off several months to help out your sister. You're beautiful and talented and thoughtful. Good with kids. What's not to love?"

Something like fear rushed through her from head to toe. "Are you trying…not to…love me?"

Ben turned to face her, curled his hand around the back of her neck and drew her up against him. "Oh, yeah," he said, almost in a growl. "I'm fighting as hard as I know how." He touched his lips briefly to hers. "And losing."

Cait hadn't let herself think about kissing him. There was no advantage in dreaming about what she couldn't have. But now his arms enfolded her and his mouth was taking hers and it seemed she could have anything she wanted.

She twined her arms around his neck and pressed close, trailing kisses across his cheek, along his jawline, before returning to his beautiful, devastating mouth. His hands slipped under her sweater, and Cait felt the rough pads of his fingers smoothing her spine with a gentle stroke, tracing her ribs, easing between their bodies to cup her breast. She moaned as the curve of his flesh fit hers. At the sound,

Ben nudged her lips apart, taking her into an intimacy so deep, Cait wasn't sure where she ended and he began.

Wrong. All wrong. A small, rational corner of Ben's brain screamed at him, but the caution was lost beneath the roar of desire and need and pure conquest rushing through him. For the first time in as long as he could remember, he felt *good.*

Which was why he didn't understand how Cait could be pulling back. "What? What's wrong?" He couldn't get his voice above a whisper.

She took a deep, shuddering breath, made a circling motion with her hand. "This. We can't...your family..." Propping her hands on her hips, she dropped her chin to her chest, still shaking her head. "Neither of us needs this."

With his body screaming, he couldn't agree. But a woman always had the right to say no. "Sorry." He ran a hand over his face, dug deep for some self-control. "I— I'll take out the garbage." Grabbing up the full container, he let himself out the back door before he could do or say something he'd regret.

Ten minutes of standing in the twenty-degree darkness cleared his head and tamed his body. He returned to the empty kitchen, carefully put the garbage can in its place and inserted a plastic bag, then made his way slowly to the front of the house.

Still absorbed in the movie, Maddie and Shep were eating cookies shaped like pilgrim hats. Harry had taken one of the armchairs; Cait sat on the sofa between David and Peggy. Ben glanced at her and quirked an eyebrow. Did she think she needed that much protection?

She blushed and looked away. "Help yourself to pie and coffee."

He bent to the coffee table and poured a cup, then

looked at Cait one last time. "Is it okay if I have a cookie, instead? I'm not much of a pastry fan."

"Of course. As many as you want." Ben took two, then went to his seat on the far side of the room. How soon would they be able to leave?

Conversation was sparse—the adults watched *Miracle on 34TH Street* with the kids, commenting occasionally to each other, comparing this version of the story with the one they remembered. The evening ended shortly after the movie did. Dave brought their coats, they all looked into the bedroom to say good-night to Anna, and then they were standing at the door, wrapping up to go out into the cold.

Ben knelt to zip Shep's jacket. Just behind him, Peggy gave Cait a hug. "This was just lovely. Thank you so much—it was a real treat not to have to cook this year."

"I'm so glad you could come." That voice was enough by itself to get him worked up all over again.

"So," Harry said, "I guess we'll see y'all Sunday morning."

"Not me, I'm afraid." Cait had stepped back from Peggy, as far away as she could get and still be in the hall. "I'm leaving for Las Vegas early tomorrow to do some shows. I'll be back on Tuesday."

Harry gave a low whistle. "Very impressive. Well, good luck. Or break a leg—whatever is the right thing to say."

Wishing he could break something himself, Ben got to his feet. "Must be important, to travel so far for such a short time."

Cait looked up at him. "My career is important. To me." The emphasis was slight, but real. "These shows will help me get more performance dates."

"And that's the name of the game," he said, as lightly

as he could manage. "Have a good weekend. Night, Pastor Dave. Come on Shep, Maddie. I'll race you to the car."

Both kids had to give Cait a hug before they came outside, so there was no race. After buckling them in, he turned on the engine just as Harry and Peg passed on the way to their car.

"Bring Maddie and Shep anytime tomorrow," Peggy told him when he rolled down the window. "I want to make some Christmas cookies—get an early start on the season."

"Oh, boy, oh, boy." Maddie clapped her hands. "We'll be there right after breakfast."

"Or maybe sometime in the afternoon," Ben suggested. "I'll call first."

Peggy waved and disappeared into the dark. As the two cars drove away, the Remingtons' front porch light clicked off.

Good-night, he thought. *Goodbye.*

"Daddy, did Miss Caitlyn say she was going to do some concerts?"

"Yes, she did."

"Can we go to one?"

"Not this time. She'll be way out in Nevada. You have to go to school Monday."

"Oh." Maddie thought for a minute. "But maybe she'll do one close to us, since Miss Anna's here, too. I'd really like to see her sing her songs with a band and everything."

At the moment, Ben couldn't think of anything more frustrating. "We'll try to do that sometime, sweetheart."

But if he was lucky, he could delay so long that Maddie would forget her crush on Cait and move on to another passion.

He only wondered if he ever would.

LANDING IN Nevada was like going to another planet. After the relatively simple pleasures of Goodwill—blue mountains and white snow, green pines and black night skies filled with glittering stars—Cait felt disoriented in the brashness of Las Vegas.

Russell met her at the airport. "Hey, babe. Glad you made it." He took her arm, dragged her along as he dashed toward the exit. "We've got a rehearsal at ten, sound check at four. First show's at eight. Band's waiting for you. Wardrobe's already in your room. Got you a nice suite, whirlpool, the works. Rooms are packed for each show. Not sold out—but I'm betting that'll happen after you knock 'em dead tonight."

In the back seat of the Cadillac—she didn't yet rate a limo in Vegas—Cait slumped down and closed her eyes. She hadn't slept much. She'd left the kitchen as clean as she could, since Peggy would be in and out all weekend. Then she'd gone to bed, only to relive the interlude with Ben over and over and over. She should have slept on the plane, but Cait hated to fly. She had to stay awake to keep the damn thing in the air.

So she'd spent the last four hours thinking about Ben, about that word he'd used—*love*. He hadn't meant *love*, the kind he'd had for his wife. Had he?

That would complicate everything beyond belief. Because it would be perfectly easy to love him back. What would they do then?

She got to the stage a few minutes before rehearsal was due to start and spent time catching up with the guys in the band. They hadn't played together since September, so there were rough spots to smooth, some changes to make, innovations to work in. For a good three hours, Cait stopped thinking about anything outside the notes and the words. It was a relief to get back into the songs, to know that she could lose herself in her work. Problems always took a back seat to music.

In her hotel room at last, she collapsed on the bed, exhausted enough to sleep through the ringing of the phone when Russell called at three to get her up again for the sound check. He had to bang on her door and pour coffee down her throat before she could function.

But then the adrenaline started leaking into her system. The spotlights in her eyes, the bounce of the stage under her feet, the smiles of the guys as they played around with the songs—this was what she'd always wanted. This was where she truly felt at home, where she knew exactly what she was doing. This was her world.

She dressed for the show—boots, black leather pants and vest over a soft white shirt. Her hair flowed from a black ribbon tied at the nape of her neck. Heavy makeup turned her into a person she hadn't seen for a while.

Finally…showtime. "Let's hear it for Miss Cait Gregory!" The audience obeyed the announcer's order with polite applause.

Standing at back stage center, Cait waited for her intro, the opening chords of her first number-one hit. Then she put on her show smile, tossed her head and took the stage because it belonged to her.

Two hours later she was sweating buckets, dizzy from hunger, blinded by the lights…and singing her third encore after a standing ovation. She'd put everything she had into the show. Now the audience was giving back. The waves of approval coming toward her touched her skin, wrapped her in a tangible embrace.

Why would she give *this* up for anything…anyone… else?

CHAPTER NINE

PEGGY SPENT much of the holiday weekend taking care of Anna. Harry missed having his wife at home, but he wasn't sorry to avoid her. Talking to Peg was getting harder by the day. There were so many things he just couldn't say.

When he came in Tuesday evening, after spending hours driving aimlessly through the mountains, the aroma of roast beef greeted him like a long-lost friend. He put his coat in the closet and followed his nose. "Peggy? Peg?"

She was whipping potatoes at the counter. "Dinner will be ready in five minutes."

Something about the tilt of her head, the set of her shoulders, kept him from coming close enough for a kiss. "Want me to set the table?"

"I thought we'd eat in the dining room for a change. I've set the places already."

"Ah." The two of them usually ate in the kitchen and saved the dining room for bigger groups...or important occasions. Each time Peg had told him she was expecting a baby, they'd been sitting in that room. Then, after all the miscarriages, Harry had dished up hamburgers there the night they'd brought Valerie home from the hospital. They'd eaten birthday dinners and anniversary meals at the long mahogany table.

What did they have to celebrate now?

He sat in his usual chair near the front window while Peg brought in the roast, the potatoes, hot rolls, broccoli casserole and salad. "Looks good," he said, though he really had no appetite.

Peggy bowed her head. "Let's say grace."

They passed the serving dishes back and forth without talking to each other, and ate for a long time in silence. Harry invented, then rejected, a series of comments designed to break the ice. He'd never had trouble talking to Peg before. And she was always the chatterbox. Tonight, they might as well have been strangers.

"What's wrong, Harry?"

He looked up from the potatoes he'd been pushing around the plate. "Nothing. It's all delicious."

Peg didn't answer his grin. "I don't mean the food."

In all honesty, he couldn't pretend to misunderstand her. He shrugged. "I…guess I'm at loose ends, not having the job to go to every day."

"Anna suggested you might want to talk to a therapist."

"A shrink?" His chest tightened. "I'm not crazy."

"Of course not. But if you won't talk to me, maybe there's someone else…David, perhaps?"

He couldn't imagine consulting the minister about his personal problems, not when a major financial and personal catastrophe loomed over the church. Harry pushed back from the table, got to his feet and went to look out the window. "What's there to talk about?"

"Feeling useless? Having no purpose?"

Obviously, he'd said too much at Thanksgiving dinner. "Tell Anna I don't appreciate the interference. I'm fine. Just fine."

"But you don't sleep. You're not eating. And we're not…making love."

Fear filled his lungs. "If you're not satisfied…"

Before he realized it, Peggy stood beside him. She put a hand on his arm. "Harry, please. It's you I'm worried about. You're the one who's not being…satisfied."

Pride kept him from pulling out of her hold. "I'm not complaining."

"You're not doing anything at all."

"I worked every damn day for thirty-five years. Maybe it's time I just didn't do anything. Did you think about that?"

"Harry—"

Pride be damned. "I'm going for a drive."

He walked away from his wife, away from the questions, from the knowledge that he was failing her at every level of their relationship.

But he couldn't walk away from the despair.

"WE HAVE FOUR Wednesdays left," Cait told the children's choir at their first rehearsal after Thanksgiving. "So we want to start practicing the staging for the program, along with the songs."

Maddie raised her hand. "Mary and Elizabeth and their angel come first."

"That's right. So we need Tina and Lindsey and Tiaria on the platform." Three of the older girls self-consciously climbed to their places. "Tina and Lindsey, you're sewing and talking, laughing a little." The two girls blushed, giggled, pantomimed using a needle and thread on cloth. "Right. Tiaria, you're going to come in from the right side…."

The kids were quiet as Cait worked through the scene and rehearsed with them the Advent songs that would bracket the action. Mary and Joseph arriving at the inn went well, too. "Mr. Tremaine has a background all painted—the rafters and walls of the stable, with hay in the boxes and everything. We'll start using those in a couple of weeks."

Just mentioning Ben's name was an effort. She'd spent the time in Vegas doing her best to forget him, to think of reasons why a relationship between them would never work. She catalogued every positive aspect of her career—fans asking for autographs, special tables in restaurants and waiters who knew her name, enough money to indulge her passion for good jewelry and designer clothes. There was a lot to like about being a big name.

"Okay, now for 'The Friendly Beasts.'" Slinging her guitar strap over her shoulder, she knelt on the floor in front of the youngest choir members. "Do you remember the words?" Cait strummed the opening chords. "I, said the donkey, all shaggy and brown…"

Twelve little voices picked up the verse with her, as the twelve young faces gazed seriously into hers. The rest of the choir sat silent, listening, while above them Mary and Joseph put a pretend baby on a folding chair standing in for the manger.

"Wow," Cait said as the last notes died away. "You do know the words. Excellent. And you'll all be dressed like the animals to sing the song. James's mom showed me one of the cow costumes—you'll look great!"

The shepherds weren't so well prepared. Cait propped her hands on her hips. "You guys had better get your act together. Stephen, Trace, Hal, get those lines down by next week. And all of you—learn the song. It's just one verse—you can handle one verse."

She heard noises behind her signaling the arrival of parents. "That's all we can do tonight. We'll start with the shepherds next week. Learn those parts!"

Under cover of the ensuing confusion, Cait caught Shep

by the sleeve. "Come with me a minute. I have something for you."

He followed her into the robing room, where she picked up the bag she'd carried back from Vegas. "I saw this and I thought about you," she said, pulling out a miniature Harrier jet. "I understand these planes are some of the coolest."

Shep accepted the toy with a wide grin and shining eyes, immediately taking the plane into its signature vertical liftoff. Cait watched him for a few minutes and gradually became aware that, again, the little boy was humming to himself. The Air Force theme song, of all things.

When she joined in, he acknowledged her words with a nod, and kept flying his plane.

"Can you sing the words, too?" Cait asked quietly, and started the song again. Shep shook his head.

But when she started over, his lips moved. It was a very tiny sound, barely a whisper. But he sang the words.

Her throat closed up with tears. Around the lump, she tried another song. "'Over the river and through the woods, to grandmother's house we go...'"

Shep frowned, but again he mouthed the words along with her.

"Not your favorite, huh? How about—"

"Shep?" Ben's voice came from the chancel. "Shep, it's time to go."

Once again, the little boy flashed a warning glance at Cait. Then he ran out of the room, carrying his Harrier.

Cait followed reluctantly and found Shep holding up the plane for his dad's and his sister's inspection.

"Very cool," Ben said, in a very cool voice. He looked at Cait. "Thank you."

"You're welcome. I've got something for you, too, Maddie." She brought a silky white stuffed puppy out from behind her back. "She looked like she belonged in your room."

"Oh, Miss Caitlyn. She's beautiful." Maddie took the toy into a reverent hold. "I'll call her Sunny."

Cait grinned. "Sunny's a great name."

"Isn't she beautiful, Daddy?"

"Amazing, Maddie. What do you say?"

"Thank you, thank you." Maddie threw her arms around Cait's waist. After a second, Shep took hold, as well. Cait put her arms around both of them and hugged back.

Ben closed his eyes. This was what having Cait in their lives would be like—she'd fly in with presents for the kids, stay a day or two and then take off again, leaving them lonely, bereft. Leaving *him* alone. Again.

So why couldn't he get her off his mind?

He opened his eyes to see the hug breaking up. "Get your coats on, kids. It's late and there's homework on the schedule."

Maddie and Shep pulled reluctantly away from Cait and went to the back pew to collect their coats. Cait watched them, obviously avoiding looking at Ben.

Which, perversely, made him want to see that she did. "How was Las Vegas?"

She faced him, chin up. "Great, thanks. My last three shows were sold out."

"I'm glad to hear the people out there appreciate good music."

Her grin discounted the barriers between them. "Me, too. It was a fantastic hotel and they want to book the band and me for a couple of months next summer."

"Vegas in summer?" He shook his head. "Not my idea of the perfect vacation."

Maddie stepped up beside him, the stuffed puppy

clutched to her chest, her coat still carried on her arm. "We go up into the mountains in the summer. Me and Daddy and Shep put up a tent and cook over the fire and swim in the mountain rivers. Boy, are they cold."

"It's cold outside tonight, too." Ben took his daughter's coat and held it out. "No sense trying to get sick again."

"'Specially with the school concert coming up," Maddie said. Then, with only one arm in the coat, she whirled to Cait. "Can you come, Miss Caitlyn? We have a holiday program where we sing the other kinds of Christmas songs—'Rudolph' and stuff like that, you know? This year we're doing a play, too, and I have a part. Can you come? Can you?"

"I'll do my very best to be there. When is it?"

Ben turned Maddie around again to finish with the coat. "The last day of school is the fourteenth, I think. It's usually that morning, around ten."

"Sounds like fun."

After the briefest of goodbyes, he herded the kids to the car and got them buckled in. With one foot on the running board of the Suburban, though, he hesitated. He couldn't leave without making sure Cait understood the seriousness of her commitment.

"I'll be right back," he told Maddie and Shep. "You two stay in your belts and leave the doors locked." It was a risk he'd never have taken, day or night, in Washington. But here in Goodwill, he knew the kids would be okay for a minute or two.

As he opened the door to the church, Cait was just coming up the aisle. All but the lights nearest the front had been switched off.

She stopped when she saw him. "Forget something?"

"I wanted to say…" He had a hard time remembering,

now that they were alone. The woman simply mesmerized him.

"You wanted to say?" she prompted, when he didn't go on.

Ben shook his head clear. "That Maddie's really excited about this school program. If you don't intend to be there, let me know as soon as possible so I can let her down easy."

Those green eyes flashed in the dim light. "I don't go back on my commitments. Any of them."

"I'm just suggesting you check your calendar really closely, in case there's a show or something you've forgotten."

Her hands went to her hips. "I didn't get this far in the business by forgetting to show up for a performance."

Backing up a step, he lifted his hands in surrender. "Okay, okay. I just wanted to be sure. Taking care of Maddie and Shep is my main job. That includes trying to keep them from getting hurt."

Those green eyes widened. "You think *I'll* hurt them?"

"I think…" He dragged in a deep breath. "I think with your career and your commitments, the potential exists. Yes."

There was a long moment of absolute silence. "Thanks for clearing that up," Cait said finally. "I always like knowing where I stand." She brushed past him, headed for the door. "Now I need to lock up and get home to Anna."

"Cait—" He caught her with a hand on her arm.

"Let go." She shook him off and went to stand at the door. "Come on, Ben," she said, not looking at him. "It's late and I'm tired." *And I'm finished with you,* her tone said, quite plainly.

So be it. "Sorry." Ben stepped through the door, then

caught a trace of her perfume in the cold, crisp air. He turned back. "Cait, listen."

"I'm done listening." She turned the big key in its heavy lock. "Good night." Back straight, head high, she strode to Anna's Toyota and was gone before Ben got himself moving again.

"What did you say to Miss Caitlyn, Daddy?" Maddie's question greeted him as he climbed into the car.

"Nothing important," he told her, with standard parental evasion.

Just all the wrong things.

REGINA THORNE stopped by the organ after choir practice Thursday night. "Remember, Cait, dear, that tomorrow is our choir Christmas party. We hold it at the beginning of the season, before everything gets so terribly hectic."

"Oh." She'd forgotten, even after being reminded every week for the past month. And even if she'd remembered, all she'd been able to think about since last night was Ben Tremaine and how pigheaded, shortsighted, narrow-minded...

"That's seven o'clock at my house," Regina continued. "We'll have a potluck dinner, some games and carols. It's always a lovely evening."

Cait dredged up a smile. "I'm looking forward to it."

"So are we." Regina patted her arm and left the church.

The one hope Cait held out for missing the dinner—Anna—fell through. "I think you'll have a good time," she said. "The games *sound* intimidating, but turn out to be fun."

"Is David going to be home tomorrow night?"

"Who knows? If he is, he'll probably be in his study."

She sighed. "I can reach him on his cell phone if I need to. Even in his study."

"Annabelle, he *is* worried about you. Maybe more than you realize."

"I know." Anna put her hand over her eyes. "I just didn't expect…"

Cait waited, and finally said, "Didn't expect what?"

"I thought having a baby—a baby you wanted desperately—was supposed to bring you closer together. But…"

She didn't finish, and Cait didn't need her to. She'd seen the way David avoided being home with his wife. Maybe the excessive worry he'd confessed to explained his behavior.

But as far as she was concerned, nothing excused the way he was hurting her sister.

So she was waiting for him when he came through the kitchen door that night at eleven o'clock, long after Anna had fallen asleep.

"I'd accuse you of cruising the bars," she said as he stood staring at her, "but Goodwill only has one."

"No." He shook his head slowly. "I was at the office. Working." Rubbing his fingers in his eyes, he walked blindly toward the door into the hallway. "Man, I'm tired."

"David."

He stopped, but didn't face her. "Can we talk tomorrow, Cait? I told you, I'm really exhausted."

"Will you be around long enough tomorrow to say anything meaningful?"

His shoulders slumped. Turning, he leaned back against the side of the refrigerator. "What is it?"

"Do you know what you're doing to Anna?"

To her surprise, he laughed. "I'm trying to make things right for her. What else can I do?"

Cait stared at him. "By ignoring her?"

"I don't—" A yawn overtook him and he covered his face with both hands. "I see her, talk to her, every day. But I'm running this church on my own and I just don't have a lot of time. There's so much to do…Anna understands." He yawned again, then looked at Cait with red-rimmed eyes. "Anything else?"

"Why don't you ask for assistance from the people of the church? Get somebody else to do what Anna used to— typing, answering the phone. There are lots of people out there who would be glad to help the two of you in any way they can." She had a sudden brainstorm. "You could let someone take care of the paperwork. Harry Shepherd, for instance. He's got the time now."

"No." The word was harsh, implacable. "I have things under control. I do," he insisted, in response to her skeptical frown. "I'm going to get it finished up by the middle of the month, and then when the baby's born…*if* the baby's born…I'll be able to give Anna all the help she needs. Good night, Cait." He didn't give her a chance to stop him again, but went quickly across the hall into his study, shutting the door firmly behind him.

Cait only hoped he slept as poorly on the couch in there as she did in Anna's guest room.

AFTER SPENDING just a few minutes with Harry and Peggy on Friday night, Ben was tempted to take the kids out for dinner and back to the house for a movie, leaving the older couple to themselves. Last week's lack of enthusiasm had become even more noticeable. Both of the grandparents looked tired, tense and preoccupied, even with Maddie and Shep demanding their attention, as usual.

Add to that his own reluctance to attend the party he'd

been invited to tonight, and the case for him taking his children home was pretty strong.

"Don't be ridiculous," Peggy said, when he suggested they call off the visit. "We've been looking forward to seeing Maddie and Shep all week. I'll be very, very disappointed if they don't get to stay." She gazed up at him with tears in her eyes. "Please, Ben. Let us keep them tonight."

A woman's tears always turned him to mush. "Sure, Peggy, if that's what you want."

So now here he was, with a potted poinsettia in hand, waiting for Regina Thorne to answer the doorbell. Behind him on the walk, a brisk set of footsteps approached. He turned to greet another guest...and looked down into Cait's shocked face.

Regina Thorne opened her door. "Hello, Ben. What a lovely poinsettia. Oh, and Cait, you're here, too! Did you two drive together? What a good idea. Please, come in."

Ben backed up against the rail of the narrow steps to allow Cait to go past, but he couldn't avoid the brush of her hip against his thigh. He caught the drift of her scent in the cold air and nearly groaned. How long would this night of torture last?

Two minutes inside the house convinced him he'd been set up. All the other guests were choir members and their spouses. He knew them, of course, and they'd asked him more than once to join their group. This could be a recruiting ploy, he supposed. Get him involved and then get him to sing.

But when the only seat left at the table was the one next to Cait, the real purpose of inviting him became clear.

However, placing them side by side at dinner was only the opening move in the evening's matchmaking campaign. The first game, Miss Thorne announced, would be Christmas charades. She proceeded to assign partners, which meant that he and Cait were together, of course. Then she handed out cards with the phrase they were supposed to act out. Ben took one look and groaned.

"What is it?" Cait pulled the card from between his fingers. "Oh, no. How could they?"

He shook his head. "I can't tell you. But we can march out in righteous anger—which will have them all believing there's something going on we don't want people to know about. Or we can play the game as if it's no big deal." Without looking at her, he shrugged as if he didn't care. "It's up to you."

"We'll play," Cait growled.

Other pairs had funny assignments—reindeer on the roof, visions of sugarplums, dashing through the snow, chestnuts roasting on an open fire. Then it was Ben and Cait's turn.

"Give me your ribbon," he whispered as they took the center of the room. Before she could say yes or no, he slipped the bright-green strand from the end of her braid and tied it quickly in a double bow.

All eyes were on them as they faced each other. "What are you going to do?" Cait said desperately.

Ben grinned. "Just close your eyes. It'll be over in a second."

She did as he asked. He took a step that brought them toe to toe and raised the bow over their heads with one arm. With the other hand, he tilted Cait's face up, and touched his mouth to hers.

"Kissing under the mistletoe!" "No fair, too easy!" Other comments filled the room, but Ben scarcely heard them through the roaring in his ears. One simple kiss had jolted him to the soles of his feet. Even after he drew back, Cait was still standing with her eyes closed, as if she didn't want to lose something precious.

We're in trouble now, Ben thought. Somehow, though, he couldn't be sorry.

The next game was Pictionary. Ben ended up on a different team from Cait, with a line from "Blue Christmas" to draw out. Poor Cait's challenge was just as bad: "On the fifth day of Christmas, my true love gave to me five gold rings." Blushing all the time, she drew five interlocked circles and won the game with the shortest time necessary for her team to guess the answer.

After that they gathered around the piano for carols, which sounded really good, since the choir members sang in parts. Ben actually started to relax—the evening would be over soon.

But Regina Thorne had one more surprise in store. "Cait, would you sing 'White Christmas' for us?"

Cait held up a defensive hand. "Why don't we all sing?"

"Because we want to hear you. Or—or maybe Ben would sing with you—he has such a nice voice, but he's always refused to join the choir."

With an expression that said, *Let's humor them and get this over with,* Cait sat down at the piano and ran through an introduction. The glance she gave him told Ben to begin the lyrics and he did so without trouble. Like the professional musician she was, she pitched the melody perfectly for his voice.

Then she joined him on the second line, in a harmony that wove through the tune like moonlight through bare tree branches. It was all Ben could do to keep his own part going. He wanted to listen to hers.

The room stayed quiet for a long moment when the

song ended. Miss Thorne finally drew a breath. "That was…"

"Perfect," Ellen Morrow said. "You couldn't ask for a nicer Christmas present."

Couples began to say good-night shortly afterward. Somehow Ben and Cait ended up standing next to Regina Thorne, saying good-bye until they were the only guests left.

The schoolteacher finally brought them their coats. "Thanks so much for coming, both of you. You really made the party special."

Ben decided not to laugh at the double meaning of her comments. "Thank you. It was a lot of fun." He held Cait's black, curly wool coat for her to slip into.

She turned to their hostess. "Thanks, Regina. I had a great time."

"Oh, you're welcome, dear." Before Cait could move away, Miss Thorne gave her a hug and a kiss. "You've done so much for us."

Red-cheeked, Cait scurried out the door and down the steps without even buttoning her coat. When Ben caught up with her, she was shaking her head. "These people…they make me crazy. What am I supposed to say to something like that?"

"Just accept the compliment," he suggested. His own car was parked to the left of the walk, but when Cait turned right, he went with her down the dark, empty street. "In the same spirit of love."

"How can they love me? They don't even know me." Hands in her pockets, she strode beside him, head down, obviously upset.

"They see what you *do* and, for them, that's who you are. You're helping Anna, you're teaching their kids, you're directing the choir. Those are the acts of a lovable person.'' He cleared his throat. ''Not to mention bringing chicken soup to sick families and toys to little kids who miss their mother.''

She stopped beside Anna's car and wiped her cheeks with the heels of her hands. ''You're making me cry. Stop it.''

Twice in one night, he'd made a woman cry. Shaking his head, he walked in front of her and took hold of her shoulders. ''A few tears are a good thing, now and then.''

She chuckled. ''Not when you wear mascara.''

''Ah. I can take care of that.'' Pulling out his handkerchief, he tilted her chin up with one hand and dabbed lightly at the slight smudges under her eyes.

''I didn't think men carried cloth handkerchiefs anymore.'' Her warm breath blew against the skin on the inside of his wrist. Ben felt everything inside him tighten up.

''Maddie sewed my initials on them as a Scout project. I wouldn't go anywhere without one.''

''You're such a good dad,'' she whispered. ''They're so lucky to have you in their lives.''

He gently knuckled back the wispy curls at her temple. ''Want to share? There's enough of me to go around.''

''Ben...'' She started to pull away...but stopped and gazed up at him, her eyes dark, her lids a little heavy, her lips slightly parted. ''Oh, Ben.''

Reaching up, she took his face in her hands, cold fingers over his ears, warm palms against his cheeks.

And then she drew his head down until their mouths met.

CHAPTER TEN

"THIS IS CRAZY." Ben's voice rasped in her ear even as his palms, warm and calloused and possessive, moved over her bare skin. "My house is empty tonight. Come home with me."

Before she could answer, he took her into another kiss and she was lost again, indifferent to anything but Ben—his hands, his mouth, the hard weight of his body leaning into hers.

But his leather jacket deprived her of the chance to touch him in return. Cait struggled with the zipper, finally breaking the kiss to lean away so she could see what she was doing. Ben's hands slipped over her ribs to cover her breasts, only the thin silk camisole she wore separating his skin from hers.

They both gasped, and Cait pulled hard on the tab of the zipper. The jacket opened; she plunged her hands into the warmth next to his body, feeling the planes of his chest, the strength of his arms, the breadth of his shoulders. Ben leaned over her again and found her lips with his.

In just a minute—or it might have been an hour—he pulled back again, chuckling breathlessly. "If we keep this up, I'm going to have you stretched out on the hood of this car in the freezing cold, and neither of us will have enough clothes on."

He drew his hands from beneath her sweater, cupped

his palms around her face. "Let me take you somewhere warm and safe and comfortable. And private," he added as a car rounded the corner just a block away, drenching them in its headlights. The driver beeped the horn as the vehicle drove by. Cait knew chances were excellent, given the size of Goodwill, that whoever it was had recognized Ben, and her.

The thought cooled the heat in her brain. She took her hands out of Ben's jacket. Her fingers were shaking as she buttoned her coat.

"Cait?" Ben took hold of her shoulders again.

She closed her eyes. "I can't go home with you."

"Why not?"

"This isn't smart. We both know that and we should never have let ourselves forget."

"How can you be so sure?"

Her heart pounded with the need to get away before she did something really stupid—like agreeing to sleep in his bed tonight. Or not sleep, as the case would be. "There are too many reasons to count, but I'll give you a couple. Everybody in town will know by tomorrow night that we were standing out here, and what we were doing. If I go home with you, they'll know that, too, and they'll jump to conclusions. In another week gossip will have us married and I'll be pregnant and—and—" Cait shook her head. "You don't need that kind of complication in your life. Neither do I."

"Would marriage be such a terrible prospect?" His voice was low, reasonable. His words were insane.

Cait struggled for good sense. "Ben, you don't want to marry me. I don't want to marry you. Why put ourselves in a position where that becomes something other people expect us to do?"

His hands dropped to his sides. "You sound awfully sure of yourself."

Good to hear, since she felt anything but confident she was speaking the truth. "Tomorrow, we'll both be really glad we didn't give in to—to—"

"To uncontrollable lust? Insatiable need?" His face twisted with frustration. "Or how about just a desperate desire to be close to someone we care about? Someone we could even—might even—love?"

"Go home." Turning, she fished in her coat pocket for the car key and fitted it into the lock. Ben stood behind her for a minute, his body heat reaching her through the cold air between them, through their clothes, melting her resolve. If he didn't back off, all her good intentions would go for nothing and she'd end up taking everything he offered.

In the instant before her determination vaporized, he stepped away. "Get in," he said, his voice cool again. "I'll see you...later."

She took three stabs at fitting the key into the ignition. The motor cranked briefly, then died. Biting her lower lip, Cait tried again. And again. Ben stepped forward, approaching her window as she tried one last, desperate time. If she had to talk to him...

The engine caught, roared as she gunned the gas pedal. Without glancing to the side, she slipped the car into gear and pulled away from the curb, only daring to look at Ben through the rearview mirror. Hands in his pockets, feet firmly planted and head held high, he stood motionless in the street for as long as she could see him.

And he remained that way in her mind's eye until she finally fell into a restless sleep, sometime near dawn.

BEN ARRIVED at noon on Saturday to pick up Maddie and Shep—too soon, as far as Harry was concerned. Having the kids in the house was the first time he'd seen Peg relax since he'd come back to the house Tuesday night. Make that Wednesday morning…he'd driven to a truck stop up on the interstate and drowned himself in coffee until after 2:00 a.m.

Since then they'd been polite to each other, and that was all. Peg seemed to have given up trying to talk to him; Harry told himself that was for the best. Talking wasn't going to get him his job back. He slept in his recliner—good thing he was an early riser or the kids would have found him there Saturday morning.

Meanwhile, whenever he talked to David Remington, the minister stalled him on reporting the missing check to the police. Or to the governing committee of the church. Out of deference to Anna's condition, Harry hadn't pushed the issue. But somebody needed to know and soon. Waiting would only make things worse.

Across the lunch table, he noticed Ben didn't look any more rested than he felt. "I think you've been working too hard, son. You're supposed to take the night off while Magpie and Shepkin are with…us." He wasn't even sure there was an "us" anymore.

Ben gave his half smile. "I did take last night off, remember? I went to Regina Thorne's party."

Peggy set a plate of tuna sandwiches on the table. "Did you have a good time?"

"Uh…sure. Did *you* know it was a setup for me and Cait?"

Harry saw his wife's cheeks turn bright pink as she took her seat. "As a matter of fact…"

"Miss Caitlyn was at the party, Daddy? Did she sing Christmas songs?"

"We all did. It was a...festive...event. Even if it had an ulterior purpose."

Maddie frowned. "What's ulterior mean?"

Ben looked at Peggy again. "It means people aren't telling you what they really want—they're hiding the reasons for what they're doing, or wanting you to do. Sometimes it's a good thing to have ulterior motives—like sending somebody off to look at the toys while you buy them clothes for a present. And sometimes—" he pulled in a deep breath "—sometimes, there's no hope whether your motives are hidden or out in the open."

"I'm confused."

Her father ruffled her curls. "So are most of us, Maddie. Don't worry about it."

After lunch, the kids helped clean up the kitchen. Harry led Ben to the den. "Want to catch a ball game?"

His son-in-law shook his head. "No, thanks. We'd better get out of your way. But first, I'm going to be a pain in the rear."

Harry snorted. "There's a first time for everything."

Ben flashed that half smile again. "So you won't mind telling me what the problem is?"

He kept his face blank. "What problem?"

"The one that has you and Peggy talking to everybody but each other. The one that has you looking like a man twenty years older than you are. The one that sends my kid home saying, 'Grandpa was grumpy last night.'"

The last accusation stung. "I didn't mean to be harsh with the children."

"I didn't say you'd been harsh. But Maddie and Shep are used to a grandpa who laughs, jokes, plays with them. You haven't done much of any of those things for the last few weeks."

Haven't made love to my wife, either. Not something he would confess to Ben. "I just…" He shrugged.

"You just hate having lost your job."

Harry swung away and went to stare out the window at the rainy, gray day. "I didn't lose my job. I retired."

"Does the word you use make a difference?"

"Sure it does. I wasn't fired because I couldn't do the work. I left after thirty-five years with an excellent reputation, a decent retirement package and a gold watch."

"Because you were the oldest VP, the one the company felt would be cheapest to eliminate."

"Dammit, Ben. Drop the subject."

"I would if I didn't see it consuming you."

"I'll be okay."

"Before you ruin your marriage and your health?"

"Butt out, son. I'm telling you everything is just fine." He didn't lie often, which might explain why his heart and head were pounding and his hands were clenched in his pockets.

Ben shrugged. "Okay, I quit. For now. But you need to talk to somebody, Harry. Soon." Without waiting for an answer, he left the room. A few minutes later, Harry heard the sound of the kids saying goodbye to Peggy, heading out the door.

And then Peg's footsteps sounded on the stairs and in the hallway above him. She'd retreated to her sewing room, leaving the whole downstairs free for him.

Free. Free of the burden, the constraints, the regimentation of a job. Free to do whatever he pleased with his days and nights. No business trips, no reports to generate, no endlessly boring meetings to sit through.

No purpose.

In his mind, Harry backed away from that idea, the way he would an arcing electrical wire. Sitting in his recliner,

he picked up the remote, found the ball game he wanted
to watch.

Sometimes the best thought was no thought at all.

BRENNA AND Maddie and Shep arrived ahead of the rest
of the choir on the next Wednesday. They joined Cait at
the organ in a puff of cold air.

"It's supposed to snow," Maddie announced. "Maybe
we'll get days off from school again."

Cait modulated the chords into "Let It Snow." Maddie
and Brenna joined her on the chorus. She glanced at
Shep—he was sitting on the edge of the stage, swinging
his legs. Humming? It was hard to tell over the girls'
voices.

When they finished the song, Cait stood up. "Maddie,
Brenna, could you go into the robe room and get the box
of music folders?" They raced each other to the doorway,
leaving Cait alone with Shep.

She sat down beside him, singing the same song, softly.
He began humming with the first line. Then Cait felt her
heart stop as the little boy whispered the words to the
chorus, clearly, on pitch.

Afraid that hugging him would drive him back into his
shell, Cait stayed still by sheer determination, and kept
singing. Shep joined her on each repetition of the refrain.
When they finished, she held her breath and looked at
him. He stared back at her, his brown eyes serious, a little
questioning.

"I like singing with you," Cait said gently. "Can we
do it again sometime?"

After a moment he nodded. Then his friend Neil came
running down the aisle and Shep was back to being his
usual happy, if silent, self.

"Three Wednesdays," Cait told the choir as they

started. "Shepherds, did you learn your song?" The boys nodded. "Good—let's hear it."

The shepherds had exaggerated quite a bit, so she held them after the rehearsal for extra practice, ignoring the waiting parents as best she could. When she finally let the boys go, Maddie and Shep had already left with Karen and Brenna Patterson. No chance to talk to Shep again tonight. No chance to see Ben, either. And that, she told herself, was just as well.

The next opportunity to realize both of those desires came from an unexpected direction. Ben called her Friday morning. "I have a favor to ask."

Just hearing his voice made staying calm a challenge. "What is it?"

"This is the weekend for choosing the Christmas tree."

She had to grin. "Did I hear a few unspoken epithets preceding the words 'Christmas tree'?"

"Yeah, you probably did. Anyway, Maddie and Shep...and I...wondered if you would like to come with us to the tree farm tomorrow."

"Ben, I don't think—" She didn't want to think. She wanted just to say yes.

"With two eagle-eyed chaperons along, what can happen? We'll take a lunch, drive up in the mountains, spend a couple of hours tramping around in the snow comparing identical trees, finally choose one and chop it down, tie it to the roof of the car and come home. Just a friendly holiday outing." *Holiday* came out sounding like a curse word.

"I get it. You're using me as a shield, right? So you don't have to be all Christmassy with the kids."

"You caught me. Will you do it?"

Cait gave in to her own weakness. "I'll have to make sure David will be here tomorrow."

"Why wouldn't he be? It's Saturday."

"That's what I'm wondering. Let me check with him and I'll let you know."

She called David at the church office and on his cell phone, but got no answer at either number.

"So much for being able to reach you in an emergency." Cait met him outside the house that evening when he pulled in the drive. "Where have you been all day?"

"I—I had a meeting up in Winchester. Is something wrong? Is Anna okay?" Without waiting for an answer, he started for the kitchen door.

But Cait stepped in his way. "Does it really make a difference to you? How could you be so completely unreachable? Where is your head these days, David?"

His hands clenched and, for a second, he looked as if he would tear his hair out. Or reach out and tear her apart.

Then his shoulders slumped. "Look, there are some…problems with the church accounts. I've been working on them, trying to get it all straightened out, that's all. I had my cell phone, see?" He held it up, then looked at the screen. "But I didn't know the battery had run down. I'll charge it tonight."

"What kind of problems?"

David avoided her gaze. "Just some columns that don't add up, you know how that goes."

She could only think of one reason he would be so preoccupied with the books. "Is there money missing?"

"No. No, of course not." He reached under his glasses and rubbed his eyes. "It's just a matter of adding and subtracting right. I'll get it taken care of. Though I have to say, one reason I'm a minister is because I knew I'd never make it as a math teacher or an accountant." He grinned, obviously trying to joke her out of her suspicions.

Cait wasn't amused. "Well, in case you've forgotten, Anna could go into labor at any minute. You'd damn well better stay in touch. And," she said as he started to turn away, "I'd like to go to the mountains tomorrow with Ben and Maddie and Shep. So unless you have something critical to do, you'll need to stay here with your wife." She put some extra emphasis on the last two words.

"Sure. No problem. I'll be glad to." He stood in front of her like a chastised schoolboy. "Can I go in to see her now?"

Cait stepped aside and let him through the door. Then she stood for a long time in the backyard, watching the stars come out while she tried to decide why life in a small town had to be so complicated.

SATURDAY MORNING dawned clear and bright, with tree shadows lying crisply across the four inches of snow they'd gotten this week. Ben served orange juice and oat-meal for breakfast—instant oatmeal, cooked in the micro-wave. But each of the kids ate two envelopes, so he thought they'd be good to go until lunch. And lunch would be decent because he'd ordered sandwiches, cook-ies and hot chocolate from the diner. All they had to do was pick up the basket on their way out of town.

He happened to be at the front window when Cait parked Anna's car in front of the house. She ran lightly across the shoveled walk, wearing a bright-green coat and a crazy hat—a green-white-and-red knitted stocking cap, with bells tied onto the point with ribbons. Even through the closed windows, he could hear her jingling as she came up the steps.

"Santa's elf, I presume," he said when he opened the door.

"I thought so—but Maddie looks more like an elf in

her Christmas sweater. And Shep looks like he's ready for combat patrol."

To Ben's surprise, Shep giggled. Aloud. It wasn't a sound he made very often at all. But Cait always seemed to be getting reactions that Shep withheld from almost everyone. Including his own father.

On the way into the mountains, Maddie and Cait sang carols along with the disk in the CD player. Ben pleaded the need to concentrate on the snowy road as a reason not to join in. But he caught himself humming along with "Jingle Bells" and "The Little Drummer Boy." Except for the night at Regina Thorne's house, he hadn't sung Christmas tunes in a couple of decades. Cait had him and his family behaving in strange and unpredictable ways.

Ben was forced to admit it was a change for the better.

"These surely are beautiful mountains," Cait said during a quiet moment after the CD ended. "Not so aggressive as the ones out west. I like the gentleness."

"The Blue Ridge has its share of hazards. Maybe not as dramatic as the drop-offs in the Rockies, but it can be a long way down."

As he spoke, they came out of a wooded area onto the top of a peak. The left side was still protected by a high dome of rock. But the right shoulder fell away into a steep-sided valley, white snow streaked with bare trees and the occasional green of a cedar or pine.

Cait took a deep breath. "I see what you mean. Not a place you want to underestimate the risks."

"Especially not when there's a foot of new snow." He glanced to the west, where clouds had piled on the peaks. "Or when more is predicted."

"More snow?" Maddie bounced in her seat. "Cool! Maybe we won't have school all week."

"Then you wouldn't have your holiday program," Ben

pointed out. He glanced at Cait, to see if she had remembered. Her gaze was waiting for him, sardonic, a little reproachful. Yeah, she remembered.

"Are we almost there, Daddy?"

"Almost. Give me ten minutes, okay?"

"Okay."

In about eight, he took the turnoff onto the narrow, crooked gravel road leading to Dove's Tree Farm. There was no parking lot, just the front yard of a small log cabin standing on a slight rise. Behind the house, spruce trees filled the landscape all the way to the rocky sides of the valley.

"Okay," Ben said, cutting the engine. "Lunch, or tree?"

"Tree!" Maddie shouted. Shep wrestled with his seat belt in agreement.

"Why did I even ask?" He glanced at Cait.

She shook her head. "I don't know. The answer was pretty obvious." Her smile turned the barb into a gentle tease.

And her presence made the tree search less of an ordeal. She romped through the snow with the kids, inciting snowball fights and snow angel contests. Maddie and Shep sought her opinion on every tree they passed, and Cait took to making up silly evaluations.

"Too conceited," she judged one specimen.

Ben stopped in his tracks. "A conceited tree?"

"It is, Daddy." Maddie dragged at his arm. "Come on."

With a wave of his arms, Shep presented the next candidate, which looked exactly like the last one. Cait shook her head. "Doesn't like children. Wants a house with two adults, no cats and only an old dog. No pets would be even better."

Shep laughed. Ben heard him, and for a few seconds his heart thudded against his ribs. Was his son finally coming to terms with what had happened in his life? Would he speak again?

And was Cait somehow responsible for the change?

The sky clouded over as they wandered through the trees. A little after noon, Ben glanced up and realized they were definitely in for more snow. At the thought, it seemed, the first flakes came drifting down.

"Oh, boy. We're looking for a Christmas tree in the snow!" Maddie and Shep dodged in and out between the green branches.

Ben hefted the ax onto his shoulder. "And we need to find one, get it cut, and get back to the car. I'd like to beat the snow down the mountain."

"Okay, kids, that's a direct order." Cait surveyed the trees around them with her hands on her hips. "Let's figure out which of these trees is yours and take it back to Goodwill."

An *hour* later, they dragged their choice up to the log cabin. Farmer Dove, who looked like a retired college professor in a heavy tweed jacket and with a pipe clamped between his teeth, helped Ben tie the tree onto the roof of the Suburban. "Better go the short way home," Dove recommended. "Weather channel's calling for another six, eight inches."

Ben climbed into the driver's seat. "I don't think there is a short way home. But thanks."

Farmer-Professor Dove nodded and went back inside.

As soon as the car doors were shut, Maddie said, "What about lunch, Daddy? I'm hungry."

"You can eat as we drive." He turned on the windshield wipers to clear away snow. "A traveling picnic. If Cait will do the honors."

"Sure." But she gave him a concerned glance. "Can you eat and drive?"

"On a flat interstate, with no traffic, in the summer, maybe. Going down the mountain in the snow, no way." He grinned at her. "I won't starve between here and home."

The wind picked up as the storm drew close, driving snow against the windows. Going around exposed turns, Ben could feel the tree shifting the car's balance. He tightened his hands on the steering wheel, sat up straighter. Too bad there really wasn't a shorter way down. They should have left the tree farm much earlier. He'd known it at the time, and allowed emotion to sway his judgment.

Just as Cait started passing sandwiches into the back seat, Ben spotted blue lights flashing up ahead. Two highway patrol cars had been parked across both lanes of the road. When Ben eased to a stop, a frozen-looking patrolman walked up to his window.

"There's a bad accident up ahead. You'll need to detour, sir."

Ben swallowed a few choice words. "I'm not really familiar with the area. Can you give me some directions on this detour?"

The patrolman seemed to swallow a curse of his own. "Got a map?"

Cait had already searched the glove compartment and come up with his Virginia map. Ben gave her a grateful smile and stepped out into the quickly falling snow to get directions.

"Okay." He got back in the car feeling chilled and tired, and only hoping he could follow the officer's instructions. "First we take this left turn, here...."

THE PHONE WOKE Anna on Saturday afternoon, but before she could reach it, the ringing stopped. While she was still trying to get her eyes open, David came to the bedroom door.

"Anna?"

"Hmm?" She'd been dreaming she was working outside, digging up a new flower bed.

"Your dad is on the phone."

Completely awake now, she put the phone to her ear. "Hi, Dad. How are you?"

"Very good. I hadn't heard from you in quite some time. Has your baby been born yet?"

She got a kick in the bladder from the person in question. "No, we're still waiting, thank goodness."

"You're being careful this time?"

As if she hadn't been careful with the last two babies? "I'm on complete bed rest. I haven't lifted anything heavier than a glass of milk for weeks now."

"That sounds wise. David is taking care of you, I'm sure."

"Of course." *As long as he doesn't actually have to communicate with me. Or touch me.* Some impulse drove her to add, "And Cait's been here since the beginning of October."

"I...see." The Reverend Allan Gregory cleared his throat. "That's very nice of her, I'm sure. The weather down here has been so warm, it's hard to believe we're in the Christmas season. But I can tell from the increasing workload. I've got three extra messages to write before the twentieth."

For once, she wouldn't let him off so easily. "Cait is directing our annual Christmas pageant. And she's written a song for it, as well."

"Commendable."

Anna wanted to scream. "This will be the first Christmas she's celebrated since she left home."

Her dad made no reply to that piece of news.

She gave up the subtle approach. "Don't you think it's about time you ended this stupid feud with your own daughter?"

He remained silent so long, she began to think he wouldn't answer her question at all. "I have never been treated with such a complete lack of respect."

"That was ten years ago, Dad."

"I have not received an apology, or any kind of communication at all."

"Cait left home with the impression you never wanted to hear from her again."

"She made her choice."

The temper she'd been holding in check for months broke free. "And that's the problem, isn't it? You can't get over the fact that Cait didn't do what you told her to. She didn't follow the path you laid out for her, like I did. And to make the whole situation worse, she was right, wasn't she? You have to have heard how successful she is, how much people across the country like her music. You were wrong. And you can't deal with it."

This time, she knew he would hang up on her. After a long pause, he said, "I hope you will stay well and that the baby is born safe and healthy."

"Thank you." She made one last attempt to change his mind. "'Do unto others as you would have them do unto you.' That's the rule, Dad. It's the reason for Christmas. If you can't forgive, how can you be forgiven?"

Another stretch of emptiness on the line. "Take care of yourself."

She'd failed. "You, too."

"Call me when the baby is born."

"Of course."

"Goodbye."

"Bye." Anna clicked off the phone and rolled onto her back, crossed her arms over her face and let herself cry.

THE AFTERNOON darkened and the snow came faster and thicker as they rode slowly through the mountains. Maddie had long since given up her cheerful chatter; the car was very quiet. Cait hesitated to say anything at all, for fear of distracting Ben from the treacherous conditions. She couldn't look away from the road, either, as if her attention was required to keep them on course.

Just outside her window, the mountain dropped at a sharp angle into a deep hollow, thickly filled with trees. Gusts of wind buffeted the evergreen they carried on the roof. It was almost like having a sail tied to the car. In the middle of a hurricane.

Ben flexed his fingers around the steering wheel. "There should be another turn coming up on the left. That road—"

A blast of wind hit his side of the car, pushing them toward the drop-off on Cait's side. She gasped, then sat stiff as he gentled the Suburban back to the center of the road.

"What's wrong?" Maddie's sleepy voice meant she'd missed the worst of that adventure. "Are we home?"

"We're getting there, darlin'." Cait reached backward over the seat to pat the little girl's knee. "It won't be long now."

As she spoke, the wind attacked again. Above them, the tree shifted to Cait's side of the car.

"Damn," Ben muttered under his breath. The windshield wipers barely cleared the glass before it was covered again. "I'm going to pull over, see if we can wait out the worst..." He put his foot gently on the brake.

The antilock system kicked in with a rumble. That meant they were driving on ice, invisible under the new layer of snow. Their forward motion slowed just as the wind drove into them yet again, pushing the big vehicle toward the hollow.

Holding his breath, Ben turned into the skid, fighting for control, but the wind had taken the possibility out of his hands. "Put your head on your knees," he yelled. "Cover your face with your arms."

A picture of Valerie laughing with the kids flashed through his mind. Then he heard Cait gasp as the Sub-urban slid onto the narrow shoulder...and over the side of the mountain.

CHAPTER ELEVEN

"TALK ABOUT MIRACLES." Ben pushed the airbag away from his face. "I can't believe this."

The Suburban had careened through the trees growing on the bank of the hollow without smashing into any of the big ones. As far as he could tell from looking out the side window, the car had come to rest about halfway down the slope on a nearly level platform of four or five fallen trees. Big trees, thank God. Their position seemed about as secure as possible, given what had happened.

And nobody had been hurt. No glass was broken, though the windshield was blocked by debris and uprooted bushes. He wasn't sure where the Christmas tree had ended up. He was pretty sure he didn't care.

"Do we have to stay here Daddy? Can we get out and play in the snow?"

Beside him, Cait gave a groaning chuckle.

"No, Maddie. We're staying where we are until somebody comes to help us get out. I'm going to call the police right now." He felt for the cell phone in the console between the front seats praying that there would be service down in this hole.

The relief that rushed through him when he got a ring on 911 was evidence of how worried he'd really been. "Yes, hello. I need to report an accident...."

When he disconnected, he realized Cait hadn't said anything—except for that chuckle—since the car had come to a stop. He reached out, feeling for her arm, her hand. His fingers found hers, twined between them. "Are you okay?"

"Sure. Just still...um...getting my heart rate down. I'm not a fan of roller coasters."

"Neither am I, anymore." He left their hands joined. The contact felt too good to abandon. "Given where we are, it'll take them an hour or two to find us, especially in this weather. I'll run the motor at intervals to give us some heat, and we all should be fine."

"But, Daddy, what can we *do?*"

"We can sing," Cait said. "How about 'Jingle Bells'?"

Surprising himself, Ben joined in, but had to stop, laughing, when they reached the second verse. "We got 'upsot,' all right."

Cait groaned. "Life imitates art. What's the next song?"

Maddie called for "The Twelve Days of Christmas," which kept them busy for a while, then "We Wish You a Merry Christmas." Ben thought his teeth would begin to ache from an overdose of holiday sweetness.

He opted out of the next song and let his mind drift, noting how fast it was getting dark outside, thinking that he was tired of being penned in, wondering when one of the kids would need to go to the bathroom. Any time now, he was betting. When he brought his attention back to the music, he realized that Cait had started singing "Silent Night."

And that he was hearing three separate voices.

Couldn't be. He closed his eyes, holding his breath, listening hard. Did he really hear Shep singing?

Humming, actually. No words. But there was definitely a third voice there. His son was making sounds again.

How? Why? Did it have something to do with being in yet another car accident, with everybody coming out safe this time? What kind of sense did that make?

Ben looked over at Cait. She was gazing at him, smiling as she sang, her eyes shining. He grinned back at her, glad to share the moment...until he received yet another revelation. Cait was not surprised to hear Shep's voice.

She had *known* the little boy could sing.

But she hadn't told Ben.

He was still figuring out his reaction when the flash of blue-and-red-and-yellow lights on the snowy windshield caught his attention. "Looks like the police are here." His voice was rough with the tears he didn't want to shed, the fear and relief of the last couple of hours, the indignation at being left out on such a vital matter as Shep's voice. He cleared his throat. "Let's sit tight and see how this is going to work."

Getting the four of them out of the Suburban was hard work. The firefighters and police judged the fallen trees under the car pretty stable, but they did some rigging with ropes and chains, just in case. They took the kids out first, since their weight was light and would disturb the balance least. Ben felt slightly crazy, believing Shep and Maddie were safe but not knowing exactly where they were anymore.

In the lull while they waited for their own rescue, he looked over at Cait again. "You knew Shep was singing?"

"Just in the last couple of weeks. I heard him by accident one afternoon after choir practice."

"And you didn't tell me?" He couldn't control his voice enough to keep the outrage hidden.

"I'm sorry, Ben. He didn't want anyone to know."

"Shep said that?"

"No. But it was obvious. And I was afraid that if I betrayed him, he'd stop altogether."

"Yeah." The indignation faded, replaced by hurt. Why wouldn't his son want to talk to him?

He didn't realize he'd voiced the question until Cait answered. "Why did he stop talking to begin with? The reasons for both behaviors must be connected somehow. Maybe being silent was something he felt he could control, when he couldn't do anything about his mom. Maybe he was angry—at himself, at the world?—and not talking was a means of punishment. You'll probably be able to ask him one day soon. And he'll tell you."

"I guess I need to find a new therapist."

"I think… Never mind."

"What do you think?"

"It's none of my business."

He reached for her hand again. "That's not true, and you know it. My family is most definitely your business."

Cait was quiet for a breathless minute. "I think you need to give him more time before bringing in a stranger to ask questions and make demands."

"I would hope a therapist would be more sympathetic than that."

"However it's done, if he feels the least pressure, he might stop."

"So I just wait for the day he decides to talk to me?"

"Give him opportunities to sing. That's what happened this afternoon, it's what happens at choir. I've been singing with him, to him. Sometimes Shep chooses the song, sometimes I do, and it's like a game. The more fun you make it, the more often I think he'll play."

The door on Cait's side of the car opened. "Howdy, folks." A red-faced firefighter in turnout gear grinned in at them. "How about a lift back up to the road?"

Ben went last, to find that they'd brought in a crane. The trip to the top of the bank was a short cold ride standing in the electrician's bucket attached to the end of the crane's arm. And then he was on solid ground. His knees were shaky, but they held him up for the quick walk to the ambulance where Cait and Maddie and Shep sat huddled under blankets.

"Daddy!" Maddie flew toward him over the snowy ground, flung her arms around his waist and squeezed tight. Ben cupped her head with one hand and with the other arm scooped up Shep when he arrived.

"Hey, son." He spoke with his mouth against the blond hair. "I heard you singing, back there in the truck." Shep pulled away a little to meet his gaze. "Are you thinking about starting to talk again?"

After a couple of false starts, the little boy said, huskily, "Maybe."

Ben squeezed his eyes shut, swallowed hard. "That's terrific. I'm so glad."

"Me, too." Shep leaned close and put his arms around his dad's neck. "Me, too, Daddy."

Ben hugged his son even tighter, thanking God for this newest miracle of Christmas.

THE SUBURBAN was not driveable, so the police gave them all a ride down to Goodwill. Since they weren't expected home at any particular time, they had decided to call Anna and the Shepherds once they'd returned to town.

"Believe it or not," Cait told her sister, "the firefighters even rescued the Christmas tree. Ben and Maddie and Shep are setting it up right now."

"There must be some kind of Christmas jinx you and Ben share. Are you sure you're all okay?" Anna sounded tired, stressed.

"We're fine. How are you feeling?"

"The same as always these days. Bored, frustrated, alone…" She broke off with a gasp. "I'm sorry, Cait. I didn't mean to say that."

"Why not, if that's the way you feel? Nobody likes being forced to stay in bed when they aren't sick."

"But there's a good reason for me to be here. I shouldn't resent doing whatever it takes to keep the baby safe."

Cait heard a burst of laughter from Maddie in the living room. She moved to the doorway so she could see the little girl steadying the tree in its stand.

Ben was lying on the floor, only his legs visible under the green branches. "Is it straight yet?"

Maddie looked at Shep, standing across the room. "Is it straight?"

Shep nodded, and Cait turned back into the kitchen. "Annabelle, you're entitled to your feelings. What matters is what you do with those feelings. Ben has always hated Christmas, but he's spent the whole day helping his kids get ready to celebrate."

"Still—"

"You like to be up and doing things—you'd probably be really happy to decorate your house yourself, instead of looking forward to having the women of the church do it for you."

Anna sighed. "Oh, I would."

"You're not though, because you care about your baby the way Ben cares about Maddie and Shep. Be proud of what you're doing. It says what kind of person you are."

"Oh, Cait." A few telltale sniffs came over the line. "Thank you. We'll see you when you get home."

"Sure. I won't be too late."

"Oh, wait a minute. Cait? Are you there?"

"I'm here."

"You had a call today from your agent. He wanted you to get in touch with him as soon as possible, that it was very, very important and you could reach him all weekend at his number in Palm Springs."

"Thanks. I'll get back to him tonight." She hung up the phone, wondering what new havoc Russell was about to cause in her life. After the Vegas date, she'd put her foot down—no more shows until after Christmas. He hadn't liked it, but he'd agreed. Now what?

Maddie called from the living room, "Miss Caitlyn, come see the tree—it's so tall!" and Cait decided not to worry about Russell until she had to. Tonight, for the first time in ten years, she had a Christmas tree to help decorate.

Much later, after the tree had been made beautiful, after Maddie and Shep were in bed, Ben walked her out to Anna's car. The snow that had been so heavy in the mountains was just a light dusting down here in the valley.

"What a day." He took a deep breath and lifted his chin to stare at the cloud-covered sky. "I ought to apologize for risking your life."

Cait shook her head. "Accidents happen, Ben. You did everything you could to keep us all safe."

"Maybe." After a long silence, he looked at her again. "I've always wondered if there was something Valerie could have done to save herself, to avoid being killed."

"And I bet you've wondered if *you* could have changed what happened somehow."

"You know too much." But he gave her his half smile. "Today answered that question, I think. Valerie did everything possible, in those last seconds, to save Shep. She turned the car so that her side took the impact. She made a choice—the same one I would have made today, if I'd had to. If I could have. So…that's the answer. We do our best at any given moment. And what happens…happens.''

He studied her face for a minute, his expression serious, his eyes dark. "Like this," he said finally. Taking her face in his hands, he gave her a sweet, deep kiss.

And then drew back. "Can I take you to the Christmas dance?"

Still reeling from his touch, Cait wasn't sure she'd heard right. "The what?"

"The Goodwill Christmas dance. Held in the town hall. I've never been, but they tell me it's a nice evening.''

"W-when?"

"Tomorrow night. It's short notice. I wasn't going this year, either, but—'' he ran a fingertip lightly down her cheek "—I just changed my mind. What do you think?"

She thought about dancing with Ben in front of the entire town, the kind of mistaken expectations which would arise.

Then she thought about leaving Goodwill in less than three weeks without ever having danced with Ben at all.

"What time should I be ready?"

"No. ABSOLUTELY NOT."

Three thousand miles away, Russell sighed. "C'mon, Cait. This is a big chance for you—standing in for a major name in a sold-out concert.''

"It's a week off. She'll be over the flu by then."

"Uh, well…let's just say she's checked into a California facility to deal with this particular virus on an in-patient basis.''

"Oh.'' So much for that excuse. And why did she need one? Six months ago Cait would have given anything for this opportunity. She wouldn't have so much as breathed before jumping at the offer.

And at any other time, she still would. But not this particular week. "I told you, no more shows until after Christmas."

"Don't make me go through the tough-guy routine again. Hell, the gig's in D.C., an hour away from that little hamlet you're trapped in." He sounded like he'd been drinking, as was usual for Russell on most nights. And afternoons. "You drive in Friday morning for rehearsal, drive back Saturday at the latest. What's wrong with that?"

"I have a-an appointment Friday morning. I wouldn't be able to get to D.C. until midafternoon." Maddie's Christmas program was this Friday. Cait had promised to be there. She did not intend to renege on her word.

"Appointments are made to be rescheduled, babe."

"This is a one-shot deal. No rescheduling." Through the phone line, she heard the clink of ice, the gurgle of liquid.

After a minute, Russell said, "Well, *this* is a deal breaker, Cait." His words were more slurred now. "You don't show up for this gig, we don't have a contract anymore. And—excuse me for borrowing somebody else's line—if you dump me, you'll never work in this town again."

For an instant, she was ready to tell her so-called agent what he could do with his contract. Who needed this kind of pressure? If she couldn't choose when she wanted to work, what kind of career did she have, anyway?

Reason kicked in before she did something stupid. Give it all up? Throw away ten years of work? Prove that her father was right, that she should've settled for the safe, manageable career he wanted her to have?

Maddie's program was at 10:00 a.m. "Can you schedule the rehearsal for noon?"

"That's cutting it close. Sound check's at three."

"We played six shows two weeks ago. I think we all remember the basics."

He sighed again. "Yeah, okay. Just be there on time. I've got press meetings lined up before the show."

Her least favorite part of the job. "See you Friday, Russell."

"Cheers."

Dropping the phone, Cait flopped back on the bed and stared up at the ceiling. D.C. was more than an hour away by car. How was she going to be in two places at once on Friday morning?

Why would you want to? Think about the audiences in Vegas. Then decide what matters most—your career or an elementary school play in Goodwill, Virginia.

For better or worse, she fell asleep before she'd forced herself to choose.

"I'LL BE BACK sometime around midnight."

At the sound of Peggy's voice, Harry drew his gaze from the newspaper he wasn't reading. She stood in the doorway of the den, wearing a deep-red dress that showed off her figure and made her hair shine silver, the pearl necklace and earrings he'd given her for their thirtieth anniversary, and high-heeled red shoes.

"You look nice." When they hadn't spoken for days, he couldn't use a more enthusiastic word without sounding hypocritical. "Where are you going?"

"Tonight is the Christmas dance. As I said, I'll be home around twelve." Her heels clicked briskly on the floor as she went toward the front of the house.

Pushing himself out of the recliner, Harry followed. "You're going alone?"

Peg pulled her coat off its hanger. "I assumed you

weren't interested.'' When he tried to help with the coat, she gave him a cold look, jerked it out of his hands and put it on.

"Peggy—"

She picked up a large tray of her famous Virginia ham biscuits from the table by the door. "Don't wait up." Before he could move, she'd opened the door herself, and was heading down the front steps.

Harry closed the door and leaned back against it. *Well, okay.* He didn't have to go to the dance this year. That was a relief.

Except that he always enjoyed dancing with his wife. Used to, anyway. There wasn't much of anything he enjoyed these days.

As he glanced around the front hall and the living room, he saw that Peggy had brought out the Christmas decorations. Preparing for Christmas had always been a family activity for the Shepherds, especially these last two years without Valerie. They'd needed each other to get through the holiday with any kind of spirit.

This year, Peg had gone on without him. What did that say, except what he already knew? He wasn't much use to anybody.

On the way back to the den, he stopped by the refrigerator for a beer. The case he'd bought just a few days ago was more than half gone. Had he drunk all those beers by himself? And why was he drinking alone on a Sunday night during the Christmas season? Why was he putting off the confrontation with David Remington over the missing money? He'd always been one to face a conflict head-on, get it solved and move on to the next. What was wrong with him?

Harry didn't have any answers.

Or maybe he just didn't *want* the answers anymore.

CAIT SHOWED OFF her outfit to Anna. "Think this is okay?"

"No, I think it's fabulous." Anna motioned her to turn around. "Especially if your purpose is to have every man at the dance watching you instead of their date." Then she sighed. "Remember all those nights you watched me get dressed for dates and whined because you wanted to go along?"

"I was a real pain, wasn't I?"

"Now I know how you felt. It's terrible, watching someone else get dressed for a party you can't attend."

Sitting down on the edge of the bed, Cait brushed the curly bangs back from her sister's eyes. "Next year, you'll have a baby-sitter come over so you and David can get out."

"A year from now, who knows what will have happened?"

In the soft light of the lamp, Anna's face was pale and thin, her eyes shadowed. She wasn't the picture of health an expectant mother should be, though the doctor said the baby was growing as well as they could hope. But instead of being relieved that the baby hadn't been born too early, Cait was beginning to think that the longer Anna was pregnant, the more she suffered. And David's erratic behavior didn't help at all.

So much for the joys of marriage and parenthood. If Anna couldn't be happy as a wife and mother, who could?

The doorbell rang. "That's Ben." Standing up, she looked down at her sister. "Try to sleep," Cait suggested. It was all she could think of.

Anna shrugged, avoiding her gaze. "What else can I do?" Then she shook her head and attempted a smile. "Have a great evening."

Grinning, Cait nodded. "I'm going with Ben. What else can I do?"

"THE TOWN HALL'S been here since the 1870s," Ben said as he parked the sedan he'd rented across the street, "when they rebuilt after the war."

Cait glanced at him and smiled. "'The war'? Should that be capitalized?"

"Definitely. This place takes its history seriously." He was babbling, had been since they'd gotten into the car. But he still hadn't recovered from the sight of Cait in red and black, her hair piled high, her arms and long, slender neck bare. Then there was the view from the back—the low cut of that crinkly top, the snug fit of those slacks...

"So, should we go in?" Cait's voice brought him back to reality.

"Uh...yeah." Grateful for the bitterly cold night, he got out of the car and came around to open her door. The heels she was wearing added a couple of inches to her height, which would make kissing her so incredibly easy—just a tilt of his chin would bring their mouths together.

Ben cleared his throat. "Let's go see who's out on the town tonight."

He spotted Peggy right away, beautiful and elegant as usual in her red dress. She waved, but continued a lively conversation with Ellen Morrow. Harry wasn't as obvious. All Ben knew for sure was that he wasn't among the men staring at Cait when he took her coat. He wanted to tell the bunch of them to pick their tongues up off the floor.

"Dance?" he said to Cait, instead. And couldn't restrain a rush of masculine pride when she smiled up at him and moved into his arms.

The music was supplied by a deejay and compact disks

rather than a live band, but at least the tunes weren't exclusively Christmas. Big band, easy listening, contemporary country and...

"Oh, no," Cait said, resting her forehead against his shoulder.

"They're playing your song." Ben obeyed an impulse and pressed a kiss lightly against her temple. "I like it."

"Rainbow Blues" had been her first number-one single, he knew, a torch song, with jazzy chords showcasing the husky voice he'd grown to love.

Yes, love.

The recognition didn't come as a surprise, but more like greeting an old and dear friend who'd been gone for a long time. He drew back a little to look into Cait's face. "I haven't danced in years. But it's easy with you."

"I wouldn't have known," Cait said. "I guess we just naturally share a rhythm." Even as she finished the sentence, her cheeks flushed, her eyes darkened. "I mean—"

"I think you're exactly right." He placed another kiss along the curve of her jaw. "Sometimes, two people just...fit." Then he took the kiss he wanted from her lips.

Cait felt her knees shake as that kiss went on and on and on. There was something different about Ben tonight, in his eyes, in his hands on her back, in the sweet caress of his mouth. She couldn't define the change any more than she could break away from the kiss. For the first time in years, she wished "Rainbow Blues" would play all night long.

But it didn't. The music stopped and, eventually, Ben lifted his head. "Something to drink?" His voice was as unsteady as her pulse.

Cait nodded and followed him off the dance floor, her hand tightly wrapped in his. But she wasn't so bemused that she didn't notice the glances they got, the whispers around them, especially among the women.

"They're talking about us," she told Ben as he handed her a plastic glass of golden punch.

He surveyed the room as she'd seen Secret Service agents do on TV. "I'd say you're right about that, too." Over the rim of his glass, his gaze met hers. "Do you care?"

His eyes held the promise of something she thought she might have been searching for a long, long time.

Cait smiled and touched the rim of her glass to his in a toast. "Not at all."

"Don't you make a gorgeous couple?" Peggy appeared beside them and put an arm around Cait's waist. "I don't have to ask if you're enjoying yourselves. It's a good party, isn't it?"

Ben nodded. "As long as you brought your ham biscuits."

Peggy reached up to kiss his cheek. "Of course I did, since you always ask for them."

"I guess that's where we'll find Harry. He comes in second in number of biscuits consumed," Ben told Cait, "but he pushes me hard."

Peggy seemed to withdraw a little. "Um, Harry didn't come tonight. So," she said, too brightly, "that will leave you his share of the biscuits. Works out well, doesn't it?"

It wasn't hard to see the glitter of tears in the older woman's eyes. Cait looked at Ben, wondering whether to disappear or offer comfort.

"Harry's still having trouble with the retirement issue?" Ben handed over his handkerchief. "Do you want me to beat some sense into him?"

That got a watery chuckle. "Not just yet. I've made an appointment with David. I'm hoping Harry will go with me." She looked at Cait. "I'm sorry. I know this must be terribly embarrassing—having to sit through my pitiful problems."

Cait took Peggy's fine-boned hand. "Not pitiful or embarrassing. I wish I could help, is all."

"Well, you can." Peggy sat up straight and squared her shoulders, gave a final sniff and handed back Ben's handkerchief. "You two go back out on the dance floor and have a wonderful time. That's the best thing you could do for me. I'm so glad to see Ben getting out, having fun...." She leaned over to Cait. "Falling in love," she whispered. Then, with a watery smile, she went to talk with the deejay.

Without a word, Cait and Ben put their glasses on a tray and moved back to the dance floor, back into each other's arms. "White Christmas" came over the speaker system.

"That night at Regina's, you really blew me away," Ben said in a low voice. "Your harmony was incredible. I know you're not crazy about this time of year, but you ought to record a Christmas album. Give all your fans a chance to hear what you can do."

She drew back a little to look up at him. "I just might do that."

He smiled. "I heard what Peggy said, you know."

Cait felt her cheeks heat up. "What she said?"

"'Falling in love' was the phrase."

"Oh. Yes." She looked down at their feet. "Well, even Peggy doesn't know everything."

"Maybe not. But she's right about that. I love you, Cait."

Suddenly, it hurt to breathe. "Ben—"

"I know there are issues to resolve. But I'm more convinced every day that we belong together." He brought their joined hands up, kissed each of her knuckles. "So I think it's time I put this question on the record, so to speak. And the town hall seems like the perfect place."

The music stopped, and so did Ben. Even through the sudden increase in conversation, she heard him very clearly.

"Caitlyn Gregory, fellow grinch, will you marry me?"

CHAPTER TWELVE

BEN HADN'T EXPECTED an immediate yes—the situation was too complicated. But he hadn't expected Cait to be quite so surprised, either. Stunned, to be exact.

The music started up again—"Unchained Melody" by the Righteous Brothers. With few other options, he drew Cait close again and started dancing. "What are you thinking?"

She took a deep breath. "I'm not sure I'm able to think."

He danced her halfway around the room to a spot near the door. "You can slap my face and stomp out of here, if that's your inclination."

A laugh shook her shoulders. "Not necessary."

"You can just say no," he said more seriously. "That's allowed."

She lifted her chin to look up at him. "I wish it was that simple. The problem is…I love you, too."

Ben kissed the words off her mouth. "Sorry, but a statement like that deserves instant positive reinforcement."

"Spoken like a true parent." Her sweet smile faded. "A subject I only know secondhand. Have you thought about that?"

"Nobody's a parent until they have a child. And then we're all in the same boat, learning how to row and steer and navigate as we go along. You're great with Maddie and Shep.''

She glanced up at him, smiling again. ''You make things seem so easy.''

He shrugged. ''Life supplies the tough stuff without any help. I'm just trying to keep the situation from being worse than necessary.''

''You were married before. I don't know anything about being married, either.''

''Being married to Valerie was…what it was. Being married to you will be totally different, and I'll be starting at the beginning of the process, just like you.'' He heard his own words and shook his head. ''Damn. I sound like the man with all the answers.''

Pulling Cait with him, he went to an empty corner and sat down, seating her in the chair facing him. ''I thought I had it all worked out, Cait. Your career, my life—no possible common ground. My kids didn't need an intermittent mother. I wanted the standard package—both of us home together in bed every night, Saturdays spent fixing up the house or playing in the park with the kids.''

She looked down at their joined hands, but Ben tightened his hold until she met his eyes again. ''The truth is, Valerie and I didn't have that kind of life together, either. I was on the road or pulling some kind of weird duty, she had business trips…and then, all at once, she wasn't there at all.''

''But—''

''There are no rules, Cait. No guarantees. That's what yesterday showed me. And I care about you so much that I'm willing to settle for what we *can* have, instead of holding out for a perfection that might never happen.''

Gazing at Ben, Cait thought she'd never been so tempted to stop thinking altogether, to let her heart and her body choose which path to take. She wanted to believe they could work everything out, that there would be feasible compromises and sacrifices that didn't cost too much to accept.

Mostly, she just wanted to keep seeing the love on Ben's face, as she saw it now. And she wanted to spend as many nights as possible in his arms.

"Give me some time," she said finally. "I can't make this decision on the spur of the moment. Not because I don't want to," she said, as the hope in his eyes dimmed, "but there are other people involved, contracts and commitments and—and a hundred details to be taken care of."

He pulled in a deep breath. "Makes sense, much as I hate to admit it." His smile was rueful. "Take whatever time you need. The kids and I aren't going anywhere. And if you do, well…I won't feel any different. I guess there's one advantage to having been married before—I recognize when love is strong enough to last a lifetime. And that's what I feel for you."

Cait pulled her hands free and wiped her fingers gently under her lower lashes. "You shouldn't make me cry in front of all these people. My mascara will run and I'll look like a raccoon."

"Then let's go back to dancing, and I'll try to keep from saying anything more serious than 'You stepped on my toe.'" He pulled her up from the chair and out into the crowd again.

"I don't step on anyone's toes when I dance," Cait said indignantly.

"Then why am I limping?"

She grinned, and let him lead her into a mock argument. "You aren't—that's just your uneven sense of rhythm kicking in."

They danced until the music stopped and stayed after

to help with cleanup, which in Ben's case meant being sure Peggy didn't carry any ham biscuits home with her. Then he drove Cait back to the Remingtons'.

"I love you," Ben told her at the front door. He touched a finger to the tip of her nose. "When you start coming up with all the reasons not to marry me, just remember that."

"As if I could forget," Cait murmured, watching him jog back to the car. She remembered seeing Ben in the Food Depot all those weeks ago, remembered thinking that here was a man who could tempt her to settle down. Now he'd done exactly that.

Be careful what you wish for, she reminded herself ruefully. *You just might get it.*

WEDNESDAY'S CHOIR practice was a disaster. Shep and Neil fell to wrestling with each other whenever Cait's attention wasn't on them. Brenna had a sore throat and Maddie pouted because Cait wouldn't let her sing the angel song alone. The shepherds still didn't know their song, and the wise men weren't much better. Most of the girls who would be angels spent their time giggling and whispering behind their hands.

Cait held on to her temper with an effort. "You guys have been singing this carol since you were in nursery school," she told the wise men. "How hard can it be to learn one extra verse?"

Mothers had attended the rehearsal to fit costumes, and kept calling singers out—always, it seemed, just when Cait needed their voices. She'd never been so glad to see five o'clock arrive.

"One more Wednesday," she told the kids when she managed to get them quiet for a second. "Then a dress rehearsal on Saturday and—boom!—it'll be Christmas

Eve. If you're ever going to know your lines and your songs, next Wednesday would be a really good time.''

As the choir scattered, she saw David and Ben standing together at the back of the church. She glanced at them surreptitiously, studying Ben as if she'd never seen him before. He still looked like a marble statue of a Roman emperor. Yet he was anything but cold and stony. Now she knew what that beautiful mouth felt like on hers, and how his rough palms could heat her skin, and how hard his heart thudded when she kissed the pulse at the base of his throat.

And how his eyes laughed when he was having fun with his kids. How meticulous a craftsman he was, whether building his own furniture or the backdrop for a children's Christmas pageant. How much he loved his family and friends and his town, how he never resented the considerable time he spent taking care of them.

This was the man who wanted her to marry him. Why couldn't she just say yes?

Ben glanced her way and grinned, then started down the aisle with David following. "How's it going?" he said when he reached her. "Not too many rehearsals left, are there?"

Cait groaned. "Don't remind me. Remind them." She looked at David. "What time do you think you'll be home? I'll get dinner ready. More turkey leftovers, do you think?"

David didn't even smile. "I'll be here awhile yet. I really need to get this work finished up before the baby comes. You and Anna eat without me, and I'll grab a sandwich when I come in."

"David, you really need—" She was talking to thin air. Her brother-in-law had already left for his office.

"Hi, Daddy." Maddie joined them, still subdued and

unhappy. "Brenna couldn't sing today so we didn't practice the angel song."

Ben put an arm around her shoulders. "Sounds to me like there were a lot of other people who needed more practice than you do. You already know your song."

"Yeah." She sighed. "And I get to sing Friday in our program at school." The light came back into her face. "You're going be to there, right, Miss Caitlyn? Daddy said he'd save you a seat on the front row."

"I wouldn't miss it."

Ben thought Cait's smile looked strained. He sent Maddie to get Shep and collect their coats. Then he took Cait's hand and pulled her a little farther away from the kids. "What's the problem?"

Watching Maddie, she shook her head. "Nothing, really. Except—" she glanced at him, obviously worried "—would you mind if we didn't sit on the front row on Friday?"

"No problem. Why?"

She drew her hand out of his. "It's just…I may have to leave before the program ends. I—I'm supposed to be in D.C. at noon."

He waited for her to continue, but she didn't volunteer any more information. A tiny crack formed in the rose-colored lenses through which he'd been viewing the world since Sunday night. "What's the rush? Won't one o'clock do as well?"

"People will be waiting for me." She obviously didn't want to tell him who.

So he asked. "Which people?"

"My band."

"Your band will be in Washington on Friday?"

"We have a concert Friday night."

"Ah." The crack widened. "I thought you weren't performing again until after Christmas."

"This is an emergency. One of my agent's other acts is…sick…and he asked me to take her place. It's a sold-out crowd. Really good publicity."

"I imagine it is." This had to happen, of course. And if they spent the rest of their lives together, these situations would come up all the time. He shouldn't set a precedent for raising Cain about each and every one.

Even though he was mad as hell right now. "So you're planning to come to Maddie's program and then leave when it's over?"

"Or—or maybe a little before it's over? I want to see Maddie sing, of course. But then I may need to get on the road, which is why the front row…" She gazed up at him for a few seconds. Then her weak smile collapsed entirely, and she turned away. "It's the best I can do," she said in a soft, rough voice.

Ben pulled in a deep breath. "Okay, it's the best you can do. We'll deal with it, starting by making it easy for you to slip out without disturbing the program."

Suddenly, she was in his arms, hugging him tightly. "You are such an incredible man," she whispered in his ear.

"What are you doing, Daddy?" He opened his eyes to see Maddie and Shep staring at him holding Cait.

She let him go, blushing, and turned to the kids. "I was giving your dad a hug for being such a great guy. You understand that, I bet."

Maddie nodded, her face serious. "Does this mean you're going to get married?"

Cait laughed. "Not right this minute. Right now I'm going home to fix supper for Miss Anna. But I'll see you Friday morning."

He and Maddie and Shep were at the door when Ben had a brilliant idea. "Cait," he called, stepping back into the dim sanctuary. "Do you suppose there would be three tickets left for that concert on Friday night?"

Her grin lit up the whole room. "There will be. I guarantee it!"

CAIT WAS STILL floating when she stopped the car in Anna's driveway. Maybe she and Ben could do this. With most men, having a career like hers and a marriage and children would have been impossible. But Ben was unique, so strong and completely dependable, so accommodating...

A wavering voice greeted her the second the door swung open. "David? Cait?"

Cait ran into the bedroom. "Anna, are you all right?" One glance told the story. The bed was a mess, the sheets tangled, wet. Anna lay curled up in the middle, her arms cradling her stomach.

"Dear God—are you bleeding?"

Anna shook her head. "But the contractions are every three minutes." A shiver passed through her body. "That would be *now*. Oooh, Cait..."

She reached out her hand and Cait took it, let her sister wrap tight fingers around hers, a grip so strong that Cait winced at the pain.

Finally, Anna eased her hold, relaxed into the bed. "The baby is coming. What are we going to do?"

Cait picked up the phone. "I'm calling David, first."

Anna shook her head. "I've tried for the last two hours. There's no answer at church, no answer on his cell phone."

Damn the man. Damn him. "Did you call an ambulance?"

Pale-faced, with shadows all around her eyes, Anna shook her head. "I didn't want to be carted off without anybody I knew to come with me. I'm not a—a cow." She gave a sobbing laugh. "Even if I look like one."

"You don't." Cait pushed tangled, damp curls back from Anna's face. "I'll call them. If this baby wants to be born tonight, then we'll just make sure everything goes the way it's supposed to."

She made the call, then sat through another of Anna's contractions. When it passed, she helped her sister into a clean gown and robe. The next contraction hit at two minutes. Cait stripped the bed, got it made again just as Anna gasped. Less than two minutes. The ambulance wouldn't be here for twenty minutes at least.

Ten minutes later, Anna groaned. "I need...I need to..." She bore down for the length of a contraction, then fell back, panting. "The baby's coming. I need to push."

Cait grabbed the phone and called the hospital. "I've got a woman at home about to deliver a baby several weeks premature. What do I do?"

"Have you called her doctor?" The nurse's voice was calm. Infuriatingly calm.

"She's pushing *now*. What do I do?"

The calm voice picked up some interest. "I'll get an ambulance sent. Where does she live?"

"EMTs are on the way. The baby will be here first. Tell me how the hell to handle this."

As the nurse started shooting out instructions about blankets and water and string, the door in the kitchen opened and shut again, hard. Cait put a hand on Anna's cheek. "Hold on. I'll be right back."

Taking the phone with her, still listening to the nurse, she stalked into the kitchen to find David leaning over the table, his head hanging. He looked up. "Cait, what—"

"Hold on a minute," she told the nurse. Then she walked up to her brother-in-law. "You bastard, you turned off the phone in the office, didn't you? And you let your cell phone die. Again, your wife is in labor, and you're so wrapped up in your own stupid problems, so concerned about *your* reactions and *your* worries, you let her go through this by herself. If she didn't need you, I swear, I'd put you in the hospital with a broken face."

Eyes round with horror, he stared at her for a second.

"Go, damn you." Cait pushed him toward the hallway. "Go!" David ran toward the bedroom, and Cait went back to the phone. "Blanket, warm water, what else?"

When the paramedics arrived about twelve minutes later, the hard part was over. Anna lay propped against the pillows, smiling through tears as she stared into the face of a tiny—but perfect—baby boy. David sat beside her, his glasses crooked, his shirtfront wet with his own tears.

Leaving the paramedics to their work, Cait went into the kitchen. She poured a glass of juice and only then realized her hands were shaking. No wonder. She'd received a new baby into those hands, the first person in this world to touch him. Her throat closed with awe, with relief, and she set the glass on the counter.

A song lived within this moment, she could feel it growing inside her, though she didn't have the stamina to write it out tonight. All she wanted to do, she realized, was talk to Ben.

"Anna just had her baby," she said, with no introduction and no hello, when he answered the phone. "Here at home. Can you believe it?"

"Is she okay? Is the baby?"

"So far. The ambulance is here and they have an incubator. Oh, Ben, he's so tiny."

"But he's hung on this long. He's a real fighter, and he'll make it." After a moment, he said, "Was Dave there?"

All Cait's fury came rushing back. "At the end. Only by accident—Anna couldn't reach him when she tried to call."

"I can tell how you feel about that. What does Anna think?"

"I don't know. I think she's just so relieved the baby is alive that she's not thinking beyond that fact. If I were in her place..." She stopped, struck by a sudden vision of Maddie or Shep being sick, injured, or maybe just upset; of Ben, depending on the support of his wife, the child's mom...and herself on a concert tour a thousand miles away.

"Cait? You still with me?"

"Um...sure. Just spaced out, I guess, after the excitement. Listen, Anna's getting ready to leave. I'll talk to you later, okay?"

"Give her my love."

"I will." She hung up the phone, and then heard the rumble of wheels in the living room which meant Anna was heading for the ambulance.

Standing by the gurney, she took her sister's hand. "Make sure they take care of you."

Tears rolled out of Anna's eyes into her hair. "I miss him already. Isn't that strange? I only held him for a few minutes, and now he's in the incubator and I feel empty."

Cait leaned down to kiss her sister's forehead. "He'll be with you soon, I know he will. He's a big guy, for just thirty-four weeks. I'll drive up to see you both tomorrow. Try to get some sleep."

Anna managed a chuckle. "I don't have to sleep on my

left side anymore. I think I'll spend all night lying flat on my back.''

"Do it.'' Cait stepped back as the gurney started to roll. She watched the paramedics put Anna and the incubator into the ambulance, saw them drive into the night, lights flashing. When she turned back into the living room, David was standing just behind her, holding Anna's suitcase.

"I'm following them with her clothes,'' he said, not meeting her eyes. "I don't expect to come back tonight. If anyone calls for me, give them the hospital number, okay?''

"Okay.'' She crossed her arms and waited for him to say something else. Excuses? Rationalization? An apology? At the very least, she expected a confession of relief that the baby was alive and Anna would be okay.

But her brother-in-law just turned and walked back through the house and out the kitchen door. She heard the engine of his car start up, saw the lights as he backed down the drive and headed in the direction the ambulance had taken.

Shaking her head, Cait locked all the doors, made herself a cup of tea and went back to her bedroom. She wondered what would happen between David and Anna now. How did you deal with a spouse who let you down, who wasn't there when you needed them? And if you knew that's the kind of spouse you would be, did you owe it to the ones you loved to spare them the ordeal?

Would it be better for Ben—and Maddie and Shep—if she refused to marry him?

THURSDAY AFTERNOON, Anna stood at the window of the NICU, watching her son sleep. The tubes in his tiny arms scalded her heart—how could anyone stick a needle into a little baby, even for his own good? He wore a blue knit cap and a diaper, and was no bigger than she could hold in her two hands. Dr. Hall said he was doing very well for being so small.

Not well enough that she could take him home. They let her come in and touch him, talk to him, let her squeeze her breast milk from a syringe into his feeding tube. But it wasn't enough. She wanted to cradle him in her arms.

She also wanted to name him. He'd been born, he was here to stay, according to the doctors and nurses who cared for him. He needed a name.

David had stayed through the night at the hospital, but there hadn't been time for them to talk. Once the doctor had checked her over, once they'd consulted the neonatal pediatricians and nurses, once they'd simply gazed at the miracle of their son, Anna had been too exhausted to say more than good-night before she fell asleep. And David had been gone when she woke up this morning. She'd called the house and reached Cait...but her husband appeared to have gone missing.

Again.

Through a kind of mental fog, she remembered the terror of last night, the endless ringing of the church phone in her ear, the automated message telling her the cellular customer she had dialed was not in service, the knowledge that she could end up delivering her baby without anyone to help. And then Cait had come, and David, and everything had turned out well.

But where had he been? And why, when he knew she could go into labor at any minute, hadn't he made sure the phone worked?

"Mrs. Remington?" A nurse stood beside her, his smile a little worried. "You've been standing there for a couple of hours now. Wouldn't you like to go back to your room and lie down for a while? Maybe take a nap?"

Fear struck like lightning. "Is something wrong with the baby? Are you going to do something to him you don't want me to see?"

"No, no, not at all." He put an arm around her shoulders and walked her away from the window. "He's doing very well. We were worried about *you*. You have to take care of yourself, so you'll feel good enough to take care of him."

Settled in her semiprivate room, she could hear the cries of the baby on the other side of the curtain, hear the mother's crooning voice, the sounds of an infant being fed.

Sitting in her bed, Anna put her head down on her knees and started to cry.

"Anna? What's wrong?" David took hold of her shoulders and sat her up to see into her face. "Are you okay? Is—is the baby sick?"

She wanted him to hold her, to draw her close so she could sob out the pain of last night, the desperation of the last eight months, on his shoulder.

He didn't. "Anna, please, what's wrong?"

Pulling away, she wiped her cheeks with her fingertips. "Nothing. I—I was wishing I could have the baby here with me, that's all. Everything is okay, except for that."

"Oh." He sank back into the chair by the bed, the one he'd slept in. "That's good to hear." Then he smiled and gestured toward the chest near the window. "Like them?"

A vase containing a huge spray of dark-red roses stood there. "Oh, they're beautiful. Thank you so much." She gazed at him hopefully. When was the last time he'd kissed her? Anna didn't remember. Surely, now, with the baby safe, their relationship could come back to life.

"I stopped at the NICU," David said. "He seems to be holding on."

No kiss. She stifled her sigh. "The doctors and nurses say he's doing very well. But he weighs only a little over four pounds. That isn't much, is it?"

"Not even as heavy as a bag of sugar."

"Well, he's very sweet." She smiled, and got a brief smile in return. "What shall we call him?"

David looked away from her, toward the roses. "There's plenty of time for names. I don't think we have to decide right now."

"I'd like to choose, so I can talk to him and use his name. I want him to know who he is."

"He won't understand for months, Anna. Let's not rush it."

"Rush it?" Something hot poured through her which she recognized, almost with surprise, as anger. "David, some people start working on names the day they find out they're expecting. You didn't want to think about it then, or in any of the months since. Now that the baby's here, I think we owe him a name."

He blew out a sharp, irritated breath. "Well, then, what do you want to call him?"

She gazed at the man in the chair, wondering if she knew him at all. "What is wrong with you? Why aren't you celebrating? We have a son—doesn't that make you happy?"

"I...he...still has a fight ahead of him. If we get too attached to him and he doesn't..."

"I don't believe this. You're afraid to love him because he might die?" Anna slid off the other side of the bed and walked to the window. "Is that why you've avoided me for months? Because you didn't want to care too much?"

Sitting forward in the chair, David propped his elbows

on his knees and hung his head over his clasped hands. "I was afraid, Anna. I could have lost you both."

"What kind of coward are you?" He didn't look up. "Did you ever think about the fact that I didn't have a choice? That once I was pregnant I had to stay with this baby every second of the day, worrying, wondering, always on guard?"

"Sure, I thought about that. But—"

"But that wasn't as important to you as your own fears. So you let me do it by myself, even down to the delivery. Was it just bad luck you came home early last night?"

"No!" David stood up, his face pale, his eyes round with horror. "I wanted to be with you when the baby was born. I didn't mean to let the cell phone die. I thought it was working."

"But you turned off the church phone. What's the secret, David? What are you hiding? Or hiding from?"

His shoulders slumped again and he covered his face with his hands. "I've done everything I can think of but it's no good. I'm going to have to tell the church the truth."

At one time, his words would have scared her. But right now, indignation left no room for fear. "What are you talking about? Tell them…?"

"There's money missing from the church account." He looked up, his face as haggard as she'd ever seen it. "Somewhere, we've lost that check from Mrs. Fogarty. The money was never deposited, but the check was cashed."

"Ten thousand dollars?" More than two months' salary.

David nodded. "They'll think I stole the money, Anna. Harry Shepherd already does. And as far as I can see—" he held out his hands in a helpless motion "—there's no way to prove otherwise."

CHAPTER THIRTEEN

DESPITE A COLD, dreary rain, David brought Anna home early on Friday morning. The baby wasn't strong enough to leave the hospital, but since she'd had a normal, non-surgical delivery, the insurance company refused to pay for his mother to stay any longer.

Already dressed, packed and ready to leave for D.C., Cait opened the front door as her sister and brother-in-law came slowly up the walk. "Welcome home! Do you like the wreath?"

Anna gazed at the large circle of pine boughs, decorated with royal-blue bows and shining blue-and-silver balls, which hung on the door. "It's wonderful. Christmas and baby combined."

"That's what we thought." Cait stepped back to let the new parents inside. "The women of the church met yesterday at the flower shop and put it together."

Anna stopped in the doorway to the living room. "Oh, Cait. Christmas!" A fresh tree stood in the corner, decorated with white lights and more blue-and-silver balls, garlanded with blue-and-silver beads and topped by an angel in a silver dress. Stacked underneath, presents of every size and shape had been wrapped in different patterns of silver and white and blue. Anna's collection of ceramic trees was arranged in various nooks around the room, with the lighted ones switched on and shining softly in the dark, stormy morning.

After a breathless second, Anna broke into tears. Before Cait could move, she ran into her bedroom and slammed the door. The click of the lock was clear in the silence.

Cait looked at David. "What in the world…? Is something wrong with the baby?"

His face gray, David shook his head. "He's…okay. She didn't want to leave him, of course. I told her I'd take her back after she rested for a while, but—" he shrugged "—she's pretty emotional about everything right now."

Somehow, that sounded like only part of the story.

"Do you mind if I talk to her?" Cait asked her brother-in-law.

He waved his hand in a helpless gesture. "Please. She needs somebody."

The obvious question—"Why aren't you in there?"— remained unasked. She went to the bedroom door. "Annabelle? Can I come in?" No answer. "Please, darlin'. I want to hear all about my nephew." After a long moment, the lock clicked. But Anna didn't turn the knob.

Cait pushed gently on the door and slipped through the narrow opening, closing it behind her. Anna lay facedown on the bed again, still crying. Putting her arms around her sister's shoulders, Cait kissed the mussed red hair. "What's wrong?"

Anna muttered a word that might have been "Everything."

"Okay." Cait waited through another storm of sobs. "Tell me about the baby. He's okay?"

Nodding, Anna hiccoughed. "I sat with him for about two hours this morning. Then I had to leave." More sobs.

"Do they know when he'll get to come home?"

"They want to be sure he's gaining weight and breathing well. I have to keep pumping my breast milk and freezing it for him and...oh, Cait, it hurts!"

"Poor baby." Cait could only imagine. "What else?"

"David won't let me name him. H-he won't even touch him!"

"So name him by yourself."

Face still buried in the pillow, Anna shook her head. "We're supposed to do that together. But...nothing...is happening...like it's supposed to."

Giving up on more questions, Cait applied herself to soothing her sister. Eventually the sobs faltered and died away. She wiped Anna's face with a cool cloth, helped her into a clean gown, then brushed and braided her hair. Finally, she pulled the fresh sheets up under Anna's chin.

"I have to be gone today and tonight," she said, sitting on the edge of the bed. "Remember, I'm doing that concert in D.C."

Heavy-eyed, Anna nodded.

"Peggy Shepherd will be here by noon. She'll stay all day and all night, so you just ask her for anything you need. Okay?"

Another nod.

"And I'll be back early tomorrow—before noon, anyway—and we'll get everything straightened out. Until then, you rest. David or Peggy will take you back to see your son this afternoon." Keeping her voice soft and low, Cait stroked Anna's forehead until her eyes closed and her breathing deepened. Whispering, "I love you, darlin'," she pressed a final kiss on her sister's cheek and left the room.

David stood where she'd left him in the living room. Cait kept the width of the carpet between them.

"I don't really want to talk to you," she said, clenching her fists so her voice would stay calm. "But you're in charge here until noon, when Peggy arrives. I've left the number of my hotel by the phone in the kitchen." She turned and walked down the hallway, assuming he would follow. "And the numbers for the concert hall—main office, ticket booth, security. If you need me for any reason at all, tell them it's an absolute emergency and they have to get me to the phone. I'll have my cell phone on, too, in the car during the drive, during rehearsal, every time but during the concert itself. You shouldn't have trouble reaching me."

"Cait—"

"Show Peggy these numbers before you disappear again."

"I'm not going to disappear."

She looked at him with contempt. "Yeah, right. Just be sure that Anna's taken care of before you go. I swear, if she's upset when I get back, I'll…" She couldn't think of a threat dire enough to capture her feelings.

Maybe she didn't have to. David only gazed at her miserably. Cait rolled her eyes, grabbed her purse and without another word, left the house.

As far as Ben was concerned, Friday started out crazy and never recovered. Maddie woke up so excited she was hardly able to eat or sit still long enough to put on her socks and shoes. Shep, on the other hand, didn't want to wake up at all. Ten minutes before they were supposed to leave the house for school, Ben went upstairs to find his son fully dressed but back in bed.

"Shep, this doesn't work, son. We've got to go." He found a blanket-draped shoulder and shook it. "You'd better wake up, or there will be consequences. Dire consequences."

The form under the blue bedspread didn't stir.

Ben sighed dramatically. "Okay. You asked for it." With one quick jerk, he pulled all the covers completely off the bed, leaving Shep lying exposed, still pretending to be asleep. Fingers curled, Ben knelt on the edge of the mattress and began to goose the little boy's ribs.

Twitching, wriggling, fighting, Shep tried to stop the merciless assault. Soon he was laughing, panting, still trying to resist getting out of bed. All at once, Ben realized he was hearing a word in the sounds Shep made.

"No...no...no..." Whispered between giggles and gasps, the plea accomplished its task. Ben froze, hardly daring to believe what he heard. His son was talking again. For some reason known only to himself, Shep hadn't said another word since their trip to the mountains. Ben had started to wonder if that night had been some kind of dream.

After a frozen minute, Ben got his breath under control. He eased back on the bed. "I like hearing you talk," he said gently. "Do you...do you know why you stopped?"

Shep rolled away, grabbed Bumbles the Bear and pulled him close. Keeping his back toward Ben, he didn't answer for a long time.

Ben figured he'd pushed too hard. "It's okay, son, don't—"

"I talked to Mommy. After...the crash." Valerie and Shep had been driving late at night; the police estimated that nearly an hour had passed after the accident before help arrived.

"You talked to Mommy?" Ben flinched away from the

thought of four-year-old Shep strapped into his car seat, talking to his mother, unconscious in the front of the car.

"But she didn't talk back." The young voice squeaked, like a crank grown rusty from disuse.

"No, she didn't." Valerie had suffered head injuries and lingered in a coma for two days, without ever waking up.

"An' she went away. I just—" Shep shrugged "—didn't want to anymore."

"I understand." Adults escaped into alcohol, work, depression or denial. Shep had escaped into silence. "Do you know why you decided to start again?"

"I like to sing," Shep said softly. "With Miss Caitlyn."

No surprise there. He'd known for a while now that Cait could work miracles. "Well, I hope you'll keep talking, buddy. Meanwhile, it's time to go."

Ben didn't feel nearly as casual as he tried to sound, but he didn't want to pressure his son at this crucial point. He held out a hand, Shep took hold with both of his and Ben pulled him to his feet. "Your sister has probably decided to walk to school, carrying her costume but forgetting to wear a coat."

AFTER DROPPING OFF the kids, Ben went to his workshop, intending to sand down the first coat of varnish on the chest he was scheduled to finish before Christmas. The sanding quickly gave way to wishful thinking, though...about the chance to talk with Shep again, and the chance for them all to be a family when Cait agreed to marry him. Before he realized it, he had ten minutes to get to school before the holiday program began. He and Cait might lose their seats on the back row.

But she'd arrived before him and saved him a chair.

He sat down just as the curtain opened. "Here we go," he whispered into her ear, and got her grin in reply.

With a theme of "Goodwill" and including songs from many different traditions, the program couldn't fail to please everyone. Maddie sang "White Christmas" beautifully, and received a round of applause.

"That song sure gets around," Cait murmured in his ear. "Did you know that's what she was singing?"

Ben shook his head. "She wanted to surprise us, she said. But she's also been praying every night these last few weeks for snow on Christmas Eve."

Cait chuckled. "Well, wishes seem to be coming true these days. Anna's got her baby boy, and maybe Maddie will get her white Christmas." She glanced at her watch, then sat forward in preparation to stand. "I've got to go. Tell Maddie I'm proud of her."

She looked worried, he realized, and tired. "Are you—" Before he could finish his thought, Cait was gone. "—okay?" he said to the empty seat beside him.

He would see her tonight at the concert. They were staying in the same hotel, in adjoining rooms, and they could talk after the kids went to sleep. She would share her problems with him then, he knew.

But he would have felt better if she'd spared ten seconds to say goodbye before she left.

"THIS IS SO COOL," Maddie said, as they were escorted to the front row of the performance hall. "I can't believe I really get to see Miss Caitlyn sing."

Ben settled Shep on one side of him and Maddie on the other. "Looks like we're lucky to be here. The place is pretty crowded." Even though a sign outside announced that the originally scheduled artist would not perform, there were very few empty seats. If people had turned in their tickets, evidently most of them had been purchased again by people who wanted to hear Cait Gregory.

The lights dimmed, and Maddie sat up straight, her back not even touching the chair. Because of the long drive, they'd missed the opening act, arriving at intermission. Suddenly a voice boomed from speakers in the ceiling. "And now, please greet our artist for the evening, Miss Cait Gregory."

Music reached out, slow, sexy, as the curtain rose. Onstage, guitar players, a drummer and a pianist stood silhouetted against a glowing purple backdrop. The tempo picked up, and the crowd clapped in rhythm. Maddie glanced around, then joined in. Shep sat motionless in his chair, mesmerized.

A roar went up as a woman stalked to center stage. Lit by a single spotlight, she was in control—of the band and the crowd. A wave of her hand changed the music yet again, to the tune the audience recognized and saluted with an even louder furor—"Rainbow Blues."

Then Cait began to sing.

For two hours, she held them spellbound, using the listeners' emotions and reactions as surely as she used the instruments she played. Sweet love songs and rowdy drinking songs, wry commentaries on the state of the world and the state of the roads...she covered the most popular tunes of her career, plus a couple Ben hadn't heard before. And she brought down the house, as he'd known she would, with her version of "Bobby McGee."

After two encores, the applause still hadn't stopped. Cait came out on the stage alone the third time, holding her guitar. She propped one hip on the tall stool she'd used off and on during the show, adjusted the microphone and cleared her throat.

"I haven't recorded any Christmas songs," she said, her voice even huskier, sexier, after two hours of singing. "Haven't really sung them for a long, long time. But this year is different. Or maybe I'm different. Either way, I'd like to close tonight with a special piece for three very special people. I can't see them in the lights, but I know they're here."

Soft chords from the guitar quieted the crowd in time to hear the first words of "The Christmas Song."

She sang in the midst of a breathless silence, her tone as pure and clear as he'd ever heard it. When the lyrics talked about mistletoe, her voice broke a little and she smiled. Ben thought back to the night of Regina Thorne's party, and grinned.

As the last notes died away into the night, Cait whispered "Merry Christmas to you" into the mike. She sat motionless for another moment, a slender minstrel still caught in her song. Then the spotlight cut off with a suddenness that made them all gasp. When the auditorium lights came back, Cait's guitar was leaning against the stool behind the mike. The woman herself was nowhere to be seen.

"Oh, Daddy," Maddie said worshipfully. "That was so…" She shook her head, at a loss for words. "Do we get to talk to her now? Can we tell Miss Caitlyn how much we love her?"

I already have, Ben thought. But after tonight, he wasn't so sure of himself anymore. What sane woman would walk away from the chance to be revered like this? How could one man's love, even a man with two great kids, compete with the adoration of thousands?

In other words, marrying Ben might just be the biggest
mistake Cait Gregory ever made.

THE SECURITY OFFICER took them backstage. Weaving
through the crowd, Ben held tightly to Maddie with his
right hand and Shep with his left.

They finally reached a plain blue door which opened to
a sharp knock. "Tremaine," their guide said tersely. The
door opened a little wider and the crowd pushed forward,
calling Cait's name, snapping pictures, propelling Ben and
Maddie and Shep into the room beyond. With relief, Ben
heard the door shut behind him.

Then he took in the number of people in *this* room.
Cait was nowhere to be seen, though a clump of people
standing near a mirror gave him a hint as to where she
might be hiding. At least these people weren't talking all
at once. In fact, it seemed to be a press conference. Cait's
answers to the reporters' questions were made in a voice
that got quieter with each answer.

Ben glanced around, saw an empty couch against one
wall and herded the kids there. Shep immediately leaned
into his side; from the weight, he'd be asleep in minutes.
Maddie sat straight and still at first, taking in every detail.
But as the questions continued, as some reporters left and
others replaced them to ask for the same information,
Maddie began to droop. Ben thought he, too, might be
asleep before Cait got free to talk to them.

Not quite, but his eyes were burning when the group
broke up and the last reporter left. That still didn't mean
the room was empty—a couple of beefy guys stood by
the door. Bodyguards? Nearer to the couch, a woman was
cleaning up a table that overflowed with food. And in the
corner, Cait sat astride a chair, her face buried in her arms

propped on the straight wooden back. Beside her sat her agent, Russell.

"I can't believe you did that," Cait said, her voice only a whisper. "Don't ever schedule press meetings after a gig again. I can't do it."

"Hey, you're the one who was late for rehearsal. That pushed everything back so there was no time for the press till afterward." Russell stood up, his Italian suit and shoes worth every dollar he'd no doubt paid for them. "Oh, look," he said, as he saw Ben. "The country mouse came for a visit."

Cait looked up quickly. "I didn't know you'd come in—I'm so glad to see you!" She crossed the room and crouched in front of Maddie. "She's asleep, isn't she? And Shep, too. I know it's late for them." A sigh lifted her shoulders, but she gazed up at Ben with a smile. "Thank you for coming. Just knowing you three were out there made it a really special night."

Ben touched her cheek with his fingertips. "You were spectacular. Maddie was awestruck. And so was I."

Cait turned her head quickly and caught his fingers with a kiss. Behind her, Russell groaned. "I'm outta here. Cait, babe, I'll see you in L.A. on the twenty-sixth."

She dropped her chin to her chest, attempting to ease the headache she'd been fighting since the end of the concert. "Right. I'll call you."

"I'll be waiting." The door opened and closed, and Russ left, along with the two "security advisors" he'd started taking everywhere he went. In another minute, the caterer wheeled her cart out.

"Thank you," Cait called. "It was delicious." The woman lifted a shoulder but didn't turn back, and shut the door firmly behind her.

Without thinking, Cait leaned forward until she could rest her cheek on Ben's leg. "I could go to sleep right here."

He lifted her hair off her neck with one hand. "What can I do?"

She sighed. "Just holding the weight of my hair is wonderful. Who would think hair could be so heavy?" His free hand came to her neck, and his strong fingers massaged the stiff muscles. "Oh, heaven. I think I'm going to cry." She closed her eyes, because tears were really close. It had been such a hard day, except for those few minutes at Maddie's program, and she was so tired...but for once she didn't have to go back to an empty hotel room alone.

Tonight, there was Ben.

"I'll call a cab," she said, reluctantly pulling out of his grasp. "And you can get these sleepyheads in bed."

"Sounds good." Ben woke Maddie gently; she stared up at Cait with bleary eyes.

"I loved your singing," she whispered. "I hope you keep having concerts forever."

Smiling at the little girl, Cait caught a flash of something unexpected in Ben's face—regret? Disappointment? Fear? It was gone so fast she wasn't sure she hadn't imagined the reaction altogether.

The question got lost in the process of carrying two sleepy children out to a cab, into the hotel and up to the room. Cait helped Maddie into her nightgown—soft white flannel covered with red bears holding candy canes. Shep's pajamas featured blue airplanes on gray. With the two of them tucked into one of the double beds, Ben turned off all but a single dim lamp and then followed

Cait into the adjoining room, leaving the door open a few inches.

They stared at each other across the width of the sitting area. Cait didn't know what to say, and Ben seemed to have the same problem.

Finally, he shook his head. "You must be exhausted."

"I'm too wired after a gig to sleep right away. But if you're…um…tired…" She'd never felt this awkward with him before.

"Not really." He stood with his hands in his pockets, looking around as if he didn't know what to do, either. "The leather's a good look for you," he said after a minute, indicating her stage clothes, "but wouldn't you rather get into something more…unimaginative?"

His grin relaxed her a little bit. "Be right back."

It was hard to rush through a shower with her thick, heavy hair to wash, but she did her best, then stood in front of the suitcase wrapped in a towel, debating. Robe? Jeans and a shirt? Bare feet? Socks?

The number of times she and Ben had come close to making love without taking that final step crossed her mind. What made this night different? She wasn't sure about their future. Was sex a wise choice at this point?

Maybe that uncertainty was, itself, the issue. If she didn't marry Ben, this would be the only chance she would ever have to spend the night in his arms. Her heart was already involved, already primed to be broken. Couldn't she at least have the memory of a few beautiful hours to take with her when she left?

Since he was still dressed, she opted for jeans and a soft, loose sweater. Bare feet, braided hair. No makeup and no expectations of more than just conversation.

But she could hope.

Ben had ordered room service while she changed. "Wine?" He held out a glass.

"Oh, yes." She sipped the tart chardonnay and eyed the service tray. "Are you hungry?"

"Not as hungry as you, I bet. You didn't touch any of that food in the dressing room, did you?"

Her cheeks warmed as she shook her head.

"Sit down."

He served her dinner, coaxing her to try different foods as if she were a child with a delicate appetite. Her wineglass stayed full, and there was decaf coffee with chocolate truffles for desert.

"Wow." Cait fell back against the sofa cushions. "That was terrific. I could hibernate for months after that much food."

With the service cart pushed outside, Ben came to join her. "That's the idea. You looked fantastic onstage. But—" his fingertip smoothed her skin over her cheekbones "—now, you just look exhausted. And this morning, I noticed something was bothering you."

His kindness, his perception, made saying anything at all impossible for a minute. When she got control, she told him about Anna and David. "He won't help her name the baby, Ben. It's as if he expects him to die and thinks it won't bother him as much if the baby doesn't have a name. It's tearing Anna apart."

Ben took her wineglass and put it with his on the coffee table, then sat back and eased her into his arms. "It's not completely rational," he murmured, his chin propped on top of her head. "But I think he's under some kind of work-related stress, so nothing makes sense with him right now."

She thought about the books David had been working

on. Maybe he hadn't been able to resolve the figures. But how could he allow math, of all things, to ruin his marriage?

Cait sighed and felt Ben's mouth move against her hair. Excitement leaped inside her and she held her breath, hoping for another caress. He turned his head, moved her braid and then his warm lips kissed the nape of her neck, the soft, sensitive spot just behind her earlobe. His breath blew over her ear, making her shiver. Turning in his arms, she took his face between her hands and covered his mouth with her own.

Ben hadn't meant to let things get out of hand, if for no other reason than that his kids were in the next room. But his need for Cait ambushed him. It seemed only seconds before she was stretched beneath him on the couch, her hands roaming his bare back, her soft body cradling his, her mouth hot, demanding, insatiable. And he wanted her the same way. Except...

Breathing hard, he pulled out of the kiss, buried his face in the scented curve between her neck and shoulder. There were reasons not to do this. Maybe in a minute, he'd remember what they were.

"Ben?" Her warm palms stroked his skin, stoked the fire beneath. He needed her so much....

So much that he couldn't risk their future together on a single night.

With an effort that hurt, he forced his body to relax, to stay still, to be *quiet*. "Shhh," he whispered, to himself as much as to Cait. "It's okay."

With a sound like a sob, she pressed her face against his shoulder. "No, it is not okay." She was breathless, nearly voiceless. Her hands gripped his waist. "What's wrong?"

He didn't have the breath or the brains for much explanation. "Bad timing."

"Because of the children?" Confusion colored her tone. "They're fast asleep."

"Because of us." Reluctantly, he pushed away from her, moved to the end of the sofa.

Cait scooted into a sitting position at the other end. Her mouth was swollen, her eyes heavy. "I don't understand."

Looking at her was torture. He pressed the heels of his hands into his eyes. "If I could settle for just an affair with you, I'd have done it weeks ago."

"Oh. That's—" she seemed to search for the word "—that's virtuous of you."

He laughed a little. "Not particularly. I just can't take the risk. There's too much at stake."

"Risk." She stood up and walked to the window. "There's no risk, Ben. I haven't been with anybody—"

"Cait, you're tired and you're deliberately misunderstanding me. That's not what I mean. I need to know that our relationship is going to work, that we can combine our lives successfully, before we…" his voice trailed.

She turned to face him, her arms wrapped close at her waist. "You were sure last Sunday. You asked me to marry you."

Last Sunday, he hadn't seen what he was up against. "And you weren't ready to say yes, which means you have some doubts. Then, tonight, I saw how much you'd be giving up if you walked away from your career. Even if you just scaled back…" He shrugged. "That's a lot to ask. Maybe too much."

Cait couldn't believe how much hurt she was able to contain without some kind of physical breakdown.

"You'll be making…adjustments…too." She didn't want to use the word *sacrifice*. "I won't always be here for the children, or you. I get caught up in the music sometimes and forget things like dinner and laundry." He chuckled, which encouraged her. "I'm not very neat. And all I can really cook is Thanksgiving dinner."

Ben gave her one of his half smiles. "I know everything can't be perfect. But…I'm in deep with you as it is. Sex will just make goodbye harder, if you decide…" He shrugged.

Needing some support to stay on her feet, she leaned back against the wall. "You don't think I'm strong enough to change my life." She didn't add that she'd come to much the same conclusion—worrying whether marrying Ben would be the worst thing she could do for all of them.

His expression was bleak. "I just don't know that your feelings for me are strong enough to justify the kind of sacrifice you'd have to make."

He didn't seem to have her problem with the *S* word. "What will it take to convince you that I love you?"

Getting to his feet, he stood with his hands in the pockets of his cords. "Just one word, Cait. Because I know if you agree to marry me, you're putting our life together, with our kids, first."

But Cait couldn't manage that one word. Added to her own doubts, his hesitation was simply too much to overlook. Much as she wanted to be with Ben—and Maddie and Shep—she simply couldn't promise what he was asking. And so she said nothing at all.

Ben stared at her through the big, empty silence. Finally, he drew a deep breath. "Right. I understand." He turned and walked to the door between the sitting room and his bedroom, spoke with his back to her. "We'll see you in the morning. The kids and I thought we'd stay in D.C. for a while, do some Christmas shopping. Can you come with us?"

As if we were a real family? Cait couldn't bear the pretense. "I have to get back to Anna. David's no help to her, and Peggy has her own problems." She saw Ben's shoulders slump and for a moment, she was tempted...

No. Cait shut her bedroom door between them before she could do any more damage. She stood for a moment, breathing hard against the ache in her chest, and then went to work. In fifteen minutes she had her suitcase packed and was on the elevator going down to the lobby.

The valet brought Anna's beat-up Toyota to the door. Cait gave him a lavish holiday tip, gunned the engine and drove out into the night, tears dripping down her face as she started the long dark drive back to Goodwill.

CHAPTER FOURTEEN

ABOUT DAWN ON Saturday, Harry went out to the garage, turned on the space heater and started the coffeepot. No sense lying in bed if he couldn't sleep. He'd given up on TV as a way to pass the time—sex and violence everywhere without much real entertainment in any of it. Or maybe that was just his mood.

He found one of Peggy's notes on the workbench. She'd taken to leaving terse little messages out here, where he spent most of his time, so they really didn't have to talk at all. Harry figured the day would come soon—though probably not until after Christmas, for the sake of the grandkids—when the message would consist of a big envelope with a bunch of legal papers inside for him to sign, agreeing to a divorce. He wouldn't blame her. That was the least he deserved at this point. If he could change how he felt, what he did, Harry thought he would. But...there just wasn't much hope of change anymore.

This note was like the others, written in Peggy's sweet round hand on pretty pink stationery with a tulip in the corner. The information was brief and to the point: "We have a meeting with David Remington tomorrow afternoon at 2:00 p.m. Please let him know if you won't be there."

So. She was trying a talk with the minister first. A man half their age, married barely a tenth the time he and Peg had lived together, was going to give them advice on…what? How to put the zing back in their relationship? How to communicate?

How to face the rest of an empty life?

Or maybe how to embezzle ten thousand dollars from a church?

Harry folded the note along its crease and put it with the others in the cedar box he kept out here for unexpected valuables he sometimes came across. Like the tortoise-shell-framed magnifying glass he planned to give Shep one day, which he'd seen lying on the beach when he and Peg had visited Ocean City last year. Or the pretty stone bracelet he'd found when he was cleaning out a box of old toys in the attic. He remembered giving the bracelet to Valerie for her twelfth birthday, figured he would polish it up and do the same for Maddie.

There had been days, right after Valerie died, when he thought he couldn't stand to go on without her. How had he managed? What kept him going? He'd endured then. Losing his job was nothing, compared to losing his little girl.

So why couldn't he cope now?

The answer, of course, was Peggy. He had shared his grief with her, helped bear hers and Ben's and the children's. They had been bereaved as a family, and as a family they'd grieved.

Now…Peggy was part of the problem. She expected him to enjoy the free time, to jump on all the projects he'd put off over the years. The ribbing he got from his friends, the expectation that he was living the high life…nobody appreciated how empty, how worthless a man without a job could feel.

Would David Remington, a barely grown boy with less than half a decade's work experience, understand any better? Not likely.

But if Peg wanted counseling, Harry decided, he would go. At least then, when she filed for divorce, she'd know she'd done her best to save the marriage.

It was, he thought, all he could do for her anymore.

ANNA WALKED INTO her kitchen on Saturday morning and halted at the sight of her sister seated at the table, drinking coffee.

"Cait? What are you doing back so early?" Judging by the grim set of her mouth, the dark circles under her eyes, the answer to that question would not be a cheerful one. "How'd the concert go?"

"Great." Cait's tone of voice was a direct contradiction of the word. "Close to sold out. Good audience. I'm glad I did the gig."

"Did Ben and Maddie and Shep enjoy it? I can't imagine that they wouldn't, of course."

"I think so. By the time we got to talk it was really late and the kids were almost asleep. But Ben said they had a good time." The way she said Ben's name didn't leave much doubt about the source of her gloomy attitude.

With a cup of tea warming her hands, Anna sat down. "What happened afterward that's got you so upset?"

Her sister propped her elbows on the table and rubbed her eyes with her fingers. "Ben asked me to marry him at the dance last Sunday."

"How wonderful!"

"And last night, he pretty much revoked the offer."

Anna choked on her tea. "Why in the world…?"

Cait took her mug and went to stand at the sink, looking out at another rainy day. "He'd had some second thoughts, didn't know if I'd be able to put my life with him ahead of the career. And he didn't want to risk himself or the kids getting hurt."

"Oh, Cait."

She put up a defensive hand. "No, it's okay. Some things are meant to be, and some just aren't. Ben and I might fall into the second category."

This sense of defeat was not what Anna had hoped for when her sister came to Goodwill. Ben's worry had some merit—Cait had been focused on her career for a long, long time. From what Anna could tell, he seemed to be asking for reassurance, not total capitulation.

But Cait's experience with their dad might make it hard for her to hear the difference.

"Anyway, there's more important stuff to talk about." Cait returned to the table and sat down, a determined smile on her face. "How's that baby boy of yours? Did he learn to walk yesterday?"

"Took his first steps, as a matter of fact." Anna grinned at the nonsense. "Peggy and I drove to the hospital and spent the afternoon, got some dinner in Winchester and went back for a little while. He's...okay. His eyes are open a lot more, and I think he hears when I talk to him."

Cait's eyes softened. "I'll go up with you today. I know you'd rather be there than anywhere else." She swirled her mug, staring inside as if she read an important message there. "And how's David? Or maybe the question ought to be, where's David?"

Anna lifted a shoulder. "Asleep in his office, I suppose."

"Have you two...talked since I left yesterday?"

She didn't see any point keeping secrets from Cait. "Only to go over what he told me in the hospital, which is how much trouble we're in. Not how to fix it. Just what to worry about...in addition to the baby."

"What kind of trouble?" Anna's explanation about the

missing church money didn't take long. Cait sat back in her chair, horrified. "Good grief, Anna! He told me he was having some problems making the accounts balance, but...ten thousand dollars? Has he told the church committee?"

"No. He'd like to replace the money without anyone knowing."

"Do you have that kind of cash?"

Anna shook her head.

Cait muttered a rude word. "Well, I do. I'll loan you the money and you can pay it back sometime. Better yet, take it as rent for the last couple of months." She got up and crossed the kitchen. "I'll fetch my checkbook."

"You will not." Halfway through the door into the hall, Cait stopped and turned around, her jaw hanging loose in surprise. Anna shook her head, gentled her tone. "We're not taking your money and we're not pretending nothing ever happened—not to the church and not to ourselves."

"Annabelle—"

"My son won't start his life out under a cloud of deception." She'd had two days to think about this. Amazing how, with the baby to worry about, her thoughts had cleared, her emotions had finally settled down. "If we can't find the check, we'll just have to say so. After that...the committee may fire him. Or they may want the money repaid, and we'll figure out how to do that, too. But we aren't going to lie about it. We didn't steal the money and that's a fact."

"But how..." Cait thought for a moment. "How are you going to forgive David? For losing the check to begin with. For avoiding you these weeks, for—for abandoning you when the baby was born? *Can* you forgive him?"

At the stove for more hot water and a new tea bag, Anna heard the questions behind the question. She wished she had something wise to say, something that would help Cait with her own dilemma. "I don't know the answers right now. But I'm committed to David, and somehow we'll work it out. He's a good man, and he tries really hard." She smiled. "And I love him. That helps a lot." After a minute of watching her tea brew, she changed the subject to something even more difficult. "Cait, did you call Dad about the baby?"

The absence of an immediate answer was the answer in itself. "No," she said finally. "I didn't even think about him. I stopped that kind of useless self-torture years ago."

"Okay, I just wanted to know." Yet another situation that needed to be straightened out once and for all. "So, what's your agenda for today?"

"Besides spending time with my nephew, I plan to work on props for the pageant. We need gifts for the wise men to carry, and straw for the manger, shepherds' crooks or facsimiles thereof. And a camel."

"A camel?"

Cait smiled mischievously. "Keep it a secret, and I'll let you in on my grand scheme for live animals."

"A live camel? In the pageant?" The idea was insane. But the excitement in Cait's face made the possibility worth considering. "What else have you got in mind?"

EVEN IN AN indoor mall the size of a small town, shopping on a rainy day wasn't much fun.

Or maybe it was just their combined mood, Ben thought. The kids had been disappointed to wake up and find Cait gone. His explanation that she'd had to hurry back to take care of Miss Anna mollified them only slightly. As for himself—he'd knocked on Cait's door not thirty minutes after they'd separated and discovered her missing. Now he wasn't sure which of them he was most angry with—her for leaving, or himself for the stupidity he'd demonstrated last night.

At noon, as he and the kids stood in the center of the food court trying to choose somewhere to eat, Maddie looked up at him. "Daddy, do we have to stay here?"

"You want to eat somewhere else?"

She shook her head. "I want to go home. There's nothing in the stores here we don't have at our stores, and at home it's a lot less crowded, and noisy and—" she wrinkled her nose "—smelly."

Ben looked at Shep. He would have liked a word of agreement, but would settle for his son's nod. "I'm with you two. Let's go."

Traffic heading out of D.C. was fairly light, so they made good time. And just as they drove over the last hill, where the low mountains fell away to reveal the winterbrown Shenandoah Valley in all its beauty below them, the sun peeked out of the clouds.

"Winchester is where Miss Anna had her baby," Ben pointed out as they drove past the city. "In the hospital, of course."

Maddie sat forward. "Is she still there, Daddy?"

"Miss Anna's back home. But the baby is too little to leave yet."

"Can we go see him?"

"Uh—"

"Please, oh, please. It would be so neat to see Miss Anna's little boy. Don't you think so?"

He did think so. Babies were special, whoever they belonged to. "Okay, Maddie. We'll drop in on Goodwill's newest citizen."

At the wide window of the NICU, he pointed to the incubator labeled Remington. "There he is."

Maddie stood on tiptoe to peer through the glass. "Oh, wow. He's so little. And all those tubes and wires and machines..." She looked at him anxiously. "Are you sure he's okay?"

The top of Shep's head just reached the windowsill. Ben picked him up so he could see, too. "I told you, he's very small because he was born earlier than most babies are. The tubes are to help him stay healthy and grow stronger so he can go home to his mom and dad."

"Maddie! Shep!" Ben turned in unison with Maddie to see Anna hurrying down the hallway toward them. "What a wonderful surprise! Did you see the baby? Isn't he beautiful?" She swept Maddie into a hug. Shep wiggled to be let down, and Anna scooped him in with his sister.

That left Ben to watch Cait approach. Her chin was up, her eyes defiant...and hurt. She stopped at the opposite side of the window from where he stood. "I didn't realize you planned to come by."

Which probably meant she wouldn't be here, if she'd known. "A spur-of-the-moment decision as we were passing Winchester. Maddie wanted to see the baby." He closed the distance separating them by half. "Why did you leave?"

"We missed you for breakfast, Miss Caitlyn." Unaware of the undercurrents, Maddie stepped between them. "And we wanted to go shopping with you. But it wasn't much fun so we came home anyway. And now we're all here."

Cait's face smoothed into a smile. "I was worried about Anna, so I hurried back. What do you think of my nephew? Pretty handsome, isn't he?"

"But what's his name?"

Anna came to stand with them. "What do you think his name should be?"

Screwing up her face, Maddie thought hard. "Christopher," she pronounced after a minute. "Because it's almost Christmas. We can call him Chris." Standing next to Anna, Shep nodded his agreement.

"Christopher Remington." Anna stared through the window at the incubator and its tiny occupant. "You know, Maddie, I think that's perfect."

Remembering the problems Cait had told him about, Ben wasn't sure David would be pleased to have the decision of his son's name made without him. "Where's Pastor Dave this afternoon?"

"He's parking the car," Anna said, "after letting us off at the door. He should be here any second. I'm going to see if they'll let me talk to Christopher for a few minutes. Y'all stay and watch, okay?"

Cait wanted to protest, *No, don't leave me alone here with them!* Being with Maddie and Shep and Ben was like looking through the window at a doll she wanted for Christmas and knew she wouldn't receive.

Anna, of course, didn't hear her silent plea. But just a minute after she disappeared, the sound of hurried footsteps announced David's arrival. For the first time in several weeks, Cait was actually glad to see him.

"Guess what?" Maddie ran to meet him. "We found a name for your baby. Christopher. Do you like it?"

David stopped in his tracks. Emotions played over his face—anger, shame, relief. He laid a gentle hand on Maddie's shoulder. "You know, that sounds like a good name. What did Miss Anna think?" He came to the window just as Anna approached the incubator. Wearing a surgical cap and gown, even a mask and shoe covers, she was identifiable only by her red bangs and shining brown eyes.

Maddie came to the window, pressed her nose against the glass. "Why's she dressed so funny?"

Ben picked up Shep again and they all watched as Anna stroked her fingers down the baby's back. His eyes opened, and he turned his head slightly toward his mother.

"You know how we talked about germs when you had the flu?" Maddie nodded up at her dad. "Well, the doctors and nurses want to keep the babies as safe as possible. So they cover their clothes and shoes and hair, because those are places germs might land, and cover their mouths and noses so they won't breathe germs onto the babies."

The little girl shook her head. "Seems sad, not to be able to just hold him and kiss him. I bet he needs to know people love him right now."

Cait saw David's hands clench as they rested on the windowsill. "I'll bet you're right," he told Maddie, his voice hoarse. "Will y'all excuse me for a minute?"

He reappeared momentarily beside Anna, wearing the same outfit. She looked up quickly; even without seeing most of her face, Cait knew her sister was smiling. David reached out and touched the baby's cheek with one finger.

Cait turned and walked away from the window, blinking back tears.

Ben and Maddie and Shep left soon after that. There was no time for personal conversation, thank goodness, just a serious stare from Ben. "I'll call you," he said.

She stared down the hallway long after he and the kids had disappeared.

I'll call you.

Was that a promise...or a threat?

HARRY WASN'T SURE what the protocol for marriage counseling would be. Should the couple arrive separately, or in the same car? What did they say to each other the day of the appointment? Or should they save all their comments for the session?

He and Peg went to church together on Sunday morning, as usual. Garlands of pine framed the doors, and boxwood wreaths with red velvet bows hung in the windows. The evergreen scents and the tang of candle smoke brought images of Christmases past—Valerie as a teenager, singing carols from memory; as a ten-year-old speaking the part of the announcing angel in the pageant; as a five-year-old falling asleep during the midnight service on Christmas Eve.

And always Peg there beside him, to share smiles of pride and joy and love. Was that sharing over? Had he destroyed his marriage completely?

After the service, they went to lunch with Ben and the grandkids, which filled the time until two o'clock. Harry couldn't think of anything to say on the drive back to the church, and Peg didn't interrupt the silence. She didn't wait for him to open her car door, either, or look behind to see if he followed her to the office entrance.

Knowing he deserved to be ignored, but not liking it in the least, Harry tightened his jaw and determined to participate in this meeting.

David was waiting for them. "Hi, Peggy, Harry. Come on in." Harry waited for Peggy to choose one of the red velvet-covered chairs and sit down before he took the other. Just because he was a jerk didn't mean he couldn't be polite.

"So, what's this all about?" David sat back in his chair, making a tent of his fingers, looking from one of them to the other and back again.

When Harry glanced at Peg, she was staring out the window at the sunny, bitterly cold afternoon. She'd made the appointment. She should be the one to start talking. But minutes passed, and she didn't say a word.

David looked at Harry, waiting. "I...retired," Harry said, finally. "Actually, the company forced me to retire. And I didn't like it. I wasn't ready."

The minister nodded. "That's a very hard verdict to accept, that the company doesn't want you anymore."

"It was." Harry looked down at his hands. "I guess I let it eat at me."

"In what way?"

Thinking back, Harry reviewed what he'd done, how he'd felt, and tried to explain some of it. He looked over at David, now and then, finding nothing but concerned concentration in the younger man's face. No pity, no blame. Stumbling over the situation with Peggy—the way he'd avoided talking to her, his...failure...as her lover— Harry expected reassurances, condescension. David just listened.

The afternoon was getting dark when he finally ran out of things to say. David reached across the desk and turned on a low light. For the first time, Harry noticed that Peggy was watching him.

"You didn't have to be alone," she said softly. "I was there."

Harry closed his eyes. "I know. But at first I thought I had to handle it by myself. Then after a while, I couldn't...I don't know...connect. There was me, and there was everybody else, and no way to get through the wall between us." He shrugged. "I'm too old for a mid-life crisis. I guess you could call this senility."

"No, you call this depression." David came around to the front of his desk, leaned back against the edge. "Happens to a lot executives who have the world on a string one day and are out on the pavement twenty-four hours later.''

Harry didn't like the *D* word. ''So now I guess you're going to send me to a shrink for some pill that'll make it all right again.''

''Medication is one possibility. Or you could talk to me, to Peggy…use the opportunity to say what you think about what happened to you.''

''That's easy. I was royally pissed.'' He thought for a minute. ''Still am. What kind of company takes thirty-five years of a man's life and then dumps him like a trash can?'' Suddenly, he couldn't stop talking. All his anger just poured out….

When David got up to switch on another, brighter, lamp, Harry realized he'd been ranting for too long. ''Sorry. I knew once I got started, I'd have a hard time shutting up again.''

The minister nodded. ''Exactly. You needed to say all that, and a lot more besides. So why don't you come back next Sunday, same time, and talk about it again? Peggy, you're welcome, too, of course. And if either of you need a sounding board during the week, you can call. Okay?''

Feeling about twenty pounds lighter, Harry got to his feet and reached for David's hand. ''Okay. Thanks for— for listening. For being here.''

Peggy came over and claimed her own handshake. ''You're wonderful. I knew you would be.''

The minister's smile was warm, but faded very quickly. He took off his glasses and rubbed his eyes. ''Now, it's my turn.''

Harry raised an eyebrow. ''Now?''

David nodded. ''I can't do this anymore.'' He looked at Peggy. ''Would you excuse us for a few minutes? I'll try not to keep him long.''

"Of course. I'll wait in the outer room."

But Harry caught up with her at the door and followed her out into the front office. "You go on home," he said, handing her the car keys. "I can get David to drop me off."

She nodded, her gaze lowered.

He put his hand on her shoulder. "Peg. I'm so sorry."

Her eyes squeezed shut, and a tear slipped out.

Harry's throat had closed up. "When I get home, we'll talk." He bent his head to look into her face. "Or something."

His reward was her sweet, forgiving smile. "Or something," she agreed.

He claimed a quick kiss, felt the familiar jump of excitement in his blood. "See you soon." Peg nodded, blushed and backed through the outside door. Harry watched her get into the car, saw the headlights flare against the bare trees.

Then he turned and went back into the study to take his velvet seat again. "Okay, Pastor, what are you planning to do?"

His face pale, his high forehead beaded with sweat, David Remington swallowed hard. "I think I have to confess."

WAITING THROUGH the long Sunday evening, Anna had finally fallen asleep on the couch in the living room. She woke immediately at the sound of the kitchen door closing, the click of the lock. "David?"

As she sat up, she heard his slow footsteps coming down the hall. He leaned a shoulder against the doorframe. "What are you doing still awake?"

She'd turned off the lamps and left the tree lights on; in the dimness she couldn't read his face. "Waiting for you, of course. Why are you so late? What did Harry say?"

David sat at the opposite end of the sofa, slouching down to rest his head against the back. "We've called an emergency meeting of the church committee. I've been on the telephone with each member, explaining the situation. They're all upset, of course. Timothy was so appalled, he couldn't say a word." He sighed. "So...I've got one more week. If I don't come up with an answer, the committee will turn the problem over to the police. And then the whole town will know." He rubbed his fingers into his eyes. "How could I have botched things so badly?"

"It's been a very difficult autumn."

"Yeah." He turned his head to look at her. "How's Christopher today?"

"They took out the breathing tube for a little while. He did okay for a few minutes, but then his oxygen level dropped, so they put it in again." She blinked back tears, thinking about her five minutes of hope. Christopher wouldn't come home until he could breathe on his own. "They say that's not too bad for a first time, though, and he's really doing pretty well."

"I wish I could have gone with you." David sighed. "But Harry needed some encouragement in talking about his situation. He was punishing himself, trying to keep his feelings about his retirement all locked up."

"Poor Peggy. It seems to be a male characteristic, not sharing problems."

He chuckled wearily. "Don't women prefer the strong, silent type?"

Anna risked moving nearer to him. Not touching—but close enough to be touched. "Women prefer being given the chance to help the men they love get through the hard times. Just as they want the men they love to help them when they're struggling. That's part of what being married is about. Isn't it?''

David looked away from her face, toward the Christmas tree. ''I haven't done very well on that score. Lately, especially.'' Almost as if he didn't realize what he'd done, he put his left hand on her knee. His wedding ring glinted in the twinkling lights. ''I was just so...scared.''

''And that's hard to admit, when you're supposed to be the one with all the faith.'' She held her breath, wondering if she'd pushed too hard this time.

But he turned to stare at her, his eyes wide. ''Exactly. How did you know?''

Anna put her hand over his. ''It's not that much different, being the minister's wife. I feel like I always have to be at peace, always certain that all will be well.'' She shook her head. ''I haven't felt like that since we lost the first baby. I don't know if I'll ever feel quite safe again. With a child, there's always something to worry about.''

Shifting on the couch to face her, David laid his palm along her cheek. ''We haven't talked enough since then, have we?''

''Perhaps we let ourselves get busier and busier so we wouldn't have to think about it.'' She closed her eyes, savoring the warmth of his skin against hers.

''Could be.'' His kiss took her by surprise, a taste she'd been craving. ''Anna, I'm sorry. So sorry.'' He skimmed his lips over her eyelids, her forehead, then returned to her mouth.

She would have said many things...but David didn't give her the chance. Not for a long time. They lay together in the gentle light of the blue-and-silver Christmas tree, relearning their own language of touches and sighs and deep, shuddering breaths. Complete intimacy wasn't possible so soon after the baby, but by the time Anna fell asleep in her husband's arms, they had begun to regain the union of their hearts and souls.

Whatever happened in the next week, they would face the challenge together.

CHAPTER FIFTEEN

WHAT HARRY had meant to be a passionate reconciliation turned into a disaster.

"This isn't supposed to happen, dammit!" He dropped his legs over the side of the bed, felt for his robe on the floor and wrapped it around him as he stood up, then stalked out of the bedroom without waiting to hear what Peggy had to say.

In the dark kitchen, he pulled a beer out of the refrigerator and downed a good third of it before she appeared in the doorway. "I don't want to hear that it'll be okay," he told her when she started to speak. "Or that this happens to older men from time to time or you don't mind and you love me anyway. Don't even start."

Peggy flipped on the overhead light. "I wouldn't bother. But I will tell you that I'm tired of your moods, your selfishness, your certainty that the world is going to stop just because you lost your job. At an age when most men are glad to take a break and redirect their lives, you're pouting like a spoiled little boy."

Harry had to remember to shut his mouth. He didn't think he'd ever seen her this mad. "I gave them—"

"I know—thirty-five years and they dumped you like a trash can. You've made that clear. Deal with it, Harry. Taking your sense of injustice out on me, on yourself, won't change a thing."

"I can't even make love to my wife. What kind of man does that make me?"

"The same man you were before you went to work that last Monday morning. Only now you've got more free time."

He shook his head. The talk with David should have straightened him out. Working on the church financial records for five hours tonight—without finding the problem—had left him a little tired, kind of stiff, but he'd looked forward to getting home to his beautiful wife. They'd shared a glass of wine, and he'd taken her to bed, and…nothing.

The beer taste in his mouth turned flat, metallic. After pouring the rest of the bottle down the sink, he walked into the dining room to stare out the front window. His face heated with embarrassment as he thought over the last hour. Impotent. Mentally, emotionally, physically impotent. He would never have imagined feeling this way.

He'd never imagined getting pushed out of his job.

A clink of china and a rustle of cloth announced Peg's arrival. He didn't turn around. Couldn't face her.

"Have some tea." She stood next to him, holding out a holly-decorated mug. With a sigh, Harry took the tea. The appropriate drink for useless old men.

Beside him, Peg took a deep breath. "Harry, do you love me?"

She shouldn't have to ask. "I've loved you every day since we were nineteen years old."

"Why?"

"Because you're…Peggy."

"What does that mean?"

He closed his eyes, searching for words. "It means…you listen to me, you laugh with me, you argue about books and movies with me. You gave me a beautiful daughter and we brought her up to be a beautiful woman. You cried with me when she died. You—'' he lifted a hand ''—you're the other half of my self.''

''Why don't you trust me to feel the same?''

The question knocked the breath out of him. This wasn't about trust…was it?

''For better or worse, for richer, for poorer, in sickness and in health, Harry. You're a good provider, and there may never be a poor part. One day, though, there will be sickness for one or both of us. Do we just turn away from each other, then? Are you willing to let me go through old age alone?''

''No!''

''Then you have to allow me to be a part of what's happening now. You have to trust me enough to believe that it doesn't matter if you have a job or not. I didn't marry you because you made a good salary. I didn't marry you because you could give me a nice house, a new car, and take care of them with your own hands. Or because you were the vice president of a company. I married you because—because you're Harry.''

He squeezed his eyes shut.

Peg curled her hands around his arm, leaned her cheek against his shoulder. ''I don't value you for your income, your intelligence, your caring and concern, not even for your body and your wonderful ability to take me out of myself when we make love. If all those things disappeared tomorrow, I would still love what you are. The other half of me.''

''Peg.'' He put his mug on the windowsill, sloshing tea, and turned to take her in his arms. ''Hold me, Peggy. Hold on to me.''

She did as he asked, her arms tight around him as they stood in front of the window in the dark.

WEDNESDAY, the pageant started coming together. Ben and his crew set up the backdrop panels—the road to Bethlehem, the stable in the inn, the hills and fields where sheep grazed—arranged on a track to slide easily from side to side. The props were ready—Ben's manger was a rough wooden trough on legs, perfect for holding hay…and a newborn child.

There were problems, of course. The shepherds tended to duel with their crooks, the wise men couldn't keep their crowns on their heads, and Shep and Neil were still wrestling.

But the music sounded good. The kids knew where they were supposed to be and what they should say. The rehearsal went so smoothly, Cait almost wondered if a dress rehearsal on Saturday would be overkill.

She broached the subject with Anna, who had watched from the first pew. "I don't think so," her sister said. "When they put their costumes on, they'll lose focus. The little ones have to get used to their animal headdresses, and everybody will be silly at first, walking around in bath robes. You need that Saturday practice."

"Or," Cait said, as the kids started leaving, each of them stopping to talk with Anna on the way out, "maybe *you* need that Saturday practice."

Anna gave the last of the kids a goodbye hug, then turned back to Cait. "What are you talking about?"

"You could take over the pageant." She kept her eyes on the books of music she was sorting.

"Why should I?" Anna's voice wavered. "This is your program."

Cait shrugged, trying to seem casual. "I'm just thinking—you're feeling pretty well, getting around okay. We're talking about one two-hour rehearsal and the pageant itself. These are your kids, it's your church. Now that you're able, don't you want to be involved? I think everybody in town would be happy to have you back.''

"Or,'' Ben said, striding down the aisle, "are *you* simply trying to dig up a reason to run away?''

She jumped, then had to juggle quickly to keep from dropping the folders. "I thought everybody was gone.''

"I imagine you did.'' He stood in front of her, arms crossed over his chest. "I'm pretty sure you didn't expect to have to defend your decision to me.''

"It's not a decision. I was just offering Anna the chance—''

He looked at Anna. "Is that what you heard?''

Anna shook her head. "I heard her resigning from the pageant, expecting me to take over.''

"See?'' Ben was staring at Cait again. "Your sister and I heard the same thing.''

She placed the folders in their box. "I fail to see why this is such a bad idea. I'm just the substitute choir director.''

"And the author of the program, the composer of a couple of the songs. You have a stake in this pageant.''

"I came here to help my sister until her baby was born. He's here now, and Anna's feeling pretty good. Why is it so unreasonable for her to take back her responsibilities?'' Pulling in a deep breath, she picked up the box of folders and headed for the robe room to put them away. "And for me to go back to mine. I have a career, you know. Commitments.''

"A career you're hiding behind to avoid a real life.'' Ben followed her and blocked the door to the church so she couldn't get out again. "You can make an audience feel passion and pain, love and longing, joy and deep sorrow…but you don't have to take responsibility for the feelings you create. You choose an upbeat tune for the final number and walk away.''

She kept her gaze away from his face. ''T-that's my…job. It's what I'm good at.''

''Granted. But you need to remember that *this* isn't a performance. This is real.'' He caught her chin in his fingers, forced her to look up at him. ''You're trying to pull the same disappearing trick with me. With my kids. With all the people in this town who depend on you. And you know who will be hurt the most by what you're doing? It won't be the rest of us you leave behind. We still have each other.

''The person who will suffer is you.''

Cait blinked tears out of her eyes. ''Well, that's my problem, isn't it? Besides, you're the one who said I wouldn't be able to sacrifice the career for you. I'm just proving you right.''

''I don't want to be right, dammit.'' His hands came down on her shoulders. ''I want to give you what you've been missing all these years—the chance to live life, not just sing about it.''

He was too close, too persuasive. ''Who are you to pass judgment on what I do or don't do?''

''The man who loves you. The man who doesn't want to see you isolate yourself from everyone who cares about you.''

She backed out of his grasp. ''I've come up against this kind of caring before. 'Do it my way.' 'I'll love you as long as you let me call the shots.'''

''I never said that.''

''Ben, you said exactly that. You said you'd marry me if you could be sure I didn't hurt you or Maddie or Shep— meaning that I have to guarantee the career won't interfere with what you think matters.''

He passed a palm over his face. "I didn't mean that, actually. I was mad."

"But the career is *me*. It's not something I can just throw away—it's what I am. Singer, songwriter, performer. If you can't accept that, deal with it, recognize that at some points the music and the career will come first..." She shrugged.

Hands in his pockets, Ben stared at the floor for a long minute. "Okay," he said, lifting his head. "But why this week? Why does the career have to win *now?* Why won't you stay and see this—this project all the way through? What are you afraid of?"

Good question. Cait held his gaze, searching for the answer. She got only images—Anna and David leaning over Christopher's incubator, wonder and joy and worry on their faces; Shep and Maddie curled up in bed like sweet, sleeping cherubs; Ben...the sound of his laugh, the taste of his mouth, the way he could swing her mood from sober to joyous with just a smile. Or drive her to despair simply by turning away. She hadn't been at anyone's mercy like this in a long time. Ten years, to be exact.

She'd run away then, been running ever since.

Maybe the time had arrived, finally, to find out what would happen if she stopped.

"You've made your point," she told Ben. "I'll stay until Christmas." She sighed, but then managed a rueful smile. "I suppose we grinches have to stick together."

"Ah, revenge is sweet." His grin was confident, even cocky. "I told you I'd get you back for dragging me into this predicament in the first place!"

ANNA WAS absolutely correct about the Saturday afternoon rehearsal. Put the kids in their costumes and every line, every song they'd learned went right out of their heads.

Ben watched with a grin as assorted mothers, Anna, David and Cait herded the cast of the pageant into their places on the stage. Staring up at Cait from the front, the youngest children wore hoods resembling different animals—sheep, cows, donkeys, doves. Behind them sat the angels in white robes, silver-sprinkled wings and gold filigree haloes. To the left, the adolescent shepherds looked about as rugged as their prototypes would have, in bare or sandaled feet, rough robes and various styles of headdress. On the other side, the wise men and their servants shone like jewels in their purple, red and gold costumes.

Cait held up both hands and, miraculously, got everyone's attention. "We're going to start at the end of the pageant, work backward to the beginning. Then we'll break for pizza and drinks, come back and go straight through. Got it?"

The assembled kids nodded.

"Okay." Hands on her hips, she took a deep breath. "We have Mary, Joseph and manger, shepherds, wise men and servants in front of the stable backdrop, announcing angels one on either side, angel choir and animals in front. Find your places."

The kids scrambled, and Anna went to the organ. She would play the accompaniment while Cait directed the songs. Ben was glad to see the new mother looking happier, more rested than she'd been in months. Baby Christopher had made it through his first week of life in great form, even gained a couple of ounces. He'd been off the breathing tube for up to thirty minutes at a time. Soon, they hoped, the tube wouldn't have to be replaced.

"What's the last song?" Cait asked the kids.

"'We Three Kings!'" The shout echoed off the chancel walls.

She grinned. "I hope you use that energy to sing. Ready, wise men?" She lifted her arms, looking a little like an angel herself in a flowing white shirt tucked into slim jeans. "First verse, everybody."

The words started out weakly, gathered in confidence heading toward the chorus. "'Star of wonder, star of light...'" Listening, Ben assessed the paper star he'd constructed, wired and hung over the peak of the stable roof. There might be a couple of adjustments he could make to improve the shine.

"'Gold I bring...'" the first wise man sang, approaching the manger in response to Cait's wave.

"Louder," she called. He glanced at her nervously, adjusted his high-pointed gold hat, and gave it his best.

"Good," she smiled at him before taking the choir back into the chorus. Ben saw that smile, saw the kid flush with pleasure. Cait's approval was a powerful incentive.

"'Frankincense to offer have I...'"

"'Myrrh is mine, its bitter perfume...'"

"'Guide us with thy perfect light.'" The final notes faded into silence, and Cait held it for a few seconds. Then she dropped her arms, and everyone in the church took a deep breath.

She nodded. "Very, very good. Now, once that's done, we start the procession." She explained how the wise men and announcing angels would lead, followed by the rest of the cast. "Miss Anna will keep playing, and you'll keep singing the chorus, over and over again. The congregation will come out after you, and we'll all walk through the neighborhood to Pastor David's house. Right?" Completely focused, the kids nodded in unison. "So let's try it."

Several run-throughs later, the procession looked pretty smooth. But getting the kids back into place was a major undertaking. Ben picked up a can of soda Cait had been drinking earlier and joined her at the front of the church. "Wet your whistle," he suggested, holding out the can.

"Thanks." She sighed with relief as she swallowed. "I'm more accustomed to using mikes than I realized. The voice isn't ready to talk this loud and long."

"Do you think it's going well?"

"So far. The shepherds worry me."

Her concern was justified. Those boys still fumbled the words to "The First Noel."

Hands on her hips again, Cait stared at them. "What are we going to do, guys? We're running out of time."

Ben stepped forward. "Let me take them into the office and work on the words. You go on with the others."

She grinned. "Great idea. Shepherds, Secret Service Agent Tremaine is going to help you learn your part. Torture is an acceptable alternative," she told Ben in a stage whisper. The boys filed out ahead of him, looking a little nervous.

They flopped on the sofa and in the chairs in the church office. Ben cleared a space on the desk and sat. "Guys, you look like idiots out there."

The shepherds exchanged hangdog looks.

"Forgetting the words is not making you cool. Those angel girls are laughing at you for being too stupid to remember one verse."

"We got other stuff to do," protested the brown-robed lead shepherd.

"Not for the next fifteen minutes. What's the first line?"

"Uh…"

"Give me a break. You know the name of the song,

right?'' Shamefaced, the shepherds sang the first line. ''Good. Now what?''

By the time they went back into the church, the shepherds knew their song, and Ben knew why he hadn't gone to dental school. Pulling teeth was not an occupation he enjoyed.

But Cait's grin, when the song went well, was worth the hassle.

The angels, being girls, knew their parts cold. Maddie and Brenna sang beautifully together, so that Cait's song filled the air with mystery and joy. Ben blinked hard when they'd finished. He was glad he'd get another chance to listen to that particular piece.

''Angels, shepherds, wise men can take off their costumes and hang out for a few minutes while the animals practice their song.'' On her knees in front of the smallest kids, Cait encouraged them with a special smile. '''The Friendly Beasts,' right?''

The hooded heads nodded, Anna played an introduction.

One of the doves left her place and came to stand beside Cait, whispering in her ear. Judging from the shifting steps, a bathroom trip was in order. At Cait's nod, the little girl's mom came to get her, and Anna ran the intro again. Cait lifted her arms. ''Ready?''

From the end of the back row came a rumble, a thump, and a wail.

A mom and Anna rushed to pick up the fallen donkey. Wiping his tears, checking for injuries, took a couple of minutes.

''Okay.'' Their director, smiling with determination, took another deep breath. ''Donkeys, you sing first.''

A little boy in a sheep's hood stood up from the middle. ''I'm a cow.''

"No, you're a sheep." Cait put her hand on his head and eased him to sit again.

Another sheep boy stood up. "I'm a wolf." He put his hands up like fangs and growled. All the sheep and doves shrieked.

Smiling, Cait shook her head. "You're very, very silly. No wolves in this story. They're all out in the hills, but you sheep are in the stable, safe and warm. Right?" The sheep nodded. "Now, donkeys…"

Anna played her part and Cait started to sing. Sweet and clear, childish voices followed her lead. "I carried his mother up hill and down…"

Next came the cows. "I, said the cow all white and red, I gave him my manger for his bed…"

The sheep with curly horns were a little confused. Cait stopped and rehearsed, "I gave him my wool to keep him warm." Then the doves, mostly girls, finished up. "I sang him to sleep with my lullaby."

"You guys are spectacular," Cait told them. "I think you did such a wonderful job, we should stop for dinner now. Sound good?" A cheer went up, and Cait's face took on an expression of panic. "Take off your hoods first!" A contingent of mothers supervised the removal of the headdresses, then the church emptied as the kids headed for the social hall and pizza. Anna followed.

Cait sank into a pew and put her head back. "Whew," she said, as Ben sat down beside her.

"You're doing a great job."

She shook her head. "The kids are doing a great job. I'm just the TelePrompTer."

"Yeah, you didn't have anything to do with how it's turning out."

"I can browbeat with the best of them." Sitting forward, she rested her arms on the back of the pew in front of them and propped her chin on her fists. "The back-drops are fantastic. Your sliding system makes changing scenery easy." From the side, he could see her smile. Then she turned her head and finally met his gaze. "Thanks for all your help, Mr. Grinch."

"You're most welcome, Ms. Grinch." He stroked a thumb down her cheek. "I can't believe the difference you've made in my life. Christmas is just part of it."

She drew a shaky breath. "I've changed, too. I just don't know…" She looked down at her knees and shook her head. "There's so much to think about."

"And no time," Ben said, standing up as one of the mothers came in to consult Cait about a costume detail.

Cait wasn't sorry to have her interlude with Ben cut short. As much time as she'd spent thinking about him, about her feelings, her goals, her needs, her desires, she hadn't come up with a way to reach a compromise.

She could abandon her music career for life with a good man and the children she already cared about as if they were her own. She could turn her back on love, marriage and family for the career—because if she didn't take the opportunity with Ben, how could there be another man for whom she would make such a sacrifice?

Or she could choose the hardest way of all and try to embrace the music and the man and the kids, somehow build a life that transcended the obstacles and accommo-dated the inconveniences.

But Cait wasn't sure she had the fortitude for that effort. When it came to making plans and setting goals, she hadn't thought about anybody but herself for a long time. The fiasco with Maddie's program and then her own con-cert had demonstrated what kind of conflict could arise over small issues. What if she was considering a two-month concert tour, and Shep's birthday fell right in the middle? With Russell pressuring her, would she be strong enough to put off the tour to be with her son?

Assuming, of course, that Russell would still be her agent. If she decided to get married, he might very well decide not to represent her anymore. And he might make good on his promise that she'd never work again. In that case, the choice would be...Ben *or* the music.

Fortunately, she didn't have to decide this afternoon. The run-through of the pageant from start to finish had plenty of rough spots, enough uncertainty that everybody's adrenalin would be flowing when the time arrived.

Ben came up to her as the children were taking off their costumes for the last time. "This isn't the most romantic invitation you've ever received, but...would you like to come home with us? We've got movies to watch, and Peggy gave me a huge container of her world-famous chili this morning. You haven't had even a piece of pizza. Maddie and Shep would really like to spend the time with you." He gave her a half smile. "So would I."

It was such a simple suggestion—but a dangerous one. Every minute she spent with Ben and his children strengthened her bond with them. But what if she didn't stay? Wouldn't more time together make leaving that much harder?

"It sounds wonderful," she told him earnestly. "But...I think I'd better not." She prayed he wouldn't want a reason.

"Why?" His question sounded almost harsh in the quiet church. Most of the moms and kids had left, the costumes had been cleared away. Maddie and Shep were helping Anna stack the music folders.

"Because—" Cait shook her head "—because we need to be careful. As you said a long time ago, there's no sense in getting more involved if—if it's not going to last."

He shoved his hands in his pockets. "Does that mean what it sounds like?"

Maddie and Shep came running back into the chancel and flung themselves at Ben, arms around his waist. "Let's go, Daddy. Let's go."

Now was not the time to explain. "I...we'll talk later, okay?"

He shrugged, his face shuttered. "Sure. Later. C'mon, kids. We've got movies to watch." Shep waved and Maddie called out "Goodbye" as they followed their dad down the aisle. Ben didn't speak or glance back.

Cait wondered sadly if, by refusing his invitation, she had just made her choice.

THE CHURCH COMMITTEE met on the Sunday before Christmas, but the atmosphere was far from festive. Regina Thorne wore her most severe teacher's frown. David Remington was obviously nervous, to the point of looking guilty. Harry had come to the conclusion, working as closely with the minister as he had these past few weeks, that the boy didn't have enough guile to embezzle ten cents, let alone ten thousand dollars. The money was simply lost. Now they had to figure out what to do about it.

Fifteen minutes after the time set for the meeting, Timothy Bellows still hadn't appeared, and they really couldn't run this meeting without the church treasurer. Harry poured himself a third cup of coffee, watching the seven men and women around the library table glance at each other with questions in their eyes. He was about to pick up a forbidden doughnut when a sudden stillness came over the group.

Timothy stood in the doorway, in his Sunday suit and

tie. His chin was up, his full lips pressed into a thin line. The committee stared at him for a minute, and Timothy stared back.

"I have come to resign my position," he said stiffly. "I'll also be resigning my church membership." Stepping forward, he reached out and slapped his right palm against the table, then lifted his hand to reveal a crisp, new check. "There's your money. Every cent plus interest, at a higher rate than the bank would give you."

A long silence followed. Finally, Harry found his voice. "Why, Timothy?"

The tall man shrugged. "At first, I didn't even know I had that check. When I came to get the Sunday receipts for deposit that day, Pastor David and Anna were floating about three feet off the floor, hearing about their coming baby. So I just picked up the bag and went to the bank. The check must've fallen out as I was shuffling papers around in the truck. I found it a month or so later, when I was cleaning up."

No one asked the next question. Timothy swallowed hard. "The mortgage on my land had come due. The drought, these last couple of years...y'all probably never knew how deep I was in debt. I tried not to let anybody know, not even Grace. But in one hand I had this bill, and in the other I had this check, already stamped and endorsed. See, I'd taken out a second mortgage for the new irrigation system. So the harvest was looking good, for a change—I knew I'd have the money come October, but I didn't have it in July. This was my third extension, and those bankers up in Winchester weren't giving me another one. So...I borrowed from the church."

He hung his head, pulled in a deep breath. "I am sorry. If you want to put me in prison, I'll understand. The farm's up for sale starting tomorrow. Gracie knows everything. She's moving to South Carolina, near her family, right after Christmas. I'll do whatever y'all say is right.''

After a minute of absolute stillness, each of the committee members, Harry included, turned to look at their pastor. The outcome rested on his judgment.

David stared down at his hands, clasped on the table in front of him. When he looked up, finally, he smiled. '''Do unto others as you would have them do unto you.' What season, what celebration, demonstrates that idea better than Christmas?''

He got to his feet. ''As far as I'm concerned, Timothy, this issue is in the past. I think I must accept your resignation as treasurer.'' He glanced around the table and got nods from the committee members. ''But if you're leaving town solely because of what's happened, I hope you'll reconsider. You and Grace are a part of our church family. We don't want to lose you.''

Timothy broke down, then. Harry got him a chair and stood with a hand on the man's shaking shoulder while the room emptied. David came to the end of the table and crouched in front of Timothy. Harry backed toward the door. ''I'll leave you two alone.''

The minister glanced up at him. ''Thanks, Harry. For everything.'' Then he turned back to the man in the chair. ''Let's talk, Timothy.''

Harry closed the door to the library and leaned back against it. An unforeseeable answer to all their questions. Who would have thought…? He'd been ready to believe the minister had taken the money. But Timothy?

Shaking his head, he straightened up and left the church office, headed for home. David Remington was right. The problem was solved, the situation settled. Time to move on and deal with the things that really mattered. Life, love…and Christmas.

THE PHONE RANG about three in the morning on Christmas Eve. At least that's what Cait thought, given the dimness of the room, until she rolled over to see that the clock read almost 10:00 a.m. She fell back against the pillows, then scooted over to pull the curtain aside, revealing a sky heavy with dark-gray clouds. Delicate tracings of frost feathered across the windowpanes.

Anna knocked on the door. "Cait, the phone's for you."

"Thanks." But she groaned inwardly. If this was Russell, bugging her about getting out to L.A…. No, Russ wouldn't be awake at seven in the morning. "Hello?"

"Miss Caitlyn? This is Leon's mother." The tone of her rich southern accent predicted bad news. "I'm really sorry to tell you this, but Leon woke up with a sore throat and a fever this morning."

Leon was the first wise man. Nothing could happen to Leon. They didn't have anybody else to sing the part.

His mother knew that. "I just had him at Dr. Hall's office a little while ago and he's positive that Leon's come down with strep throat. I really am sorry—" she drew a deep breath "—but I don't see any way my boy will be able to sing in the pageant tonight."

CHAPTER SIXTEEN

CHRISTMAS EVE MORNING, Ben and Maddie and Shep took their traditional walk along the Avenue. The temperature hovered at about thirty-five degrees, the air felt damp, and the sky wore a flat gray blanket of snow clouds.

"It's gonna be a white Christmas, Daddy, I know it!" Maddie danced along the sidewalk, stopping to press her face against the glass of the bakery. "Look at all those tree cookies. And bells and reindeers and stars. Can we get some, Daddy? We've eaten almost all the cookies Grandma sent home with us."

"I guess we'd better get something to feed Santa when he stops by tonight. What do you think, Shep?"

Standing beside his sister, the little boy looked around and whispered, "Please?"

To hear that one word, Ben would gladly have purchased the entire shop. He settled for six dozen shaped and iced sugar cookies, enough for Santa with plenty more to take to the Remingtons' for the reception tonight.

"We're moving on now," he said, leading Maddie and Shep out of the bakery before they could persuade him to buy a dozen of every other kind of goodie. Each year, the merchants in town enjoyed a friendly rivalry over their Christmas decorations. As a result, Goodwill on Christmas Eve resembled a village in a snow globe. There were wreaths on all the doors, garlands and lights on the lampposts and displays of holiday scenes in the windows, including some with action figures—carolers who moved their mouths to sing, reindeer whose legs bent and straightened as they pulled the sleigh above the rooftops. From every doorway, Christmas music spilled into the air.

For Ben, the colors seemed almost too bright, the laughter and music too loud. Not unpleasant, but as if he'd spent his life wrapped in a cocoon, seeing only shadows, hearing only echoes, and had just broken free into the real world. *This* was Christmas. He was beginning to realize some of what he'd been missing.

They ran into Harry coming out of the hardware store. "Hey, there." He put down his sack and picked up Shep while Maddie hugged him around the waist. "It's a cold Christmas Eve, isn't it? Smells like snow, too."

"What are you buying, Grandpa?" Maddie tried to peek into the bag he'd put down.

"It's a secret for your grandmother." Harry put down Shep and picked up the bag. He winked at Ben. "She'll never guess in a million years. See?" He held the bag out for the kids to peer into.

"Skates, Grandpa? You got Grandma skates? Is that what she asked for?"

Harry nodded. "She did. I got us both a pair. Now I need to rush and get them wrapped before she comes home from the grocery. See you all at the pageant!"

He hurried up the street, happier than Ben had seen him in a couple of months. That probably had something to do with his new job. David had called Harry yesterday to offer him the position of church accountant. The pay wasn't much, but money wasn't the issue—except to keep more mistakes from getting into the books, of course.

"Let's go to the bookstore, Daddy." Maddie pulled his hand, and he followed along. As soon as they stepped inside, "White Christmas" started to play. "It *is* going to be a white Christmas," Maddie told Hunter Dixon, the owner. "I'm positive."

Grinning, Hunter toasted her with a mug of warm cider. "I'll second the motion, Miss Maddie. See y'all at the pageant tonight."

They would also see Cait, Ben thought as they walked up the hill on the other side of the Avenue, toward home. He hadn't approached her at church yesterday, and after one long glance, she hadn't looked at him during the service or afterward. Finishing up a couple of Christmas orders had kept him busy for the rest of the day—too busy to call her, he told himself. No doubt she had things she needed to take care of, as well. After all, she was leaving town in a day or two.

If he said it often enough, he thought he might possibly get used to the idea.

Back at the house, he fixed soup for lunch, carefully avoiding both tomato and chicken noodle in favor of minestrone.

"So what is Santa going to be leaving at our house tonight?" He was pretty sure he'd completed his Christmas shopping, but it didn't hurt to double check.

"A new bike," Maddie said quickly. "And a Harry Potter watch and some in-line skates and Nancy Drew books."

"Right." All those items were hidden in the Shepherds' garage. "How about you, Shep? What are you hoping for?"

Looking down at his bowl, Shep said something in a voice too low for Ben to hear.

He leaned forward and put his hand on the sleek blond hair. "I didn't hear you, son. Can you say it again?"

But Shep shook his head. Ben sat back in his chair,

cautioning himself to be patient. It would take time for Shep to come completely out of his shell.

"A mommy," Maddie said. "He wished for a mommy."

Ben felt his heart thud, then stop. "What does that mean?"

Maddie looked at her brother, who resolutely avoided her eyes. "Well, it's just…he likes Miss Caitlyn a lot. And he thinks it would be neat if she stayed to be our…um…mommy." For once, Maddie turned shy. "Me, too," she said softly.

Me, three. Ben cleared his throat. "I don't think that comes under Santa's control, kids. Miss Caitlyn has a mind of her own."

"But you could ask her, couldn't you? I mean, you like her a lot, right?"

"Yes, Maddie, I do. But I told you a long time ago, she's got a big career. She can't drop it to stay here with us."

"No, but she could come back when she had time. And we could go to her—we could fly to California, or Florida or New York. We'd get to see all those places *and* have her as our mommy."

A rosy picture, indeed. Ben only wished he could promise to bring that picture to life. "We'll just have to wait and see," he said. When Maddie tried to pursue the topic, he held up a hand. "No, we're not going to talk about it anymore. Right now we're going to clean up the kitchen, and then you guys will take a nap. It's going to be an exciting night. I have to be at the church extra early and you'll be up pretty late. You need some rest first."

Not surprisingly, Maddie complained and Shep pouted wordlessly. Also not surprising, they were both asleep within fifteen minutes.

Which left Ben alone with the silence and his thoughts. He fought the impulse to call Cait for about an hour, then took the phone to the living room, sat down beside the Christmas tree—which leaned to one side, despite Maddie's and Shep's assistance—and dialed the Remingtons' number. Busy.

He ironed Maddie's angel robe and called again. Busy. Ran a couple of loads of laundry. Still busy. Actually fell into a restless sleep for about twenty minutes. And the Remingtons' number was still busy when he woke up.

Maybe it's a sign. He took a shower and got dressed, then went to wake the kids. *The universe telling me to hang up and get on with my life.*

He'd done it before, Ben decided. He could do it again.

"Hey, Announcing Angel, it's time to put on your wings." He shook Maddie's shoulder gently, then returned to Shep. "Your master awaits you, oh, servant to the wise man. Wake up!"

The most important people in his life were these two sleepyheads. If they were safe and happy and healthy, he was doing his job pretty darn well.

So for tonight, at least, he just wouldn't think about how they'd feel when "Miss Caitlyn" said goodbye.

CAIT WENT to the church about five o'clock, to sit in the quiet for a few minutes and calm her nerves before the pageant. She still didn't know exactly how to handle the missing wise man issue. After spending nearly all day on the phone, she hadn't found a single boy or girl willing to take on the role. The idea of drafting Maddie had occurred to her, but that would leave Brenna singing alone without any warning. Even professionals could choke under that kind of pressure. Which put her back to square one. Who could she draft to be the wise man?

Ben would arrive soon to set up the backdrops. She hoped he would bring Maddie and Shep along—seeing him alone would just be too hard. She'd caught his eye once during the service on Sunday morning, had felt as if she would drown in the longing that swept through her. Given the chance at that moment, she would have agreed to stay with him for the rest of her life.

But then Russ had called on Sunday afternoon with plane flight information and show details. Anna and David came back late from the hospital after a rough afternoon— Christopher had been having some breathing problems. The first glow of having the baby alive and getting well had faded now. Anna was tired of pumping her breasts, of feeding her baby through a tube in his throat, of not being able to hold him. Cait offered what comfort she could, but the truth was that, in the first few weeks, premature babies struggled for their lives. And the people who loved them could only watch and wait and hope.

Why, Cait wondered now, in the silence of the chancel, should she take the risk of facing such pain? Living alone, responsible for no one and to no one but herself, made life so much easier to bear.

One of Barbra Streisand's earliest hits came to mind, a song about how much people need each other. Then there was John Donne's version—"No man is an island." And above all the old, familiar words, "Tidings of great joy which shall be to *all* people…Peace on Earth."

Hard to argue with such illustrious witnesses.

Behind her, the outside door opened. She heard Maddie's cheerful tones and gave a sigh of relief. At least something was going right today.

On her feet, she turned to face them. "Merry Christmas, Tremaine family. All ready for the big show?"

Holding two clothes hangers with costumes, Ben

shrugged, sent Cait a half-grin. Maddie flew down the aisle to give her a hug. "What time do we start Miss Caitlyn? It's not snowing yet, but the weatherman promises it will before morning. Do you think it will start during our procession? I think it would be so neat to walk through the snow."

"I think so, too. The program starts in about two hours, so there's still time to get lucky." Shep had sneaked up on her other side and thrown his arms around her waist. Swallowing hard, she hugged both children close, but let go quickly.

"Okay, it's time for me to get to work. Ben, the boys will get dressed in David's office and the girls in the social hall, if you want to put the costumes there. Maddie, we need to put out the candles the congregation will hold and make sure they all have little drip collars."

"Have what?"

Cait went to robe room and brought back the box of candles. "See? This little paper circle fits over the bottom of the candle, so hot wax doesn't drip on people's hands. Would you get those ready?"

Maddie settled on a pew, carefully adjusting each candle. Shep had disappeared—to be with his dad, Cait assumed. Ben and a couple of the other men would move the pulpit and chairs that sat on the stage, bring the backdrop panels in and set them up.

Meanwhile, Cait carried in a few of the bales of hay Timothy Bellows had left outside the church. The majority would be used for her animal surprise—the part of the pageant none of the children and only a very few adults knew about.

With the hay arranged where the stable would be, she began bringing the props out of the robe room—the manger, Elizabeth and Mary's sewing, the shepherds' crooks.

On her third trip into the little space, she heard the music. Shep was in there somewhere—probably underneath the hanging robes again. And he was singing. Not humming. Singing with words.

The words of "We Three Kings." The wise men's song.

Heart pounding, Cait dropped to sit on the floor. "Shep? Shep, can I talk to you a minute?"

After a second, he peeked out from between the long black robes, his expression wary.

"Shep, guess what's happened." He continued to stare at her. She took a deep breath and gripped her damp palms together. "Leon, the first wise man, is sick today. He has a bad sore throat and can't sing or even be here."

The little boy before her started to dive back behind the robes.

She caught his hand in time to stop him from disappearing. "No, wait. Would you…sing the song for us? Just that one verse about gold? I've asked absolutely everybody else and can't find anybody to help."

Wide-eyed silence greeted her request.

"If I could think of another way, I would use it," Cait continued to plead. "But I just heard you singing the words. You have a really nice voice. And the costume would fit you—it's the purple robe, you know, with the pointed crown." She held her breath, hoping for an answer. "Please, Shep?"

After a long, long time, he said, "I can't." Softly. Hoarsely. But she heard him.

"I bet you could." Cait forced herself to stay calm. "'We three kings of Orient are…'" she began to sing. By the time she reached the chorus, Shep was singing with her.

Just at the beginning of the second verse, Maddie appeared in the doorway. "Miss Caitlyn, I finished the candles." Shep vanished under the robes.

Cait clenched and unclenched her jaw. "Thank you very much."

"What are you doing on the floor? And why is Shep hiding under those long dresses Pastor David wears?"

"We were...I was hoping he would take over the part of the first wise man tonight. Leon has strep throat."

Maddie looked over at the robes. "You could do that, Shep. You could even sing the verse. I bet Miss Caitlyn would be really happy if you would."

Cait got to her knees and reached out to hug Maddie again. "You're right." She pressed a kiss on the dark curly hair tickling her chin. "Can you convince Shep to help me out?" she said softly.

Maddie nodded with a very adult confidence. "Let me talk to him alone for a minute."

Ben and his crew were in the midst of setting up the backdrops when Maddie and Shep reappeared. Cait looked at them hopefully.

"He'll wear the robe," Maddie announced. "He won't promise to sing, but...he says he might."

How many situations in this world were ever exactly perfect? Cait heaved a sigh of at least partial relief. "That's great. I'm so grateful. The other kids have started coming in. Are you two ready to put on your costumes?"

"Oh, boy!" Still holding her brother's hand, Maddie whirled and headed for the dressing rooms. "It's time to be an angel!"

AT SEVEN O'CLOCK the church was filled to capacity. Two spotlights, borrowed from a drama teacher in Winchester by Regina Thorne, focused attention on the stage. The rest of the room stayed in shadow.

David Remington stepped into one of the spotlights to welcome everyone to the Goodwill Christmas pageant. He said a brief prayer of thanksgiving for the faith and hope children offer.

Then the music started—a guitar, with rolling chords, joined by the organ singing a familiar, plaintive song of waiting. The young woman Mary stepped out of a back-drop doorway on the left, to be greeted by an angel with golden wings, coffee-colored skin and a profusion of shoulder-length braids. Cait watched, a little anxious— Tiaria had been hyperventilating with stage fright just twenty minutes ago. But she swallowed hard, then spoke the words of annunciation in her sweet, deep voice. At Cait's signal, the children came to the steps of the stage, singing another Advent hymn as Mary pantomimed telling her cousin Elizabeth about the baby. With everyone in their places, the lights suddenly went out. Eerie, uncertain, the last notes of hope died away into the dark.

When the lights came up again, Mary and Joseph stood at the door to the inn. They knocked…and knocked…and knocked again. Joseph cast Cait a questioning look and the audience chuckled slightly. Maybe this innkeeper wasn't even going to answer the door.

Fumbling, a red-faced Bobby Porter finally pulled the door panel back. With a lot of "ums" and "ahs" and "you knows" he explained to Joseph and a drooping Mary that he had no room. Then he offered them his sta-ble. "Don't milk the cow," Bobby, a dairy farmer's son, warned them. "The milk's for the paying customers." Cait glanced at Anna and rolled her eyes, while the au-dience laughed at this strictly improvisational dialogue.

"Psst." Cait called softly to the youngest singers. "Cows, sheep, doves, donkeys. It's your turn!"

One by one the little faces turned away from the stage.

Standing, they all stared hard at Cait as the introduction to their special piece began. And if some of the doves sang with the cows, if the sheep wiggled and only a couple of the donkeys remembered all the words, it was still very sweet and true. The stable animals received their own round of applause at the end of the song.

Then, with "Silent Night," "O Little Town of Bethlehem," and "Away in a Manger," the baby Jesus was born. Again the spotlights shut off. A backdrop panel slid into place with oiled ease, and the shepherds trooped onto the stage.

Cait gasped as the lights came up again, and heard the audience stir in surprise. The boys looked very much the way those long ago shepherds might have—a little surly, a little sleepy, arguing and teasing each other to stay awake for the night watch. And glory be—they sang their verse all the way through, strongly, without missing a word. Cait found Ben in the corner by the robing room door and they shared a moment of pure delight.

Then, without anyone having noticed their approach, the announcing angels stepped onto the stage. Dressed exactly alike, Brenna and Maddie complemented each other perfectly—Maddie's dark eyes and curls, Brenna's gray eyes and long, cornsilk hair. Cait played the guitar introduction for "The Angel Song" and looked up at Maddie to cue her entrance.

Maddie didn't need a cue. She sang as if it were as easy as breathing, as if she spent her life in song. Making eye contact with the shepherds, she told them the good news she brought. Brenna joined in with the harmony, the two voices weaving together in seamless beauty. Cait squeezed her eyes shut as she played, felt teardrops cool the back of her hand.

The other angels stood to join in the celebration with

"Joy to the World." One last blackout brought Mary and Joseph and the manger back to center stage, surrounded by angels and animals and worshiping shepherds.

Cait closed her eyes, murmured a quick and fervent prayer. The three wise men were about to make their entrance.

Anna started the song on the organ and the choir picked up the words. Gradually every head in the church turned toward the back where Shep stood in the doorway, a small yet regal figure. Pacing majestically, holding a wooden jewelry box filled to overflowing with gold-wrapped chocolate coins, he approached the stage. His servant came behind him, carrying the long train of the shining purple coat. At the front of the church Shep stopped just as the choirs reached the end of the chorus. Cait couldn't breathe. She closed her eyes, because she couldn't bear to watch.

"Gold I bring to crown him again..." Still a little hoarse, not as steady or as confident as it would one day be, Shep's voice rose above the gasps of the assembled crowd. Anna's accompaniment faltered, stopped. But Shep sang on, alone, finishing his verse with perfect certainty.

After a moment, Anna began to play again. The children sang the chorus, the second and third wise men delivered their equally well-done parts. Cait let her shoulders slump. The pageant was over.

At her signal, Maddie and Brenna left the stage, followed by the wise men, all singing the "Star of Wonder" chorus. Cait winked at Shep as he went by her, and got his wonderful smile in return. While the congregation shared the lighting of their candles, Mary and Joseph filed out, cradling a bundle of blankets, followed by animals and angels, and then the church full of people.

Still carrying her guitar, Cait scooted out the back door of the church and came up behind Timothy's bales of hay just in time to hear the children's collective "Ooo" when they glimpsed the scene outside.

Lit by tall torches, real sheep, two white ewes and a black lamb, grazed from a trough of hay. A red-and-white Holstein cow stared at the growing audience with placid unconcern. The same couldn't be said for the donkey, who protested being tied to a tree with loud and penetrating bray.

But the camels stole the show. Cait didn't know how Timothy had done it—especially given what had happened at the meeting with David and the church committee. But the farmer had used his miraculous contacts to produce two dromedary camels. The entire procession came to a stop as the children admired those miraculous additions to the Christmas menagerie. Cait gave them plenty of time, then caught Maddie's eye and restarted the chorus of "We Three Kings" on the guitar. The little girl's strong voice resumed the song and, with the help of a few moms and dads, the congregation moved on. Holding their flickering candles, singing in unison, the townsfolk of Goodwill advanced through the Christmas Eve darkness.

And as they walked, the snow began to fall.

CAIT FOLLOWED at a distance. She couldn't remember ever having experienced such a powerful, peace-giving ceremony, not even as a child. The children of Goodwill had shown her the meaning of love with their voices, their talent, their willingness to give. And the moment Shep started singing symbolized all that they'd done. Now Maddie's wish was coming true—the world was receiving a healing blanket of snow.

David and Anna didn't really have enough room for the whole town inside their house—every window was lighted, each room within filled to capacity with people. Cait hung back, letting everyone else enter, so she could treasure the quiet and solitude of this one special night.

After a few minutes, the front door opened with its distinctive squeak and she looked down the length of the front walk to see who was leaving. A tall man stepped out, as tall as Ben but broader, in a long overcoat and scarf—something she'd never seen Ben wear. He stood on the porch, gazing around him as the snow fell. Cait felt the moment his eyes found her in the dark. Without hesitation, he started down the steps. His walk—proud, measured, confident—identified him immediately.

She braced her fists in the pockets of her slacks. "What are you doing here?"

He stopped a couple of yards away. "Your sister invited me. She wants me to meet my grandson. And..."

The Reverend Allan Gregory knew how to pitch his voice for maximum effect, and he did so now. "Most of all, I believe, she wants me to welcome you back into the fold."

WHEN BEN FINALLY found Shep, the boy was resting high against Harry's shoulder, with his pointed crown askew, holding an iced Christmas cookie in each hand.

"Can you believe this young man," his granddad demanded. "Just coming out like that with a song?"

Ben's pulse was still thudding double-time. "I'm pretty amazed." He put his hand on his son's back. "Good job, Shep. I'm really proud of you."

"Thanks." The simple word, its matter-of-fact tone, just about wrecked Ben's control.

"What about me, Daddy? Did you like my song?" Maddie pulled on the hem of his sweater.

He picked her up and hugged her tight. "The most beautiful song I've ever heard, Maddie," he said softly against her ear. "I'm betting your mom heard it, too, and she's just as proud and happy as I am."

Maddie tightened her arms around his neck. "I love you, Daddy."

Christmas, Ben decided at that moment, was his favorite time of the year.

"But where's Cait?" Peggy joined them, carrying a glass of punch for Harry and one for herself. "I haven't seen her since the procession started."

They all looked around as if they could locate her in the crush of people filling the Remingtons' house from wall to wall. Ben set Maddie down again. "I'll find her—it's easier for one person to move through the crowd."

But he couldn't see her, though he searched all the rooms of the house. She could have been traveling in the same direction, always leaving a room just as he entered, but the people he asked hadn't encountered her either.

As he wrestled his way through the living room for the second time, he glanced out the window and saw Cait at the end of the sidewalk, confronting a man he could see only in profile. A minute's study, though, gave him a name. Cait was smaller, of course, more feminine, but the angle of their stances as they faced each other were the same, the tilt of their chins, the air of self-reliance and the power of personality.

Cait's father had come for Christmas.

CHAPTER SEVENTEEN

"I DON'T WANT or need to be back in the fold."

Ben heard Cait's words very clearly as he eased into the quiet, snowy night. Reason said he should let her handle this meeting herself. But he loved her, and this was likely to be a tough scene, however it turned out. If she needed him, he would be there.

"Perhaps I misstated that." Her dad cleared his throat. "Anna believes we should...reconcile."

"What Anna thinks, in this situation, is irrelevant." The tautness of Cait's tone revealed more stress than she probably was aware of.

Mr. Gregory put his hands in the pockets of his overcoat. "You aren't making this easy."

Cait didn't move. "Why should I?"

"Don't you care that we've been estranged for ten years?"

"Do you?"

He shifted from one foot to the other and back again. "I don't understand your attitude."

"That's nothing new. You never did."

"Can't you let go of the past?"

"No, I can't. You threw me out of your church, your house, your life. Now you want me to walk back in, without some kind of—of acknowledgment that it mattered to you in the least." She shrugged. "Sorry. I'm not so generous."

"You expect an apology?"

Her laugh sounded bitter. "That's an interesting idea, but not really accurate. I stopped expecting anything from you ten years ago tonight."

For a couple of minutes the only sound was the soft plop of snowflakes on the ground.

Finally, the older man shook his head. "I started this in the wrong manner. Let me begin again." He took a deep breath. "I...regret...my reactions that day. I should have listened to your side of the argument."

"You should have." Her voice held a hint of surprise.

"I was, however, very disappointed and hurt at being deceived by my own daughter."

Now Cait hesitated. "Hiding the applications was wrong. I ought to have stood up for myself, been open about what I intended."

"I agree. But—" Mr. Gregory actually chuckled "—I doubt I would have been any more receptive. I believed I knew what was the best course for you to take in life."

"Believed? Past tense?"

"It's obvious that the fears I had for you were groundless. I thought the career you wanted would destroy you, as it has so many others. Drugs, alcohol, promiscuity...the popular entertainment industry has always been notable for its excesses."

"I've seen my share."

"I'm sure you have. But you seem to have emerged unscathed. And if you could produce a program like the one this evening, I must conclude that your heart and your soul are sound."

Ben could only hope Cait heard the admiration, the concession in her dad's words.

"Well...thanks. I really wasn't sure—" She broke off, shaking her head.

"Of what?"

Cait shrugged. "That I could do this. That I still understood the message."

"And your lack of faith is—is my responsibility." When his daughter stared at him, without saying anything, Mr. Gregory made an open-handed gesture. "The irony of the situation isn't lost on me. How could you be expected to trust yourself, when I, as your parent, did not? Why should you forgive, if I couldn't?"

"Dad..."

He held up a hand. "Let me say it all. I am sorry, Caitlyn. I allowed my hurt feelings and my own pride to drive you out of my life. I nursed an inappropriate sense of outrage, until the breach between us became insurmountable. And yet—" he blew out a long breath "—and yet, I've missed you every day. I don't follow the news in your...profession, but I hoarded what information I could glean about you. You've done well. And you've remained what you were ten years ago—a lovely, honorable, admirable woman."

Cait covered her face with her hands and stood without moving for a long moment. When she lifted her face, Ben could see the tears on her cheeks.

"We're very much alike," she said. "Maybe that's why the explosion was so—so violent. I've spent a lot of time being mad at you. For a decade I've refused to make the first move, though I was the one who hid those papers, the one whose deception betrayed your trust. But..."

Cait took a step toward the man facing her. "But just these last two months, I've learned—remembered, maybe—about love. About forgiveness and tolerance and sacrifice. About families and friends and people who look out for each other. There's a lot of that kind of caring here in Goodwill." Her shoulders lifted on a deep breath, and she crossed the remaining distance between herself and her dad. "This Christmas Eve feels like the right time to put those lessons into practice. I'm sorry, too, Dad. Could we start over?"

"Caitlyn," he said, in a strangled voice. And then, awkwardly, he drew her into a hug.

Ben went back into the house. Cait hadn't needed him after all. Was that the problem with their relationship?

Or the answer?

GRADUALLY the crowd thinned, the rooms emptied. By nine o'clock, only the Shepherds, the Tremaines and the Gregorys were left behind, sharing eggnog and cookies with their hosts.

David came into the living room. "I called the hospital." He spoke to Anna directly, but the others stopped talking to hear what he said. "Christopher's doing fine. No breathing troubles since they took out the tube this morning."

Anna's smile was bright. "I think he's turned a corner," she told Cait.

"That's fantastic." Cait gave her sister a hug. "I bet you get to bring him home by the New Year."

"Oh, I hope so. Dad, can you stay that long? It would be wonderful to have both of you here at the same time."

"Both—" Cait stopped before she could make a mistake. Anna didn't mean *her,* because she knew Cait would be flying out late on Christmas afternoon. "The two of you" had to mean Christopher and his granddad.

"I believe I can," Allan Gregory said. "I want as much time with that little boy as possible." He smiled at Anna. "Not to mention my daughters."

Why did everyone here seem to be confused about what

was happening? *Or,* Cait thought, *am I the one who's confused?*

Harry got to his feet. "Speaking of time, I think we'd better let you folks get some rest. I know a jolly old elf who can't make his stops in Goodwill until all the children are asleep."

"Santa Claus!" Maddie scrambled to her feet. "We have to put out cookies for Santa."

Cait stood when the others did, but stayed a little separate from the general bustle for coats. Her dad, she'd discovered, had been staying with Harry and Peggy since he arrived yesterday afternoon. Tomorrow, of course, he could move into the guest room of Anna's house.

Which meant that this was the end of her sojourn in Goodwill. There wouldn't be a reason to see Maddie and Shep...and Ben...again after tonight. Somehow she had to get through goodbye.

She looked down as Maddie pulled on her sleeve. "Can you button my coat, Miss Caitlyn?"

"Sure thing." She knelt to meet Maddie face-to-face. "I hope Santa brings just what you've wished for tonight."

"You can come tomorrow morning and see, can't you? We get up pretty early, and Daddy makes cinnamon rolls for breakfast and we build a fire and open our presents and play with stuff. You should be there, too."

Shep joined them in the middle of the living room. "Please," he said softly. "Please come."

Cait felt something shatter inside her chest. "I... um...I'll be having Christmas here with my family tomorrow morning."

"So come later," Maddie suggested, and her brother nodded. "Then you can go with us to Grandma's and Grandpa's house for Christmas dinner."

She had hoped to get by without making this explanation. But maybe that wasn't fair. Maybe Maddie and Shep should be reminded that she'd always intended to leave at Christmas. "Well...see, Maddie, I'm flying out to California tomorrow afternoon. I have to get back to work. Remember?"

"But you can come over first. And then you can come back when you finish your work."

"That's not—"

Big, capable hands closed around her upper arms and literally lifted Cait to her feet. "We need to talk," Ben said, when she turned to stare at him. The intensity of his gaze made refusing, or even protesting, impossible.

"I have an idea." Peggy came over and put her arms around the children. "Why don't Granddad and I take you two home? We'll help set out Santa's snack and get you ready for bed and read stories and everything. Your dad can come along in a few minutes and kiss you good-night before you fall asleep. What do you think?"

Maddie and Shep looked at their grandmother, and their dad and Cait. Then they looked at each other, and some unspoken message passed between them. "Okay," Shep said. "We can do that."

In just a few minutes, the Shepherds were driving away from the house, with Maddie and Shep in their car. Anna looked at David, who was picking up used cups and paper plates and napkins. "Let's leave the cleanup until tomorrow," she said.

"Won't take but a few minutes." He bent for another stack of plates.

Cait saw her sister roll her eyes. "I'm tired, David. Let's go to bed. *Now.*"

At the emphasis in her voice, he looked up. "Oh. Okay. I'll just..." Anna's meaningful glance finally conveyed the message. "…I'll just leave these right here." He set the plates and cups back on the coffee table and quickly followed his wife out of the room.

"Merry Christmas," Anna called over her shoulder. And then the bedroom door shut with a firm thud.

Cait gathered together the trash David had abandoned. "You sure know how to clear a room," she told Ben, and headed for the kitchen.

He followed with a stack of empty serving plates. "It's all that Secret Service training."

"I bet." They worked without talking to tidy the house for Christmas morning.

Then Ben went to the closet, grabbed her coat and his own. "Let's go outside."

Her fingers were a little unsteady, but Cait got her buttons done and followed him onto the porch. The light snow that had graced the procession was now a steady, heavy fall, covering grass, sidewalk, driveway and street. Goodwill would have a glorious white Christmas.

"Maddie will be thrilled when she wakes up to the snow." Cait leaned her shoulder against a column by the steps. "I think she must be personally responsible. Powerful wishes, your daughter makes."

"I hope so," Ben said cryptically. He leaned back against the other column, watching her. "I heard your talk with your dad."

She sighed. "I know—I saw you. Thanks. I was glad to have the backup."

"You said you'd learned some things since you'd been in Goodwill."

"More than I could have imagined."

"Enough to make staying a possibility?" When she turned to protest, he stopped her with a raised hand. "I know. There's no way it'll be perfect. You've got ambition and drive, a need to succeed, which will take you away more than I'll like. I'll complain and you'll get mad and we'll argue. And then we'll make up and we'll figure out how to compromise and move on."

He reached out and took her hand between both of his. "Please, Cait. I won't always be a model husband, won't always understand and accept your other commitments. But I'll always, always love you. And I know that my kids and I will miss something infinitely precious if we lose the chance to share your life. Wherever it leads."

The world became a blur of white. Cait squeezed her eyes shut. "Ben…I'm so afraid…I don't want to hurt you, or Maddie or Shep."

"Then say yes. Marry us. Marry *me* and take me on this wild ride you call your life." When she opened her eyes, he stood right in front of her. "We've seen so many miracles these last few days. Make one more. With me."

She framed his face with her palms. "We're fast losing our grinch qualifications here."

"So we'll apply for elf credentials."

Cait laughed at him. "I love you."

Ben grinned back. "I'll remember that when you're being the temperamental diva." His arms came around her hard and tight. "And when you're not," he whispered over her lips.

Then he claimed the first in a long and merry lifetime of Christmas kisses.

EPILOGUE

Three years later

"C'MON, C'MON!" Shouting at the top of his lungs, Shep ran from the foot of the stairs into the den and back again. "The commercial's almost over and the show's going to start."

In their bedroom, Cait pulled a little way out of her husband's close hold. "Our son is making a lot of noise down there."

Ben grinned. "Isn't it great? I guess we'd better join the audience for this major production. But later..." He glanced at the king-size bed, piled high with jewel-toned silk pillows on a gold spread.

She reached up for one more kiss. "After these last six weeks away from home, I'm on your wavelength, Mr. Tremaine. Believe me."

On the way down the hall, Cait tapped on Maddie's closed door. "The program's starting. Tell Kevin you'll call him back later."

"Yes, ma'am." The tone of voice held all of a thirteen-year-old's dismay at being forced to follow an agenda other than her own.

When Cait reached the den, Anna and David were already curled into the corner of one couch, watching as Shep and redheaded Christopher fought a fierce air battle with toy planes. An empty baby carrier sat next to them—sweet Lisa was sleeping soundly on her mother's shoulder. Full-term at birth and now three months old, Lisa seemed determined to spare her parents the least twinge of worry. She slept through the night, smiled when she was awake and loved to watch her big brother make silly faces.

Cait only hoped her own baby would be half as easy.

"Here it is. Shhh!" Shep quieted them all down just as Cait sat next to Ben, with Maddie on his other side.

The picture blurred for an instant, then sharpened again on the branch of a Christmas tree. Widening the angle, the camera took in the entire tree, a crackling fire, and then the whole room, keeping the frame centered on a family of four gathered near the hearth.

"I look like a beach ball," Cait moaned, hiding her face against Ben's shoulder. "Why didn't somebody stop me from wearing that red-and-green sweater?" On television, the chords of her guitar introduced Maddie singing "I'll Be Home for Christmas."

"A Family Christmas," the announcer informed them. "This special holiday program featuring Cait Gregory and her family is brought to you by..."

"That was lovely," Anna concluded an hour later, when the four Tremaines singing together had closed the show with "The Angel Song."

"Not bad," Cait decided. "Except for that fat woman who kept hogging the camera. Somebody should have tied her up offstage."

"You are not fat," Ben said, helping her off the low couch. "You were seven months pregnant then and you're eight and a half now and you're beautiful all the time."

"And you're just a little biased." She smiled and kissed his cheek. "I love it."

Once the Remingtons had left for home, Maddie and Shep went back inside the house, leaving Ben and Cait sitting in the swing on the front porch, enjoying the warm night.

Cait turned sideways to put her feet up on the seat and leaned back against Ben's chest. He wrapped his arms securely around her and their baby.

"No more tours for a whole year." She sighed with contentment. "No plane flights. No fast food." Tilting her chin, she pressed a kiss to his throat. "No waking up in the middle of the night in an empty bed."

"Mmm." Ben eased her back even further, took them both into a mind-stealing kiss. "That's the best part. Will Russell survive?"

"He's got a new 'sensation' to promote. A twenty-year-old he thinks will be the next Celine Dion. Or Cher. He's happy for me just to record two albums in the next eighteen months—good money with lots less work for everybody involved. Except me, of course, since I have to write the songs."

Dismissing her agent with a snort, Ben turned to a more important issue. "What do you want to do for our third anniversary?" They'd gotten married on January 2 to be sure they started off every new year together.

Cait smiled with her eyes closed. "Sleep. Make love with you. Sleep some more. I need to be here, with you. With Maddie and Shep, and Anna and David and Christopher and Lisa and Harry and Peggy and Dad…all the people who care about me."

She sat up with a groan and curled over her stomach as far as she could, putting one foot on the porch floor. "And I need you to rub my back when it aches. Down low. Ah, that's it. You're wonderful."

"It's my pleasure." They sat awhile longer on the

swing while he massaged her muscles and her spine. Then Cait got chilled, and Ben took her up to bed…where they realized pretty quickly that this was no ordinary backache. Somewhere around dawn, they woke the kids and dropped them off at the Shepherds' house, then headed for the hospital in Winchester.

And around 6:00 p.m. that Christmas Eve, another baby was born—a beautiful, healthy little girl with red hair and a lusty voice.

Ben eased Noel Anna Tremaine into her mother's arms. "Here you go. Merry Christmas, Mom."

Cait gave him a smile brilliant with happiness, then gazed at her daughter, reaching to trace one fingertip along the path of a tiny vein under the soft pale skin of her temple.

"Merry Christmas to *you*, darlin'. And peace on Earth, goodwill to us all!"

The Christmas Wife

by

Sherry Lewis

For Gene and Vanda Lewis,
the best parents any woman could ask for.

CHAPTER ONE

"HAS ANYBODY SEEN a blue sock?" Beau Julander straightened from the basket filled with clean, unfolded clothes and closed the dryer with his hip. "Anybody?"

Late-autumn sunlight streamed into the renovated kitchen of the old farmhouse he'd inherited from his grandparents, spotlighting last night's dishes stacked by the sink, still waiting to be washed. Leaves from the huge oak trees in the yard fluttered past the window, and the autumn colors on the foothills surrounding Serenity gleamed in the warm Wyoming sunlight.

Beau kicked at the mound of unwashed laundry at his feet and turned toward the table where his twelve-year-old daughter scowled at the pages of an open notebook. "Brianne? Did you hear me?" It was an unnecessary question since he was standing less than ten feet away, but she'd been giving him the silent treatment for days, and he was growing tired of it.

Brianne slowly turned a page in her notebook and rolled her eyes toward the ceiling, where footsteps thundered overhead. Eight-year-old Nicky must still be searching for the missing math worksheet Beau had sent him to find. Brianne let out a sigh weighted with preteen attitude and big-sister irritation, brushed a lock of wheat-blond hair from her forehead and looked back at her father. "When Gram was taking care of us, we always knew where our socks were." One eyebrow arched meaningfully. "That's because they were always clean."

Beau congratulated himself on getting a few words out of her and pretended not to notice the challenge underlying them. Before her mother left, Brianne had chattered at him endlessly, sharing news of her day, talking about her hopes, dreams, joys and disappointments. She'd changed since the divorce, and things had taken another turn for the worse two weeks ago. Now if she wasn't ignoring him, she was starting an argument.

He'd been struggling to hold things together for the past year, after Heather walked out on him. But he'd been sinking fast since the night two weeks ago when he'd decided it was time to do the job on his own. All he wanted was for life to get back to normal. For Brianne to greet him with a smile once in a while. To get through just one morning without an argument.

"These clothes are clean," he pointed out. "At least some of them are. And if each day would just come with three or four more hours attached, they'd be folded and put away, too."

Brianne's only answer was an annoyed sniff, but he supposed that was better than nothing.

Beau was due at the airstrip in less than an hour to begin a charter flight that would keep him in the air most of the day. He'd be home in time for supper and a last-minute meeting of the Homecoming committee, but he didn't have time to spare, and he wasn't in the mood to explain—again—why things had to change.

He bent over the basket and dug until he found two boy-size socks that were similar, if not exact matches. Tossing them on top of the washer, he turned back to the eggs he'd left cooking.

His daughter slid a pointed glance at the stove. "Gram never burned the eggs, either."

"Gram is a better cook than I am," he said as he reached into the cupboard for plates. He flipped the mass of eggs, which had started out as fried and ended up scrambled, and turned off the burner. "But I can learn."

"That's doubtful."

Struggling to hang on to his patience, Beau put the plates on the counter and opened the drawer for the silverware. "Get used to it, Brie. Gram isn't going to be taking care of you anymore."

"Well, she should."

"I know you think so."

Brianne turned a page and shoved a stack of Homecoming flyers out of her way. "You're just being mean."

"No, I'm being practical. Your grandmother was a great help after your mom left. But *I'm* taking care of us now. We have to expect that a few things will be different."

"I don't want things to be different."

"I realize that, too." Beau pulled juice from the refrigerator, found three clean glasses in the dish drainer and carried everything to the table.

"Gram never left dirty dishes around, either," Brianne pointed out needlessly. She brushed a piece of lint from her pink sweater and tossed her hair over her shoulder.

Beau put a glass in front of her and filled it with juice. "Gram's had more experience taking care of a house and kids than I have. I just need to get organized, that's all. Once Homecoming Week is over, I'll have more time."

"You won't have more time," Brianne said sullenly. "As soon as Homecoming's over, you'll start getting ready for WinterFest, and then Christmas."

"Not immediately."

"Almost."

"I might not help with either of them this year."

"Yes, you will, because if you don't, you'll just worry about where they put the banners and whether those wire-deer decorations on Front Street are lit right." She reached for a napkin and wiped her mouth with it. "You *like* doing all that stuff. Mom said so."

He'd heard that accusation more than once. Coming from Heather, it had always made him feel slightly guilty—as if volunteering to help his community was something to be ashamed of. It didn't sound much better coming from Brianne.

"Serenity's a small town," he reminded her. "Without volunteer help, there would be very few things going on around here. But you're not the only one who has to make changes."

Brianne's face twisted in disbelief. "Bet you'll do Christmas. You always do."

"Bet I won't. I already told the mayor to find someone else. And he will." He'd better, anyway. Mayor Biggs hadn't sounded convinced that Beau intended to step down. "I've told him I'm staying just until I can get a replacement up to speed."

A skeptical roll of the eyes met that promise. "I still don't see why Gram can't come back and take care of us. That way you could do stuff like Homecoming and Christmas and you wouldn't have to worry. We wouldn't get in your way, and Nicky wouldn't be so sad anymore."

"You don't get in my way," Beau said evenly, "and

Nicky doesn't seem all that sad to me. And has it ever occurred to you that Gram might have other things to do?''

"Like what?"

He leaned against the counter and crossed one foot over the other. "Okay, fine. Gram would have kept coming over here every day for the rest of her life if I'd let her, but that wouldn't be fair to her."

"Why not? She likes doing it."

"I know she does, but taking care of us is *my* job, not hers. Gram's already raised her family—"

"*We're* her family. She says so all the time."

"Well, of course we're her family." At least, the kids were. Beau shifted uncomfortably and tried to find a way to explain the subtle nuances that seemed to be lost on his daughter. Now that the initial shock of Heather's decision had worn off and the divorce had become final in July, it felt more and more wrong to give his ex-wife's mother free rein over his house.

It wasn't that he didn't appreciate Doris's help. What he didn't appreciate was the way she watched and judged every move he made, her belief that Heather would "come to her senses" one day and return to Serenity, and her repeated insistence that Beau should be waiting for that day with open arms. He didn't like thinking that Doris was filling the kids' heads with unrealistic expectations about their mother, either. But how to explain that to a child who didn't really understand why her mother left?

"Gram's been great to help us," he admitted, "and you know how much I appreciate what she's done. But I'm starting to feel like I'm not doing my job."

"That's dumb."

Beau sat at the table and filled the other two glasses

with juice. "That from the girl who keeps pointing out everything I don't get done?"

"You're no good at housework, Daddy. That's why Gram has to come back."

Her lack of faith stung, but the "Daddy" took some of the sting away. Beau went after the plates and decided to skip that second cup of coffee. "I'm not saying you can't see Gram, sweetie. You and Nicky can visit her anytime you want."

"Anytime?"

"Within reason. You can't just disappear without asking me, though, and you should make sure Gram's home first. But if you want to stop by after school once in a while, I won't say no."

Brianne kicked the back of her chair rhythmically. "That's not the same as having her here."

"No, it's not. But that's how it has to be." Beau checked his watch and groaned. Once, he'd been a stickler about punctuality. These days, it seemed he was always late. "How about running upstairs to see what's keeping your brother? The school bus will be here in ten minutes."

"I don't think it's fair that *I* have to baby-sit because *you* don't want Gram here."

"That's enough, Brianne. I'm not asking you to baby-sit. I'm asking you to contribute to the family. Now go."

She let out another sigh, rose majestically to her feet and disappeared with one last toss of her hair. Beau spooned cold eggs onto plates with a grimace and made a silent bet with himself about how much the kids would choke down before they ran out the door. He knew exactly how much *he'd* eat.

Brianne was right about one thing, he thought with

a frown. Housework wasn't his strong suit. But that was going to change. He just needed time. A chance to focus. Then the piles of laundry would disappear and the dirty dishes would vanish. His relationship with Brianne would get back to normal, and he'd prove, once and for all, that he was more than capable of raising the kids on his own.

TWENTY MINUTES LATER, Beau stood in his cluttered study and tried to remember where he'd left his car keys. The kids had made it to the school bus on time, but he'd be late if he didn't walk out the door in two minutes. He dug through a stack of old mail, patted the bank statement beside his computer monitor and swore softly under his breath.

He had to get more organized. That was all there was to it.

He'd just lifted a pile of mail that still needed sorting when the telephone rang. He thought about ignoring it, but one glance at the caller ID changed his mind. He snagged the receiver from its cradle. "Gwen? What's wrong?"

"Well, that's a nice greeting," his sister returned. At thirty-one, Gwen was two years his junior, solid and dependable and, lucky for him, willing to take up the slack while he adjusted to the world without his mother-in-law underfoot. "What are you doing home? I've been trying to reach you at the office."

With a frown, Beau cradled the phone against his shoulder. "I have a better question. Why are you calling me?"

"Why shouldn't I?"

"I may be paranoid," he said, "but a call at this hour of the morning isn't a good sign—especially on a day when you've promised to pick up the kids after school.''

Her indrawn breath and soft sigh as she let it out again confirmed his suspicions. Her response cinched it. "Don't kill me, okay?"

"Gwen—"

"It's Riley's mother's birthday. We're supposed to take her to Star Valley to visit her sister. I forgot all about it until five minutes ago."

Beau tossed the mail back onto the desk. "You don't have to pick up the kids until three-thirty."

"We won't be back that early. We're taking Riley's brother and his family with us, and they have the whole day planned. I'm really sorry, but we'll be gone until late."

Beau stared out the window but he barely saw the autumn foliage on the hillside in front of him. "You're leaving me in the lurch because of a birthday party?"

"I have to. We're committed."

"You're committed to me, too, Gwen. What am I supposed to do now? I'll be in Jackson when the kids get out of school."

"I know, but can't they take the bus home just this once?"

"They take the bus home every day, but tonight Brianne has karate and Nicky has soccer practice." Beau turned away from the window and rubbed the back of his neck. "I can't believe you're doing this. I have to take off in just a couple of minutes. People are waiting for me in Grant's Pass—"

"I know, and I'm really, really sorry. Riley feels horrible, too. Usually one of us remembers things like this, but somehow we both spaced it this time."

Beau checked his watch and swore again. "Fine. Whatever. I'll call Mom and see if she can help."

"Don't bother," Gwen said quickly. "I've already called. Lucas says she left for King's Junction half an hour ago."

With a growl of frustration, Beau shoved aside a bunch of magazines and finally spied his keys beneath a picture Nicky had brought home from school the previous afternoon. He stuffed the keys into his pocket so he wouldn't lose them again and carried the cordless phone with him into the kitchen, where the scent of overcooked eggs still hung in the air. "Did you ask Lucas what he's doing?" Their younger brother wasn't nearly as responsible as Gwen, but he'd do all right for a few hours.

"He's scheduled to work until seven."

A tension headache began to pound behind Beau's eyes. He ran quickly through a list of friends close enough to ask a favor on such short notice, but he couldn't think of anyone who'd be home at that hour. "This is one helluva time to leave me hanging," he snarled. "I can't afford to ask another pilot to fly this trip. Property taxes are due in two months, and canceling at the last minute would shoot holes in my reputation."

"Well, of course you can't cancel. I know that. But I can't cancel on Riley's family, either." Gwen's voice trailed away thoughtfully, then brightened again. "How about Doris? I'm sure she'd be glad to watch the kids."

Beau laughed harshly. "I don't think so. She's still upset with me."

"But she's their grandmother."

"A grandmother who's convinced I'm going to fail

with the kids and who's just waiting for me to prove her right."

"This isn't failure," Gwen said reasonably. "This is a scheduling conflict. Besides, you shouldn't let her bother you."

"We're talking about Doris Preston, right? My mother-in-law? The woman who can turn stone to dust with just a glance?"

Gwen laughed. "I'll admit she's a little obsessive, but she's not that bad. Her feelings are hurt, but she'll get over it. Besides, if she knows that you really aren't going to keep the kids away from her, maybe it'll help heal the rift between you."

"I doubt it." Beau tugged open the fridge and pulled out two cans of cola, two apples and a plastic sandwich bag filled with grapes. "I saw her at the gas station yesterday," he said as he stuffed the snacks into his knapsack. "She pretended I didn't exist. She'd like nothing better than to have me begging for help today."

"Oh, please. You're a good father. You were a great husband. Heather's the one who decided she wanted a different life, and Doris feels responsible for some reason. You'll get used to caring for the kids on your own. You just need time."

Beau smiled ruefully. "Thanks, sis. Some days I need a cheerleader."

"Whatever you say. Just be realistic, okay? What other choice do you have?"

Although he tried like hell to think of another solution, Gwen was right. Doris *was* his only option. "Go," he said as he checked to make sure he'd turned off the stove. "Eat cake. Open presents. Have a great time. I'll call Doris and grovel."

"Don't grovel. Just ask."

"Right. I'll ask." He disconnected a few seconds later, but even with the minutes racing past, he couldn't make himself pick up the phone again. He didn't think Doris would turn him down, but asking a favor of her so soon sure felt like he was losing ground.

Beau had never learned how to admit defeat easily— not on the football field in high school, not in his marriage, not in any aspect of his life. Only the balance in his checking account got him to dial Doris's phone number. Only the certain knowledge that Doris adored the kids, and the hope that a visit with her might even soften Brianne's mood, kept him from hanging up when she answered.

"Hey, Doris. It's Beau. Am I catching you at a bad time?"

He sensed a slight tensing on the other end, but that might have been his imagination. "Well, Beau. This is a surprise. What do you need?"

Nope. Not his imagination at all. He kept a smile on his face and hoped it would carry through to his voice. Anything to take the chill off Doris's tone. "I'm in a bind," he forced himself to admit. "I'm calling to ask a favor. If you don't want to or if you have other plans, just say so. I'll understand complete—"

"You need help with the children?"

"Just for this afternoon. I have a charter. Gwen was going to pick them up for me, but she forgot a family obligation."

"And you need *me*."

If the warm sun hadn't been streaming through the dirt on his window, he'd have sworn he'd stepped into one of Wyoming's famous January freezes. "It would help a lot if you could get the kids from school. Brianne has karate and Nicky has soccer—''

''I remember their schedules. It hasn't been that long.''

''Of course you do.'' Beau concentrated on keeping his tone even. ''If you don't mind, I'll pick them up from your house about five.''

''You don't want me to take them to your house?''

And see everything he hadn't done? Not a chance. ''No. Thanks. I don't want to impose, and I'm sure you already have plans around home.'' He kept talking so she couldn't disagree with him. ''I won't be late. You don't even have to worry about giving them supper. I'll be home in plenty of time for that.'' Even if it was just fast food from the Burger Shack.

''I see.''

She sounded so much like Heather, Beau closed his eyes and reminded himself why he was calling Doris in the first place. ''I know it's a lot to ask, but it would really help me out.''

''It's not a lot to ask,'' Doris said firmly. ''That's the whole point. I'm glad to do whatever those children need—and heaven knows, they need plenty. It just seems wrong to me, having to schedule time to spend with them. I don't understand why you're being so stubborn when it's obvious you can't handle them on your own.''

''I *can* handle them. I'm just in a bind this afternoon, that's all.'' He could feel his irritation rising, so he took a couple of deep breaths and watched the neighbors across the street drive away to start their day. ''I need a favor,'' he said when he could trust himself to speak, ''but I'm not going to argue with you. It's time for me to get back on my feet, but that doesn't mean you and the kids can't spend time together. It's not as if I'm trying to separate you from them."

"Well, it sure feels like it." She sighed heavily and he could almost see the scowl on her face. "Is it all right if I give them an after-school snack?"

When had that ever been an issue? She really was trying to make this difficult. Beau closed his eyes and rubbed his forehead. "You can give them an afternoon snack," he said. "You can let them watch TV if they don't have schoolwork, just like always. I'll be home by five." And then, because he didn't have the patience or the energy for more, he added, "Thanks a lot, Doris. If you need to reach me, I'll have my cell phone on when it won't interfere with the instruments. If I don't answer, leave a message and I'll get right back to you."

Before she could argue, he disconnected, letting out a groan that would have frightened small children and animals if there'd been any around. He really had to get his life under control.

He knew he could do it. Like training for football season or learning how to fly. He'd keep distractions to a minimum and focus on the goal. It had worked for him before. He'd just have to make it work again.

MOLLY SHEPHERD absently tapped her fingernails on the rental-car counter at the Jackson airport while she waited for the clerk to locate her reservation on the computer. She was just two hours away now. One hundred and twenty minutes, give or take a few, before she drove into Serenity for the first time since her mother's death. Yet again, she wondered if coming back was a mistake. But after spending most of the day on an airplane, and a significant chunk of money to get here, it was a little late to be having second thoughts.

A soothing feminine voice paged passengers over the public-address system. Soft music underscored the noise of the crowd and should have calmed the nervous energy Molly felt, but every sound only added to the tension in her neck and shoulders.

The card announcing Serenity's Homecoming Week Gala had reached her mailbox at a vulnerable time. One year after her divorce from Ethan, six months after her father's funeral, one month after being downsized out of the job she'd held for five years with a graphic-design firm. For weeks she'd been at loose ends, searching for some way to tie those ends together again. When the invitation arrived, she'd jumped first and saved questions for later.

The man behind her bumped into the trolley holding her luggage. She wheeled it out of his way and glanced out the window at the towering Teton Mountains that created the valley known as Jackson Hole. The rugged peaks already wore a cap of snow, though it was only the first of October. It wasn't that she hadn't wanted to come back to Wyoming before now, just that there had never been a real opportunity. Her father hadn't wanted to return, and Ethan had never been interested in her past. Neither of the men in her life had understood how much the missing pieces of her memory bothered her.

The young man behind the counter clicked his fingers over the keyboard and glanced at her. "We're out of compacts. Midsize okay with you? It'll be the same price."

"Midsize is fine." She forced a smile and tried to shake off her uncertainty. So what if it had been fifteen years since she'd seen or heard from any of her old school friends? So what if she couldn't remember most of her senior year? There were things and people she *could* remember. Most important, she had a chance to find answers to questions that had been haunting her for years.

"Do you want insurance?"

"No," she said, making a conscious effort to stop worrying. "Thank you."

"Are you sure?" A concerned smile quivered across the young man's lips. "You're taking quite a risk. You want to make sure you're fully covered."

Driving without extra insurance felt like a minor risk compared with the others she was taking. "I'm quite sure. Thank you."

"Will there be any other drivers besides yourself?"

"No."

"And you want unlimited mileage?"

"Yes, please." Maybe she'd do some sightseeing while she was here. The butterflies in her stomach made another round, and her hands felt clammy. She silently chanted the mantra she'd been reciting all day. It didn't matter if none of her classmates remembered her. It didn't even matter if she spent the entire Homecoming Week alone. She had to take advantage of this opportunity, or she'd regret it the rest of her life.

"You want the car for how long?" the young man asked without looking away from his screen.

"Two weeks, maybe less. I don't know for sure."

"You don't want the weekly rate?"

He seemed confused, but she didn't want to elaborate. "The weekly rate is fine," she said firmly. "I'll bring it back on the seventeenth."

"Of October."

"Yes."

"You're sure? I can recalculate using the daily rate if you need me to."

The man behind Molly groaned in protest at the delay and she felt a prickle of nervousness. She hated imposing, even on a stranger. "I'm quite sure. Two weeks is perfect. No early return."

The man behind the counter typed a bit more, and Molly turned to glance at the crowd. She became aware of a deep male voice edged with tension coming from the corridor behind her. A heartbeat later, she identified the speaker as a tall blond man wearing jeans and a sage-colored shirt. He maneuvered through the passengers crowding the baggage-claim turnstiles as he set a steady course toward the car-rental area.

"Excuse me." He turned sideways to sidle past a young mother with three children and came up short behind a hefty woman weighted down by several bulging bags. Annoyance pinched his face, and it was easy to see that he was having to work to hang on to his patience. "I'm sorry, ma'am. Would you mind…?"

Molly started to turn away, but something compelled her to look back at him across the crowded area. Maybe she was imagining things, but the voice, the face, even the way he moved seemed hauntingly familiar.

Did she really know him, or was she just jumping to that conclusion now that she was back in Wyoming?

"Okay. I think we're set." The clerk tapped the counter to get her attention. "Here are your keys, and here's your contract. You'll need to keep the contract in your glove box at all times…"

Nodding absently, Molly took another look at the man who towered over most of the people around him. Broad shoulders, narrow hips. The muscular legs of an athlete. He put his hands on an elderly woman's shoulders as he slipped behind her, then pivoted toward the rental counter.

Molly's gaze flew to his face again and the niggling feeling that she knew him took form. This time she was certain it wasn't her imagination. In fact, she couldn't decide why she'd even wondered. His was a face she'd never forgotten, not even for a second.

Beau Julander. High-school jock, senior-class president, every teacher's favorite student, every girl's dream. He was hands down the hottest guy Molly had ever seen in her life—and that list included Ethan when she'd been in love with him.

Her heart raced and her stomach knotted uncomfortably. Fifteen years dropped away as if they'd never been, and she felt young and foolish and hopelessly self-conscious, just like the last time she remembered being in Serenity.

She whirled back toward the clerk and pretended to pay attention to his final instructions as Beau came to a stop at the end of the line. When she tried to swallow, her throat was parched and her mouth dry. She resisted the urge to look back at him and nodded in all the right places as the clerk talked. But even without turning around, Molly was all too aware of Beau.

Time had been good to him. No surprise there. He'd always led a charmed life. He was still tall and solidly muscled, still better-looking than any man had a right to be. She touched one hand to her cheek, then realized how silly she was acting and gave herself a stern mental shake.

So he was Beau Julander. So what? He probably wouldn't even remember her.

She stole one last peek at him. Yes, of course, she'd expected to see him at Homecoming. Homecoming probably couldn't take place without Beau Julander there. But she hadn't expected to see him so soon. Not when she looked as if she'd been sleeping in her clothes. Not when her breath reeked of garlic from lunch on the airplane.

And most important, not alone.

CHAPTER TWO

TRYING DESPERATELY to pull herself together, Molly tucked her credit card into her pocket and turned slowly toward the end of the line. She glanced at the wrinkled linen pantsuit she'd been wearing since early morning, and the blouse that bore faint traces of spilled coffee from her early flight.

"Is there anything else, Ms. Shepherd?"

Molly shook her head at the clerk, apologized to the annoyed man whose path she was blocking and stepped away from the counter. Clutching her purse like a security blanket, she was aware of Beau shifting his weight impatiently from one foot to the other.

Hands propped on his hips, he scowled at the world for having the nerve to keep him waiting. He'd always been Serenity's golden boy, so Molly shouldn't be surprised to discover that he'd grown into the kind of man who thought the world should stand still for him.

She lifted her chin and started back down the long line, dragging her luggage behind her on the rented cart, which suddenly developed steering problems and a hideous squeak in one wheel. But all the determination in the world couldn't keep her from seeking him out once more as she passed.

Like everyone else in line, he was watching her struggle with the cart, but as his gaze settled on her face, recognition flickered in his eyes. Certain her heart had stopped beating, Molly looked away and willed herself not to trip or do anything else clumsy and embarrassing.

"Excuse me." His voice sounded startlingly close to her ear and a hand landed on her shoulder.

She jumped and whipped around quickly. If she'd been wearing heels, she would have twisted an ankle. In flats she teetered just a little and did her best to hide her nervousness. "Yes?"

"Don't I know you?"

Molly's heart thumped against her rib cage, but she managed, somehow, to sound almost normal when she responded. "I don't know. Do you?" Okay. It was a lie. But she was not going to make him think she'd been dewy-eyed over him all this time. Bad enough that he'd once suspected how she felt.

"Yeah. I *do* know you. Aren't you...didn't you go to Serenity High School?"

"Yes, I did." She almost left it at that, but she was thirty-three, not sixteen, so she smiled and held out a hand. "Molly Shepherd. I was Molly Lane back then. But I'm sure you don't—"

"From Mr. Kagle's ceramics class, right?" He took her hand and his lips curved into the grin that had nearly cost Molly a passing grade in Mr. Kagle's class. "Beau Julander."

Molly nearly laughed at the idea of Beau introducing himself, but the feel of his hand around hers froze the sound in her throat. His eyes were still the most incredible shade of blue she'd ever seen. "Beau. Of course." Her voice sounded tight and high, but she prayed he wouldn't notice. "I remember you."

He let go of her and nodded toward the cart she was

clinging to with her other hand. "You're here for a visit?"

As she loosened her death grip on the cart, Molly willed her heart to regulate its rhythm. "I came for Homecoming Week. I got an invitation...in the mail."

He grinned again. "Great. We dug around for a while, but we weren't sure we'd actually found you." His eyes narrowed. "You do know that Homecoming's still a week away?"

"I came early so I could take care of a few things."

"Terrific. So are you headed to Serenity now?"

"I am." She dangled the keys from one finger. "I was just renting a car...obviously."

Beau glanced impatiently toward the front of the line. "Yeah, me, too."

"Oh. Does that mean you don't live in Serenity any longer?"

"I'm still there. I live in my grandparents' old house now, but you probably don't remember it."

Not remember? When she'd spent countless afternoons strolling aimlessly beside the creek and along the dirt road hoping to "accidentally" run into him? She nodded without looking at him. "I think I do, actually. They had that big white farmhouse out on Old Post Road, didn't they?"

"That's the one, but it's not a farm anymore. They sold off most of their land when my dad decided not to go into farming, and Hector Johnson's kids sold his place after he died, so there are houses where many of the fields used to be."

"That's too bad. I remember it being such a pretty place."

"It still is. We're sitting on an acre, so neighbors aren't under our noses."

"And you live there with your grandparents?"

He shook his head. "They both passed away a few years ago. We were there with Grandma for the last six months of her life, but it's just us now. As a matter of fact, I need to get back there in—" he checked his watch "—less than two hours. I should be flying there right now, but I ran into a slight malfunction in the plane and I can't get a mechanic to look at it until tomorrow. My car's back in Serenity, of course, so I'm stuck paying for a way home."

"You have your own airplane?" Of course he did. He was Beau Julander.

"A small one," he said, as if that somehow diminished the accomplishment. "Six seats. Twin-engine." He checked the line's progress once more and returned his attention to her slowly. "I fly charters."

Molly managed a weak smile, praying he wouldn't ask what she did for a living, then reminded herself that she was only temporarily unemployed. "That must be really interesting."

"It is when the airplane works. Not so interesting when the damn thing decides to ruin an already bad day." He shrugged and shifted his weight, then looked at her intently. "You say you're leaving for Serenity now?"

"As soon as I get to the rental car."

"What would you say to taking me with you? I'll split the cost of the car or I'll buy you dinner, whatever you want. I have to pick up my kids by five, and if I stay in this line much longer, I'll never make it."

The question caught her by surprise. "Well, I... The thing is... You have kids?"

"Two."

The line inched forward again and he moved with it, but his gaze implored her to say yes.

Molly couldn't make herself agree yet. Two hours in a car with Beau? *Alone?* She couldn't do it. Of course, children meant that he was probably married. Happily. Because what else would Beau Julander be? But two hours with him? In a car with no one to help with conversation?

She couldn't make herself say yes, but she'd really be mortified if she said no, so she bought herself another minute. "How old are your kids?"

"Brianne's twelve. Nicky's eight."

"And their mother? She's working or something? I mean…well, I mean, she's not home. To pick up the kids. Obviously." Molly let out a jittery laugh and told herself to stop babbling.

"She's not around at all. We're divorced."

"Oh." Molly tried not to look surprised. Or pleased. "I'm sorry." And she was…sort of.

"Don't be. I'm over it, and the kids will be, too, one of these days. As much as kids *can* get over a thing like that. So what do you say? Do you mind if I hitch a ride?"

Molly was barely coherent with people all around them. If they were alone together, she'd probably blather like an idiot. But what kind of person would she be to say no? And what reason could she possibly give if she did? Besides, it wasn't as if she still had a thing for Beau. It was just that seeing him again had caught her off guard. Whatever she'd once felt for him was a thing of the past, and what better way to prove it to herself?

Shaking off the last, lingering bit of childish cowardice, she looked him square in the eye. "Sure. Why not?"

Thirty minutes later, Molly drove out of town and picked up speed on the highway heading south. Though Serenity was less than a hundred miles from Jackson as the crow flew, all but about ten miles of road wound its way through mountains ablaze with autumn color. The brilliant red of oak and sumac, the burnished gold of aspen, the dark green of pine... Molly had forgotten how beautiful it could be.

She watched the passing scenery and willed herself to keep her wits during the drive. As a very young girl, she'd had a tendency to stammer when she was nervous. It had been a long time since she'd worried about that, but now, feeling sixteen again, she wanted to make sure she didn't start acting the part.

Beau leaned forward in the passenger seat and turned on the radio, adjusting the dial until he found an oldies station. When the first strains of "Hey Jude" came through the speakers, he slanted a glance at Molly. "Is this okay with you?"

"Perfect."

He sat back again with a heavy sigh. "I really appreciate this. You have no idea how much."

She shook her head and shifted lanes to pass a slow-moving truck. "It's no big deal. It's not as if I'm going out of my way or anything."

"I suppose not, but I'm still glad we ran into each other. Kind of a bright spot in a bad day." He leaned back in his seat. "So tell me about yourself. Where did we finally find you?"

"St. Louis. I've been there for the past ten years. Before that, I lived with my dad in Urbana, Illinois."

"And what kind of business brings you back to Serenity after all this time?"

The passing lane ended and Molly slowed behind a tractor-trailer. "I told you, Homecoming."

"You also said you had other things to take care of," he reminded her. "Or are they none of my business?"

Molly wasn't sure how to explain the emptiness inside her without sounding maudlin, and that wasn't the impression she wanted to make on Beau. She settled for a partial truth. "While I'm here, I'm hoping to talk to some people who knew my mother. She died near the end of my senior year, and we left town shortly afterward. I guess I need closure, and I'm hoping I'll get that by talking to some of her friends."

Beau nodded. "I remember the night she died. It shook people up pretty badly. But we've had other Homecoming Weeks. Lots of them since we graduated from high school. Why did you wait for this one?"

"The timing was never right before." The truck in front of them turned off the highway and Molly accelerated. "I got divorced last year, my dad died in March, and last month the graphic-design firm where I've been working downsized and I found myself out of a job." She shrugged as if none of those things mattered. "The notice came when I had a little time on my hands, so here I am."

"You've had a rough year," Beau said.

Molly didn't want sympathy. It was hard enough not to cry when she let herself think about her dad. "It hasn't been one of my best," she said, trying to keep her tone light. "But you've obviously hit a few rough patches, too."

"Just a divorce."

"A divorce that left you with two kids to raise."

"Yeah, but they're great kids."

"I'm sure they are. Still, divorce is never easy."

"No." He laughed without humor. "No, it's not."

"So where are your kids?" Molly asked, turning the conversation back to a subject that wasn't quite so difficult. "At some day care that charges you extra when you're late?"

Beau laughed again and shook his head. "I wish that's where they were. No, they're with my mother-in-law. My *ex*-mother-in-law, that is. Doris has been helping out with the kids since Heather left."

Molly flicked a glance at him. "You married Heather Preston?"

"Yep."

Well, that figured. Beau and Heather, a cheerleader, had dated all through high school, so it wasn't a surprise to learn that they'd eventually married. It made her curious about why they'd split up, but not so curious that she'd let herself ask. "That's kind of unusual, isn't it? Your mother-in-law helping, I mean."

"Yes, I guess it is." Beau tapped his fingers on the armrest between them. "Doris has been a big help in a lot of ways, but I'm sure you can imagine how much fun it is to have your ex-wife's mother cooking dinner in your kitchen every night, washing your boxers and making your bed."

An image of Ethan's mother digging around in her underwear drawer flashed through Molly's mind and she shuddered. "I'll take your word for it."

Beau's fingers stopped moving. "Doris is why I can't be late. I'm already on her short list for deciding I can do without her help. My daughter's not too happy with me, either. Brianne doesn't see anything wrong with having her grandma hanging around all the time."

His candor surprised her, but then, Beau had always been open and easy to read. "How old did you say she was?"

"Twelve."

The same age Molly's own child would have been if she hadn't miscarried. But the miscarriage and the news that she'd never conceive again were painful memories she didn't let herself dwell on. "Almost a teenager."

"Don't remind me," Beau groaned. "I'm barely hanging on as it is."

"I'm sure you'll do fine. You're there, and you love her. What more can she ask?"

"You don't know Brianne. She can ask more and she does. It's hard for a girl that age to be without a mother, I guess." He sighed softly. "You haven't mentioned children. Does that mean you don't have any?"

Molly shook her head and pretended that the question didn't bother her. "No, I don't."

"Well, at least you knew up front that you didn't want kids. Not that I regret having mine," he added quickly, "but it would have been nice to know Heather was going to resent the kids *before* they got here."

Molly watched the blur of trees for a few seconds before responding. Maybe she should let him assume what he wanted about her, but that teenage girl who'd been so crazy about him wouldn't let her remain quiet. "I never said I didn't *want* kids," she corrected him after a pause that felt about a year long.

"Oh." Beau looked at her. "I'm sorry. That was a thoughtless thing to say."

"It's okay," Molly assured him. "It used to be a

painful subject, but I've adjusted. I'll probably have to talk about it a hundred times over the next couple of weeks, so don't worry about it." Still, it seemed unfair that Heather had been blessed with two children she didn't want, when Molly couldn't have any.

"Well, if curiosity bothers you, better think twice about going back to Serenity," Beau said. "The town's full of good people, but you don't get to keep many secrets. I think some of my neighbors know more about my divorce than I do."

Molly was counting on it. How else would she learn about her mother? The radio switched to a Lynyrd Skynyrd song she'd loved as a teenager. She guided the car over the crest of a hill and felt herself relaxing. Beau seemed nice. Easy to talk to. A little more grounded than he'd been as a kid—but who wasn't?

"So tell me about Homecoming," she said, changing the subject. "What can I expect?"

"All the best Serenity has to offer," he said drolly. "Parade on Thursday. Football game on Friday. And, of course, the Homecoming Ball on Saturday. We even got special dispensation from the mayor." He paused. "We don't have to roll up the sidewalks at nine like usual."

She laughed, remembering how often she and her friends had complained about Serenity's lack of decent nightlife. "How long do we get? Until ten?"

"Ten-thirty. First time in Serenity's history. Quite scandalous."

She felt another layer of nervousness drop away. "I hope the police have been notified."

"Of course. We can't have folks running amok. Old Sam Harper would probably sue."

Molly had forgotten how funny Beau could be. She

took her eyes off the road just long enough to glance at his face. The familiar tickle of warmth began to curl right on cue. She had to make sure she didn't let all those old feelings get stirred up again. Not such an easy prospect, considering what was happening to her after just minutes in his company. But the past was behind her and the days of mooning over Beau Julander were long gone.

At least she hoped they were.

BEAU WAS CONVINCED he'd ground his teeth to nubs by the time he finally retrieved his car from the airstrip, where Molly had dropped him, and pulled into Doris's driveway a few minutes after six. He checked the clock on the dash and shifted into Park, as if he could turn back time if he concentrated hard enough. He'd been watching the seconds tick past for nearly two hours now, ever since he and Molly had come upon road construction forty miles outside Serenity, but so far he hadn't regained a single minute.

If he hadn't been so uneasy about being late, and so busy rescheduling the meeting by cell phone, he'd have enjoyed the ride more. He remembered Molly, of course. Their graduating class hadn't been large. But she'd been too quiet to catch his eye, and he'd been too focused on Heather to give other girls more than a passing glance.

She'd certainly grown up nicely. Waves of long, dark hair that fell to the middle of her back. Something in her deep-brown eyes that made a guy think she was ready for anything. More than once during the drive he'd found himself wondering how accurate that impression was, but he'd probably never know. One thing he *was* sure of after three hours in her company—still waters run deep.

He climbed out of his car into the already dark evening, shivering a little in the sharp breeze and hoping the weather would hold until Homecoming was over. The living-room curtain fluttered and he knew that Doris was watching him, assessing, drawing conclusions, making judgments.

Vowing to be quick, he started up the walk. He wouldn't let her engage him in a discussion. Wouldn't let himself get into an argument. It would be in and out. *Hello, Doris, thanks a bunch. Come on kids, let's go.* It didn't have to be more complicated than that. But even as he rehearsed his lines, he knew their conversation would be far more involved. Heather had never done anything quick or easy, and that was just one of the lessons she'd learned at her mother's knee.

He climbed the steps and raised his hand to knock, but the door swung open and revealed Doris. She peered at him, a deep frown pursing her lips and knitting her brows. Though she was much shorter than Heather and at least fifty pounds heavier, the similarities were strong.

"We were getting worried," she said, pushing open the screen door to admit him. "It's *way* past five."

Beau stepped inside and the tangy scents of hot potato salad and bratwurst enveloped him. "Didn't you get my messages? I called from my cell phone three times to let you know about the plane and the construction."

"I got messages, yes. It's too bad you didn't build a little extra time into your schedule." She closed the door and glowered up at him. "But then, maybe you got sidetracked. Things like that happen when you're with someone else.''

''Like I said on the phone, I ran into an old friend at the car rental counter. We decided to ride together, that's all.'' He sidled toward the kitchen, where he knew Nicky would be watching television and Brianne would be doing some girl thing. ''Are the kids ready?''

''They've been ready for nearly an hour. It started getting so late, I made enough supper for everyone.''

''That was nice of you,'' Beau said, keeping his smile in place, ''but I told you I'd take care of dinner.''

''Yes, you did. But it's already after six, and by the time you get dinner on the table, it will be too late for them to eat. They need time to digest their food before they go to bed.''

''I'm sure they'll survive if dinner's a little late one night.''

''But will it *be* just one night?'' Doris stopped under the arched doorway into the kitchen and folded her arms tightly across her chest. ''Who is this old friend you spent the day with, anyway?''

Beau would have liked to tell her that it was none of her business, but he'd opened the door on her interference by accepting her help for so long. If closing it again was difficult, he had only himself to blame. ''I didn't spend the *day* with anybody. Only a few hours in the rental car. It's just someone I went to school with who's come back for Homecoming,'' he said, and slipped past her into the well-lit kitchen.

He found the kids exactly where he'd expected them to be. Nicky lay on the braided rug, shoes at his sides, eyes glued to the television. His hair had grown too long, Beau realized, and he'd changed socks since morning. The pair he had on now actually matched.

Brianne sat at the round wood table with her feet on a chair, one eye on the TV while she swiped lazily at her fingernails with a file.

Nicky glanced up when Beau entered. Brianne pretended not to see him.

Beau didn't want his daughter's aloofness to set the tone for the evening, so he pretended a heartiness he didn't feel. "Hey, you two. Sorry I'm late. The magneto went out on the plane, so I had to leave it in Jackson. If that wasn't bad enough, the road was torn up and it took forever to drive home."

Nicky bolted to his feet and his bright blue eyes filled with an emotion Beau couldn't read. Brianne looked up from her nails, and her expression hit Beau like a kick in the gut. He'd seen that look of bored irritation on Heather's face too often over the years, and he didn't like seeing it on his daughter's.

"You're late," she said. "I thought you weren't coming."

"Of course I was coming. I left three messages on Gram's phone telling you what was happening so you wouldn't worry. Now, why don't you two gather your things and we'll get out of Gram's hair?"

"Out of my hair!" Doris sniffed in disapproval and busied herself stacking Nicky's books. "Don't you dare make these children think I don't want them around. It wasn't my idea to change everything. I was perfectly content the way things were."

Beau's neck and shoulders tensed. "I didn't mean it that way," he assured Doris, but he kept his gaze on Brianne. "Do you want me to help you?"

No hint of a smile relieved his daughter's annoyed expression. "Why can't we stay for supper?"

"Because I already told Gram I'd feed you."

"But it's late and I'm hungry."

"So we'll stop at the Burger Shack." He could almost feel Doris bristle as he retrieved Brianne's backpack from the floor. He zipped it open on the table, but managed to keep himself from gathering her books. "Make sure you get everything. No coming back for forgotten homework or hairbrushes."

Brianne's forehead crunched into an exact replica of her mother's and grandmother's when they were ready to lodge a complaint. "Why do we have to go somewhere else to eat? Dinner is ready, and Gram made enough for all of us."

Because Beau didn't *want* bratwurst and hot potato salad. Because he was tired of feeling manipulated. There were a dozen reasons, dammit, but none that Brianne would understand. "Dinner smells great," he said, "but it's been a long day and I'm tired. I think we should just go home."

"All the more reason to stay," Doris said, looking smug. "Especially since you need to talk to Nicky about his math worksheet."

Beau shot a glance at his son. "What about it?"

"He got a ten on it," Brianne announced with obvious relish.

"A ten, huh?" Beau grinned down at his son and ruffled his fair hair. "Good work, kid."

"*Not* good work," Brianne said, shoving her hairbrush into her pack. "Ten out of forty isn't good."

"Ten out of forty?" Beau's smile faded and Nicky's gaze dropped to the toes of his white socks.

"He can do much better than that," Doris put in before Beau could gather his thoughts and decide how to respond. "You should be disappointed."

"I know he can do better." Beau sat on a chair and

tilted Nicky's chin so the boy had to look at him, but Nicky's eyes were so filled with misery Beau didn't have the heart to make him feel worse.

"Kids let their homework slip if they don't have supervision," Doris warned. "It's only natural."

"They have supervision."

"You know what I mean."

"Yes, I do, Doris. It's hard not to understand what you mean—even when I try not to." She didn't seem to realize that the harder she pushed, the more resistant Beau became. He'd always been that way. He stood and picked up Nicky's backpack, struggling to swallow the words that hovered on the tip of his tongue. He and Doris might not see eye to eye, but she was still his children's grandmother.

He put a hand on Nicky's thin shoulder. "Do you need help with your shoes, buddy?"

Nicky shook his head and managed a shaky smile, but the relief in his eyes made Beau's chest squeeze painfully.

"You really shouldn't let a problem like this go," Doris warned.

"I'll handle it," Beau assured her. "Later." He tempered his sharpness with a tight smile, put an arm around Nicky's shoulders and motioned for Brianne to hurry.

Still frowning, the girl slowly zipped up her backpack and slipped the strap over her shoulder. But for once she didn't argue. Maybe she realized that he'd been pushed far enough for one evening.

He ushered the kids toward the front door, then turned back to Doris, who stood at the table, glowering at him. "Thanks again, Doris."

She crossed her arms high on her chest and nodded, but she didn't say a word. She just watched in stony silence while Beau led the kids out the door.

CHAPTER THREE

MOLLY'S HEAD started pounding the instant she opened her eyes the next morning, and the painful hollow in her stomach convinced her that skipping dinner the day before had been a mistake.

She rolled onto her side in the darkened motel room and took a few seconds to acclimate herself. Serenity. The Wagon Wheel Motel. Nothing had changed in all this time. She could have sworn these were the same curtains that had been here when she'd spent a miserable two months one summer cleaning rooms for the motel owners. They still didn't have coffeemakers in the rooms, and the closest restaurant—the *only* restaurant that would be open so early—was two blocks away.

Her stomach growled loudly and she decided that breakfast had to be the first order of business. She'd just slip into sweats and a T-shirt, eat first, then come back to get ready for the day.

She got out of bed and reached for her suitcase, but one look at her face and hair in the mirror had her moving toward the bathroom shower, after all. Even if she hadn't been in the same town as Beau Julander, she wouldn't have gone out in public with *that* hair.

She showered quickly and finger-combed her hair, then looked out the window to check the weather before she dressed. The sun was just cresting the mountains on the eastern side of the valley, and a web of gold seemed to hover over the trees on the hillsides.

In this light, the fall colors were jewel-toned, and Molly forgot about her hunger for a minute. She opened the window a few inches so she could breathe the crisp, autumn-scented air. Memories of other mornings rushed her from every side. For a moment she almost believed that if she closed her eyes, she would hear her mother urging her to dress for school.

She did close her eyes then, allowing herself to live that moment for as long as it lasted. She saw her mother's long, dark hair and wide, dark eyes. The scents of pine and earth became the sweet, musky scent of her mother's perfume, and wind chimes dancing in the breeze somewhere nearby reminded her of the tinkle of her favorite jewelry. Ruby Lane hadn't gone anywhere without her hair done, her makeup on, a spritz of perfume and jewelry. Always jewelry. Always original. Always pieces she made herself.

Molly felt the familiar pang of longing for just one necklace, one bracelet, one set of earrings, but she pushed it aside. There were things she could change and things she couldn't. The grief that had driven her father to get rid of all her mother's belongings was on the second list, and she wasn't going to waste time wishing.

The memory faded and Molly let it go, knowing it was a mistake to hold on too tightly. She wanted the memories to come and go as they pleased. They would be more meaningful that way, and maybe, if she was lucky, she'd eventually remember something about her mother's final year that she could hold on to.

She reluctantly closed the window and dressed in a pair of jeans and the oversize Chicago Bears jersey that had been a present from her dad their last Christmas together. Wearing it gave her confidence, and she needed all the help she could get this morning.

Just as she was putting the finishing touches on her makeup, a knock on the door startled her into dropping the shell-shaped compact that held her powder. It seemed early for housekeeping, but then, Serenity had always functioned at its own pace.

"Just a minute," she sang out. She picked up the compact and crossed the small room to open the door. When she saw Beau standing there with the sun in his hair and a twinkle in his eye, the compact slipped from her fingers again.

Beau bent to retrieve it and handed it to her with a grin. "Good morning. You're all ready, I see. That's good. Obviously my timing is perfect."

As Molly closed her fingers around the compact, her hand brushed Beau's. It was only an instant, but heat traced a pattern up her arm that didn't diminish even when she pulled away. "What timing? What are you doing here? Did you leave something in the car?"

He frowned playfully. "What kind of greeting is that? Let's try it again, shall we? I say good morning, and you say…"

Her cheeks flamed, but the smile in Beau's sky-blue eyes took away the sting. "Good morning," she said apologetically. "*Then* I ask what you're doing here."

"That's much better." He held out a hand as if he expected her to take it. "I'm here to treat you to breakfast."

It was all Molly could do not to gape at him. "Breakfast? Why?"

"Because you did an incredible favor for me yesterday, and I didn't thank you properly." He checked his watch and glanced behind him. "And don't give me any excuses, because I know you haven't eaten yet. The diner won't be open for another ten minutes."

"You're serious?"

He wiped the grin from his face, but his eyes still danced with laughter. "Don't I look serious?"

"Very." She glanced past him into the parking lot. A green Cherokee sat in a space near her door, but she couldn't see anyone waiting inside. "Where are your kids? Don't tell me you left them home alone."

"No, they're at my sister's. She teaches them piano on Saturday mornings. Their lessons are forty-five minutes apiece, which means that we have exactly—" he tapped the crystal on his watch "—eighty-three minutes all to ourselves."

A shiver of anticipation shimmied along Molly's spine, but she ignored it. Beau hadn't meant anything by that, and she was far too hungry to let insecurities left over from long ago make her hesitate. "You're on." She slid the room key into her pocket and stepped into the cool morning air. "You're talking about your sister, Gwen?"

"The only one I have."

"I think I remember her. Pretty girl with light-brown hair and a great smile? The one who played the piano at WinterFest?"

Beau closed the door behind him. "That's Gwen. She was a pain when we were kids, but I don't know what I'd do without her now."

"You're lucky to have her. I used to wish for a brother or a sister, but it never happened. Being an only child can get lonely sometimes." She realized she was becoming too serious and looked pointedly at her watch. "Technically, we have less than eighty-three minutes, you know. If it took you seven minutes to get here, it will take seven to get back. That means we have only seventy-six minutes—and I'm *very* hungry.''

Beau laughed. ''We have as long as we need. Gwen owes me a favor or two.'' He motioned her toward the street and fell into step beside her. ''You don't mind walking, do you? The diner's only two blocks away.''

''I don't mind at all. I didn't see much on my way through town last night.''

''That's my fault, I'm afraid.''

''Not at all. I was too tired to see anything. I'll make up for it today.''

Beau stuffed his hands into his pockets and slid a sidelong glance at her. ''Need a tour guide?''

''Around Serenity? Has it changed that much?''

''We have a new apartment building by the bowling alley, and ten new houses went up over the summer. Olene Whitefish got married again. She and her new husband put in a food mart at the gas station. If you take off on your own, you're likely to get lost in all the expansion.''

Molly's laugh echoed in the early-morning silence. ''Thanks. I'll keep that in mind.''

When they reached the sidewalk, Beau turned toward the still-dark diner on the next block. ''How's your room at the Wagon Wheel?''

''It's fine. The bed's firm and the room is clean. I can't complain.''

''And what are your plans for the rest of the day?''

''Nothing set in stone. Why?''

''We have that rescheduled meeting of the Homecoming committee later this morning. I was thinking you might like to come along.''

They drew abreast of the diner just as the lights came

on inside, and Molly shook her head quickly. "I don't want to get in the way. Besides, I probably wouldn't know most of the people there."

"You'll know everybody there. It's our year to plan this thing, so the whole committee comes from our graduating class. You know Aaron Clayton and Michelle Reeder?"

"Yes, but—"

"Elaine Gunderson and Kayla Tucker?"

"Elaine was one of my best friends in school."

"Ridge McGraw?"

An image of a bowlegged young man flashed through her mind and she smiled. "Ridge is still here? I thought for sure he'd be riding on the pro rodeo circuit by now."

"He was. Hurt his back a couple of years ago and came home. He's married. Two kids. Nice wife."

Molly hesitated another minute before agreeing. She'd come back to find answers, not to jump into small-town life just because Beau Julander crooked his finger at her.

Then again, she did have two weeks to spend in Serenity. That should give her plenty of time to connect with old friends and still talk to people who knew her mother.

And really, what was so wrong about living out an old fantasy for one day?

THREE HOURS LATER, Beau led Molly up the sidewalk toward Ridge and Cheryl McGraw's tiny frame house on the north end of town. He'd spent a couple of hours with the kids before dropping them off for a brief visit with his mother and rushing back to the motel. His mother had been thrilled to see the kids, but Brianne had been in one of her moods again.

In response to her dour prediction that he *might* make it home in time for dinner, Beau had promised to buy dinner at the Chicken Inn if he was late. He didn't mind paying for the meal, but his daughter's trust was riding on his ability to conduct this meeting and be out of here before noon so he could spend time with the kids.

The McGraws' entire front yard was buried beneath a bed of fallen leaves, and slick spots on the pavement created by old, decaying leaves made the walk a little tricky. Beau had grown so used to Ridge's aversion to yard work, he barely noticed it anymore. But this morning, with Molly behind him, he saw the mess with a fresh set of eyes and wondered what she must think after being away for so long.

He swallowed the apology he felt rising in his throat and pretended not to notice the sagging porch railing and the windows splattered with dirt from the last big storm that had raged through the valley. His own yard and windows weren't much better, and the realization didn't sit well.

He stepped around a piece of broken bicycle frame and turned back to make sure Molly didn't trip. "You'll like Ridge's wife, I think. They met while he was on the circuit. Pretty girl. Friendly. She likes having the committee meetings here. It lets her keep an eye on him and make sure he doesn't volunteer for something that'll hurt his back again." He motioned her toward the short flight of steps leading to the door. "If Ridge had his way, he'd still be riding bull."

Molly climbed the steps and moved aside to let him

ring the bell. "I'm sure I'll like her. Does this mean Ridge is the committee chair?"

"I wish." Beau pressed the buzzer and rocked back on his heels to wait. "They voted me head of the committee, but I should have said no. I enjoy being involved. I'm like my dad and grandpa, I guess—kind of a family tradition. But if I'd known how rough things would be with Heather gone, I would have stepped aside, at least for one year."

Molly looked at him oddly. "You miss her a lot, don't you."

"Me?" He let out a sharp laugh. "I wouldn't say that. The kids miss her, though, and that's rough. Brianne's had some tough times with her mother out of the picture, and I'm about as inept as a person can be about things like hair and fingernails and makeup." He shook his head, nostalgic for the days when those were his biggest problems with his unhappy daughter. "But we'll get through this. I'll make sure of it."

He thought Molly was about to say something else, but the door opened, and whatever it was, was lost in the flurry of introductions, shouts of surprise, hugs and chatter as everyone tried to catch up at once. Eventually Cheryl, a tall, blond woman with substantial curves and hair big enough to make any self-respecting rodeo queen proud, herded them all into the kitchen and settled them around the table.

Beau watched Molly covertly as she reconnected with old friends, but when he realized that he was watching her a little too closely, paying a bit too much attention to her hair and eyes, to the curve of her cheek and the sound of her laugh, he forced himself to look away. It wasn't that he was interested in her, he told himself firmly. He just wanted to make sure she was in good hands before he got down to business.

Pulling the list he'd been making for three days from his pocket he spoke loud enough to be heard. "Okay, folks, let's get with the program. Nobody wants this to take all day."

The conversations faded almost immediately, but it still took another fifteen minutes to pass out lemonade to interested parties, decide who wanted coffee, instead, and handle the debate over whether to serve chocolate cookies now or wait until they were ready for a break. No wonder he couldn't get anything done at home. He was stuck in half-day-long meetings that should have taken half an hour at most.

He made a mental note to call Mayor Biggs about his replacement on the planning committee and ignored the flicker of disappointment that came with the thought of stepping down. "Where are we with the parade, Aaron? Did Hinkley Hardware work out whatever the problem was with their float?"

His best friend, Aaron Clayton, leaned back in his chair and linked his hands behind his head. He was as dark as Beau was fair, and the fact that his hairline was receding and Beau's wasn't had become a source of good-natured contention between them. "Everything's fine," he said now. "Betty Hinkley drove into Jackson and found crepe paper in a shade close enough for them to finish making the damn thing, so Alf decided not to withdraw, after all."

"Alf needs a reality check," Kayla Tucker muttered. The faint scent of old cigarette smoke warred with her perfume, and she gestured broadly, putting Ridge's lemonade at risk. "It was *green*. He's never heard of leaves being slightly different colors before?"

Beau met Molly's amused glance across the table, then looked away quickly. "He's happy now," he said. "That's what matters. What about the marching band? Is Mr. Cavalier still upset over that song—whatever it was?"

Ridge moved his lemonade to a safer spot and stroked his thick mustache with a thumb and forefinger. Seeing everyone as Molly must, Beau realized how gray Ridge had grown lately, but it wasn't surprising for a man who'd spent fifteen years being tossed around by livestock.

"He's proposed another compromise," Ridge said. "If we let them play one song by Eminem, they'll add a Sousa march in place of the other one."

"I suppose that's all right," Cheryl put in from the spot she'd taken up near the sink. "It's not as if they're going to be singing, and it's the words people find offensive…isn't it?"

Hoping to avoid another lengthy debate on the evils of rap music, Beau glanced around the table. "Are you okay with this?" he asked Michelle. "More importantly, is Sam Harper okay with it?"

Michelle lifted one shoulder in a gesture of acquiescence. "We talked about it last night and he agreed that as long as nobody sings—and that means all the kids on the sidelines—he won't sue."

"I don't think we can guarantee that," Aaron said. "I'm not even going to try. What's wrong with Sam, anyway?"

"He finds rap music offensive."

"I find the political statements he puts on his shop marquee offensive," Aaron muttered, "but I don't threaten to sue the city over them."

Cheryl rolled her eyes. "That's different. Sam doesn't put profanity on his signs. Just ask him and he'll tell you all about it."

Ridge drained half his lemonade and set the glass down with a thunk. "Some of his opinions sure *feel* profane. The way he's always trying to regulate everything chaps my hide. You can't force people to do what you want them to do."

"Which is all beside the point," Beau said, raising his voice to make sure he stopped the inevitable argument before it got started. "The point is, Drake Cavalier and the marching band are willing to compromise with us, and I think we should adopt the same spirit. All in favor?"

He counted the vote quickly and congratulated himself on the victory, but he had less success in concluding the hour-long debate that followed over whether or not Sally Townsend's homemade sugar cookies constituted a health hazard. Only Molly's quietly offered opinion that Mrs. Townsend's sugar cookies were a necessary tradition and Michelle's grudging compromise to have the food handlers wear latex gloves when serving them brought the discussion to an end.

Thirty minutes to go, and they still had the Homecoming Ball to deal with. Beau wanted to be optimistic about his chances of getting home on time, but he had a sick feeling that he'd not only be shelling out for dinner but paying in other ways for a long time to come.

"Okay, folks, listen up. We have a lot to get through, so let's get to work." He felt the familiar flush of victory as he called for Michelle's report on the decorations and she delivered it quickly and without embellishment. To avoid reneging on his promise to Brianne, he didn't think twice about agreeing to meet with the entire committee on Wednesday evening to finish decorating the school gymnasium.

With only two more areas to cover, Beau began to feel the familiar charge he always got when victory was in sight. Sometimes he thought it was this heady feeling, along with family loyalty, that kept him so heavily involved in the committees. He liked the idea of making a difference in the world—even if it was just in his own little corner of it. "What about the half-time show on Friday night? Any problems there?"

Aaron leaned back in his seat and rested an ankle on his knee. He linked his hands behind his head and set the raised foot jiggling in that peculiar way he had. A stranger might have mistaken his posture for that of a man without a care, but Beau recognized that jiggle and his heart sank.

"We have just one little snag," Aaron announced. "Old Sam Harper has a problem with the fireworks. He thinks we should light them at the other end of the field this year."

Ridge threw himself back in his chair and tossed his pencil onto the table in disgust. "Can't we force that old pain in the shorts to move away?"

"Not in this lifetime." Aaron locked eyes with Beau. "I hate to break it to you, buddy, but he's got Mayor Biggs dancing all over the place. If we want those fireworks, we have to find a way to light them from the north end of the field without setting the scoreboard on fire."

Good thing old Sam wasn't sitting in the room right now, Beau thought. He might not have made it out alive. But Beau wasn't ready to admit defeat yet. "An emergency meeting on Monday, then."

"Nope. Mayor Biggs wants this resolved today or

we can forget the fireworks altogether. Give everybody a five-minute break and then settle in for the long haul, because I got a feelin' none of us are goin' anywhere for a while."

A LITTLE AFTER five o'clock, Beau climbed the back steps and let himself into his mother's kitchen. The aroma of freshly baked cookies filled the air, and everything from faucet to floor gleamed. He was learning about housework, but the past year had made him realize how hard it was to do those "simple" things that kept a house running smoothly. His mom made it look easy, but he wondered if he'd ever get the hang of it.

He tossed his keys onto the little shelf that served as a catchall and closed the door behind him. "Mom?" he called out to the silent house. "Anybody here?"

"We're in the sewing room," his mother replied. "Help yourself to some cookies if you want. They're by the stove."

Beau didn't have to be told twice. He nabbed three from the cooling rack and polished off one on his way down the hall. He started on his second as he stepped into his mother's favorite room in the house. Years ago, it had been Gwen's bedroom, but the lavender paint had long since been replaced by a more practical off-white, and a quilting frame, sewing machine and chests filled with craft supplies sat where Gwen's bed, dresser and stereo had been.

Vickie Julander, still slim, blond and attractive, sat in front of the sewing machine, piecing a quilt square in bright red, yellow and blue diamonds. For a while Beau had convinced himself that Heather was a lot like his mother, but he couldn't have been more wrong. It wasn't that his mother was a saint, but her natural calm made Heather's personality seem…well, overly excitable was probably the kindest way to put it. He wondered sometimes if she still suffered from the rages that had kept him in the marriage even when he'd been tempted to leave. Hard as it had been to live with her, he'd never once seriously considered leaving the kids to cope on their own with Heather.

He winked at Nicky, who sat beneath the quilting frame, quietly drawing something in one of his grandmother's sketch pads.

Nicky grinned back and popped the last piece of a cookie into his mouth. "Brianne's mad again."

Big surprise. Beau hadn't expected her to be happy. "I guess I'd better talk to her. Where is she?"

His mother glanced up from the quilt square. "You didn't see her when you came in?"

"Should I have?"

"I thought you might. She said she was going to wait outside."

"Great." He finished the second cookie and pushed away from the wall. The look he shared with Nicky convinced Beau he wasn't the only one growing tired of Brianne's sulks. "You want to wait here while I go find your sister?"

Relief filled Nicky's eyes. "Yep. I bet she's out by the rose garden. That's where she was when I went to the bathroom."

His mother glanced up briefly and peered at Beau over the wire rims of her glasses. "Remember, Beau, honesty is always best. Children are no exception."

He nodded, even though he didn't understand why she felt the need to warn him, then made his way back through the house. He was tired and frustrated, but there was no sense putting off the inevitable.

Thanks to Nicky, Beau found his daughter pacing the oval-shaped rose garden his father had planted years ago. The roses had already been pruned and packed for winter, but that didn't seem to matter to Brianne. Her blond hair blowing about in the wind, she was gesticulating and exclaiming as she walked.

Beau knew she was venting. He even dared hope that maybe she'd burned off a little steam already.

He stopped a few feet away and waited for her to notice him, which she did almost immediately. Her nose and cheeks were red from the cold, and she ground to a halt and glared at him. "You're late."

"I know, sweetheart, and I'm sorry."

"You *promised* you wouldn't be."

"I know. The meeting didn't go very smoothly. I tried to finish on time, but I guess I didn't do a very good job of estimating how long it would take."

Her eyes narrowed. "You're late because of the *meeting?*"

"Yes. Of course. That's where I was."

"Nowhere else?"

He considered mentioning his two brief stops at the Wagon Wheel, but decided against it. He'd spent less than ten minutes there, picking Molly up and dropping her off again, and he didn't see any reason to make things more complicated than they already were. "I went to the meeting," he said firmly. "Homecoming Week starts in just a few days, and we had a lot of last-minute details to take care of."

"Oh, poor Daddy." Sarcasm made her voice bitter, and Beau could feel his temper rising. He could have been looking into Heather's eyes, listening to her voice, and he had to struggle to remind himself that he was talking to a child—*his* child.

"I don't know what's bothering you," he said evenly, "but your attitude is getting real old, real fast. It's okay to feel angry sometimes, but it's not okay to treat people as if they just crawled out from under a rock. I'm your dad, not your enemy. I suggest you remember that and start making a few changes."

"Maybe you should make some changes, too," she shot back. "Maybe *you* shouldn't lie to me."

His mother's warning sounded in the back of his mind, but he still didn't understand. "What are you talking about? When have I lied to you?"

"Right now. Why didn't you tell me about the lady you were with?"

"What lady?" So that's what was really bothering Brianne. He wondered how she knew.

"The one I saw you with at the motel."

Beau glanced back at the house. Why hadn't his mother warned him about what he was walking into? "I didn't tell you," he said carefully, "because she's just an old friend who's in town for Homecoming. I picked her up for the meeting and gave her a ride back to her motel afterward, but I wasn't *with* her. We weren't on a date or anything."

Brianne folded her arms and glared at him. "Breakfast wasn't a date?"

Damn grapevine. "Breakfast wasn't a date," he assured his sullen daughter. "She gave me a ride from Jackson yesterday, and I thought it would be a good idea to do something nice to pay her back."

Brianne considered his reply for a moment, then tilted her head to one side. "Do you *want* to date her?"

He shook his head. "I'm not interested in dating anyone right now," he said, ignoring the flicker of guilt that told him he wasn't being entirely honest. "I have too much to do at home. Too many dishes to wash. Too much laundry to do. Even if I wanted to, I don't have time to date.''

"And don't forget Mom."

Beau froze. "Mom?"

"What if she comes back and you're going out with some other woman? She might think you didn't want her to come back and then she might leave again."

Beau took another step closer and weighed his words carefully. "I don't think your mom is coming back, Brianne. And even if she did—"

"But she *is* coming back. Gram said so. She said that Mom's coming back soon. That she's tired of living in Santa Fe and tired of her new friends. Gram *said!*"

"That's what Gram wants, honey, but that's not what's going to happen."

"How do you know? Have you talked to her? Did she tell you she's not coming back?"

Beau couldn't let himself answer that, so he turned the challenge around on her. "Has Gram talked to her? Has she told Gram that she's coming back?"

"Probably."

"I don't think so, sweetheart. And even if she does come to Serenity to be near you and Nicky, she and I won't be getting back together." There was too much heartache, too many angry words and accusations between them. And Heather's one big decision that Beau would never forget. He couldn't understand why Brianne didn't seem to remember the shouting matches, the slamming doors, the nights when he'd slept in the old cabin or on the couch in the family room, the mornings when the coldness between Heather and him had filled the house. Had it not been as bad as he remembered? Or was his daughter living in denial?

He couldn't blame her for that. He'd spent a fair amount of time there himself. There'd been so many things he hadn't wanted to see, so many clues about what the real problems were between Heather and him, but his pride hadn't let him see the truth until the bitter end—not until it had been thrown in his face and there'd been no possible way to dodge it.

CHAPTER FOUR

MOLLY WAS STILL thinking about Beau hours later when she stepped out of her room to get some air. She'd spent the time since the committee meeting cooped up in her room, making a list of people she wanted to talk to and looking up phone numbers and addresses in the small area phone book, but she was ready for a change of pace.

She'd been a little surprised by the reception the committee members had given her. She hadn't expected so many of them to remember her, but their welcome had certainly bolstered her courage.

As she stretched to work out the kinks from sitting in one position for too long, she let her gaze travel along the motel office fronting the street, then to the L-shaped building that housed the individual rooms and on to the tiny playground in the grassy courtyard. The buildings had recently received a fresh coat of paint, but small signs of age and neglect were in evidence, from the pitted sidewalks to the listing porch railings and the potholes in the parking lot.

Making a hasty decision, she reached back into the room for her key and slipped it into her pocket, then crossed the parking lot and climbed the two short steps to the glass door of the office.

This part of the motel hadn't changed in fifteen years, either. The same curtains hung at the windows, the same postcard tray and brochure sleeves sat on the counter. She even thought the same postcards were on sale. Only the computer looked new.

Behind the counter, an open door led to the Grahams' living quarters. Last night it had been the Grahams' daughter Brenda who'd been on duty. Today Phyllis Graham sat on the same old green velvet couch Molly remembered, probably watching the same television programs she'd watched all those years ago.

Molly crossed the room to the counter before the bell over the door stopped tinkling. Mrs. Graham pushed out of her easy chair and hurried toward the counter, patting her gray-streaked hair as she walked. The changes in the older woman left Molly momentarily speechless as the realization sank in that her own mother might have changed as much if she'd lived.

Mrs. Graham had aged and put on weight, but the changes went deeper than that. Her shoulders sagged as if she carried a great weight, and the spark in her eyes had grown dim. Was it just time? Age? Life? Or had something else happened to change her?

"You caught me putting my feet up for a minute," Mrs. Graham said with a self-conscious laugh. "It never fails, does it? Sit down for a minute, and that's when somebody will come through the door. Not that I'm complaining. Don't want to give the wrong idea." She drew closer and her step faltered. "Well, now, *you* look familiar. You're Ruby Lane's girl, aren't you?"

"I am."

"Molly, isn't it?"

"That's right." She extended a hand. "It's Molly Shepherd now. I just arrived last night. It's good to see you again, Mrs. Graham."

"Mrs. Graham?" A hint of that old spark lit her

eyes and she wagged a finger in mock irritation. "None of that, now. We're old friends. Call me Phyllis." She gave Molly a quick once-over and shook her head in wonder. "Just look at you. You're the spitting image of your mother."

The words filled Molly with pride and gratitude. "I knew there was a resemblance, but I didn't realize it was so strong."

"Take one look at a picture of her at your age and you'll know. Gracious, but it's a little startling." She laughed again and sank onto a stool behind the counter. "But don't mind me. I tend to run on when I shouldn't. What can I do for you?"

Molly couldn't bring herself to admit that grief had driven her father to throw out all the pictures of her mother. Much as it had hurt to discover what he'd done, she didn't like the judgment she saw in people's eyes when she told them about it. "Actually I'd like to talk to you for a minute if you don't mind. I'm hoping you can tell me what you remember about my mom's accident."

Something hard and cold flickered in Phyllis's eyes and she drew back sharply. "What is it you want to know?"

Her reaction was completely unexpected, but the coldness in her expression disappeared so quickly Molly told herself she'd only imagined it. "I don't know, really. I don't remember much about that night, so almost anything you could tell me would be helpful."

Phyllis straightened some papers on the edge of the counter, then reached for a stack of mail. "Goodness, Molly, what a thing to ask. That was a long time ago, and a lot has happened since then.'' Her gaze danced across Molly's face, avoiding her eyes. "Especially for someone my age. There are days when I have trouble remembering the names of my grandchildren. Besides, if you ask me, there's nothing to be gained from delving into the past. It's best to keep your attention focused on the future, I always say.''

"Normally I'd agree with you," Molly said, "but we're talking about my mother. I really need to fill in a few blanks.''

"If you want to know about that night," Phyllis suggested, giving a nonchalant shrug, "wouldn't it be best to ask your dad? I'll bet he remembers things the rest of us don't, and I'm sure he wouldn't appreciate me talking. Unless he's had a life-changing moment somewhere along the way, he doesn't like it when folks talk.''

Molly's smile faded. "I can't ask him. He died six months ago.''

She couldn't be sure, but she thought Phyllis faltered slightly as she tossed an envelope at the trash can. "Oh?''

"Cardiac arrest. It was very sudden and unexpected.''

"Frank's gone?" Phyllis gave a weighted sigh and shook her head. "That seems almost impossible. He was so...full of life.'' The remark should have been a compliment, but it sure didn't sound like one. Phyllis turned away to reach for something on a shelf behind her. "Family. That's who I'd go to with questions if I were you. Go to the people who'd remember best.''

"But that's the problem. I have a stepmother, but she doesn't know anything. Mom was an only child and her parents both died before she did. And I never knew Dad's family. You and Mom's other friends are really my only hope.''

Phyllis found whatever she was looking for and carried it back to the counter. "Well, I wish you luck, dear. But as I said, it was all so long ago. I just don't know how successful you'll be. There's been a lot of water under the bridge since then.'' She flashed an apologetic smile, then swiftly moved on to another topic. "I'm looking at your room portfolio here and I see that Brenda left off your departure date. Why don't we fill that in right now, along with anything else we need?''

It took Molly a second to recover from the abrupt shift. "I'm staying until the seventeenth," she said when Phyllis looked at her expectantly.

"Lovely. But how long are you staying *here?*"

"The entire time of course. Is that a problem?"

Phyllis pursed her lips. "Oh, dear. Yes, I'm afraid it is. You didn't make a reservation?''

"I didn't think I'd need one."

"Well, you wouldn't usually, but Homecoming is a different story. We're full up—or will be in a day or two.''

Molly stared at her in disbelief while she tried to process that piece of news. "You don't have *any* rooms?"

"I have one for tonight." Phyllis tapped on her computer keyboard and stared in concentration at the screen. "Looks like I'll have one Sunday and Monday night, too. But nothing after that until Homecoming Week is over.''

Molly could have kicked herself for not realizing that lodging might be a problem. "Is there a bed-and-breakfast in town? Or another motel, maybe?''

"Hon, we're the only motel for fifty miles in any direction. Joe Walker rents apartments by the month over on Spring Street, but you probably wouldn't be interested in something that permanent."

"I won't be here that long."

"Well, that's a shame. A real shame. But listen, there's always a chance that someone will cancel at the last minute or just not show at all. Keep the room until we need it, and we'll keep our fingers crossed that something will open up, or someone in town will have a room to spare." She stopped abruptly, sniffed twice and clapped a hand to her bosom. "My applesauce. Can you believe I forgot all about it? You'll forgive me of course. We'll talk later, I'm sure."

And with that, she was gone.

Molly stepped out into the dwindling light and stood for a moment, taking in the shadows stretching across the road, the occasional swish of cars passing on the street, the sounds of dogs barking and muted laughter in the distance. She wrapped her arms around herself and pulled in a deep breath of fall-scented air.

The one thing she *didn't* smell was the distinctive and unmistakable aroma of cooking apples. She had no idea what had made Phyllis so nervous or why she'd lie to avoid discussing the night Molly's mother died...but she intended to find out.

SHORTLY BEFORE NOON the next day, Molly walked quickly along Front Street toward the Chicken Inn. She'd spent the evening trying to find another place to stay in case she had to leave the Wagon Wheel, but everyone she knew had family coming in or homes too small.

Molly refused to be discouraged. There was a solution out there. She just had to find it. And maybe her friend Elaine would have some good news for her at lunch.

A weak storm had moved into the valley overnight. Clouds had turned the sky a heavy, gunmetal gray, and without even the autumn sun to warm it, the air in the valley had become almost frigid. She shivered and hunched more deeply into her favorite sweater, but it didn't help.

She considered going back for the car, but she was almost halfway to the restaurant, so she walked faster, keeping her head down to protect her face from the cold. When she reached an intersection, she looked up long enough to check for traffic, then protected her face again.

As she passed the FoodWay grocery store, she caught sight of a green Cherokee slowly making its way along Front Street toward her.

A chill gust of wind swept around her ankles and sent a shiver up her spine, but she couldn't make herself move. Beau pulled to the curb a few feet away from her and got out. He strode toward her, grinning as if he was really glad to see her. "Doing a bit of sightseeing?"

She laughed and shook her head. "Not exactly. I'm on my way to the Chicken Inn. What are you doing out and about on a Sunday? I thought you'd be with your kids."

"Family dinner at Mom's. She needs whipping cream, and I volunteered to go get it." He slid a slow glance along the length of her. "Do you want to join us? There's plenty."

"Thanks, but I'm meeting Elaine for lunch."

"Sounds fun. What are you doing later?"

Molly shrugged. "Hopefully finding someplace to stay."

"I thought you were comfortable at the Wagon Wheel."

"I am, but I didn't exactly think ahead. I have a room through Monday night, and then, if nobody cancels, I'm out on the streets."

Beau glanced down at her. "You didn't have a reservation?"

"I didn't think I'd need one."

"For Homecoming Week? You really have forgotten what things are like around here, haven't you? There are three times of the year when the motel fills up early—all fifteen rooms. You have to plan in advance for Homecoming, Thanksgiving and Christmas. The rest of the year, you're fine to take a chance."

The breeze blew hair into her eyes and she swept it back with one hand. "I wish I'd known. Now that I'm here, I don't want to miss all the fun."

"You *can't* miss it. That's not even an option. I have it on good authority that this is going to be one of the finest Homecoming Weeks Serenity has ever had, no matter what you might think after that meeting yesterday. There has to be someplace you can stay. I'd ask Mom, but my cousins are staying with her, and Gwen's sister-in-law and her family are going to be at Gwen and Riley's."

"That's the story I'm getting from everybody. Jennifer Grant offered me her couch. I can take that if I can't find anything else, but with a husband and four kids in a three-bedroom house, they're bursting at the seams. I hate to impose."

"It's a small house, that's for sure." A car rounded

the corner and he instinctively put an arm around her to pull her farther away from the curb.

Feeling warm beneath his touch, she drew away casually. "I'm not giving up, though. Besides, Phyllis says that someone might cancel."

"I wouldn't count on it. But I'm sure there's another solution. I can make a few calls if you'd like. I have friends in high places...sort of."

Molly caught another wisp of hair and pushed it back from her face. "I've seen how influential you are, and I'd appreciate the help. I've about exhausted my connections. I just hope you have better luck than I've had."

He frowned in mock annoyance. "You *doubt* me?"

She laughed lightly. "Umm...no?"

"Excellent answer." He hooked his thumbs in his back pockets and surveyed the world around him for a long moment. "Tell me how you'd feel about staying in a cabin."

"Does it have a bed?"

"Yep."

"Then I'd feel very happy if it's not too expensive."

"How does 'free' work into your budget?"

"Free?" She eyed him skeptically. "Almost too well. I don't want to take advantage of anyone."

"Right. But that's not a problem. This place has its own kitchen, but you'd have to go to the main house for bathroom privileges and the shower. It's a guest bath, though, so it would be almost like having your own."

"Sounds too good to be true. Do you really think I could get it?"

"Oh, I'm sure of it. The place is a little dusty. It

hasn't been used in a while. But it wouldn't take long to spruce it up.''

"Maybe you should check first,'' Molly suggested. "I don't want to get my hopes up for nothing. Whose cabin is it?''

"It belongs to a real nice family.'' A strong gust of wind whipped around them, and he took a couple of steps toward the Cherokee, walking backward so he didn't have to break eye contact. "A single dad with two great kids.''

Molly gaped at him. "You?''

"It's the original house my grandparents built when they bought the farm. You remember it?''

"I don't want to be rude,'' Molly said, "but all I remember is a tumbledown old shack behind your house. Is that what you're talking about?''

"It's not so bad. We've done a little work on it since you were here last. I used to sleep there sometimes before Heather and I split up. The only inconvenience is having to cross the yard to use the bathroom, but it's not far.''

Molly didn't know what to say. Surely he didn't expect her to stay in a falling-down old shed, so it must be habitable. She needed a place to stay, but she wasn't sure she'd relax for a second at Beau's. When he didn't break into laughter or wave off the suggestion as a joke, she forced herself to speak. "I'm not so sure that's such a good idea.''

"Why not?''

"Well, for one thing, what would your kids think?''

"It's just for a couple of weeks. They'd be fine.''

Molly still wasn't sold. "There'd be gossip,'' she reminded him.

"So? You need a place to stay. I have one. It's no big deal. Don't make it one."

Heat rushed into her cheeks, but he didn't seem to notice. She opened her mouth to argue with him, but the words wouldn't come.

"I thought you wanted to find out about your mom's accident," Beau reminded her. "Isn't that worth staying for?"

"Yes. Of course it is. But—"

"Okay, then. So you'll stay. If you want privacy, you've got it. If you want a friend, you've got that, too. Sound like something you can live with?"

She stared at him, still unable to make herself say yes.

Laughing softly, he swung away. "Think about it as long as you want to," he called back over his shoulder. "You know where to find me when you make up your mind."

She stood frozen, watching him cross the street and stride through the supermarket's parking lot past one car after another. He waved at someone in a pickup truck and stopped to chat with an elderly woman who came outside just as he reached the doors.

Molly couldn't take her eyes off him, but he never once looked back. She told herself that staying in his cabin would be wrong, wrong, wrong. She even argued with herself for a full ten minutes, but there was never any contest. In the end, she did exactly what Beau knew she would do—she crossed the parking lot and stepped into the FoodWay, telling herself that if this turned out badly, she had only herself to blame.

"I *KNEW* IT!" Brianne shouted as Beau cleared away dishes after dinner the next evening. She stood so quickly her chair toppled to the floor behind her. "You lied to me, didn't you?"

"I told you the truth." Beau stashed the plates next to the sink and turned back for more. "It's not what you think."

"Oh, yeah. Like I'm going to believe that." Her cheeks were flushed and her small chest heaved with emotion. "You can't let some stranger stay in the cabin. All Mom's stuff is in there."

Beau glanced at Nicky, who watched his sister closely but didn't seem to share her outrage. "We can move Mom's stuff," Beau said. "There aren't that many boxes. They'll fit in the equipment shed."

"I don't *want* to put Mom's things in the stupid equipment shed!" Brianne shouted. "There're spiders in there."

"I'll spray."

Brianne wrestled with her chair for a moment and finally got it back on its feet. "You want to move Mom's things, don't you? I heard Gram say that you probably wanted to throw everything away."

"Well, Gram's wrong." The muscles in Beau's jaw knotted painfully, but he took a deep breath and picked up the bowls that had held cheese, onion and tomato respectively. "But maybe it's time for us to realize that Mom doesn't want the stuff she left behind."

"She does so want it! There are things I made for her in there. Pictures Nicky drew. The candleholder I gave her for Christmas, even. She'll be really mad if you throw all that away."

Hope and defiance mingled in Brianne's expression, and even Nicky's wide blue eyes filled with worry. Beau turned away so the kids couldn't see the weariness in his own eyes. "You're right, honey. I don't know what I was thinking. We'll keep Mom's things safe and sound for her. Where do you think we should put them?''

''They should stay where they are. In the cabin.''

''Then we'll put them back after Molly leaves. She's only staying for a couple of weeks, not forever.''

Brianne dropped heavily into her chair and propped her feet against Beau's empty one, pushing on it until it teetered dangerously on two legs. ''She should stay at the motel. Why can't she do that?''

A wave of exhaustion nearly convinced Beau to leave the dishes, but he forced himself to keep working. ''She can't stay at the motel because she didn't make a reservation. Mrs. Graham doesn't have a room for her after tonight.''

''So?''

''So she came all this way for Homecoming, and it would be mean to make her leave over some simple mistake.''

Brianne pulled her feet away and the empty chair rocked back onto all four legs. ''So what? It was *her* mistake.''

Beau shut off the water and strode over to look his daughter in the eye. ''What's going on with you, Brianne?''

Her gaze swung to his face, then away. ''I don't know what you mean.''

''I mean that you've never been rude or mean to me or to anyone else, but lately that's *all* you are. I know you're unhappy with me for changing the arrangement we had with Gram, and I was willing to give you a little time to adjust. But enough is enough. It's time to get over it.''

She shot to her feet and glared at him, hands on hips

and thunder in her eyes. "You don't get it, do you. I don't *want* to get over it. I don't want everything to change all the time. First Mom left, and then you told Gram to go away, and now you're bringing *that lady* to live here. Well, it's not fair, and it's not right. I don't want to be nice, and you can't make me." She raced from the room, heading for the stairs.

Angry and confused, Beau took off after her. If he lived to be a thousand, he'd never understand females, no matter what age they were. Brianne was already halfway up the stairs by the time he reached the hallway. "Get back here," he demanded. "I'm not through talking to you."

"Well, *I'm* through talking to *you.*" She raced up the last few steps and bolted for her room. "Just leave me alone, Daddy. Find somebody else to help you get rid of Mom's stuff because I'm not going to."

Beau took the steps two at a time, but Brianne's door slammed shut before he could reach the top of the staircase. He stopped in his tracks and stood, panting and uncertain, staring at the unyielding slab of wood that separated him from his daughter.

He argued with himself for a moment about what he should do. He didn't want to be too lenient and let Brianne grow into one of *those* teenagers, but he wasn't going to force his way into her room and make her talk to him. Even if he'd been that kind of dad, he had no idea what he'd say to her right now.

As he started back down the stairs, the telephone rang. He was in no mood to talk to anybody, but he had too many irons in the fire to ignore the call. He made it into his study by the third ring and recognized the number of the mechanic in Jackson when he glanced at his caller ID.

Finally some good news—he hoped. Pushing aside his irritation with Brianne, he lifted the cordless phone and punched the talk button. "Smitty? That you?"

"The one and only. I tried you at the airstrip, but I didn't get an answer."

"Not much reason to hang around there when I don't have an airplane." Beau dropped into his chair and nudged open a bottom drawer to use as a footrest. Overhead, music blared to life inside Brianne's sanctuary. "Just tell me you have good news."

"I guess that depends on what you consider 'good.' I'm going to need to replace the magneto on your Cessna. The part's available, but I can't get it here for a couple of days."

Beau ignored the driving bass beat overhead and kneaded his forehead with his fingertips. "Why so long?"

"They have to fly it in from New Mexico."

"Which should take a few hours at most," Beau said sharply. "Certainly not longer than overnight."

"In a perfect world, maybe. They'll ship the part out on Wednesday. We should have it by Thursday or Friday."

"That leaves me out of commission for a full week."

"Sorry. Can't be helped."

Beau leaned back in his chair as the music overhead grew louder and a high-pitched sound track from a video game filtered out from the family room, where Nicky was obviously honing his hand-eye coordination.

He tuned out the slight ache forming behind his eyes and focused on what Smitty was saying. No plane meant no income. No income, no business.

"Just tell me I'll be back in business by Friday."

"That'll depend on the manpower I have when the part gets here. I know you need your plane, but I got two mechanics out with some kind of kick-ass flu and the other one's got a baby due any day now. No tellin' where he'll be when the part arrives."

"What about you, Smitty? Or are you just window dressing these days?"

"I'd make some mighty sorry window dressing," Smitty said with a chuckle. "I could do it for you, and I will if it comes to that, but I've got other jobs ahead of you. First come, first serve. That's always been my policy."

"You'd make an exception if I were one of those celebrity clients of yours. What if I told you I'm supposed to fly Mel Gibson to a location shoot near Yellowstone?"

Smitty laughed again. "I'd say you were a bad liar."

"Yeah? Well, this honesty thing is a real curse sometimes." Brianne turned her music a little higher, and something on the wall began to buzz. "How about if I remind you that we've been friends for about a hundred years?"

"Well, then, I'd buy you a drink if you stop lying to me. But I *still* wouldn't move you ahead of my other clients. We'll get you up and running as soon as we can, Beau. I can't promise you anything more than that."

Beau closed his eyes in frustration, but he was smart enough to recognize a brick wall when he ran into one, and old enough to have learned the futility of going to battle against one. "You'll call me?"

"The very second I can tell you anything."

It wasn't much, but apparently it was all he was

going to get. Even worse, it was the best thing that had happened all night. People had always seen him as lucky, but lately he couldn't seem to catch a break to save his life.

Something had to give—and soon.

CHAPTER FIVE

THE NEXT MORNING at breakfast Beau accidentally charred the toast, broke a plate loading the dishwasher and stepped on a sharp piece of ceramic as he cleaned up. The one piece of good luck that came his way was that the kids had left for school before he put Brianne's favorite blouse through the wash and turned it into a potholder.

He was holding that shriveled scrap of pink in his hands and fighting the urge to let loose some of his favorite curses, when the sound of knocking from behind brought him around. When he recognized his mother looking in through the back door, he was glad he'd kept a little control on his vocabulary.

He tossed the blouse aside and made a mental note to tell Brianne what he'd done before she could discover it for herself. After motioning for his mother to come in, he headed toward the coffeemaker to start a fresh pot. "You're out and about early," he said as he dumped old grounds into the trash. "What's up?"

"I'm on my way to a meeting of the music committee," she said, slipping out of her light jacket and draping it across the back of a chair. "We need to get started on plans for WinterFest, and I came by to get your notes from last year. We don't want to accidentally repeat ourselves."

"Sure. My file's in the study. If you'll finish this,

I'll get it.'' He left her in charge of the coffee and burrowed around in his desk for a few minutes until he found the file he was looking for. When he carried it back into the kitchen, he found his mother holding Brianne's ruined blouse up to the window.

She grimaced as she returned the ruined garment to the top of the washer. ''What are you going to tell Brianne?''

Beau shook his head and handed over the file. ''I have no idea. She was fit to be tied the last time I ruined one of her things. The way she feels about me lately, she'll probably come completely unglued.''

''She's still impossible?''

''Worse than ever.'' He dug two mugs from the cupboard and found two clean spoons in the dishwasher he hadn't yet unloaded. ''I don't know how this happened, Mom. I've tried everything, but she won't listen to reason. Everything I do, everything I say, is wrong.''

His mother sank into a chair and flashed a sympathetic smile. ''She's upset, honey. When Heather left it threw her whole world into disarray. Just when it looked like things were beginning to settle down again, you decided you could do without Doris.'' She glanced at the mounds of laundry and piles of dishes. ''All those changes would throw anyone for a loop. With an emotional child like Brianne, you have to expect a strong reaction.''

''I could handle a reaction,'' Beau growled. ''But what she's been doing goes way beyond that.'' He paced to the other end of the kitchen, scooped up a mound of laundry that had been begging for attention for days and began stuffing it into the washer. ''It's like she's decided I don't deserve any space on the planet.''

His mother laughed softly, then, getting up from her chair and crossing the room, she nudged him out of the way and began layering the clothes into the washer one piece at a time. "Don't overreact, Beau. She's upset, that's all. And you have to admit, she does have reason to be."

Beau's shoulders stiffened and a warning bell went off in the back of his head. He turned away and rubbed his face with one hand. The room was fragrant with the scent of fresh coffee, but unfinished chores loomed everywhere. Floors that needed vacuuming. Windows that needed washing. Phone calls that needed to be returned. Then there were piano lessons, soccer practice and karate on top of committee meetings, town-planning meetings and work. Life was getting away from him, and he wondered for a moment if he could ever catch up.

Even so, he wasn't about to move backward. "What did you want me to do, Mom? Let Doris stay around forever? Do you have any idea how it felt to have her here all the time talking about Heather? Trying to convince me that she's just a little 'confused' and that she'll be coming back? Filling the kids' heads with that garbage? It's hard enough wrapping my brain around what happened and moving on with life, without someone purposely dragging us all backward."

His mother added soap and fabric softener to the washer and closed the lid. "I know it was rough, honey. I'm just thinking about the other things—the more practical things that make up everyday life, like dishes and laundry and dusting."

"All the things I'm not doing. Is that what you're saying?"

"Now *you're* being too sensitive. I didn't say a word about your housekeeping."

Beau laughed. "No, but you were thinking it." He sobered and let out a sigh of frustration. "I know I'm behind. I know I have a lot to learn. But I'll get there."

"There are people willing to help you, Beau, if you'd just let them. I'm sure if you talked to Doris and explained how you're feeling, she'd make a few adjustments. In a strange way I can sympathize with her. She wants what she's saying to be true."

"You don't think I *have* talked to her? She's so convinced she's right she won't listen to anything I say." The coffeemaker stopped and Beau turned away gratefully. He poured a cup for his mother, then one for himself. Gripping his mug in both hands, he returned to the table and sank into a chair.

"It's not just that, anyway," he said when he felt a little more in control. "I need to do this on my own."

She turned toward him with a scowl. "Why?"

"Because it's my job."

"Not all of it."

"My house. My kids. My responsibility."

Shaking her head in exasperation, his mom slipped into the chair across from his. "Haven't you heard that it takes a village to raise a child? Everyone needs help at one time or another. There's no shame in accepting it when it's your turn."

Beau shook his head sharply. "I don't want help and I don't need sympathy. It's just a matter of time until I have everything under control."

"Oh, honey." She eyed him over the rim of her cup. "Are you really going to let stubborn pride get in the way?"

The question stung, and her tone of voice made him

feel like a child again. "I'm just being responsible," he insisted, but his voice came out too harshly. He took a few seconds to compose himself. "I'm taking care of my kids. I'm taking care of my home. I'm pursuing a career."

"But you can't do everything alone, honey. It's too much."

He laughed without humor. "Would you say that if I were a woman?"

His mother's eyes narrowed. "I don't know what you mean."

"I mean that single mothers do it all the time and nobody thinks twice, so why is it such a stretch to believe that a man can do it just as well? Or is it only me who's not quite up to the challenge?"

The smile on his mother's face vanished. "That's not what I meant. I would never question your abilities. You've always excelled at everything you've taken on. But you're not used to doing everything you need to do around here. And the kids—"

"So I can be counted on to toss a football or change a tire, but not to fix a casserole or clean a toilet?"

His mom glanced toward the washer, where Brianne's ruined shirt seemed to take on a special glow.

In spite of his irritation, Beau laughed. "Okay, so I still have a few things to learn. I'll get used to doing what needs to be done, Mom. Just have a little faith in me and support me in this—please. If my own family isn't on my side, what chance do I have?"

Leaning across the table, she cupped his face in her hands. "We are *always* on your side. You must know that."

And he did. His parents' love, trust and support were

three things he'd never had to question. But he wondered for the first time whether his own children would be able to say the same thing about him, and how he'd ever make up for the damage Heather's life-altering decision had done them.

By comparison, a few piles of laundry and some unwashed dishes seemed utterly insignificant, and he couldn't even do those right. He had a sick feeling that if someone tossed him a life preserver now, it would probably hit him in the head and send him under for the third time.

BY TUESDAY MORNING Molly was beginning to have second thoughts about her decision to accept Beau's offer. She'd spent nearly all of Monday with Elaine, meeting old friends, dredging up memories and giggling like schoolgirls over sodas at the Burger Shack. After school let out, reality set in. Dinner with Elaine's family had left her wondering if she'd ever really be able to accept the fact that the miscarriage had left her unable to have children of her own and envying Elaine's relationship with her husband.

To make matters worse, she'd spent entirely too much time thinking about Beau, remembering his laugh, his smile, the sound of his voice and the color of his eyes. She'd been around him for less than a week, but she was as attracted to him as she'd ever been—maybe even more.

Not smart.

Now she was about to move into the cabin he'd offered and spend the next ten days practically living under his roof. Also not smart.

The past year had been hard on her. She didn't need to set herself up for almost certain disappointment. And yet here she was, wedging her last suitcase into the trunk and closing it, as if this was actually a good idea.

And maybe it was.

Spending so much time around him might be for the best. She might find out that he had atrocious habits. Rude table manners. A secret gambling problem. Trouble with alcohol. Maybe he scratched his crotch in public. Belched for sport. With a little luck, maybe she'd finally get over this silly girlhood crush that had resurrected itself without invitation.

She'd told Beau that she'd arrive around noon, but instead, she lingered over a salad at the Burger Shack, then spent some time window-shopping before finally heading toward the farmhouse. His property lay at the west end of town, surrounded by new houses where once there'd been only rolling fields. It was a great piece of land nestled beside a stream. Probably one of the most beautiful lots in town.

She drove across the wooden bridge and a few minutes later pulled into a driveway that led to his sprawling white farmhouse. Rows of trees and a lawn that was easily the size of half a football field separated the house from its neighbors.

Halfway to the house, the drive turned to dirt. She slowed cautiously, aware of the sound of her engine in the stillness and the dust kicked up by her tires. As she pulled to a stop, a curtain in a window twitched, and by the time she opened the car door Beau was striding down the walk to meet her.

Her heart gave a little skip when she saw him coming toward her in snug, well-worn jeans and a black T-shirt that emphasized the muscles in his arms and shoulders. Did he dress that way on purpose, or was he really oblivious to his charms?

A slight breeze lifted a lock of wheat-gold hair from his forehead, and a welcoming smile curved his lips. Her heart skittered again, but she ignored it. If she was going to stay here, she had to start seeing Beau as a friend. A buddy. Just another guy.

Yeah, right.

She got out of the car and rested her arms on the open door, trying to ignore the blue of his eyes and the way the sun lit his hair. "I wasn't sure where to park. Is there somewhere better?"

"This is fine." He nodded toward a copse of trees behind the house. "The cabin's back there by the stream. Walk with me and I'll show you."

Molly fell into step beside him as the kitchen door opened again. This time a young girl with light-blond hair came outside. She wore a frown so fierce Molly could have sworn she felt its weight across the distance. A young boy with hair the same shade as Beau's bounced out the door. The girl sidestepped him, brushing the sleeve of her sweater as if she'd picked up germs simply by standing on the same ground as her brother.

Molly's heart gave an uncomfortable squeeze at the girl's obvious displeasure, but she told herself to push it away. No getting wistful about Beau. No getting soft with his kids. Those were the rules from this moment on.

Beau performed introductions quickly and waved for the kids to join them without ever breaking stride. "Come on, you two. You can help."

"The kids don't have to help me," Molly protested as she struggled to keep up with him. She was pretty sure Brianne would object, and she didn't want to start off on the wrong foot. "I don't have much, and my bags aren't heavy."

"You're a guest."

"I feel like a pest."

Beau's gaze settled on her face and a frown tugged at the corners of his mouth. "I invited you to stay here, and I always take care of my guests."

Molly managed a weak smile and decided not to annoy him by arguing the point.

He nodded toward the willows, their branches still thick with leaves beginning to lose their color. "I hope the cabin's okay. I've had the windows open all morning to air it out, and the kids helped me clean up a bit."

Glancing at the kids, Molly saw that Nicky had already reached the edge of the lawn, but Brianne was taking her time and making no effort to hide her annoyance. Molly could only hope that the girl would relax once she realized that her father's guest wasn't going to be around much.

They rounded the copse of trees, and Molly got her first glimpse of the small log cabin nestled among the willows near the stream.

Far from a run-down old shack, it was utterly charming. Two large windows looked out over a long wooden porch that stretched the cabin's length. Rusted farm equipment, horseshoes and strands of barbed wire twisted into Western shapes decorated the outside walls and porch railings. Two green Adirondack chairs flanked a wide wooden porch swing, and Molly immediately saw herself spending lazy afternoons there while she read or listened to music.

She realized Beau was watching her, waiting for her

reaction with a mixture of pride and vulnerability. "So? What do you think?"

"I think it's wonderful," she said. "I can't believe this is that old run-down shack I remember. You're probably the luckiest guy I've ever met."

Beau's expression changed subtly. "I wouldn't call it luck. My grandparents left the farm to my dad, but he and my mom were settled in town and Mom didn't want to give up her house to move out here. My sister and her husband built a brand-new house on the East Bench about five years ago, and my kid brother was too busy dating and partying to take care of the property. That leaves me here by default."

The East Bench, Molly knew, was a small subdivision of houses mostly built at least forty years earlier. Nice, but nothing compared with this wonderful old home. "It doesn't matter how you got it," she said as she stepped onto the porch. "The point is that you have something that's been in your family for generations. I'd love to have *anything* that had belonged in my family for that long."

Nicky caught up to them and threw his arms around Beau's legs. Beau absently wrapped an arm around the boy's shoulders. "Maybe you will someday."

Molly shook her head and looked away. "It was just my dad and me for the last fifteen years of his life. I don't have anything belonging to my mom, and her folks are gone, so there's no hope of getting something now."

"Your dad didn't keep anything?"

"He was so upset when she died he got rid of all her things." Funny that she could admit that to Beau when she didn't like sharing it with anyone else. "I have one pair of his glasses and one of his sweaters.

My stepmother has the rest. And if we ever had any family heirlooms, they're long gone."

Beau tousled Nicky's hair. "My family is completely opposite from yours, then. I don't think my dad's ever thrown away anything in his life, and my mom's nearly as bad. She still has pictures I drew in first grade and every report card I ever brought home." He grinned at Brianne and seemed not to notice that she didn't smile back. "My kids are going to end up with more mementos from my life than they could possibly want."

He nudged Nicky forward and opened the cabin door for Molly. She stepped inside and took in every detail with a hunger that surprised her. Two matching windows in the back wall let sunlight stream through the room and brought the outdoors inside. A queen-size bed covered with a dark blue comforter and white lacy throw pillows nestled between the windows. A small kitchen took up some of the area in the front, and a living room complete with blue plaid couch and easy chairs in pale blue took up the rest. Dried flower arrangements in varying shades of yellow and ochre added just the right accents.

Beau nodded toward the rock-faced fireplace on the far wall. "Nicky and I will bring some wood for you. Nights can get cool this time of year. There's running water, but unfortunately the sink drain's not hooked up. You'll have to use the washtub and then carry the water outside to dump it. It's more rustic than you're probably used to, but I haven't had time to finish the plumbing yet."

"It won't be any trouble," Molly assured him. "I think this is the most charming place I've ever seen in my life." She put her purse on the wood dining table and let her gaze wander around the rest of the room one more time. "Did you decorate this?"

He laughed and shook his head. "Me? No." He glanced over his shoulder at Brianne, who'd moved into the doorway and stood glowering at the world in general. "Brianne and her mother did most of the decorating, didn't you, Brie?"

"Mom did it, not me." The girl's petulant voice filled the entire cabin like a blast of cold air.

Molly took her cue from Beau and pretended not to notice. "Well, it's beautiful. Your mother always did have a way of putting things together just so."

Brianne's gaze shot to Molly. "You know my mom?"

Molly nodded. "I went to school with her, too."

"Were you friends?"

"Not exactly. Your mom was a cheerleader and your dad was a football player, and I was...kind of a nerd. We didn't hang out with the same crowd."

Brianne's gaze hardened slightly. "Then what are you doing here?"

"I came back for Homecoming Week." She allowed herself a self-mocking smile and added, "Even nerds get invited back."

"Don't let her fool you," Beau put in from somewhere behind her. "She wasn't a nerd."

The ever-so-slight smile on Brianne's lips vaporized. "I didn't think so."

"Oh, but I was," Molly insisted. "At least, I wasn't one of the popular crowd like your mom and dad were. Your dad's just trying to be polite, but he doesn't really know. We weren't friends back then, either."

Hopping on one foot for reasons only an eight-year-old boy can understand, Nicky came in to stand in front

of her. "You don't look like a nerd to me," he said
after studying her for an uncomfortably long time.

Molly couldn't stop her pleased grin. "Why, thank
you, Nicky. I think that's one of the nicest things anyone's ever said to me."

"You're welcome." He tossed a triumphant grin at
his sister as he began hopping around the table. "See,
Brianne? She *is* nice. You were wrong."

Brianne's face flamed. "I never said she wasn't nice,
dummy. I said she was going to be trouble—and she
will be, too. Just you wait and see." She spun away
and dashed off the porch before Molly could absorb
what she'd said.

Beau was after her like a shot, slamming the cabin
door behind him. Nicky stopped hopping and stared at
Molly with huge blue eyes filled with questions Molly
couldn't even begin to answer. "I'd better go," he
whispered, and then he was out the door behind his
father, leaving Molly staring after him.

The rapid footsteps and Beau's voice faded away.
Molly let out her breath in a *whoosh.* "Well," she said
to the silent cabin. "I think that went well, don't you?"
But the silence that rang in answer convinced her that
the less time she spent around Beau and his kids, the
better it would be for everyone.

IT WAS NEARLY six o'clock by the time Molly finished
settling into the cabin. She'd unpacked her suitcases
and spent some time familiarizing herself with the hot
plate and refrigerator. She'd tried every chair in the
cabin, tested the bed and given the books in the small
bookcase near the bed a thorough inspection.

When she finished that, she'd spent a leisurely hour
or so on the porch making a list of things to pick up

at the FoodWay. But as the afternoon sun slipped behind the western mountains, time and the two large glasses of water she'd downed while she worked combined to force her to make her first trip to the house.

She wasn't eager for another encounter with Brianne, but maybe Beau had calmed her down by now. Besides, it wasn't as if she was going over to visit. She'd slip in quietly, find the bathroom and leave again before Beau and the kids noticed her.

After grabbing her purse and the list, she turned out the cabin lights and began the trek across the deep lawn. The temperature had dropped sharply with the setting sun, and the air had the crisp feel of autumn. She shivered slightly and walked faster toward the old white farmhouse.

Light gleamed in almost every window and she recognized the enticing scents of garlic and oregano on the breeze. Ignoring the rumble in her stomach, she stepped onto the porch and knocked. The door opened almost immediately, and Beau stood before her, framed by light, surrounded by the rich scents of dinner and wearing a shirt liberally spotted with something that looked suspiciously like spaghetti sauce.

Molly held back a grin while her heart did its now familiar tap dance in her chest. While she waited for the sensation to pass, she did her best to find a few faults. But his face was as close to perfect as a face could get, and the splotches of spaghetti sauce added a vulnerable appeal she didn't have the strength to fight.

Beau beamed when he saw her—which didn't help—and pushed open the screen door. "Come on in. I was wondering when you were going to wander over."

Molly stepped into a spacious kitchen that had obviously been recently renovated. Two of the walls, including the one behind the stove, were exposed brick. The other two were painted a shade of blue so soft they were almost white. Just like in the cabin, huge, multipaned windows looked out on Beau Julander's world. A perfect world in Molly's view—if you didn't count one angry daughter, heaps of laundry in the bricked alcove with the washer and dryer, and a stack of dishes by the sink.

She took another look around and realized that—from the laundry to the dishes to the mail stacked on the chopping-block work island—clutter seemed to dominate every surface. Finally! A flaw! Maybe Beau and his world weren't perfect, after all.

When she realized Beau was watching her and waiting for something, she grinned self-consciously. "I thought I should find out where the bathroom is. You know. Just in case."

Beau laughed and tossed a faded kitchen towel over one shoulder. "The guest bath is just down the back hall, second door on your left. And there's no need to knock when you come over. I'll leave the door unlocked while you're here, so just let yourself in when the need arises."

Molly caught another breath of warm garlic bread and her stomach growled again. "What if I need to leave and you're out somewhere? Will it be safe to leave the door unlocked, or would you rather give me a key?"

With a shrug, Beau turned back to the stove. "It'll be fine. This is Serenity, not St. Louis. How's the cabin?"

"It's perfect." She started toward the hallway, stepping over a bright yellow toy bulldozer on her way. "I meant what I said earlier. I think it's the loveliest place I've ever seen."

His pleased smile was almost boyish, and Molly turned away, hurrying down the hall to the guest bath as if she could actually outrun the warmth that curled through her.

Like everything else she'd seen so far, the bathroom was beautifully decorated. White walls were accented with lavender and green accessories, from the shower curtain and towels to the toothbrush holder and the scale on the floor. Heather Preston—Heather *Julander*—had always been perfectly put together as a girl, and obviously marriage and motherhood hadn't changed that.

Time hadn't changed the feelings of inadequacy Molly battled when she compared herself with Heather, either. She caught a glimpse of her reflection in the mirror and turned away quickly. Thick brown hair. Mud-colored eyes. Freckles across her nose and cheeks—even at thirty-three. An unspecified number of extra pounds on her hips and thighs. Molly was about as far from Heather's willowy blondness and subtle grace as a person could get. She probably looked as out of place next to Beau as Raggedy Ann would have looked if she'd started dating a Ken doll.

She had no idea what had brought about the end of Beau and Heather's marriage, but she felt uncomfortable in this big house where Heather and Beau had lived as husband and wife. She wasted no time taking care of business, washing her hands and heading back to the kitchen. She told herself to plow through the clutter and let herself out the door before Beau could sidetrack her with conversation, but the sight of

Brianne and Nicky at the table made her step falter, and Beau spotted her before she could get away.

"Dinner's almost ready," he said as Molly tried to get her feet working in rhythm again. "I know there's nothing to eat at the cabin, so why don't you join us?"

Brianne's head jerked up and color flooded her cheeks. Nicky began to bounce in his chair. "Yeah! Sit right here beside me. We're having s'ketti. It's my favorite."

Molly shook her head and tried to look regretful. "Thanks, but I can't."

"Why not?"

"Well, I...I have things to do." She lifted her purse as if it would prove how busy she was. "I was on my way to the store."

"Now?" Beau picked up a wooden spoon stained red and plunged it into a pot on the stove. "The market closes at seven. You don't have time to go shopping tonight."

"I'd have time to pick up a few things."

"Barely. And why bother?" He stirred carefully and made a face at the pot. "It's not homemade, but I have enough sauce here to feed half of Serenity. There's more than enough for the four of us."

"Yes, but—" Molly looked from Brianne's sour expression to Nicky's eager one "—our deal was that I'd stay in the cabin," she said, turning to Beau. "Not that I'd impose on your family."

"You're not imposing. We'd love you to join us. Meals are always better when they're shared...and we *can* be kind of fun to hang out with." He looked beyond Molly to Brianne. "As a matter of fact, Brianne has something she wants to say—don't you, Brie?"

Brianne looked so unhappy Molly's heart sank, but

she tried not to show any reaction. The girl cleared her throat, shot an impossible-to-miss dagger glance at her father, then swung her gaze to Molly. "I'm sorry."

How was Molly supposed to respond to that? Only a fool would have believed that Brianne was sincere, but Molly wouldn't have said so aloud for anything in the world. Apparently Beau thought that making his daughter say she was sorry would accomplish something. Molly didn't agree. If anything, he'd just made her chances of getting a civil word out of the girl a hundred times harder.

Hoping that *something* would ease the tension, she sent the girl her best smile. "Thank you. That's very nice of you."

Brianne looked away pointedly and focused on the book in front of her. "Okay."

Beau smiled as if something positive had actually happened. "So you'll stay for supper, right?"

Molly could think of a dozen things she'd rather do, but to refuse now would be a slap in the face of Brianne's "apology." And that would be a bad way to repay Beau's generosity.

Like it or not, she was stuck.

CHAPTER SIX

BEAU WATCHED a dozen different emotions filter through Molly's eyes before she finally gave in. "I'll stay," she said, "but only if you'll let me help."

He smiled, hoping she wouldn't guess how relieved he was that she'd accepted. He knew she wasn't fooled by Brianne's apology. Neither was he. But his daughter had been growing more difficult by the day, and he was at his wit's end. He didn't care if she was sincere. He only cared that she'd finally done *one* thing he'd asked her to—although *asked* wasn't exactly the right word to use, either.

"That's a deal I can live with." He ignored the poisonous looks still coming from Brianne and nodded toward the refrigerator. "Salad fixings are in there. Knock yourself out."

Molly looked around for someplace to leave her purse, finally settled on the top of the washer, then pushed up the sleeves of her sweater. "Any particular likes or dislikes I need to be aware of?"

Beau's gaze fell on the softly rounded breasts barely visible beneath the oversize sweater, and the sudden surge of heat he felt caught him by surprise. He looked away and tried to remember what she'd asked. Something about the salad. "Whatever you like," he said, hoping that came close to answering her.

He tried to focus on the spaghetti sauce, but his attention returned to Molly over and over as she pulled vegetables from the fridge and lined them up on the chopping block. She reached into a high cupboard for a bowl, and her sweater hiked up over one hip, accentuating the tuck of her waist and the curve of her bottom, and Beau nearly forgot what the spoon in his hand was for.

It wasn't that he didn't recognize the sensation, but it *had* been a while. He hadn't given women much thought since Heather walked out on him. He hadn't had the time, the energy or the inclination.

He chanced another glance at Molly, who'd moved back to stand at the chopping block while she tore lettuce into the bowl. Those dark eyes and hair combined to make her a strikingly beautiful woman. Her curves were enough to make a man lose his head. But with Brianne going through...whatever she was going through, Homecoming activities the next few nights in a row and an airplane stranded in Jackson, this was a bad time to even think about entanglements.

Besides, Molly wasn't permanent, and he wasn't interested in temporary. Heather had been temporary enough. If he ever got involved with a woman again, it would be someone capable of making and keeping a commitment to him and his kids. Someone who knew who she was and what she wanted. He didn't think Molly fit a single requirement on the list.

He pulled a large pot from a hook on the wall and filled it with water, turning his back on Molly in the process. But he wasn't blind, and by the time he had dinner on the table, Beau knew one thing for certain. Having Molly living in the cabin for the next ten days was going to be a much bigger distraction than he'd anticipated.

AN HOUR LATER, Beau scooted Brianne and Nicky upstairs to do homework while he and Molly cleaned up
the kitchen. As if they'd done this a thousand times,
Beau carried plates from the table while Molly scraped
garbage into the disposal and fit dishes into the dishwasher.

After only a few minutes, he turned on the CD player
and the sounds of big-band music filled the kitchen.
Molly looked surprised by his choice, but only for a
second. She turned back to the dishes and fit the last
of the plates into the rack, then straightened and
brushed a lock of dark hair from her eyes. "I think
that's everything that'll fit tonight. Tell me where to
find the dishwashing soap and I'll start the cycle."

Beau glanced at the overloaded dishwasher with a
grimace of embarrassment. "I keep it in the cupboard
beneath the sink, but you'd never know I even had any,
would you. Can I just go on record as saying how
embarrassed I am by the mess?"

"You can, but it's not necessary." She opened the
cupboard and sent him an understanding smile. "You
forget that I lived with a single dad. I know what life
is like when one parent has to do everything to hold
house and home together." She filled the soap holders
and snapped the second one shut, then slid the soap
box beneath the sink and closed the door.

Beau gathered the butter, salt and pepper from the
table as if he put them away after every meal. "I guess
it's too much to hope that you hated your dad for a
while, got over it magically and lived together peacefully after that."

Molly shook her head slowly. "I don't think so.
Sorry."

"You don't *think* so?"

"I don't actually remember, but Dad never said any-thing about me being difficult." She reached for a dish-cloth and set to work on the stains on the stovetop. "But our circumstances were different from yours. I could hardly blame my dad for Mom's accident." Glancing over at him, she flushed the most charming shade of pink he'd seen in a long time. "Not that I'm saying you're to blame for Heather leaving."

He laughed softly. "I know what you mean. No of-fense taken."

For a few minutes, only the riffs of clarinet and pi-ano filled the room, then Molly stopped working and looked over at him. Her eyes grew thoughtful and her expression a little distant. "I think the only real argu-ment I ever had with Dad was when I told him that Ethan and I were getting divorced. Even then, I wasn't angry. But *he* was."

Beau wasn't sure what to make of that or how to respond. He only knew he couldn't stand around while Molly cleaned up after him. He grabbed a broom from the closet and tackled a corner that seemed to scream for attention. "Your dad liked Ethan, then?"

Molly let out an abrupt note of laughter. "No. He had no use for Ethan at all, but marriage? That's what he believed in. For better or worse. He couldn't un-derstand anything making life so horrible that we couldn't work through it."

"Yeah? Well, I agree with him—to a point. I thought Heather and I would be together forever. It sounds funny to say that now. Things weren't good between us for a long time before she left, but I still never thought we'd divorce."

"Nobody goes into marriage expecting to get di-vorced, do they?" Molly said, avoiding his eyes.

"Of course not. But I'm sure some people are smart enough to get a clue when they spend three or four years doing nothing but fighting with their spouse."

Molly's expression sobered and she went back to scrubbing. "Is it possible to be sure you've done everything you can to save the marriage in less time?"

"You're saying that your divorce dragged on for a while, too?"

She looked up at him under bangs that had fallen into her eyes, and Beau had a sudden and unexpected feeling of rightness. As if she belonged there as much as he did. As if this kitchen without her in it would feel wrong.

"Ethan and I fought almost constantly toward the end," she said with a sad smile. "It didn't matter what it was about. By that point, the sound of his breathing irritated me and he hated the way I chewed, but I still thought we were working on the marriage. Living up to our vows. Trying to stay together."

"Sounds familiar," Beau admitted. "What happened?"

Molly sighed. "He found someone else. Someone more like him. Someone who came from money and who understood all the nuances of being a rich man's daughter-in-law, which he'd decided I would never learn."

"Ah. Nice. So your husband came from money?"

"I think he was made out of it." She laughed. "I, most definitely, am not."

The urge to put his arm around her came upon Beau without warning. He gripped the broom handle to keep his hands where they belonged. "There are worse things than being regular folk."

"Not according to the Shepherds." Molly glanced

at the dishcloth in her hand with wry amusement. "Finding out about Bambi was a shock at first, but it only hurt for a little while."

"That's her name? Bambi?"

Molly laughed and shook her head. "It's Emily, but I think Bambi fits better." She sobered again and glanced toward the stairs. "Of course, I didn't have children who were hurting and who needed me to help them understand why their world had just been tossed upside down. Only a father who thought I should fight the divorce and stand by a man who didn't want me."

"So you're telling me this Ethan Shepherd guy is a total idiot?"

The corners of Molly's mouth curved with pleasure.

Beau could tell that he'd caught her off guard. He'd also strayed into territory he'd be smart to avoid. He changed the subject before he could go any further. "I'm afraid I haven't done a very good job of helping my kids understand what happened. It's…complicated. I was too numb at first, and I let their grandmother step in and take over. It seemed great for a while. The house was always clean and the kids knew just what to expect. But then the other problems got too big to ignore. I'm afraid I let Doris influence the kids too long as it was."

"Doris sounds like my dad. And you and Heather *were* together a long time. A lot longer than Ethan and I were."

"Yeah, but time doesn't count for much when one person decides they want something else." He didn't know how to explain that his relationship with Heather had become habit long before they'd gotten married, or that he'd wondered for years if he'd ever actually loved her. Everyone else had thought it romantic for high-school sweethearts to get married and they'd both been swept up by other people's expectations. But saying that part aloud made him sound like a jerk, and he still wasn't ready to admit the truth. He could barely admit it to himself.

He concentrated on creating a nice mound of dirt with the broom. "I just want Brianne to forgive me for taking her grandmother out of our daily lives."

"She will. Eventually." Molly leaned against the stove and watched him. "You're her whole world now, and she loves you."

"She has a funny way of showing it."

Molly's lips curved in a smile again. "Cheer up. She'll come around. She's just trying to make a point in the only way she knows how. She's twelve, not twenty. She's still learning how to discuss things calmly."

"I hope you're right." Beau switched gears again. "The Homecoming committee is getting together tomorrow night to decorate the gym. You're planning to come along, aren't you? We could use an extra hand."

"Are you sure I wouldn't be in the way?"

"Are you kidding? You heard how much we have to get done this week. Trust me. Everyone will welcome you with open arms."

She grinned shyly. "Okay, then. I think I'd like that."

"Great. Plan on having dinner here with us before we go."

Her smile faded and she glanced toward the stairs again. "Thanks, but that's not necessary. I've already intruded enough."

"You haven't intruded. The salad was great, you saved me some work by making it, and I enjoyed having another adult to talk to. You'll be doing me a favor. Besides, it might do Brianne good to have a woman around. Someone without an agenda—that is, if you can stand her attitude.''

Molly hesitated, but only for a heartbeat. ''All right, then. I guess it would be okay for one more night.''

One more night. Beau felt a ridiculous grin stretching his face, but he didn't even try to hide it. It had been a long time since he'd felt like a winner. Too damn long, in fact.

THE NEXT MORNING Molly made herself wait to take a shower and use Beau's phone until she was certain he and the kids had gone for the day. Last night's conversation had left her tossing and turning for hours after she'd said good night—not because of their discussion, but because she'd realized that it would take almost nothing to convince her that she was head over heels in love with him.

Again.

But that wasn't why she'd come to Serenity, and she wasn't going to let herself get sidetracked—especially since she didn't trust her feelings. It wasn't just Beau, she'd realized around midnight. She couldn't trust her feelings for *any* man right now. She might downplay the devastation of her marriage to Ethan when she spoke of it aloud, but his betrayal had ravaged her emotionally. Her self-esteem had taken a direct hit when he'd decided to replace her with someone his family would approve of, and she wasn't about to use Beau to soothe her hurt feelings.

She was far too vulnerable, but at least she knew it. Imagine the trouble she could get into if she didn't.

There was fresh coffee in the kitchen, along with a

note from Beau to help herself. She ignored both and hurried down the hall to the guest bath. She'd watched Beau drive away, but she couldn't shake the feeling that he might return at any moment. Only after she'd dressed again did she allow herself to pour a cup while she studied the list of people she wanted to contact about her mother.

She had no clear idea what she wanted to ask them, but she hadn't come all this way to let uncertainty stop her. Biting down on her bottom lip, she found Beau's cordless phone and dialed the first number on her list.

Louise Duncan had been her mother's closest friend, and Molly had vivid memories of spending time as a little girl in Louise's big, sunny kitchen while the two women laughed and chatted. She held her breath while the phone rang and felt the flutter of nervous excitement in her stomach when a familiar voice came on the line a few seconds later.

Molly's heart was thumping, but she forced herself to remain calm. "I don't know if you remember me," she said when she'd verified that she was talking with Louise. "You used to be friends with my mother, Ruby Lane."

"Molly?" Louise's voice rose in excitement. "My word, child, is it really you?"

Unexpected tears stung Molly's eyes. "You remember?"

"Well, of course I remember." Louise gave a soft laugh and the years fell away. "My, but it's good to hear your voice. Where are you calling from?"

Her obvious delight made Molly feel young again, and cradled by familiar things. "Actually I'm here in Serenity. I came back for Homecoming Week."

"And you thought to call me while you're here? Aren't you sweet!"

Molly battled a twinge of guilt. Would she have called if she hadn't wanted something? "I'd love to see you while I'm here. Is there any chance the two of us can get together?"

"What a question! Of course we'll get together. I'm tied up today, but you'll come to my place tomorrow. No excuses."

"No excuses." Molly laughed and felt herself relaxing. "I'd love to come. It'll be great to see you again."

"And you. Do you remember how to get here?"

"You'd better give me your address and directions," Molly said. "I don't think I could find it without help." She glanced around for paper and something to write with, then added, "I really do appreciate this. I have so many questions about my mother, and the two of you were so close I'm sure you're the best person to ask."

There was a brief pause before Louise's voice came again, and this time she sounded slightly less enthusiastic. "Questions?"

"I hope you don't mind. It's just that I don't remember anything about that night." Molly dug into the stack of papers beneath the phone until she found a spiral notebook and the nub of a pencil. She carried everything back to the table and sat. "I don't know why it's a blank, but for about six months on either side of the accident, I don't remember anything. Dad never talked about Mom much, and now that he's gone, it's too late to find out what he remembered. I don't know anything except that she went off the road somewhere. I don't even know where it happened."

"Your father's gone?" This time there was no mistaking the change in Louise's tone.

But Molly still couldn't think of any reason for it. "He died of a heart attack six months ago."

"Oh." A brief pause, then, "I'm sorry to hear that. I wish I'd known. I'd have sent a card or flowers."

Molly cradled the phone between her shoulder and ear. "I probably should have let someone here in Serenity know about his death, but I honestly didn't think of it."

"Well, of course you didn't, and no one could have expected you to. It wasn't as if we ever saw you after you left, and Frank never bothered to let us know where you were." Louise paused briefly, then sighed. "But listen to me going on. You don't want to hear about all that. Let me tell you how to find me, and tomorrow we'll talk about happier things."

While Louise gave directions, Molly scribbled notes. The edge in Louise's voice had disappeared, and Molly wondered if she'd only imagined it.

"I'll expect you around eleven," Louise said. "If that's okay with you, that is."

"It sounds perfect. I really appreciate this, Louise. I have so many things to ask you."

"Don't be silly," Louise said after another brief pause. "But I hope you don't expect too much. It's been a long time, and I'm not sure how much I'll be able to tell you."

She rang off before Molly had a chance to ask what she meant by that. She stared at her notes for a long moment, telling herself one more time that she'd only imagined the wariness in Louise's voice. But this was the second friend of her mother's who seemed unwilling to talk about the accident, and she didn't believe for a second it was merely coincidence.

MOLLY'S NEXT FEW CALLS were even less satisfying than her first one. Eleanor Peck's phone rang at least eight times before Molly conceded that no one was home. Charmaine Wilkinson's went to voice mail, and the number she had for Belinda Hunter had been disconnected.

Frustrated, she drove to the grocery store and wandered up and down every aisle, picking up everything on her list and a few impulse items, as well. She spent a few minutes in the pharmacy talking with Mrs. Dooley, whose daughter Katelynn had been a school friend of Molly's. According to her mother, Katelynn had moved to Tulsa with her husband nearly ten years earlier, and she wasn't planning to come back to Serenity for Homecoming Week.

Molly was a little disappointed to learn that, but she was even more discouraged by Mrs. Dooley's insistence that she hadn't known Molly's mother well, and that she didn't remember any details about the night Ruby Lane died.

Was there *anyone* who remembered her mother? Anyone who'd admit to remembering? Serenity was a small town. Too small for a fatal accident to go unnoticed. People *must* remember…

So why wouldn't they talk about it?

She thought about trying to find the spot where her mom had gone off the road, but she wouldn't even know where to look. And even if she went to the effort to find out, she was pretty sure that going there alone wasn't a good idea.

Back at the cabin she put her groceries away, pretending that the place was really hers and that it mattered where she put the tuna, bread and mayonnaise. By the time she saw Brianne and Nicky getting off the school bus at half-past three, Molly was so eager for company she convinced herself that her previous encounters with Brianne hadn't been that bad. Molly was an adult, after all, and Brianne was a hurt child. She could make more of an effort to get along with the girl.

Armed with fresh determination, she closed up the cabin, crossed the lawn to the house and knocked on the door. She hadn't forgotten Beau's instructions, but she wanted to make sure the kids knew what he'd told her before she barged in on them.

Through the glass in the door, she could see Brianne enter the kitchen. She wore a pair of jeans and a pale blue sweater, and her hair skimmed her shoulders when she walked. She recognized Molly and her step faltered, but she came to the door, threw it wide and turned toward the refrigerator. "You don't have to knock, you know. I thought my dad told you that."

"He did." Molly stepped inside and closed the door behind her. "I just didn't want to come barging in and frighten you."

Brianne pulled a can of soda from the fridge, opened it and drank deeply. "We're not babies," she said when she paused for a breath. "We wouldn't get frightened just because you came into the house."

"I know you're not," Molly assured her. "That's not what I meant. I saw you and Nicky get off the bus. Are you here alone very long before your dad gets home?"

Brianne shrugged. "A little while. Why do you care?"

The question caught Molly by surprise, but if Brianne wanted direct, Molly was happy to oblige. "I don't, really," she said with a shrug and a smile. "I'm just trying to make conversation."

Brianne's eyes widened almost imperceptibly, then immediately narrowed again. "Why?"

"Because you and I are standing in the same room, and it would be rude to ignore you."

"It's not rude to ignore somebody you don't like," Brianne said with a smirk. "And it's worse to pretend to like somebody when you really don't."

"Does that mean you don't like me, or that you think I don't like you?"

Beau's daughter leaned against the fridge and folded her arms. "What do you think?"

"Well, since I have no reason not to like you, I think I know the answer. Are you going to tell me why? Or do I have to guess?"

Brianne's shoulder rose in a nonchalant shrug. "My dad might not know what you want, but I do."

"Oh? And what do you think I want?"

"I don't think, I *know*." Brianne met Molly's gaze with a challenging glare. "You're after my dad, aren't you?"

Molly gaped at her. "Ex*cuse* me?"

"I said, you're after my dad and you think you can make him like you. That's why you're here. That's why you're staying in the cabin. And that's why you had dinner with us last night."

The girl looked so sure of herself Molly knew she'd have to choose her words with great care. "That's not true," she said. "I do like your dad, but we're friends, that's all. I've never even thought about making him like me." *Not since high school, anyway.* "I'm here for Homecoming, and to talk to people who used to know my mother. I'm staying in the cabin because the motel is full and I didn't make a reservation. And I was planning on taking care of my own dinner last night, but your dad invited me to stay.''

Brianne tilted her head and looked at her from behind a curtain of pale-blond hair. ''Why should I believe you?''

''Because I understand how important your dad is to you and I wouldn't insult you by lying.''

''Then why do you look at him that way?'' Brianne asked, flipping the pull-tab on her can with an annoying pinging sound.

A denial rose to Molly's lips, but Brianne would never believe it. ''I'm not sure how I look at him,'' Molly said with a sheepish smile, ''but you have to admit that he *is* a pretty good-looking guy. He always has been.''

''So you're in love with him.''

''Not at all.'' Molly moved to stand beside the counter. ''There's a difference between appreciating a good-looking man and being in love. I don't know your dad well enough to be in love with him.''

''But you could fall in love with him, couldn't you?''

Molly laughed uneasily. ''I'm not sure what to say, Brianne. If I say no, you'll think I'm insulting your dad. If I say yes, you'll think I'm lying about the rest. I don't think there is a good answer to that question.''

Brianne's lips actually curved into a semblance of a smile, but the challenge still burned in her eyes. ''I won't think you're insulting him if you say no. Why should I? You're not his type at all.''

Ouch! But it wasn't exactly news. ''So we agree that it's highly unlikely that I'm going to fall in love with your dad. What do you say the two of us try to get along while I'm here?''

"That's not a real no.''

Shaking her head, Molly laughed in disbelief. "You drive a hard bargain, kid. But I'm old enough to know better than to say 'never.' You're going to have to be content with highly unlikely, extremely remote, and it would take a miracle.''

With another shrug, Brianne pushed away from the refrigerator. "That's what my dad said, too,'' she announced as she headed down the hall toward the front of the house. She stopped at an open doorway and glanced back at Molly. "You can have a soda if you want one,'' she said, then disappeared, leaving Molly staring at the empty hallway and trying not to admit how much Brianne's offhand comments hurt.

CHAPTER SEVEN

SICK TO DEATH of blue and gold crepe paper, Beau followed Aaron out of the gymnasium and into the darkened corridor that led to the school's cafeteria. They'd been working for hours, tying banners and stringing streamers until Beau's fingers were stained with the school colors.

But his attention had only been partially on the job.

Every time he climbed the ladder, his eyes sought Molly across the cavernous room. Every time he went down, he caught himself straining to hear what she was saying. Her laugh intrigued him. Her walk fascinated him. He was acting like a man who hadn't had sex in years. Three. And a half. But who was counting?

He was having a hard time staying focused on anything but Molly, and his inability to think was starting to annoy him, so he'd jumped at Aaron's suggestion that they pay a visit to the snack machines outside the cafeteria. Maybe a short break would help him clear his head and put his fascination with Molly in perspective.

Music from Ridge's portable CD player trailed after them as they walked through scraps of crepe paper trimmed from streamers.

"Tell you what," Aaron said with an old man's groan. "If I never see another roll of that damn stuff again in my life, I'll die a happy man."

"You're not the only one." Beau caught a fluttering bit of blue and stuffed it into his pocket to throw away later. "I'll be glad when this is over. I need a few nights at home."

Aaron trailed his fingers along the lockers as they passed. "You won't get many. Mayor Biggs has already called a meeting of the WinterFest planning committee for next week."

Beau moaned in protest. "I hope he finds my replacement soon. I need a break."

"You don't really think he's going to replace you?"

"He has no choice. I've already told him that I have to resign."

"So? There's always been a Julander on the WinterFest committee. The town's entire Christmas is inside that thick head of yours." Aaron snorted a laugh and palmed his thinning hair. "You know what? I'll believe it when it happens."

Before Beau could argue, they drew to a stop in front of the darkened cafeteria and Aaron pulled a handful of change from his pocket. "So what's the story on Molly?" Aaron asked, as Beau dropped quarters into the vending machine.

Beau's first instinct was to punch Aaron for bringing the subject up. They'd been friends as long as he could remember and gotten into more scrapes together than he could count. They'd played on the same teams from Little League to their trophy-winning, high-school football squad, and each had been best man at the other's wedding. He trusted Aaron like no one else—but he had no idea how to answer his question.

He shrugged and culled a few quarters from the change in his own pockets. "No story." He fed four quarters into the coin slot and made a selection. "Why do you ask?"

Aaron snagged his bag of corn chips and tore it open. "No reason. Just curious. How did the two of you hook up, anyway?"

Beau dropped more coins into the slot and punched the buttons for another bag of chips. "We didn't hook up. She's staying in the cabin for a few days, that's all. No big deal, okay?"

"Whoa, buddy!" Aaron froze with a chip halfway to his mouth. "It was just a question. I didn't mean anything by it."

"Yeah? Well, then, don't say it like that. You could give somebody the wrong impression."

"Okay. Whatever." Aaron glanced over his shoulder toward the gym. "Is it just me, or is she a lot prettier than she was in school?"

Beau didn't want to think about pretty. He moved to the soft-drink machine and held out an impatient hand for some financial input from Aaron. "Not everyone reaches their peak at seventeen."

"You saying *I* did?"

"You? No. But there are times when I wonder about myself."

The laughter in Aaron's eyes faded almost immediately. "You're serious?"

Beau gave up trying to figure out what he wanted to drink and leaned against the cool brick wall. "Tell me what you think of me."

"What I *think* of you?"

"Yeah. You know. What do you think of me? If you had to sum me up in a few words, what would they be?"

"You're my friend. A pain in the neck sometimes, but still my friend. Why?"

A distant burst of laughter echoed through the empty hallways, and Beau could have sworn he could tell Molly's laughter from the others'. He just couldn't understand why, when he'd been perfectly content to be alone and get his life together, he had to start letting things become complicated. He raked his fingers through his hair and told himself—again—to stop thinking about her.

"It's just...well, Molly said something the other day that's been bugging me. She has this image of me as lucky, and I know she's not the only one who feels that way."

Aaron quirked an eyebrow. "You? Lucky?"

Beau smiled halfheartedly. "I didn't say it, she did. But when I put that together with some of the things Heather used to say, it makes me wonder if *everyone* sees me that way."

"Well, *I* don't."

"I'm not sure you count," Beau said grudgingly. "You know me too well. You know what I've screwed up and you know where I've failed. But what about other people?"

Laughing, Aaron dumped the last of his chips into his hand and crumpled the empty wrapper. "Did Molly give you a reason for this assessment of hers?"

Beau thought back for a moment. "Well, she thinks I'm lucky for inheriting the house and the farm."

"And you are."

"Yeah, and I'm the first one to admit it," he said, though the instant the words left his mouth, he realized they weren't quite true. "My lousy marriage wasn't lucky. My divorce wasn't lucky. Having an ex-mother-in-law who still wants to run my life isn't lucky.''

"So you're an unlucky SOB instead. What do you care what Molly Lane thinks?''

"I *don't*.'' Beau pushed away from the wall and tried once more to figure out what kind of soda he wanted. He punched a big flat green button with his fist. "I was curious, that's all. It's no big deal.''

"Get me one of those, wouldja?'' Aaron fished a bill from his pocket and handed it to Beau. "You had a great run in high school. Senior-class president. Captain of the football team…and whatever else you were. You got good grades. Girls were all over you. You could have dated anybody you wanted.''

"And you think I lucked out in all that? All the hours I spent working on my game and hitting the books meant nothing?''

"No. But what's the big deal?''

"It's not a big deal,'' Beau said. "But if you work hard for something, it's nice to know your efforts are appreciated. Nobody wants people to write off their skill and hard work as dumb luck.''

"And you think that's what people do with you?''

"I don't know.''

"Well, hell. You've had some bad luck, too, and everybody knows it. So even if some folks did think that when we were kids, they don't now.''

Beau handed over change and a cold can of root beer to his friend, and started back toward the gymnasium. "Then there *are* people who feel that way?''

"No. No!'' Dumbfounded, Aaron ran a hand along the back of his neck. "I don't know. Nobody ever said anything to me. I said *if* they'd felt that way. But even if they do, what does it really matter? You know who you are, so what does somebody else's opinion matter?''

Beau had no answer for that. These days, it seemed that there were a whole bunch of questions he couldn't answer. When they reached the gymnasium again, he glanced through the open doors and his gaze flew to Molly. She stood in the center of the crowd, smiling broadly, basking in the attention of her former classmates. Even from a distance, he could see the glow in her eyes, and his heart turned over twice before he could pull himself together.

It had been too long since he'd been with a woman, he told himself. That was all. He was reacting the way any man would react to the sight of a particularly beautiful woman. Hell, if circumstances were different, he might be tempted to let nature take its course.

But circumstances *weren't* different. Molly would be here for just ten more days. Then she'd go back to her life and Beau would stay in his. Another man might have taken advantage of the situation, anyway, but marriage to Heather had cured him of any interest in a superficial relationship, and temporary just didn't cut it.

He *did* care what Molly thought of him, even if he wasn't ready to admit how much.

"I STILL CAN'T believe you're really here," Jennifer Grant said from atop a ladder a few hours later. She'd been another of Molly's friends when they were girls, and it had taken only a few minutes to rediscover their former closeness.

"To be honest, I can't, either," Molly admitted. She stretched high to hand Jennifer one end of the soft blue netting they'd been assigned to drape over the plain walls of the gymnasium. Only about ten people had showed up for tonight's work party, so there hadn't been much time to chat, but they were nearly finished and the mood was beginning to lighten.

Even Beau, who'd been working nonstop all evening, had disappeared. She glanced over one shoulder to see if he'd come back, but there was still no sign of him. "You can't imagine how glad I am you've all been so welcoming," she said, turning her attention back to Jennifer. "I was a little worried about coming back. I was afraid that you'd have all forgotten me."

"You're one of us, Molly. Always have been. Moving away didn't alter that."

Unlike some of the others in their class, Jennifer hadn't changed much since high school. She'd put on a few pounds, but she still had tons of energy and wore too much makeup and flirted outrageously with every man in sight. But the flirting had always been harmless, and her husband—a good-looking guy Molly remembered only vaguely—didn't seem to mind.

Jennifer secured the netting in place and started down the ladder again. "The only thing I can't figure out is why you're suddenly so...insecure."

The comment threw Molly and she nearly missed Jennifer's cue to pick up her end of the ladder. "Insecure?" she asked when they were finally in sync again and moving toward the next patch of bare wall. "Is that how I strike you?"

"A little." Jennifer set her end of the ladder on the floor and headed back for the bolt of netting. "You're less confident than you used to be. But you're still smart. Funny. Lots of fun to hang out with. Don't you realize that?"

Molly shook her head. "It's been a while since I had

any close friends," she admitted numbly. "Dad was a bit of a loner, and I'm probably a lot like him—but not because that's what I want. I like being with people and I'm having a great time tonight."

"I'm glad." Jennifer carried the netting over to the ladder and wedged it against a folded stack of bleachers. "I guess losing your mom didn't help—especially not the way it happened."

For the second time in less than a minute, Molly felt as if she'd been hit hard. She picked up the basket holding scissors, tape and string, and walked over to join Jennifer. "You remember the accident?" she asked, setting the basket on the floor

"Of course I do." Jennifer seemed oblivious to the fact that she was discussing something that everyone else had decreed off-limits. "It shook everybody up practically forever."

Or maybe Molly had misinterpreted everyone else's reticence. "Would you mind telling me what you remember?"

"Sure." Jennifer shrugged. "But you must remember more than I do."

"Actually, I don't remember anything at all. The year around my mom's accident is a blank."

"Seriously?"

"I'm afraid so."

"You don't remember anything?"

"Not a thing. The only things I know are what my dad told me, but he didn't like to talk about it. Now that he's gone, the people here in Serenity are the only ones who can tell me about that night."

Jennifer reached into the basket for the scissors and tape, tucking them into the waistband of her jeans. "Well, that stinks."

Lanie Byers interrupted long enough to get the keys to Jennifer's Suburban so they could bring in the disco ball. When they were alone again, Jennifer's expression grew thoughtful. "I remember that night really well. It was cold. Sometime in January, I think."

"April tenth." That much Molly did know.

Jennifer looked confused. "Yeah, but we had a storm. A blizzard. A white-out. That's why she went off the road, wasn't it? That and the ice?" She paused. "I guess you could be right. It was probably one of those freak spring storms we sometimes have. I just remember the phone ringing and someone telling my mom about the accident. It happened out past the Trego ranch, I think. The car hit a patch of ice and went through the guardrail. They figured Ruby died on impact. I know it's not much, but at least you can feel better knowing that she didn't suffer."

Molly nodded slowly, letting those few details filter in to mingle with what she could remember about the town. "The Trego ranch..." she said after a few seconds. "Isn't that way out on the East Bench?"

Jennifer nodded. "Past the houses out there, on the way to Beaver Creek."

Molly could picture the road—a narrow, winding strip of asphalt barely wide enough for two lanes of traffic and usually closed during bad weather. "Did they ever say what she was doing out there?"

"Not that I heard." Jennifer tilted her head to one side. "It does seem like an odd place to be in the middle of a bad storm, doesn't it?"

"Very. I thought that stretch of road was closed when the weather was bad, so how did she get out there in the first place?"

"It is closed—usually. They lock the gates in late

October and don't open them again until almost Memorial Day, except in mild winters.''

Molly nodded thoughtfully. She didn't know what to think, but she didn't want to be guilty of blowing things out of proportion. Still, her dad's refusal to discuss the accident had never seemed so unfair or so wrong. She should already know the details of her mother's accident. She shouldn't have to beg people to tell her about it.

"I wonder if anyone knows what she was doing out there," she said, more to herself than Jennifer.

"One of her friends might."

"I've talked to a couple of her friends," Molly said, "but nobody seems willing to say much. What about your mom? Do you think she might know?"

"I don't know." Jennifer fished a piece of gum from a pocket. "I'll ask. She still wears the jewelry she bought from your mom."

Molly realized they'd slacked off with the decorating and grabbed the bolt of netting to unwind a length of it. "Really?"

"Yeah. She's got some really great stuff." Jennifer pulled out the scissors and waited for Molly to stop. "I keep trying to convince her to give me those turquoise earrings your mom made when we were seniors, but she won't even consider it." Molly stopped unwinding and Jennifer cut the netting to the proper length. "I'll tell you what I really wanted—that beaded choker she made for you that Christmas. That's still the most elegant piece of jewelry I've ever seen. Do you still have it?"

Although she struggled to remember something— anything—about a choker, Molly's mind was a blank. "I wish I did, but Dad gave away all her jewelry and clothes to charity after she died. By the time I realized what he'd done, it was too late.''

"But that choker was yours," Jennifer protested.

"Dad must have given it away with all the rest." Molly tried not to feel the cold spikes of anger that bumped around inside her, but they were getting harder and harder to ignore. She understood her father's grief. She knew how painful it must have been to see reminders of his beloved wife, but why hadn't he realized that Molly might feel differently? That she might *need* the reminders? Or had he just not cared?

A faint wisp of memory stirred—a shadowy image surrounded by anger and shouting, though she couldn't make out the words. A vague sense of uneasiness ran through her, but she didn't know why. Had she been angry, or had she been frightened by someone else?

Frightened?

Yes. There was anger all around her, but she was frightened and nearly overwhelmed by sadness. Just as quickly as the image came, it was gone. She let out a shaky breath and rubbed her temples with her fingertips. "I don't *think* I remember, but I'm not sure. It's like there's something right outside my line of vision. I see this shadow, but then I turn to find out what it is and it's gone.''

Jennifer grabbed one end of the netting and climbed the ladder. "Maybe it would help you remember if you could see some of the jewelry your mom made."

"I'd love to. You can't imagine how much."

"Okay. I'll talk to my mom and let you know. And who knows? Maybe Mom will be able to tell you something about the accident."

A faint spark of hope stirred in Molly's chest, but she tried not to let it grow too large. Jennifer's mother probably did know something. The real question was, would she be willing to talk about it?

Molly was almost afraid to hope.

SHE WAS ASLEEP the second her head touched the pillow and slept straight through until eight the next morning, something she hadn't done since her father's heart attack. She awoke slowly, stretching beneath the light blanket and reveling in the autumn sunlight that streamed into the cabin through the windows.

Other than a few brief moments during her conversation with Jennifer, she'd had a wonderful time at the school, and even that conversation seemed less sinister in the daylight. The possibility of seeing her mother's jewelry after all this time got her up and out of bed, but she tried not to let herself get too excited or hopeful. After all, Jennifer's mother might be as reticent as the rest of Serenity when it came to Ruby Lane.

Almost without thinking, she crossed to the front windows and looked at the main house, remembering the drive home with Beau well after midnight. Had she really seen a spark of something different in his eyes last night, or had exhaustion and excitement made her imagine it?

She yawned and started to turn away, then realized that the Cherokee wasn't in the driveway. The kids would be at school and Beau was gone. Maybe she could save herself a few steps. She crossed the lawn wearing her robe, pajamas and slippers, and carried shoes and clean clothes with her so she could dress after her shower.

Weak sunlight filtered down on her, and the sounds of Serenity coming to life surrounded her. It was such a lovely morning, maybe she'd even have coffee on the porch. But when she let herself into the kitchen, she saw Beau standing in front of the washing machine. She came to an abrupt halt and one of her shoes dropped to the floor with a thud.

He wore a pair of faded jeans slung low on his hips. No shirt. No socks. He turned as Molly entered, and the sight of his bare chest, whisker-shadowed cheeks and lopsided smile sent her heart into overdrive. Her mouth went dry and she clutched her clothes in front of her like a shield, but she couldn't do anything about her makeup-less face or the hair poking out from her head at all angles.

His gaze swept her from head to toe, but his expression gave no clue as to what he thought. "Morning," he greeted her, as if disheveled women wearing pajamas burst into his kitchen every day of the week. "Coffee's on. Toast and jam's on the table. I can fix a couple of eggs if you're not particular, or I saved you two of my mom's peach muffins. They're on a plate near the microwave."

"Muffins are fine," Molly croaked out around the lump of pure mortification lodged in her throat. She tore her gaze away from his flat stomach and made herself meet his eyes, but that wasn't a whole lot safer, since they seemed exceptionally blue this morning. "I didn't see your Jeep in the driveway. I thought you were gone."

Beau checked the pockets of a Nicky-size pair of jeans and tossed them into the washer. "I had to leave for a while. The kids missed the bus. By the time I got back, Mom was here with muffins so I parked on the street." He pulled a pair of Brianne's jeans from the mound at his feet and checked the pockets. "Guess I'm finally getting that chance I've been wanting to catch up around here.''

Molly poured herself a cup of coffee and leaned against the counter. She made herself look at the swollen mound of laundry, instead of Beau. ''I'm not a very good houseguest. I should offer to help with something.''

''With what? My dirty laundry?'' Beau laughed and shook his head. ''Even if you did offer, I'd turn you down. The kids and I made this mess. We'll clean it up.''

''Your laundry wasn't exactly what I had in mind.'' When she realized she was staring at a pair of men's boxers, she looked away from the clothes. ''You keep feeding me, though, so maybe I should pay you back by cooking dinner one night.''

Beau dropped a sweatshirt into the washer and fixed her with a skeptical look. ''You know how to cook?''

It had been a long time since anyone had teased her, and she'd forgotten how it felt to view life as something to be enjoyed rather than simply endured. She managed to keep a serious expression on her face and shook her head. ''No. Is that a problem?''

''Not if you can keep from giving us all food poisoning.''

''I can certainly try.''

He grinned and turned back to his laundry. ''Well, what more could a guy ask? When do you want to fix us this feast?''

''How about tonight?''

''Tonight's the parade and I need to be there early. I'm afraid you'll have to join us for a quick bite at the Burger Shack.''

''Tomorrow, then.''

"Football game. Pizza. And Saturday's the Homecoming Ball. The kids will be at my parents' house, and I don't think you should have to toil over a hot stove before you need to get dressed. I thought we could have dinner at the Chicken Inn on our way to the school." His gaze shot to hers and she saw a glimmer of uncertainty in his eyes. "If that's okay with you of course."

Somewhere way in the back of her mind a voice whispered caution, but she ignored it and nodded. "It's fine. So I'll fix dinner on Monday, then. What do the kids like?"

"Oh, they're pretty fussy. They insist that the food be at least semiedible."

"Don't you think that's a bit demanding?"

"Well, yes, as a matter of fact." He dumped laundry soap into the washer and closed the lid. "I've tried talking to them about their extreme demands—three meals a day, clean clothes, a roof over their heads…" He shook his head in mock exasperation. "It's this younger generation. They think they're entitled to things we never had."

Molly chuckled. "How about chicken? I have a great recipe. It has to be marinated overnight, but it makes the meat so tender you won't believe it."

Beau crossed to the coffeemaker and poured a fresh cup. "Sounds great, but you don't have to get fancy. We're just small-town folk here."

"It's not fancy," Molly assured him. She carried the plate of muffins to the table and made herself comfortable. "It takes hardly any time at all. And living in a small town doesn't mean you can't gussy up from time to time, does it?"

Beau pretended to consider that for a moment. "No,

I suppose not. We gussy occasionally. We just don't gussy our chickens.''

"Cute.'' She broke off a piece of muffin and popped it into her mouth. "Well, Monday's chicken *is* going to be gussied, and I promise you it's semiedible. I'll just have to remember to stop at the FoodWay for garlic and oranges.''

"You should find 'em there. We're small, but we do have produce.'' He looked at her over the rim of his cup and her heart took off at a gallup. She knew she was playing with fire, but she couldn't make herself look away. He was still the best-looking man on the planet, bar none.

CHAPTER EIGHT

AFTER WHAT SEEMED like hours, Beau finally broke eye contact and took up the conversation as if the moment had never been. "So now that you've been here for a few days, what do you think? Disappointed?"

Molly drew a breath and tried to follow his lead. "In the town? Of course not. I'd forgotten how much I like it here."

"It's not too unsophisticated for you?"

"Not at all. Did you really think it would be?"

Beau shrugged and joined her at the table. "Lots of people have gone in search of something bigger and better since we graduated."

"Yes, but I didn't leave by choice. I left because my dad left. I didn't go out to look for something better, and I came back to find what I lost." She ate another bite of muffin and made a mental note to ask for his mother's recipe. "What about you? Do you ever regret staying?"

Beau lowered his cup to the table and nodded. "Once in a while."

"Really? I didn't know you'd ever thought of leaving."

"Of course I did. I thought about it all the time when I was a kid. Not that I don't love it here. I do. And I love my family. I don't really regret my choices, but there are times when I look at some of the other guys in our class and wonder what might have been."

"Like who?"

"Dave Marbury, for one. He's on the coaching staff at the University of Wyoming. Hank Hilton writes for the *Denver Post*. Steve Cummings just bought a summer house on an island off the coast of Maine. And here I am, living in my grandparents' old house and flying my little airplane from one place to another."

"Yeah, but most of those guys would have given a limb to be you back in school."

Beau's lips curved into a wistful smile. "That was a long time ago, Molly. It's a little disheartening sometimes to realize that the best thing you'll ever do in life happened before you were twenty."

"But I thought…"

"You thought an achievement or two during high school should be enough to carry a guy through life?"

She laughed uneasily. "I guess not."

Beau spread butter on a piece of toast and followed it with blackberry jam. "Don't get me wrong. I do love my life. I have great kids and a terrific career, and I'm following in the traditions that mean so much to my family. It might not be what I originally wanted to do, but it's close. Still, every once in a while—usually around Homecoming when the guys come back—I think about what might have been and I feel a twinge of envy."

"What did you want to do?"

"I was going to be a commercial airline pilot," he said. "I had dreams of traveling all over the world, seeing everything, soaking up different cultures."

"So why didn't you?"

"Life got in the way." He took a bite of toast and

washed it down with coffee. "Heather and I took a few wrong turns and weren't as careful as we should have been. She got pregnant before the end of high school, so we got married and settled into life here in Serenity, and that was that."

Had Molly known that at the time? Was that another thing she'd forgotten? She shook her head in confusion. "But Brianne isn't old enough—"

"No, she's not. The baby was stillborn." Old heartache flickered across his face, but he went on quickly, "I think some folks expected us to split up after that, but losing the baby after everything we'd been through was almost too much for Heather. I couldn't walk out on her. I loved her. I wouldn't have married her if I hadn't."

Molly finished her muffin and wrapped her hands around her coffee mug just to have something to hold on to. "I'm so sorry. I had no idea."

He shrugged away her concern. "How could you? You were gone."

"Well, yes, but—"

"It was rough," he said, "but we got through it. We gave up one set of dreams and worked on another. That's life." He finished his toast, then stood and stacked plates and silverware. "Like I said, I don't even think about it much except when Homecoming rolls around."

His thoughts must be especially poignant this year after Heather walked out and left him holding that new set of dreams by himself. Molly bit her lip to keep from asking if Heather had run off to chase her old dreams, and if he resented her for leaving him to raise the kids alone. She knew the answer, anyway. Even if he harbored some mild resentment, he clearly adored his children, and would have been heartbroken if Heather had taken them with her to Santa Fe.

She drained the rest of her coffee and carried her mug to the sink, where Beau had started scraping dishes and loading the dishwasher. "It's a funny thing about comparisons," she said. "I've been thinking how lucky you are and what a great life you have, and here you are comparing yourself to other guys. I wonder why we can't ever just be happy with the life we have."

Beau shot a glance at her. "I *am* happy."

"I wish *I* could say that and mean it."

He shut off the water and turned to face her. "You're in the middle of a rough year. I couldn't have said I was happy when the baby was stillborn. I'm not sure I could have said it when I stopped working for my dad and opened the charter company. And I sure as hell couldn't say it last year when Heather walked out. But I *wanted* to be happy, and sometimes that's enough."

Molly smiled slowly. "I can say *that* and mean it."

"So there you go."

She shook off the slight melancholy that had taken hold and turned back to the table for the rest of their dishes. "I'm a happy person most of the time. It'll take a while to get over Dad's death. I know that and I'm prepared for it. Losing my job bothers me in a different way—probably because it's the one thing I should have been able to control. There are so many people out of work now that it's not easy finding something else."

"You've been looking?"

"Since the day I was let go." Molly sighed. "I've probably sent out seventy résumés, and I've only been called in for two interviews—and both of those were disastrous. One was for a different position from the one they advertised—at about half the pay. The other was for a company that declared bankruptcy a week later.''

''Are you trying to stay in the same field, or would you consider branching out?''

''I'd love to stay in graphic design, but I'm not sure if that's because I enjoy it or because it's all I know. I'm pretty good at crafts, but there's not much money in popsicle-stick birdhouses. But the graphic-design field is glutted right now, so I don't know what I'll do. I'm just lucky I have a little time to get on my feet again. My dad had a couple of life insurance policies. My stepmother was the beneficiary on one, but I was named on the other, so I don't have to take the first minimum-wage job that comes along.''

''Well, at least you're not destitute.''

''No, or I wouldn't be here. But I don't want to live off the insurance money indefinitely. I know Dad would want me to use that money for something big and wonderful. He wouldn't want me to fritter it away month by month on rent and utilities.''

''Then we'll both keep our fingers crossed that you won't have to.'' Beau shut the dishwasher and looked over the kitchen with a satisfied smile. ''And that the perfect opportunity will come knocking soon.''

''I hope so, but with the job market the way it is right now, I'm not going to hold my breath.''

''So maybe you should think about doing something else. Make your own opportunity.''

Molly laughed. ''If only it were that easy.''

''Maybe it could be. What do you know how to do?''

''Not a whole lot, that's the trouble.''

"And the crafts? No possibilities there?"

She crossed to the trash can and tossed in their napkins. "I need more than a little pocket money. I don't think a hobby is the answer."

"Depends on the hobby, doesn't it? Look at your mom. She did all right for herself with her jewelry business. I'll bet every woman in town bought stuff from her, and I'll bet most of them still have it. If she'd been able to launch a business on the Internet, Ruby Lane would probably be a household name by now."

Molly started to shake her head, but something stopped her and a tiny seed of excitement took root. "I do know how to make jewelry," she said, testing the idea as she said it aloud. "At least I used to. It's been a while, but I helped my mom a lot when I was younger."

Beau held out both arms and grinned. "You see?"

"There's just one problem," she said, trying to be practical. "My mom's jewelry was special. Unique. She was a genius at design, but I'm not. I might be able to do all right if I had her sketches, but I'm sure my dad threw them out along with everything else."

Beau waved off her argument with one hand. "You could copy your mom's designs, couldn't you?"

"Maybe."

"So we just find everybody in town who has your mom's jewelry and you go from there. You've got a little capital of your own, and I'll bet Pete Gratz over at the bank would be willing to talk to you about a loan if you need one."

Molly was having trouble keeping up. "But I'm not staying here, and I—"

"At least think about it," he urged. "It's an option,

and five minutes ago you didn't have one. You're already ahead.''

His optimism was contagious, but Molly wasn't Beau. Life didn't go the way she wanted it to simply because she wanted it.

"At least think about it," he urged again.

And Molly nodded. Because she *would* think about it, even if she knew that it was too much to hope for.

MOLLY SET OFF for her appointment with Louise Duncan at a little before eleven. She tried to put Beau's suggestion out of her mind, but the possibility of resurrecting her mother's jewelry designs was awfully appealing, even if she couldn't make a living at it.

She considered various possibilities as she drove through town and into East Bench subdivision. Even though the homes there were aging now, they still sported manicured front lawns and wide driveways filled with boats, snowmobiles on trailers and recreational vehicles.

Once she'd found Louise's sprawling rambler, she pulled up to the curb and sat for a moment, remembering. The house hadn't changed much since she'd last seen it. The trees in the front yard were taller, and there were more flower beds along the sidewalk, but memories of time spent here with her mother swirled all around her.

Only a few fallen leaves littered the carefully tended lawn; someone had gathered the rest into orange trash bags, which now formed a neat stack at the end of the driveway. Those bright pumpkin-shaped bags forced her to acknowledge something she'd been holding at arm's length for months—the holidays were just around the corner.

She'd been dreading Thanksgiving and Christmas ever since the funeral, but she couldn't ignore them much longer. She was going to have to find some way to get through them alone.

With an effort she shook off the melancholy and smiled at the leaf bags. Unlike most of the folks around Serenity, Louise had always turned up her nose at the practice of burning leaves in the fall.

Ruby had teased her relentlessly, but nothing she'd said had changed her friend's mind. Molly could almost hear the two women bantering now, and she smiled as she imagined the sound of her mother's delighted laughter.

Her father had grown to hate Serenity, but Ruby had loved living here. She'd been artistic and passionate, ruled by her heart rather than her head, and she'd loved the volatile springs, the hostile winters, the heat of the summer and the glorious autumns. She'd found joy in everything, from the first buds of leaves in the spring to the sting of sleet on her face in the winter. But she'd found that joy because she'd looked for the best in every situation and always expected to find it.

A whole lot like Beau.

Molly wished suddenly that she'd inherited more of her mother's ability to find the good and less of her father's tendency to expect the worst. Ruby wouldn't have balked at the idea of embarking on a journey into the unknown. She'd never been the careful, cautious type.

Then again, if she'd been more cautious, maybe she'd have stayed off the road to Beaver Creek and would be here still.

That possibility made Molly's heart ache, but she didn't want to spend the day filled with regrets over things she was powerless to change, so she resolutely pushed everything out of her mind and took a few deep breaths of crisp, autumn-scented air. She wanted to find out about her mother's accident, but maybe not today, after all, despite the fact that it was her main reason for visiting Louise. Today, she wanted to spend the time celebrating her mother's life, remembering her spirit and talking about the things that had made her happy.

She climbed out of the car and started up the curving sidewalk to the front door, but she'd only gone a few steps when someone called out to her.

"Molly? Molly Lane, is that you?"

She wheeled back around and found a blond woman in her late fifties striding across the road toward her. It took only a second for Molly to recognize Joyce Whalen, a friend of her mother's she hadn't yet tried to call.

With a glance at Louise's still-closed front door, she changed direction and walked back toward the street. Joyce looked exactly the same as she had the last time Molly saw her. Trim. Athletic. Full of energy. She wore a pale-blue warm-up suit and new tennis shoes, and she still had a spring in her step.

She swept Molly into a hug and released her again just as quickly. "I heard that you were back in town. When did you get here?"

Molly frowned slightly when she realized how many days had slipped away already. "I've been here nearly a week."

"You've been here all this time and I haven't seen you? Where are you staying?"

"Believe it or not, I'm staying in the cabin on Beau Julander's property."

"Oh?" Joyce's eyes flickered with interest. "That's a nice place, if I do say so myself. I worked with Heather on some of the decorating."

"Did you really? I had no idea you were a decorator."

Joyce laughed and shielded her eyes against the glare of the sun. "Well, I wouldn't go *that* far, but I do like to dabble from time to time. Ruby used to encourage me to take a risk, and I finally got my courage up. But what about you? Are you married?"

"Divorced."

"How many little ones?"

Molly shook her head. "None."

Joyce didn't so much as blink, just motioned at a white brick house across the street where a tennis racket and a tube of bright yellow balls sat on the driveway beside a dark-colored Buick. "I just got back from a match, but I'd love to visit with you for a while. Would you like to come over? I was just going to make a pot of coffee. I even have some of that lemon poppyseed cake you used to like so much."

Another wave of memory swamped Molly. "It's been years since I've had that cake," she said with regret, "and I'd love to take you up on your offer. But I made arrangements to spend some time with Louise this morning, so I'm going to have to say no. I'd love to come by another time, if that's all right."

Joyce squinted toward Louise's house. "Louise is expecting you?"

"At eleven." Molly glanced at her watch and realized that she was already a few minutes late. "I should hurry. I don't want to keep her waiting. Are you in the book? Do you mind if I call you tomorrow?"

"I don't mind at all," Joyce said. "But are you sure

Louise is expecting you? I saw her getting ready to leave early this morning. She said she wouldn't be back until Sunday tonight.''

"Oh, but that can't be," Molly said. "I talked to her just yesterday.'' But the words were a token protest and a sick feeling settled in her stomach. She knew that Joyce wasn't lying, just as she knew that Louise had skipped town to avoid talking to her.

"Well, then, I must be wrong.'' Joyce's eyes filled with sympathy, but that only made Molly feel worse. "Or maybe something came up at the last minute," she said, trying to sound as if she actually believed it. "You know how that can happen.'' She squeezed Molly's arm and smiled encouragement. "Tell you what—you run over and check, but if Louise isn't there for some reason, just come to my place and let yourself in. Tom's out of town this week and I could use some company—and I'd love to hear what's been happening in your life since I saw you last.''

Molly nodded, almost too numb to think. She turned away and started up the sidewalk again, but the joy she'd felt earlier was crushed beneath a wall of doubt and fear. When she reached the front door, she lifted her hand to knock, but a piece of paper taped inside the screen door caught her eye. And when she realized that her name was scrawled across the note, the disbelief and anger she'd been fighting got the upper hand.

She jerked open the door and tore the note from the glass, read Louise's half-baked explanation for taking off without a word of warning and crumpled the paper in her fist. For a long time she stood there, trying to decide whether to cross the street and take a chance that Joyce might actually talk to her when she found out what Molly wanted.

She couldn't bear to set herself up for more disappointment, but what if Joyce *was* willing to talk?

With one last glance at Louise's empty house, she crossed the street to Joyce's front door. But she refused to get her hopes up. Ruby hadn't been as close to Joyce as she was to Louise. If Joyce had any ideas about why her neighbor left town, she'd have said so already. The idea of company was appealing, however, and it might be a good thing to spend some time talking about her mother's life, instead of always worrying about her death.

"OKAY, BUDDY, do you have them all?" Beau settled a jacket on top of the load he'd already piled on Nicky's outstretched arms. "Are you sure you can carry all that?"

Nicky scowled up at him from beneath a too-long sheaf of hair. "Of course I can. I'm not a baby." He pivoted away, eager to help, but still a little young to handle much responsibility. A jacket sleeve dangled from the pile and nearly tripped him on his way out the door. Beau watched until he was certain Nicky wouldn't fall down the stairs and called after him, "If your sister's out there, tell her it's time to leave."

He'd spent the day getting ready for the parade—roping off prime viewing areas, making sure the banners were draped on the cars of local dignitaries, shuffling the order of parade entrants to allow Melvin Greenspan more time to fix the brakes on the float entered by the high-school science department.... He'd been running on high for hours, and he was ready for the part that made all the work worthwhile.

If any problems arose now, they were Ridge's responsibility. For the rest of the evening, Beau was just another spectator, and he was determined to enjoy every minute.

Whistling softly, he turned back to the list of last-minute details he'd made that morning and checked off another item. A shadow passed in front of him and he glanced up to find Molly standing in the open doorway.

She wore a pair of jeans and a shape-hugging white sweater, but she seemed completely unaware of how incredible she looked. "Rope and jackets delivered safely, sir. Two blankets tucked into the back seat as ordered. What next?"

He grinned, marked off the items on his checklist and patted his pockets, searching for his keys. "Next, we head out—unless there's something else you need." When she shook her head, he checked the stove one last time to make sure he'd turned off all the burners. "Did you happen to notice if Brianne is out there?"

Molly nodded. "I saw her coming around from the front as I came back here. But are you sure she's going to be okay with this? I mean, I don't need to stay with you all evening. I'd be happy to meet up with Elaine or Jennifer if that would make things easier."

"Absolutely not!" He spied his keys near the phone and crossed the room to get them. "I invited you and I'll be insulted if you don't come. It's time Brianne realized that she doesn't get to call all the shots around here."

"O-kay," Molly said hesitantly.

Beau laughed at her obvious lack of enthusiasm. "It's going to be okay. We'll have a great time, I promise. Just relax. Brianne's a great kid, and once she realizes that she can't run you off with a tantrum or two, she'll give up and you'll get to see the good parts of her personality."

Molly still didn't look entirely convinced, but Beau appreciated her willingness to give Brianne another chance. He followed her out and locked the door, then fell into step at her side as they strode across the lawn toward the Cherokee.

"How did your meeting with Louise Duncan go?"

"It didn't." She slanted a glance at him. "But let's not talk about that, okay? I just want to have a good time tonight."

"Okay. Sure." As they approached the car, Beau realized that Brianne had already buckled herself into the front seat. He scowled and swore under his breath. What was *wrong* with this kid of his, anyway? It wasn't like her to be so rude.

Not wanting to start the evening on the wrong foot, he pasted on a smile and opened the car door. "Hey, funny face, how about sitting in back with your brother so Molly can sit up here?"

Brianne smirked at him. "Why should I?"

"Because I asked you to." He kept the smile but put a little heat into his voice so she wouldn't misunderstand.

Either she didn't understand, or she just didn't care. "I don't want to sit back there. I want to sit up here. With you. There's lots of room in the back seat—" she looked at Molly with all the haughty disdain Heather had shown toward the end of their marriage "—unless she's too big to fit."

Beau's smile vaporized. He shot a glance at Nicky and jerked his head, and his son jumped out of the back seat without hesitation. Brianne folded her arms and stared straight ahead through the windshield.

Still determined to save the evening, Beau leaned into the car and lowered his voice so that the others couldn't hear him. "This is completely uncalled-for, young lady. Molly is my friend and my guest. I want her here even if you don't, and I won't tolerate rudeness. Is that clear?"

Brianne's glare was hostile. "Well, I *don't* want her here. Don't I count for anything?"

"Of course you do. And when you behave like the young lady I raised you to be, you'll get a voice in the way things are done around here. If you're going to behave like a baby, you don't get a vote. Now get in the back seat and sit with your brother, and if I hear one more rude comment or see one more dirty look directed at Molly, you and I are going to have some real trouble."

A muscle in Brianne's jaw twitched, and for a minute Beau thought she was going to refuse again. Finally she sighed and released the lock on the seat belt. "I thought you didn't like us to lie."

"I'm not asking you to lie. I'm telling you to be civil."

She climbed into the back through the space between the front seats. "What's Mom going to say when she comes home and finds her here?"

"Mom's not coming home," Beau snapped. He regretted it immediately and tried to soften his tone when he spoke again. "I know you want her to come back, but wanting it won't make it happen. You're going to have to accept that, because it's how things are."

"Gram says—"

"Well, Gram's wrong," Beau cut her off before she could spout more of Doris's delusions. He leaned farther into the car and gripped the seat as if hanging on to it might help him keep a grip on his temper. "Gram wants your mom to come back because she's unhappy with the choices your mom made and she feels guilty. It's not Gram's fault. It's nobody's fault. Your mom is who she is. But I think Gram blames herself for what your mom did. She thinks that if Mom will just come back to live with us again, it'll prove that Gram was a good mother.''

The anger in Brianne's eyes seemed to break apart, and whatever had been holding her so stiff and unwieldy for weeks crumbled. In a flash, she was young and frightened and vulnerable again. "But what if Mom's wrong? What if she isn't really...like that?''

Her inability to say the word *lesbian* aloud filled Beau with a mixture of sympathy for her and outrage at Heather. He understood only too well how hard it was to say the word aloud. The realization that Heather had never been sexually attracted to him had bruised his ego badly, but he would eventually learn to live with that. What he couldn't understand—what he would never be able to forgive—was the hell she was putting their children through.

"Your mom isn't going to change her mind," he said gently. "It isn't easy for me to admit it, but she was never happy with me. The life we lived wasn't right for her. She's much happier in Santa Fe with Dawn, and I hope they have a great life together.''

"Then you're not angry with her anymore?''

If she walked back into his life this second, swearing she'd been wrong and begging for his forgiveness, he wouldn't have been able to grant it. But he shook his head and forgave himself the lie for his daughter's peace of mind. "I'm not angry with her. In fact,'' he said, switching to the truth, "I'm grateful to her. If she hadn't married me, I wouldn't have you and Nicky, would I?''

"I guess not." Brianne dragged her gaze away from his and settled it on Molly, who'd moved to stand on the lawn near Nicky. "Are you going to marry her?"

"Who? Molly?" Beau laughed, but there was no humor in it. "No. We're friends. I think she's kind of pretty, and it makes me happy to have a pretty woman to spend time with, but she's only going to stick around for another week, so I think you're safe."

"But you'll marry somebody, won't you?"

"I might someday. But not yet, Brie. I'm still trying to figure out which way is up, and I don't plan to turn our lives upside down again until I know where my feet are."

Brianne smiled sadly and Beau reached through the seats to brush her cheek with his fingertips. He wasn't naive enough to think they were out of the woods, but for the first time in weeks, he actually believed they might make it through this.

And that was enough—for now.

CHAPTER NINE

BEAU TRIED HARD to maintain his equilibrium during the parade, but it wasn't easy. Now that Brianne's hostilities were on hold, he had plenty of time to think about Molly. And Molly was giving him plenty to think about.

He watched in amazement as she slowly, patiently and carefully lured Brianne into a conversation about a group of boys who stood nearby. He felt his heart swell with gratitude when she listened to Nicky's convoluted story about something that had happened at school. When the football team rode past in a convoy of pickup trucks, Molly cheered as if she was single-handedly responsible for the team's morale, and even Brianne started getting into the spirit.

By the time the parade ended, he'd begun to regret that Molly wasn't going to stay around longer. Not for himself, but for his poor, confused daughter and for the son who held Molly's hand as if he'd known her forever.

Well...maybe a little bit for himself.

Just after dark, the marching band rounded the corner and the last strains of the school's fight song faded away. Beau picked up an empty French-fry holder and tossed it into the trash, followed it with two half-empty cups someone had left leaning against a lamppost and tried to figure out what had happened this afternoon.

He turned back to the three people who waited for him near the curb. Brianne stood a little apart from Molly, but the high level of hostility was gone. Nicky walked the curb like a tightrope, carefully placing one foot in front of the other and using his arms for balance. Molly stood to one side, watching him with an expression he couldn't read and looking nothing short of stunning.

Overhead, the stars began to show in the gathering darkness, and a surprisingly warm breeze stirred the air. Laughter faded as people began to move off toward whatever they had planned next, but Beau was frozen in place by a longing for something he could never have.

He shook off the feeling and forced a smile as he walked toward them. He'd been feeling a little strange since his conversation with Brianne, and it wasn't surprising that the desire to be part of something real and right would be hovering around after that. He could pretend all he wanted, but Heather's bombshell had done some damage. Yet even if Molly had been planning to stick around, he wouldn't have rushed into a relationship with her. It wouldn't have been fair to any of them.

"Well," he said as he stopped in front of Molly. "What did you think? Impressive, wasn't it?"

Her lips curved into a smile. "You think I'm going to say no, don't you?"

"Come on, admit it. It was a little small-town compared with what you're used to."

She made a face at him. "I'm not admitting any such thing. I haven't been to a parade since I left Serenity, Mr. Know-it-all, so this is *exactly* what I'm used to. And I think it was wonderful. A perfect size, too. Not so many entries that you get bored watching. Not so many people in the crowd that you can't see. Just perfect.''

Beau laughed softly and called for Nicky to follow, then turned toward the Burger Shack. Brianne fell into step beside him, and he decided to take a risk and actually touch Molly's arm to help guide her through the crowd. "So we lived up to your expectations?"

"As a matter of fact, you did. It really was fun, Beau. Thank you for inviting me to come along.''

Brianne plucked at his shirtsleeve. "You need to walk faster, Dad, or we won't get a table.''

They were less than a block from the Burger Shack, and a lot of people appeared to be heading in the same direction, but Beau wasn't quite ready to start battling crowds for a place in line or position at a table. "So we'll wait a few minutes. It won't be the end of the world.''

"But I'm hungry.''

"Okay, then, why don't you and Nicky go on ahead and get your food? We'll be along shortly.''

Brianne needed a minute to think about that, but she finally held out her hand. "Okay. Fine.''

Beau gave her a few bills from his pocket. "Off you go, then. Keep an eye on Nicky. And save us a place!''

His daughter set off running with Nicky right behind. Now he was alone with Molly. As alone as they were going to get in Serenity on a night when the entire town and everyone in the outlying areas were crammed into the center of town.

She smiled up at him, and the light in her eyes made the breath catch in his throat and desire flame deep in his belly. He shrugged and tried to toss off a casual response. "I'm glad you liked it, and I'm glad you came with us. I think there's a law about watching a parade alone.''

"And you were simply trying to save me from spending time in jail?''

"What can I say? I'm just that kind of guy." To keep from wanting to kiss her, he glanced away. But he caught their reflections in the window of a store they passed, and that brought up a whole new set of emotions. They looked good together, and his fingers tightened on her arm.

Her gaze shifted toward him and their eyes met for only a second, but it was enough. He saw recognition dawn quickly, followed by a glimmer of shared yearning, and he knew she wasn't completely immune to him, either.

Well, well, well. That was going to be hard to forget. He wasn't even sure he wanted to.

His shoulder collided with something solid and jerked him back to reality. He looked up sharply and found himself face-to-face with Eve Donaldson. Eve had graduated the year before Beau had, and she'd been Heather's closest friend for years. She was one of the few people in Serenity who knew the truth about his divorce. She'd never breathed a word, but the chip on her shoulder when she was around Beau was the size of a bull moose. He had no idea why she resented him. He wasn't the one who'd lied about who he was. He hadn't forced Heather into the life they'd created. But in Eve's eyes he was still somehow to blame for Heather's misery.

Tall and willowy, with pale-brown hair and disconcerting gray eyes, she laughed and put out a hand to steady herself. "Goodness, Beau. You nearly broke my shoulder running into me like that." Her curious eyes lingered a moment on Molly, then returned to Beau's. If it hadn't been for the glint in their depths, he might have believed her friendly smile was sincere. "I looked for you in our usual place, but I didn't see you. Doris was looking for you everywhere. We didn't think you'd come."

He merely smiled as if there were no undercurrents. "Well, as you can see, we're here."

The glint grew a little sharper as she turned to Molly. "You look familiar. It's Molly Lane, isn't it?"

Molly must have felt the chill emanating from Eve. It was impossible to miss, and Molly wasn't naive. But she smiled as if she'd just been invited to dinner. "Thanks. It's Molly Shepherd now."

"Oh? You're married?"

"Divorced."

"Oh." As if Eve cared. "So much of that going around these days." She shot a look at Beau as if he'd been the one to walk out on Heather. "It seems like nobody wants to stay for the long haul."

"Isn't that the truth?" Molly's smile never slipped, but her voice dropped a few degrees. "One person decides to walk away, and the one who *was* in for the long haul is left to pick up the pieces. It's definitely not right."

Beau was torn between irritation with Eve and admiration for Molly. He didn't need her to defend him, but he couldn't deny that he liked knowing she would do it. He gave her arm a gentle squeeze of support and changed the subject. "Where's Cal?" he asked Eve.

"With the kids, getting the car. When did you two start seeing each other?"

"Oh, we're not—" Molly began.

"Molly's been staying with us for nearly a week.

You don't have any objections to that, do you?'' The night and the mood worked together to make Beau a little reckless.

Eve's eyes narrowed dangerously. "Why would I object?"

"Well, I don't know. I guess you wouldn't." He grinned and slipped his hand from Molly's arm to her back and urged her to start walking—which she did in spite of the stunned expression on her face. "My best to Cal," he called over his shoulder as they walked away.

"Why did you do that?" Molly asked when they'd put a few feet behind them.

"Do what?"

"You know what. Why did you leave her with the impression that you and I were an item?"

"Do you mind?"

She blushed. He could see it even in the dim light spilling onto the sidewalk from the small businesses they passed. "That's not the point, Beau. You deliberately misled her, and now there's going to be talk."

He stopped walking and took her by the shoulders, pulling her gently around to face him. "I'm sorry. I shouldn't have done it. I don't care if there's talk, but it obviously bothers you."

Her eyes shuttered. "I don't think you and I are the issue here, do you? I can survive the talk. I won't be around. But what about Brianne and Nicky?"

Her question brought about the strangest reaction. On the one hand, Beau knew she was right. He'd let his irritation with Eve get the best of him. On the other, Molly's worry about Brianne and Nicky almost made him glad he'd done it. Heather had been so consumed by her own identity crisis for so long, she'd barely noticed the kids. Doris loved them, but she was also soothing her own battered conscience through them. Beau tried to put them first, but he sometimes wondered just how well he succeeded. And here was Molly, who had no reason to care, and yet she did.

Without thinking, he pulled her close and lowered his mouth to hers. It lasted no longer than the space of a heartbeat and probably didn't even qualify as a kiss, but it ignited a fire inside him, and judging from the look on Molly's face when he released her, it did the same to her.

Someone behind them let out a whistle and someone else howled, and Molly's face turned redder than ever with embarrassment. Without saying a word, Beau found her hand and laced his fingers through hers, then set off walking toward the Burger Shack, feeling better than he had felt in years.

MOLLY PACED restlessly around the cabin, still buzzing from that half-second kiss on the way to dinner a few hours ago. Somehow—she didn't know how—she'd managed to follow the conversation over burgers and fries and had made arrangements to meet Jennifer in the morning so they could talk with Jennifer's mother. She'd even answered Nicky's nonstop questions on the way home.

But now that she was alone again, she couldn't stop thinking. She couldn't read because of it, and she couldn't sleep, either. And her heart seemed to beat just one message over and over again.

Beau Julander had kissed her.

The teenager that still resided somewhere inside her was jubilant. The adult was numb and a little worried. Had he meant anything by it, or had it simply been an impulse? Did he feel something for her, or had he put it out of his mind as soon as it happened?

Did she care?

She could have just asked him, but she didn't trust herself to discuss it. She was quite sure she couldn't talk to him without giving away her feelings. And what if he *didn't* feel an attraction for her? What would she do then?

More than a little confused, she microwaved water in a mug, stirred in powdered cocoa and made a mental note to buy marshmallows next time she was in town. After pulling on a sweatshirt over her pajamas, she carried her cocoa and a blanket to the porch. She settled into one of the Adirondack chairs and let her gaze drift across the lawn, the neighboring houses, then finally to the sky with its full moon and an endless field of stars.

Except for one lone porch light, Beau's house was dark. That ought to tell her something, shouldn't it? Obviously Beau wasn't losing sleep over her.

She leaned back in the chair and searched her heart for clues to what she was really feeling. When she was a girl, she'd spent endless hours dreaming about sharing a kiss with Beau. But instead of contentment over a dream realized, she found herself wanting the kiss to be the beginning of something new and wonderful.

Sighing softly, she cradled the mug in her hands and turned her thoughts, instead, to people's huge reluctance to tell her the details of her mother's accident. Like in her conversation with Joyce, which had been pleasant, but certainly not informative. Half her time in Serenity was gone, and she was no closer to learning the truth than she'd been a week ago. Now she wondered what had possessed her to think that coming back to Serenity after so long would be the solution—to anything?

Just as she was about to set her cup aside, the sound of a footstep on gravel reached her ears. A second later she saw the glint of moonlight on Beau's hair as he came around the trees and started toward the cabin. He disappeared into the shadows, but not before her heart began to race and her hands to tremble.

He was walking so slowly she'd have had plenty of time to gather her things and disappear inside. But she didn't want to disappear. She wanted to make sense of where she was and what she was doing. She wanted to figure out what she wanted from life and how she was going to get it. And she couldn't do that by running.

She pulled the blanket up to her chin and waited till Beau reappeared. In seconds he did, and she saw he was still wearing the jeans and leather jacket he'd had on at the parade. When he reached the patch of lawn in front of the cabin, he paused for an instant before starting toward her. Her breath caught in her lungs and all her senses were on high alert by the time he reached the bottom of the steps.

His eyes met hers and held. "You're awake."

She nodded, but the intensity of his gaze took her voice away. When at last she felt she could speak, the world's most inane response came from her lips: "So are you."

He propped one hand against a post, still without looking away. "I tried sleeping, but I couldn't get comfortable. Must have been the excitement of the parade."

"And the stress of being in charge," Molly suggested. "Stress can do strange things to a person."

Beau's eyes danced with amusement. "That was a joke, Molly. The parade had nothing to do with it."

Heat rushed into her cheeks, and her gaze faltered. "Oh."

Laughing softly, he motioned toward the chair beside hers. "Mind some company?"

"Of course not." She sat a little straighter and slipped one hand from under the blanket. "Please...sit down." He closed the space between them and spent a few seconds getting comfortable. Every cell in her body felt as if it was on fire, but she tried not to let that warp her perception or cloud her judgment. "So, if it wasn't excitement over the parade that kept you awake, what was it?"

Beau leaned back in his chair and stared up into the sky. "A little bit of everything, I guess. Brianne. Nicky. Laundry. Nosy neighbors. Wondering when I'll be able to work again." He rolled his head to the side and looked straight at her. "You."

The blanket Molly held slipped from her grip and puddled around her waist. Even wearing a sweatshirt over her pajamas, she felt exposed and vulnerable, but she didn't let herself reach for the blanket again. "Me?"

"You."

"I don't understand." She sounded foolish. He was being clear enough, but how could she let herself believe after wanting this for so long?

Beau covered her hand with one of his and heat spread up her arm. "You're a beautiful woman, Molly. Surely you realize that. You're intelligent and funny. You're easy to talk to and great to hang around with. And you're a whole lot more of a distraction than I ever thought you'd be."

He looked sincere, but she still wouldn't let herself believe him. "Do you want me to leave?"

"No, Molly. I want you to stay." He reached out and gently ran one finger along her cheek. The touch robbed her of the ability to speak again, but she wouldn't have known what to say, anyway. "It's been a long time since I tried to make a move on a woman," he said, still holding her gaze. "I'm really rusty and I could use some help."

The confession astonished her. "What kind of help?"

"Well, you could say something to help calm the butterflies in my stomach. Tell me if I have a chance or stop me if I don't."

If he hadn't sounded so sincere, Molly might have laughed. "You're asking if *you* have a chance with *me?*" Was he nuts?

He drew his hand away slowly. "I don't know what I'm asking. I mean, it's not as if you're going to be around after next week, so it's not like there's a chance that we could become anything permanent, and yet…"

Molly swallowed convulsively and her gaze traveled slowly across his features. Her heart stuttered with heightened awareness. She noticed everything from the curve of his brow to the tone of his skin, from the slight indentation beneath one ear caused by a long-forgotten scar to the faded scent of aftershave.

His gaze left her eyes and followed the line of her chin, locking on her lips and remaining there for so long she was afraid she'd never breathe again. She wondered what he'd say if he knew how many times she'd dreamed of this, but she didn't want to find out. So much had gone wrong in her life lately that she couldn't resist the pull of having just one dream come true—even if she knew it couldn't last.

He trailed a finger along her jaw and tilted her chin, then edged forward oh, so slowly and touched his lips to hers. The chill disappeared and sensations flamed to life inside. Molly drew in a ragged breath as his lips brushed hers tentatively, uncertainly, as if asking permission for more.

He leaned back and searched her eyes. She tried to hang on to her reason, but the moon and stars seemed to work together to create a magic that made rational thought impossible. He moved in close again, and this time when he kissed her, all that had been tentative before vanished.

He claimed her with an energy and passion she couldn't have resisted if she'd wanted to—and God help her, she did *not* want to. She gave herself over to the moment and let the sensation envelop her. His lips were soft and warm...so very warm. He pulled her close and caressed her with hands that were at once gentle and demanding. His tongue brushed her mouth and she parted her lips to offer him entry.

It was more than a dream, and she never wanted it to end. His hands seemed possessed by a need that matched her own. His mouth spoke silently of longing deep as the night and endless as the sky, and she knew that whatever was passing between them in this moment was larger than them both.

Too soon, the kiss ended and he pulled away. Their eyes met again and he smiled almost sheepishly. "Too much?"

Too much? Not enough!

Molly shook her head and whispered, "I have no complaints."

His smile grew and he briefly kissed her lips once more. "You have no idea how good that is for my poor, battered ego."

"Your ego?" Molly laughed softly. "I don't think your ego needs rescuing by me."

He cupped her face in his hands. "You might be surprised."

Somewhere nearby a lone cricket that hadn't noticed the colder weather began to sing. The sound and the touch of Beau's hands soothed her, and she pressed her cheek into his palm. "I think you're probably the last person around who should be worried about your ego. There wasn't a girl in our high school who wouldn't have sold her soul to go out with you, and I have a hard time believing that anything's changed."

Something flickered in his eyes, and she felt a sudden *ping* as she realized there was another Beau hidden behind the mask he presented to the world. She studied his expression carefully and the sensation grew. "You could have anything or anyone you want just for the asking," she said softly, "but you really don't know that, do you?"

He crooked a smile and drew his hands away. "That might be the way it looks to you, but that's not how it was in school, and it sure isn't how things are now. I'm a castoff, Molly. An old shoe that Heather grew tired of wearing."

She started to protest, but the look in his eyes stopped her.

"I'm just trying to find my way through life again, that's all." He sighed heavily. "There are a million other guys out there just like me, walking around in a daze and wondering if we'll ever figure out what the hell happened."

His voice had changed, and a shadow drifted across his expression. Molly didn't want to pry, but something stronger than her normal reticence made her ask, "What did happen between you and Heather?"

"She left me…" He took a deep breath and let it out slowly, and the agony on his face kept Molly from interrupting while he worked out what came next. After a long time, he stood and walked to the edge of the porch. He stood there, bathed in shadow and obviously struggling for a long time.

Molly wished she could take back the question.

"It's been a year," he said at last. "You'd think I'd have adjusted to this by now."

"Please don't feel like you have to answer me," Molly said quickly. "I shouldn't have asked."

He waved away the offer with one hand, but tempered the gesture with a thin smile. "It's all right. Like I said, it's just my poor bruised pride that's hurting." He ran a hand along the back of his neck and looked her in the eye. "She left me for a woman," he said at last. "After seventeen years together and the birth of three children, she suddenly realized that she preferred women."

Somehow Molly managed not to gasp, but her mind had trouble processing the bombshell. "Heather Preston?"

Beau actually grinned. "Yes, ma'am."

"But how… Why…" She stopped and tried to pull her thoughts together. "I would never have guessed. She seemed so interested in boys…in you."

"If it's hard for you to believe, imagine how I feel." He leaned against the post with one shoulder. "She wasn't exactly reluctant when we were dating, and I always figured we created the mess we made together. Now I wonder if I just wasn't paying attention.''

Molly stood, still shaken, but needing to do something more than stare at him. ''I don't think you can blame yourself. If it's true that Heather felt that way, she had a responsibility to tell you.''

His laugh held no humor. ''Well, I kinda thought so, too, but I have it on good authority that I never paid attention to her, never listened to anything she said and didn't give a damn about anything that was important to her. I'd like to think that if a woman finds sex with her husband repellent, it might be a good idea to give a stronger clue than 'Not tonight.' But apparently I'm wrong about that, too.''

Molly still couldn't completely wrap her mind around the news, but the numbness was beginning to wear off a little. ''So she's living somewhere. With…''

''Dawn.'' He made a face and added, ''That's D-a-w-n, not D-o-n.''

''And the kids? Do they know?''

''Brianne does. Nicky knows as much as he can comprehend—which isn't everything.''

So many things about Brianne came clear to her all at once. The girl obviously felt betrayed and lied to on top of being deserted, and it was no wonder she had so much anger inside her. Molly's heart ached when she thought of someone so young carrying such a heavy burden. ''How are you dealing with it?''

''That depends on the day, and sometimes on the minute.''

''Have you considered getting counseling?''

He nodded and looked at the tops of the trees. ''I considered it, but the counselor at the county mental-health department is a good friend of Heather's, and I don't think she's the right person to be talking to the kids right now.''

"There's no one else?''

"No one close enough to do any good. Rural Wyoming isn't exactly bursting with options.''

He looked so lost, so confused and so angry all at the same time that something in Molly shifted. She'd carried around an image of him for so long that she'd practically turned him into an icon. Now, for the first time in her life, she saw clearly beneath the surface to the man inside, and she liked what she saw even more than the image she'd created. "You're a good dad, Beau. You'll figure out what the kids need. I have no doubt of that. You're open with them, and that's very important.''

"It's funny,'' he said, moving close again. "You don't even know my kids, but you've shown more concern for them in the few days you've been here than Heather did in years. She walked out on us a year ago, but she was gone a long time before then. Thank you for that.''

He brushed a kiss on her cheek and let his gaze linger on her for a long moment before turning a regretful glance toward the house. "I'd love to stay longer, but I should get back. Nicky doesn't always sleep through the night, and I swear Brianne has some kind of internal radar that goes off when I'm not there.''

Molly nodded quickly. "Of course. You need to be there with them.''

"Thanks for that, too.'' He started down the steps, but he paused at the bottom and looked back. "I'll see you tomorrow?''

"Of course,'' she said again, and the sudden smile

on his face did the strangest thing to her heart. She watched him walk away, waiting until he disappeared again into the shadows before she went back into the cabin. But as she closed the door on the night, she wondered how easy it would be to walk away from him in a week.

CHAPTER TEN

THE PHONE RANG promptly at six-thirty the next morning—before Beau's eyes were completely open, before he had coffee on, and long before he was ready for trouble. He'd slept like a log after his late-night visit with Molly, and he had a feeling it was going to be a very good day. He'd much rather start by sneaking a few kisses before the kids woke up than talking to someone who thought six-thirty was an acceptable hour for phone calls, but kickoff was just twelve hours away and there were bound to be problems. Smitty might even be calling to tell him the Cessna was ready.

He rolled onto his side and picked up the phone a split second before his sleep-blurred eyes registered the name and number on the caller ID. Holding in a groan, he flopped onto his back and draped one arm across his eyes. "Hello, Doris."

"You're awake?"

Her voice was harsh and cold, but Beau tried not to respond in kind. "I am."

"I realize it's a bit early," she said, "but I didn't want to miss you. I looked for you at the parade."

"We were there."

"Not in our usual place *or* at the Chicken Inn afterward."

He resisted the urge to explain and said only, "You're right. Is that why you're calling so early?"

"Not exactly. I heard something last night that upset me so much I barely slept a wink."

Still groggy, Beau sat on the edge of his bed. "Let me guess—this thing you heard has something to do with me?"

"Eve called after the parade. You know what she told me."

Beau stood, stretched and started toward the stairs. He kept his voice low so he wouldn't wake the kids. "I have a pretty good idea what she told you, but Eve needs to mind her own damn business."

"She's concerned."

"She's trying to make trouble."

"That's not true. She sees smoke and she's worried about fire."

Beau wasn't wide enough awake for this argument. "It's nothing. She's overreacting."

"Is she? You're over there with a woman who isn't your wife. Parading all over town with her—and right in front of the kids. What on earth are you thinking? What's gotten into you, letting some other woman stay in my daughter's house with my grandchildren under the same roof?"

The fog of sleep evaporated by the time he reached the bottom of the stairs, and a slow anger began to burn. He pulled a fresh filter from the cupboard and scooped coffee from the can, hoping the everyday actions would help him hang on to his self-control. "There are a couple of things wrong with your argument, Doris. This isn't your daughter's house, and Molly isn't in the house, she's staying in the cabin. It's all perfectly safe and harmless, and the kids aren't being exposed to anything sinful."

Doris snorted in disbelief. "Harmless? Please, Beau,

you're not exactly a naive young boy. You know how these things work. You're there with this woman, making a spectacle of yourself and completely disregarding the children.''

''The kids,'' he interrupted sharply, ''are the *only* thing I think about. I would never do anything to hurt them.''

''So you say, but what's going to happen when their mother comes back?''

''If you're concerned about the kids, I suggest you talk to Heather. She's the one who's completely disregarded them, not me.''

''We're not talking about Heather. We're talking about you. Even if what you say is true, you're only confusing those poor children needlessly.''

Why was the woman so determined to settle the blame for this mess on his shoulders? He filled the coffee-machine reservoir with water and flipped the switch. ''Heather isn't coming back, Doris. It's time you accepted that.''

''Of course she is. You've known her all your life. You know what she's like. You know what she wants. She's going through a phase, that's all.''

''Well, it's one helluva phase.''

''One of these days she's going to wake up and realize what she's lost, and then she'll be back. What will she think if you've been dating other women— setting them up in the cabin—while she's gone?''

Beau leaned on the counter and looked outside at the rising sun, the glory of autumn, the mountains uncluttered by human mistakes and heartbreak, and he wondered how long he had to drag this heartache around with him. ''So it's a phase when Heather finds a new girlfriend, but it's a sin if I do?''

"Don't be smart."

He closed his eyes in frustration. He didn't want to throw up walls between them, but he couldn't keep letting Doris back him into a corner. "Even if you're right and she does come back, it's over between us. I can learn to forgive her if this really is something she can't change. But if it's a phase, if this is a choice she made, I don't think I can."

"You're trying to divert me," Doris snapped. "The point is you and that woman."

"She's a friend. I'm not 'setting her up' in the cabin, but I'm enjoying her company. And I know you won't like hearing this, but who I date and what I do isn't any concern of yours."

"I don't believe this! You've been in love with Heather since you were a boy."

"Things change."

"Love doesn't just die like that, Beau. After all the years you've been together?"

"She *left* us, Doris. And you know why she left. She doesn't want me and apparently she doesn't want the kids, either. Love *does* die, and so does trust."

"You make her sound like a horrible person. Don't you understand that she's just confused?"

"If that's the case, then I'm sorry for her, but it doesn't change the way I feel."

"The two of you married so young, and then losing the baby... I don't think she ever recovered from that. All her hopes and dreams were gone. All the things she once wanted to do."

He didn't know how to answer Doris's desperate need to clear Heather of responsibility. Apparently she couldn't release herself of blame until she'd lifted the burden from her daughter. "My dreams didn't survive, either," he reminded her, "but I didn't spend a lifetime lying about who I was or take off and leave my wife and kids in the lurch."

"You're stronger than she is," Doris wailed. "You always were. You're the rock in the family, I won't deny that. But you and Heather are family, and you'll always be family. You need to be there for her when she comes to her senses."

Beau sank into a chair and chose his next words carefully. "Listen to me, Doris. I want you to really hear me this time. I know she's your daughter and you love her, but what we had died a long time ago. I don't love her anymore, and you're going to have to accept that it's over between us. Heather and I will never be together again, and I don't want you filling the kids' heads with the idea that we might be. It's not going to happen and I'm not going to discuss it with you again. Heather will get on with her life and I'll get on with mine, but we won't do it together."

"Beau—"

"No, Doris. I want Heather to be part of the kids' lives, but only if she can give them security and stability. Those are two commodities that have been in short supply around here for the past few years. But frankly, I'm not sure she's capable of providing those things, and until I'm convinced, I'll do whatever it takes to keep her away from the kids."

"She's a good mother."

"Not right now she's not." He kneaded his forehead where a dull ache was forming above his eyes. "I meant what I said before. I'm not going to keep rehashing this. I'm sorry you're upset, but this conversation is pointless and I'm hanging up."

He disconnected and tossed the phone onto the table.

Lowering his head into his hands, he tried to put the call out of his mind. A soft noise behind him brought his head back up, and he turned to find Brianne standing in the kitchen door, feet bare and hair still tousled from sleep.

Nicky stood just behind her, his eyes wide with shock. He said something Beau couldn't hear, and Brianne rounded on him. "Don't you get it, Nicky? He doesn't love Mom anymore, and he doesn't *want* her to come back."

She jerked her sweatshirt from its hook by the door before Beau could get up, then slipped her feet into an old pair of shoes and raced outside.

The door banged shut, but Beau took off after her. He threw it open again and shouted for her to come back, but she was halfway across the lawn and it was clear she had no intention of listening to him.

"Dad?"

Nicky's trembling voice stopped him in his tracks. He whirled back to find the boy leaning against the wall. The look of misery and disbelief on his face twisted Beau's gut. He didn't know whether to follow Brianne or stay and comfort Nicky. Both kids needed him, but he'd been giving Brianne more than her share of attention lately, and he had to trust that she'd do what she'd done a hundred times before when he and Heather fought. She'd head into the field and run off steam, but she'd be fine. Right now, the stricken look on Nicky's face worried him a whole lot more than Brianne's volatile anger.

He hunkered down in front of his son and touched the boy's shoulder gently. "Nicky? Are you okay?"

The boy's blue eyes lifted to meet his slowly, and

the fear in them made Beau feel about two inches high. "Is it true, Daddy? Do you hate Mom?"

"I don't hate her, son." And he didn't when he was thinking clearly. "But Mom and I aren't going to live together again."

"Because you hate her?"

"No. No, son. Because Mom and I don't love each other anymore. Sometimes that happens with parents." He picked up his little boy, straightened to his full height and winked in a lame effort to lighten the moment. "But we're doing okay on our own, aren't we? I got some laundry done yesterday, so you'll even have matching socks today."

Nicky smiled slightly, but his eyes still looked sad. "It's okay, Dad. I don't mind if my socks don't match."

"Well, I appreciate that, but every kid deserves to wear matching socks to school."

"Okay. But Brianne says I shouldn't bug you. She says maybe you'll stop loving us."

Beau felt as if someone had punched him in the gut. "She said what?"

"She says we were a pain for Mom and that's why she stopped loving us. She said maybe if we're a pain to you, maybe you'll stop loving us, too."

A searing pain tore through Beau's heart. If that's what Brianne thought, why did she constantly push his buttons? To see how much she could get away with? How much he'd take before he broke? He felt broken now. "I could *never* stop loving either of you," he assured Nicky. "You're my kids, made right from a piece of my heart."

"But you stopped loving Mom."

Beau could have kicked himself for ever saying that

aloud. "Well, now, that's not entirely true," he back-tracked. "I still love Mom, just in a different way than I used to." He kissed his son's cheek soundly and tried to smile. "How could I stop loving the woman who gave me you and Brianne? You two are the very best thing that's ever happened to me."

Some of the clouds cleared from Nicky's eyes, but he still wore a worried frown. "Then why did Mom stop loving us?"

"She didn't stop," Beau said with a heartiness he didn't feel. "She loves you as much as I do. You're the greatest kids in the world. How could anyone *not* love you?"

"But she left."

"Yes, she did." Still carrying Nicky, Beau started into the kitchen. He wanted to buy a few seconds to think, but the only thoughts he could put together were how small his young son was and how much he wanted to wring Heather's neck for making their children doubt their worth, even for a second.

After a quick glance out the window for Brianne, he settled Nicky at the table and poured him a glass of orange juice and a coffee for himself. "I want you to listen to me, Nicky," he said as he carried both to the table. "Your mother did not leave here because she doesn't love you and Brianne. She left because she has some things to work out. You know how Brianne runs outside when she gets mad and walks around the field until she stops being angry with me?"

Nicky nodded solemnly.

"Well, Mom's doing the same thing."

There was a moment's silence while Nicky took a swallow of juice and wiped his mouth with his pajama sleeve. "Is Mom mad at you, too?" he asked at last.

Beau smiled sadly. "I don't know, son. I think she's just confused. But she loves you. And one of these days she'll come back to see you. I guarantee it."

Nicky grinned as if Beau's word was good enough for him. After another drink of juice, he began to hum softly. But Beau had a sick feeling that he'd just lied to his son. He only hoped Nicky would eventually forgive him for it.

MOLLY WAS ON PINS and needles the next afternoon as she sat in the gleaming kitchen that belonged to Jennifer's mother. She'd spent many hours here as a kid, and even more as a teenager. From this very chair, she'd giggled with Jennifer and Elaine over boys and downed more tortilla chips and sodas than anybody should ever consume. Today she felt an odd mixture of strangeness and familiarity as she watched Jennifer and her mother working together.

Like everyone else, April Dilello had aged since Molly had seen her last. Her hair had once been a rich shade of auburn; now it was a shade of red that could only have come from a bottle, and even that color had faded. But her eyes were still filled with the same caring that had drawn the girls to her kitchen in the first place. And she could still carry on two conversations at once.

"I just can't get over how wonderful it is to see you again, Molly. You look... No, Jennifer, the other box. Lemon cookies will be better, don't you think? You really do look beautiful, Molly. Stunning, in fact." She brushed her hands on the plaid apron she wore and wagged a hand toward a door near the refrigerator. "Napkins are in the pantry. Will you grab them, dear?"

Molly was halfway to her feet when April gasped and motioned for her to sit again. "You stay put, Molly. Jennifer will get them. Tea will be ready in a minute, and I know you're eager to get down to business. I understand you're interested in your mother's jewelry."

Sinking back into her chair, Molly nodded. "Yes, I am. Jen says you still have a few of the pieces she made."

"Not just a few. I still have everything I ever bought from Ruby. I wouldn't dream of parting with them. They're the nicest jewelry I own."

"And you don't mind if I look at them?"

"Mind? Oh, heavens no." April patted Molly's shoulder and turned away with a wave toward the stove. "Just keep an eye on that kettle and I'll be back in a minute."

"I'd be glad to help," Molly called as she disappeared through the door.

April laughed and stuck her head back into the kitchen. "Not on your life. My bedroom is a disaster area, and it'll destroy my reputation if you see it."

She disappeared again and Molly shared a grin with Jennifer. "She hasn't changed a bit, has she?"

"Not much." Jennifer finished arranging cookies on a plate, took two more from the box and handed one to Molly as she joined her at the table. "So how's it going over at Beau's? Anything fun and exciting to report?"

Memories of those knock-your-socks-off kisses swept through her mind, but Molly laughed them away. "Yeah," she said. "We were up half the night making out."

Jennifer stuck out her tongue and broke off a piece

of cookie. "Nothing, huh? Figures. You have a golden opportunity and you're throwing it away."

"I'm not here for Beau," Molly reminded her. "I'm here to find out about my mom. I keep telling myself that Mrs. Duncan had a good reason for standing me up yesterday, but I know she's hiding something."

Jennifer slid down on her tailbone, just as she used to do when she was a teenager. "I wouldn't worry about it. It's probably because you've showed up suddenly after such a long time. Nobody expected you, and in a town like Serenity, people tend to circle the wagons to protect each other."

"But I'm from Serenity, too," Molly said. "And who are they protecting? My mother? From *me?*"

Her friend tried to look reassuring. "Don't read too much into it. It's just the idea of answering questions about a friend that gets them nervous. They'll soon think it through and change their minds. Meanwhile, *you* should relax. Try to have a good time." She leaned close and waggled her eyebrows suggestively. "Now, tell me what's really going on with you and Beau."

The abrupt change of subject made Molly laugh. But after what she'd learned last night, she didn't want to stir up gossip Beau would have to deal with once she'd left. She shrugged and glanced at the kettle on the stove. "There's nothing going on with me and Beau. He offered me a place to stay because I didn't think about making reservations and the motel was full."

"Oh. Right." Jennifer leaned back in her chair again and wagged a hand between them. "Beau's always inviting women to stay in his cabin. He has a new one there at least once a week. Come on, Moll. You can tell me."

Friendship pulled at her, but the wounded expression

on Beau's face was stronger. "There's nothing to tell. Honest."

"The two of you went to the parade together. You went to the committee meeting with him. You've been seen all over town together, *and* you're staying in his cabin."

"All of which means absolutely nothing."

Jennifer popped another piece of cookie into her mouth. "Everybody was blown away when Heather left, but nobody expected Beau to stay single as long as he has. I swear you're the first woman he's looked at in all this time—and he *is* looking. Everyone's noticed."

Molly's cheeks burned, but the rush of pleasure inside her more than made up for it. "He's only been single since July," she pointed out. "That's not very long."

"But Heather's been gone for nearly a year."

"I know that, but..." Molly shook her head. "Beau and I are friends. That's all."

Tucking a leg beneath her, Jennifer settled in more comfortably, as if she still expected a story. "Everyone knows how much you liked him in high school—" She broke off as if she realized she'd said the wrong thing, then grinned sheepishly. "At least, you know, the old gang knows. Not everyone."

Molly laughed. "Sorry to disappoint, but that's as exciting as it gets."

"Okay. But there's nothing that says you can't make it more exciting, right?"

Molly stared at her friend in amazement. "And how do you think I should do that?"

"Figure it out. You've been in love with Beau for your entire life."

"With a short fifteen-year hiatus during which we both married other people."

"Whatever." Jennifer waved an impatient hand at her. "The point is, you're there right under his nose, and he's certainly available. You have the chance of a lifetime. I want to know what you're going to do about it."

"Absolutely nothing."

"Nothing? Are you crazy?"

A loud thud sounded from the bedroom and Molly thought she had a reprieve, but a laugh from April and her call that she was fine put a quick end to it. "He has kids," Molly said when she realized Jennifer was waiting for an answer. "Have you forgotten that?"

"Well, I wasn't suggesting that you jump him at breakfast. You can wait until the kids are safely asleep in the house and then lure him to the cabin."

"*Lure* him?"

"Put on something sexy and offer him a glass of wine."

A wave of nostalgia swept over Molly. She hadn't had a close girlfriend in years, and she'd missed this kind of teasing banter. "I didn't bring anything sexy with me, and I don't have wine at the cabin." She tapped her cheek and pretended to consider. "But maybe I could lure him with my sweats and T-shirt, and seal the deal with a straight shot of root beer."

Jennifer bobbed her head enthusiastically. "I say, if it works, go for it."

What would Beau do if she took Jennifer's advice? Molly wondered. It made a nice fantasy, but letting herself get carried away would be a big mistake. "I can't seduce him. Not only am I a little rusty at the fine art of seduction, but I don't want a one-night stand—and that's all Beau and I could ever be. It wouldn't be worth the trouble it would cause.''

Jennifer opened her mouth to argue, but her mother chose that moment to burst into the kitchen, talking as if they'd all been carrying on a conversation the entire time. ''I *knew* that pair of garnet earrings was behind the dresser, but do you think Jim would pull it out and find them for me? Sometimes that man is enough to try the patience of a saint—though heaven knows I'm no saint.'' She held out her hand and showed Molly a pair of earrings so delicate the stones seemed to be suspended on strands of spun silk. ''Do you remember these? I think they're my favorites.''

Molly gasped and reached for the earrings, then instinctively pulled back her hand and looked to April for permission.

April moved them closer. ''Go ahead. Take them. Your mother did exquisite work, didn't she?''

Molly nodded and carefully picked up one of the earrings. They'd been made for pierced ears, and two thin strands of wire curved away from either side of the hook, then swept downward and met to form a delicate cradle for the gemstone. ''They're so beautiful. It's hard to believe my mother made these.''

''She had a real gift,'' April said wistfully.

''I used to help her when I was younger, but I know I disappointed her when I got into high school.'' Molly returned the earring and battled a stab of guilt. ''I was too caught up in my own little world. School and friends and boys.''

''And that made you a typical teenager, so don't you feel bad.'' April lowered a small jewelry box to the table and lifted the lid. ''Take your time. Look them over. You don't find craftsmanship like this every day.'' The kettle began to hum, but she didn't turn away. "I hope looking at them will help.''

"I've been thinking about taking up where she left off,'' Molly admitted aloud for the first time. "I'd like to sketch these before I go, if you don't mind.''

"Well, of course I don't mind. In fact, why don't you take them with you for a day or two? I think I can survive that—as long as I get them back.''

"Thank you.'' Molly couldn't believe her luck. She lifted an intricate bracelet made of tiny seed pearls and turned it over in her hand. "I don't know if Jennifer told you, but I don't remember Mom's accident or the last six months she was alive. That's really why I'm here.''

Jennifer took charge of the kettle. April pulled several pieces of jewelry from the box and took what felt like forever to spread them on the table for Molly's inspection. Molly held her breath, afraid to do anything that might disturb her.

"Your dad never told you?''

"He wouldn't talk about it.''

"No.'' April smiled sadly. "I suppose he wouldn't. That time probably wasn't something he liked to think about.''

Something in her tone left Molly oddly unsettled, but she told herself it was only her imagination. "I'd be happy if I could just remember what happened the day she died. I don't even remember the last conversation we had. I'd love to know the last thing I said to her.'' Her voice cracked, but she made herself go on. "Or the last thing she said to me.''

Jennifer started back with the tea tray and Alice made room for it on the table. "I suppose there's nobody left who can really tell you those things, is there.''

Molly's throat tightened, but she managed to speak. ''No. And maybe I'll just have to accept that there are some things I'll never know.''

April set out three small plates and put the cookies in the center of the table. ''The only two people who know what happened in your parents' marriage is the two of them. The most anyone else can do is speculate about why things happened the way they did.''

Molly's heartbeat slowed ominously. ''If you know something, won't you please tell me?''

April seemed surprised by the question. ''But I don't really know anything at all. There was a lot of talk at the time, but it was mostly just guessing. I don't suppose any of us will ever know for sure what came between them.''

For a moment Molly could have sworn that time stopped. ''Are you saying that my parents were having trouble in their marriage?''

''She didn't know?'' April shot a confused glance at Jennifer.

''*I* don't know,'' Jennifer said, and at her mother's expression of outraged disbelief, added, ''I was a teenager. I didn't care about things like other people's marriages. I was completely freaked out by the idea that somebody's mom could actually die. I didn't want to even hear about it.''

''You must be wrong,'' Molly said to April, her head beginning to pound. ''My dad would have told me if they'd been having trouble in their marriage. And besides, surely I'd remember something like that.''

Jennifer nudged the cookies toward Molly. ''Not necessarily. Remember Stacy Edwards? She married this guy from over in Star Valley who turned out to be an alcoholic and abusive. Things were really bad for several years before she left him. Even after all this time, there are things she doesn't remember about the years she was married. It's like her mind went into self-protective mode or something.''

Molly shook her head sharply. "That's not the same thing at all.''

"Your mind has shut out those months for some reason.''

Before Molly could protest, April continued, "Honey, I know this must upset you, and if I knew anything more for certain, I'd tell you. But all I can tell you is gossip and hearsay, and that won't help. I'll tell you who you ought to talk to, and that's Clay Julander.''

Although Molly scoured her memory, she came up blank. "*Clay* Julander?''

"Beau's uncle,'' Jennifer explained. "You remember him, don't you? Big guy. Worked for the police department for years. He's retired now, but he used to drive around town in that old blue truck with his dog in the back.''

Molly nodded slowly. "He used to say the dog was his deputy, didn't he?''

"That's right. You remember him, then?''

"Yes, but…'' Way in the back of her mind, a horrible possibility tried to reach her, but she ignored it. "I don't understand why you think I should talk to him.''

April's eyes filled with sympathy and Molly knew what her response was going to be. She battled the urge to leave, to run, to plug her ears and scream so April's words couldn't reach her. But maybe for the first time in her life, the need to know was greater than the need to forget. She forced herself to sit in her chair and hold on to a teacup covered with delicate yellow roses, while April said what she must always have known.

"Sweetheart, Clay's the one who responded to the calls every time your parents had one of their disagreements. You talk to him. If anyone knows what went on at your house the night your mother died, he will."

CHAPTER ELEVEN

MOLLY DROVE BACK to Beau's house in a daze. A sense of unreality and inevitability left her shaken and uncertain. She'd have to talk with Beau's uncle soon, but she didn't want to face it just yet. She needed time to adjust to what April had told her, and she wasn't sure she could face Clay alone.

The sudden need to have someone with her seemed odd. She'd spent so much of her life alone. Without family, except her dad. Without close friends. Without emotional support. Before she came back to Serenity, she'd felt strong enough to handle anything on her own.

Now, even with April's small jewelry box on the seat beside her, she felt weak and shaky. She wanted to talk to Beau before she did anything else. She just didn't understand why. She could have turned to Elaine. She'd have found a willing shoulder and a listening ear if she had. But whether or not it made sense, whether or not it was smart, she *wanted* to talk to Beau.

He had his hands full with Homecoming, with his kids, his house and his job. He didn't need Molly's problems on top of his own.

She pulled into the driveway a few minutes before three o'clock, and when she realized that his Cherokee was gone, her bleak mood grew even bleaker. Already, afternoon shadows stretched across the lawn and clouds had begun to gather on the horizon. The temperature had dropped sharply while she'd been with Jennifer and April, and the chill she felt now matched her mood exactly.

Still hoping that Beau might be home, she climbed out of the car and started toward the house. She'd only gone about halfway up the long walk when a movement caught her attention. She looked more closely and realized that someone was sitting on the corner of the back porch. Brianne.

The girl's feet dangled off the edge of the porch and she was leaning forward, elbows propped on her knees, and holding a small black box in both hands. Molly spotted a toy car turning circles on the sidewalk and realized that Brianne was playing with one of Nicky's toys. Even so, the set of her small shoulders and the look on her face didn't belong to a happy child.

Molly wasn't sure she could handle one of Brianne's moods, but the girl had already seen her, and her obvious unhappiness jerked Molly out of her own misery. She might be nursing old pain, but Brianne's crisis was happening right now.

As she stepped onto the walk, the toy car stopped spinning circles and began to race down the sidewalk toward her. Brianne's lips curved into a sly smile, but Molly dodged the car easily and kept walking toward the house.

The high-pitched whine of toy tires on cement told her that the car was on her tail. She glanced over her shoulder just in time to avoid a second near-collision and sidestepped the car once more before she reached the porch.

One look into Brianne's pain-filled eyes wiped away her irritation. Brianne was a child. Hurt and confused and, judging from the expression on her face, extremely upset about something. Molly had no idea what to do for her, but her own longing for someone to talk to was too strong, and Brianne's distress too evident to ignore.

For the first time in years, she didn't run away from the questions about the child she'd lost. Would she have been like Brianne? If her child had lived, Molly would have learned how to handle the sadness, joy, misery and pain that came along with adolescence, but her child hadn't survived, and she felt completely out of her element now.

To avoid future car attacks, she stood on the bottom step. "You're home early, aren't you? Didn't you have school today?"

Brianne met her gaze slowly, and the disdain on her face made it clear that she found Molly's presence offensive. "Why do you care?"

So they were back to square one. Molly shrugged and let her gaze trail away so the girl wouldn't feel challenged. "I don't, really. I'm just talkin'."

From the corner of her eye she saw Brianne register surprise, but the sullenness quickly returned and she brought her attention back to the box in her hand. "You don't have to pretend to like me just to impress my dad."

Molly felt a stab of pain at the girl's unhappiness and a flash of anger with Heather for walking away from her children and leaving them to work through all the issues her departure had created. She lowered her purse to the step and slipped her keys into her pocket. "Is that what you think I'm doing?"

"Isn't it?"

"Actually, no, it isn't." Molly moved a few inches

closer to where the girl was sitting. "I don't pretend to like people, Brianne. That's dishonest." The girl cast her a skeptical look and Molly smiled. "I was always taught to tell the truth, and I'm not going to change that now."

For a heartbeat Molly thought she'd made an impression. But Brianne looked away again and gave a snort. "You really expect me to believe that you like me?"

Molly's heart twisted. How was a child supposed to believe in herself when her mother didn't appear to care? At least Molly had never had to experience that kind of rejection, and she wished she could take it from Brianne. She sat on the edge of the porch, almost close enough to touch the girl, but far enough away to leave her space. She let her legs dangle over the side and kicked her feet gently.

"The truth is, I don't know whether I like you or not. We really haven't had a chance to figure that out yet, have we?"

Brianne raked her gaze over Molly before looking away again. "I know that I don't like *you*."

"You don't know me, either. I think what you do know is that you don't *want* to like me." Molly watched the toy car circle on the walk while Brianne pretended to ignore her. When she figured the girl had had time to absorb what she'd said, she pressed on. "I understand a little of how you feel. My mom died when I was a bit older than you, so it was just my dad and me for a long time. Then one day, he brought home this lady."

Brianne's eyes flickered toward her, then darted away again.

"She was very nice," Molly went on, "but it took

me a while to figure that out. I did just what you're doing. I decided that I wasn't going to like her, and I made sure she knew it.''

"That's not what I'm doing,'' Brianne said, but her protest didn't hold much conviction.

"I didn't have a remote-control car,'' Molly said with a conspiratorial grin, "but I think I might have used it on her if I'd thought I could get away with it.''

The car stopped spinning and silence stretched between them for a long time. "What did you do to her?'' Brianne asked at last. Her voice sounded slightly less hostile—at least, Molly thought it did.

"Well, I was older than you are when she came along, so I couldn't put too much salt in her dinner or food coloring in her shampoo, but I thought I could talk my dad out of falling in love with her in other ways.'' She grinned sheepishly. "Dad liked to jog, and staying in shape was really important to him, so I thought he might not fall in love with Cassandra if I helped him notice that she ate too much. And he really hated owing people money, so I made sure he realized that she liked to shop, and every time I saw her wearing something new, I told him.''

Brianne's lip curled into something resembling a smile. "Did it work?''

"No. He married her, anyway. And now she's the only family I have in the world.''

"That's too bad.''

"No, I'm very lucky, really. At first, the only thing we had in common was the fact that we both loved my dad, but we became friends eventually. She's a nice lady, and without her I'd be completely alone. My dad's gone, I'm divorced, and I don't have kids of my own. The holidays are right around the corner, and I *really* don't want to be alone. With Cassandra around, I might have somewhere to go for Thanksgiving and Christmas, and there's still someone in the world who'll call on my birthday. I'm awfully glad I didn't manage to run her off.''

Brianne didn't say anything, but she swept Molly's face with a slow, assessing glance.

And that was enough. For now.

Molly stood and dusted the backside of her jeans. "It's okay if you don't like me, Brianne. I'm not here to stay. But one of these days, your dad might bring home somebody new, and I hope that you'll give whoever she is a chance before you start attacking her. She might turn out to be pretty cool once you get to know her." Molly turned away, then decided to take another gamble. "If it's okay with you, I've decided that I really do like you, and I'd like to be friends. You can think about it and let me know."

Brianne still didn't speak, but Molly didn't expect her to.

It didn't occur to her until she'd closed the door behind her that while she'd been talking to Brianne, she'd forgotten all about her own worries for a few minutes.

THE NEXT MORNING, Molly pushed a cart filled with groceries across the nearly empty parking lot at the FoodWay. A handful of cars and two mud-splattered pickup trucks were parked close to the store. She didn't recognize any of them, but the instinctive expectation that she might surprised her a little. She'd only been in town a week, but in her unguarded moments she was already beginning to feel as if she belonged here.

Like coming home.

Beau had been so busy the night before during the game, she'd only seen him for a minute. Just long enough to learn that he was bringing his plane back to Serenity later this morning. Aaron would be picking him up in just an hour, and Molly wanted to do something to make the day easier for him.

He was on the go so much it was no wonder he got a little behind on the laundry and dishes. Overnight, Molly had come up with a plan to surprise him with breakfast, and she'd slipped away early to buy what she needed for the stuffed French toast she wanted to make.

Now, with everything in her cart, she stopped behind her rental car and began to load bags into the trunk. She worked quickly, enjoying the morning and softly humming a tune that had been playing on the PA system in the store. When she picked up the small bag holding the needle-nose pliers she'd found in the hardware aisle, a rush of pleasure made the whole day seem brighter.

She'd spent hours after the game making rough sketches of her mother's jewelry and wondering if she really could re-create some of the designs. Finding those pliers on the rack had felt like an omen. Buying them had been much more than impulse. Even standing in the parking lot with them in her hand felt like a life-changing commitment.

But maybe she was just being fanciful again.

"Excuse me?"

The voice so close behind her startled her. She turned quickly and found herself face-to-face with a stout woman of about sixty, whose disapproving expression wiped the smile from her face.

"Molly Lane, isn't it?"

She bobbed her head once and tried to chip the years away so she could remember the woman. She looked familiar, but Molly had met so many people the past week she couldn't place her. "Yes, but it's Molly Shepherd now."

The woman surveyed Molly critically from the tip of her head to the toes of her shoes. "Well, you certainly do look like your mother, don't you?"

Molly had lost track of the number of times she'd heard that since she'd arrived in town, but this time it was *not* a compliment. The woman's hostility confused her, but she wasn't going to be the first to look away. "I've been told that a few times. Were you a friend of my mom's?"

She knew what the answer was even before it came. "Not exactly. But I certainly knew her."

Trying not to let the woman unnerve her, Molly put the bag she was carrying into the trunk and reached for another. "Do I know you?"

"You should. Doris Preston. Heather Julander's mother." Her eyes narrowed and a direct challenge glimmered in them. "I *know* you must remember Heather."

Molly froze with a bag halfway from the cart, and she had to force herself to keep moving. "Of course I remember Heather. How is she?"

"She's doing well." Doris lifted her chin as if she dared Molly to argue with her. "She's living in Santa Fe...for the time being. Of course, she'll be coming home again soon. To her children. And her husband. Just in case you had any idea that she might not be."

The woman's intensity was hard to meet straight on. Molly couldn't imagine how Beau had lasted a full year with her peering over his shoulder. She knew she should stay calm for Beau's sake and for the kids, but the past few days were beginning to take a toll and she'd had just about all she could bear of hints and innuendo. "Why would I have any ideas about Heather's plans?"

"Are you saying you don't?"

Molly felt another wave of sympathy for Beau and a rush of understanding for poor, confused Brianne. She straightened and looked hard into the older woman's eyes. "It's pretty obvious that you're trying to make a point, but it's been a long week and I'm not in the mood for games. Why don't you make this easier on both of us and just say what you mean?"

"I think you already know what I have to say. You're interfering with my daughter's family. I want you to stop."

"I see." Molly shut the trunk carefully. "I think you're under the wrong impression, Mrs. Preston. Beau has been kind enough to let me stay in the cabin for a few days. There's nothing more to it than that." To signal that the conversation was over, she pushed the empty cart toward the collection point near the front of the store.

Doris trailed behind her. "You think I don't know what's going on over there? You think the whole town doesn't know?"

Molly shoved the cart into the metal cage and turned back. "Even if there were something going on between us, it wouldn't be your concern."

"Heather only left because she needed time and space to find herself," Doris insisted, grabbing Molly's arm to keep her from walking away. "She has always intended to come back."

"Beau told me why she left, Mrs. Preston. But out

of respect for him and the kids, I'm not going to discuss it with you in the parking lot of the grocery store.''

Haughtiness gave way to desperation in Doris's eyes. ''He told you? Everything?''

''Everything. But I have no intention of telling anyone else, if that's what you're worried about.''

The older woman seemed to sag. ''I don't know why she wants to hurt everyone this way. It's just not like her. But she'll come to her senses one of these days. She wasn't raised to walk out on her responsibilities.''

The change in Doris cut through Molly's irritation and she almost felt sorry for the poor woman. Molly had never known Doris well. Unlike April, the woman had been a little aloof around the kids her daughter's age. But it wasn't hard to see that she was hurt and afraid. Obviously Beau and the kids weren't the only ones having trouble accepting Heather's decisions.

Molly wasn't sure of the right thing to do under the circumstances, but it seemed mean to let the poor woman worry about something that wasn't an issue. A kiss or two didn't make a commitment, and nothing had changed because of them. ''I'm not here to stay,'' she assured Doris. ''And I'm sorry if you've worried about my relationship with Beau, because we simply don't have one beyond friendship. If he ever wants to patch things up with Heather, I certainly won't come between them.''

She started toward the car again, but Doris put out a hand to stop her. ''Then you won't object to finding another place to stay while you're in Serenity?''

Molly turned back slowly, trying to recapture some of the sympathy she'd been feeling just seconds before. ''The motel is full until the middle of next week, and there *is* no other place to stay.''

"I understand that, but you're giving people the wrong impression. There will be talk. Folks will think there's something going on between you, even if there's not. And what about Brianne and Nicky? The two of you are setting a bad example for them. I just can't allow that."

Molly was the first person to admit that she knew very little about how families worked, but this much interference seemed way over the top. No wonder poor Brianne had such a suspicious nature.

"The kids aren't in any danger from me. They're not seeing anything they shouldn't. And they couldn't have a better father than Beau. I understand that you're upset, but that doesn't give you the right to toss around accusations without any regard for the truth."

"I call it like I see it."

Molly struggled to remain patient. "Well, you're wrong, and you're being terribly unfair to Beau."

"I don't blame Beau. I know you've always had a thing for him, and I'm not at all surprised that you'd go to such lengths to get what you want. You're obviously just like your mother."

Everything inside Molly turned to ice. Her heartbeat suddenly seemed way too loud and she wasn't absolutely sure she was still breathing. "If you're unhappy with the way things are," she said, speaking slowly to make sure Doris understood her, "talk to Heather. She's the one who walked out on her husband and children, not me, so don't blame me for her mess."

Molly pivoted and walked back to the car, keeping her gait slow and firm when what she really wanted to do was run. Her heart thundered in her chest, and her throat was dry. Her hands trembled and tears filled her eyes, but she refused to let them fall.

Even after she'd driven away, the accusation against her mother rang in her ears. She tried to tell herself that Doris was mistaken, but she could feel something stirring deep within her, far beneath the shock and the outrage.

Like a stick in a muddy pond, her return to Serenity had stirred things up. It was only a matter of time before the truth rose to the surface.

HOURS LATER, Molly stood on the sidelines of the dance floor, trying to catch her breath. She was determined not to let anything ruin the dance, so she hadn't mentioned her conversation with Doris to Beau. She'd done her best not to think about it herself.

For the first time in her life, she'd danced nearly every dance since the music began—first with Beau, then with a succession of other partners, half of whom she hadn't recognized. She'd be dancing even now if she wasn't in such desperate need of fresh air.

Smiling with remembered pleasure, she scanned the crowd for Beau without success. It had been several minutes since she'd last seen him, but she was also making a conscious effort to keep some space between them. She didn't want to think about Doris's accusations, but she couldn't forget them, and she wasn't going to make things worse for Beau and the kids.

She turned toward the outside doors, humming as she walked. Someone had done a good job picking out the music, she thought idly. The selection spanned several decades, but every song was familiar and easy to sing along with. From older couples to teenagers, everyone could dance to tunes they knew. Molly wouldn't have been surprised to learn that Beau was responsible. It seemed like the kind of touch he'd bring to the job.

Funny, but when she'd imagined herself in love with him all those years ago, she hadn't had a clue just how great he really was. She learned something new about him every day, and she liked him more all the time. Despite her assurances to Doris, she was close to losing her heart completely—and this time she wouldn't be able to get over it so quickly.

Dancing with him had been heaven on earth. The touch of his hand. The feel of his arm around her waist. The scent of his aftershave and the rhythm of his breathing. It had all been so intimate and wonderful. But it had also been an illusion, the product of her own imagination. What she felt for him wasn't real. What he felt for her...

What he felt for her was probably just a reaction to Heather's leaving. No matter how much Molly might want things to be different, that was the unvarnished truth. Beau's ego had suffered a tremendous blow when Heather walked out on him. He'd said so more times than she could count. And she'd be a fool to let herself believe that he was doing anything more than bandaging his pride by sharing a few kisses with a willing woman. She might have been insulted, but she'd started out doing the same thing, and she still had no illusions about creating a lasting relationship.

She pushed open the outside door and stepped into the evening air. The temperature had dropped sharply after the sun went down, and she realized immediately that it had been a mistake to wear the dress she'd chosen. The fabric felt paper-thin in the mountain breeze, and with only thin straps and a light shawl to cover her shoulders, she might as well have been naked.

That would teach her to choose fashion over function.

Vowing to stay outside for only a minute, she took a deep breath and caught the scent of a cigarette somewhere nearby. She glanced around and saw a red-tipped glow hovering near the corner of the building. The shadow moved, and the shape of a man came into view.

He stepped into the beam of light from a security lamp, and Molly recognized Whit Sharp from her graduating class. He'd grown tall and broad in the years since she'd seen him, and his once-thick brown hair had receded. But his eyes were still filled with laughter, and the hesitant smile she remembered so well hadn't changed a bit.

She grinned as he approached her. He glanced at his cigarette with a grimace, crushed it underfoot and pulled her into a quick hug that was over before she could return it. "Sorry about that," he said with a jerk of his head at the crushed butt. "Nasty habit I can't seem to break."

"I haven't seen you around. I thought maybe you weren't living in Serenity anymore."

"I'm not. I just got in this morning. I'd have come earlier, but I was in trial and couldn't get away."

"In trial?"

"Believe it or not, I'm an attorney. And you probably had me pegged as headed for a life of crime."

"No! Of course not. It's just…" She broke off with a laugh. "Well, okay, yes. You weren't exactly the shy, retiring type, and as I recall, you never missed a chance to get into trouble. And now you're an attorney. Defending juvenile delinquents?"

He laughed and reached for another cigarette in his jacket, caught himself and stuffed his hands into the pockets of his pants. "Corporate law. Bankruptcy, mostly." A surge of music from inside the gymnasium filled the space between them, and he studied her. "You look good, Molly. It's great to see you again. I didn't think I ever would."

For once Molly didn't want to talk about the strange set of circumstances that had kept her away. "You know how life is," she said. "You get busy with one thing, and then that leads to another. Pretty soon you've been gone fifteen years."

"But you're here now."

"Yes."

Whit pushed away from the wall and smiled down at her. "I heard you've been asking questions about your mother's accident."

Molly nodded and told herself not to be surprised that he knew. In Serenity news traveled fast. "I'm trying to find out what happened, but I'm running into a little resistance."

"You don't remember it at all?"

"I've lost about a year." She shivered and moved out of the wind. "Six months before the accident and nearly the same after. The last thing I remember clearly is getting ready to start our senior year. The next memory I have is of living in Illinois."

"So you have amnesia?"

"I don't know if it's officially amnesia or whether a doctor would call it something else."

Whit's scowl deepened. "Are you telling me you haven't seen a doctor?"

"Well...no. Dad wasn't terribly worried about it, and by the time I was out on my own, I was used to it."

"O-o-o-kay."

That old, protective urge she felt toward her dad rose to the surface. "He didn't neglect me," she said. "I was perfectly healthy. It's just that we never had health insurance, and you can't just run to the doctor over every little thing under those circumstances."

"Amnesia isn't exactly a little thing."

"It didn't affect me," Molly insisted. She wasn't in the mood to discuss her father's shortcomings or tear apart his decisions. "I went to college. Made good grades. And I've always done well at work. It's just a little chunk of memory that's gone, after all. Besides, it's a beautiful night and I'm having a wonderful time so far, and I don't want to think about anything unpleasant."

Whit nodded slowly. "Fair enough." She could tell he wasn't convinced they should change the subject, but he did, anyway. "I hear you're staying with Beau Julander."

Molly rolled her eyes. "You've only been here a few hours and you already know that?"

"It's a small town, and people have been worried about him since Heather left."

"Well, to set the record straight, I'm not staying *with* Beau, I'm staying in a cabin on his property. We're not an item now, and we're not going to be an item."

Whit held up both hands and backed a step away. "Whoa, put the sword away, I didn't mean to offend you. Frankly, I'm glad to see him looking like himself again. It's about damn time."

"Oh." She flushed, embarrassed by her reaction. "Well, then, I'm sorry. It's just that some people seem to have a problem with it, and I guess I'm a little touchy."

He adjusted his collar and grinned. "Really? I never

would have noticed. So, 'some people' aside, the two of you are getting along well?''

"So far, so good, I guess. He's a great guy and he's been incredibly generous. But I don't have to tell you that. The two of you have been friends forever.''

"Yeah, we have. He's a good friend. Salt of the earth and all that. So what do you think of Serenity now that you're here?''

"It hasn't changed much.''

"It never does. That's one of the best and the worst things about it.''

The music from the gym switched to an old Smokey Robinson song, and a memory flashed through Molly's mind. A dance, just like this one. Her mother swaying to the music in the arms of a man she couldn't remember. It was gone again in a heartbeat, as quickly as it came. Molly tried to call it back, but the image wouldn't form, and after a second or two she realized that Whit was still talking.

"…year after year after year. You always know what you're going to get when you come home again, though. That's one thing. It's predictable.''

Molly pulled herself back into the conversation. "I don't dislike it here. It's just a little small, that's all. And too far off the beaten track.''

Whit slanted a glance at her. "I'd say that's a pretty generous attitude…considering.''

"Considering what?''

"Well, *you* know. Considering what happened and all. Must be hard for you to come back here after all that.''

Something deep inside warned her not to ask. Not tonight. Enjoy the music. Dream through another dance or two with Beau. Indulge her fantasy for a few hours more. She could ask questions tomorrow.

But none of those arguments kept the words from rising to her throat and spilling from her mouth. "After all *what*?"

"Well, *you* know," Whit said again, but his eyes flickered from her to the nearby cars uncomfortably, and he looked as if he might have realized that she really didn't know anything. "Just the divorce and all, and then the accident and your mom dying. And all the talk afterward." He pulled back to look at her. "That must have been hard."

Molly met his gaze. "What divorce? What talk?"

"Your mom and dad. You know how this town is. All the news that's fit to spread in twenty-four hours or less."

She nodded impatiently. "What about my mom and dad? Why did anyone think they were getting divorced? What did people say?"

Giving an uncomfortable laugh, Whit drew back a step. "I don't know the details, Molly. That's just what I heard. I mean, first your dad changed the way he did, and then your mom got killed. There was all kinds of crazy talk right after the accident, especially when your dad decided not to have the funeral here. I figured that was why you and your dad left so soon."

The lights from the parking lot began to swim, and the chill night air suddenly felt too warm. Her senses pulsed with her heartbeat so that the music was alternately loud, then soft, and Whit's face was close one moment and distant the next. "What do you mean, my dad changed?"

"You don't remember that, either?"

"I don't remember *anything*. How did my dad change? Why?"

"I don't know why. I always wondered, though. He was scout leader when I was about eleven, and we all liked him. And then just a few months before your mom died, he changed. I don't know how to describe it. He was *different*. Moody. I mean, one day he's everybody's friend, and the next he's the guy you avoid when you see him pumping gas or eating a burger, y'know? How's he doing now, anyway? Better, I hope."

Molly answered automatically. Apparently there were a few things the grapevine had missed. "He passed away in March."

"Oh. I'm sorry. I didn't know."

She smiled, but her lips felt cold and stiff. "Thanks. I'll get used to having him gone one of these days, I guess." She put a hand on Whit's sleeve. "Is there anything else you remember about what happened? Anything at all?"

Whit shook his head. "I never did know what happened to change him. That's the weird thing about small towns. Just when you start to think there are no secrets at all, you find out that's just a fallacy. If someone wants a secret kept badly enough, it'll be kept."

The magic she'd felt earlier evaporated and she let out a tight laugh. "I'm beginning to find that out. But what secret? That's what I can't figure out. And why doesn't anyone else know about it?" But even as she asked the question, she knew the answer. People did know. But after all this time, someone still had a reason for wanting the truth to stay buried.

But who? And why? And what did it have to do

with her? She couldn't put it off any longer. She had to talk with Clay Julander and find out what he knew. But she had a feeling deep down in her bones that she wasn't going to like what he had to say.

CHAPTER TWELVE

MOLLY MIGHT HAVE been determined to learn the truth, but with Beau back at work, it was Wednesday evening before they could coordinate schedules and work out a meeting with his uncle. It gave her too much time to think, far too much time to fret and wonder and imagine what Clay Julander would tell her.

She was practically jumping out of her skin by the time they left the kids with Beau's mother. A thousand things raced through her mind as Beau drove along the quiet neighborhood streets, but she couldn't seem to get any of them into words.

Beau must have sensed her need for quiet because he didn't say much until he pulled into the driveway of a small, well-kept split-entry house with an extended driveway that held an RV and a sailboat that looked as if it had cost more than the house.

He turned off the engine and shifted in the seat to look at her. "This is it. You sure you're ready?"

Nervousness made Molly's stomach churn, but she nodded and opened the car door. "Ready as I'll ever be."

She started to get out, but Beau put a hand on her arm to stop her. "You don't have to do this. Knowing what happened back then isn't going to change who you are."

His touch threatened to weaken her resolve, so she

pulled away. "You're wrong. It's already taken away what I thought I knew. My parents' relationship was the one constant in my life, but now even that's gone. If I don't find out what happened to them, I'll always have a hole I can't fill."

"You aren't your parents, Molly. You aren't their decisions."

"Of course I am. And so are you and everyone else." She smiled, but she could feel her lips quivering and she knew she looked more frightened than brave. "If I don't find out the whole story, I think I'll go crazy."

Beau climbed out of the Cherokee and came around to stand beside her. "At least let me talk to Clay first."

"Why? So you can decide what to tell me and what to leave out?" She rubbed her arms for warmth and smiled up at him. "I know you're just trying to be nice, but if my dad hadn't censored everything he told me after the accident, I wouldn't be here. I need to hear the truth for myself—all of it."

Beau put an arm around her shoulders and squeezed gently. "I just don't want you to be hurt by what you find out."

It would have been so easy to let herself believe that he felt something for her, but nothing could have been more dangerous to her heart. Still, she allowed herself to lean on him for a minute and draw on his strength. "Maybe I won't be hurt," she said. "Maybe everyone else is wrong."

The look in Beau's eyes told her he didn't believe that any more than she did. He kept his arm around her as they walked to the front door. Too soon, she heard the sound of approaching footsteps and she stiffened in anticipation.

"Don't worry," Beau said softly. "Everything will be okay. I'll make sure of that."

Molly would have given almost anything right then to believe him, but this was just another illusion, and she knew how quickly it could disappear. The only thing she could count on—the only thing she'd *ever* been able to count on—was herself.

The door to Clay Julander's house swung open and he stood before them, every bit as imposing a figure as Beau himself. Molly tensed at the sight of him, but she wasn't sure if she remembered him or if she was just nervous.

At well over six feet, with broad shoulders and a thick head of dark hair streaked with gray, Clay looked years younger than the fifty-plus he must have been. He grinned and pushed open the screen door so they could enter, but once he'd closed the door behind them, he got right down to business. "So you're Molly Lane. It's been a while since I saw you."

"It's been a while since I was in town." She shook the hand he extended and followed him through the living room into a large kitchen at the back of the house. Beau trailed behind her, solid, steady and sober, and her heart filled with gratitude.

Clay motioned them toward the table and opened the refrigerator door. "Can I get you two anything? A beer or a soft drink? I've got some chips, but nothing to go with them. Your aunt Shannon's at work or I'd have her whip up some of that crab dip she makes."

Molly had trouble treating this like a social visit, but she wasn't about to say so. She shook her head, but Beau asked for two sodas and she didn't argue. Holding one would give her something to do with her hands.

Clay carried three cans to the table, set one in front

of Molly and lowered his long frame into a chair. He slid another can toward Beau and popped the top on the third for himself. "So you're here to find out about your mom, are you?"

Molly clutched her cold drink nervously in both hands. "April Dilello suggested that I talk to you. She said you might be able to help me."

"I might. What do you want to know?"

"I was just seventeen when my mother died, and I don't remember much about the accident." She flicked a glance at Beau and went on quickly, "Actually, I don't remember the six months before or nearly that long afterward. That whole year is a big, empty blank in my mind. I came back to Serenity to find answers. Unfortunately it seems that nobody wants to talk about the night Mom died, and I'm hoping you can tell me why."

There was silence for a long moment while Clay took a drink. When at last he set the soda aside, he nodded. "I remember your mother well. Nice lady. Pretty." He tilted his head and regarded Molly for a long moment. "You look like her."

"So people keep telling me," Molly said with a weak smile. "But that's about all they'll tell me—except that she made jewelry."

"That's right. She did. Made some awfully pretty things in that studio of hers. You remember, don't you, Beau?"

Beau shook his head. "I was just a kid obsessed with football and girls. I didn't pay attention to things like that."

His uncle laughed. "Man, those days seem like just yesterday in some ways. I gave a couple of rings to Shannon one Christmas, and a set of earrings for

Mother's Day. Must have been fourteen, fifteen years ago.''

''Fifteen,'' Molly said automatically. ''Why does April Dilello think you can help me? What do you know that she didn't want to tell me?''

With a shrug, Clay took another swallow of his drink and set the can down. ''I guess it's no secret that I spent a few evenings over at your place before your mother died—in a professional capacity of course. I didn't really know them to socialize with.''

Molly's breath caught and she thought for a moment that she might be sick. She hadn't realized until that moment how much she'd hoped that April had been mistaken. But if what she and Clay said was true, why couldn't she remember? She rubbed one temple with the tips of her fingers. ''Why were you there?''

''We were called there. Several times. Neighbors worried about the fighting—wanted us to do something.'' Clay studied her face for a long moment, assessing her reaction. He must have decided she was strong enough to hear more, because he settled more comfortably in his chair and went on, ''Your parents were having trouble, Molly. Lots of arguments. Loud ones. Had to haul your dad down to the jail a couple of times just to separate 'em for the night.''

The words cut like cold steel through Molly. ''Are you saying that my father... That he...'' She couldn't get the words out, but she felt Beau's hand close over hers, and that gave her courage to keep going. ''Was there abuse?''

Clay shook his head quickly. ''Not physical, no. Never saw any evidence of it, anyway. But verbal, a whole lot. On both sides.'' His gaze met hers again, and she saw the same kindness she'd always seen in

Beau's. "They were angry as hell with each other, and they didn't mince words."

Her head swam and she felt the last remaining bit of solid ground beneath her feet begin to crumble. Her father's love for her mother was the one thing she'd always counted on. Now it appeared that it had been just a figment of her imagination.

She could feel her mind recoiling, shutting down the way it always did when she got too close to the truth. But this time she wasn't going to let it happen. "Do you have any idea what she was doing on the road to Beaver Creek the night she died?"

"She had several suitcases in the car with her. We figured she was leaving him."

Molly let out a shaky breath and held on to Beau's hand for dear life. It was nothing more than she'd imagined since her conversation with April, but hearing it aloud made it so much worse—and real. Her mother had run away and left her. The same way Heather had left her children. The realization tore through her, burning itself in her mind and her heart. Was that why she'd blocked out the memories? Because her mother had walked out on her? Because she couldn't bear to remember that her mother hadn't loved her enough to stay?

Freeing her hand from Beau's, she thrust her fingers into her hair and cradled her head in her hands. She'd been so sure Whit was mistaken. "I don't understand. My dad hated divorce. You should have seen the way he reacted when I told him that my marriage to Ethan was over. He didn't care what was wrong between us and insisted I should stay and make it work. And now you're telling me that he and my mother were on the verge of divorce when she died?"

"I don't know what happened to your dad after he left here, Molly. I don't know what he came to believe, or why he felt the way he did. But I do know what happened here. There was a petition for divorce filed with the court just two days before your mother died."

She sank back in her chair and tried desperately to process what she'd just learned. But the biggest question of all was still unanswered, and she knew she couldn't put it all together until she heard the words for herself. "When my mother died," she said, lifting her gaze to meet Clay's again, "was she leaving *him?* Or both of us?"

"She was leaving him."

That was so different from what she'd been expecting, Molly narrowed her eyes and looked at him hard. "Are you sure? Or are you just saying that to make me feel better?"

Clay glanced quickly at Beau, then back at her. "I'm sure."

She dropped her hands and sat up a little straighter. "How can you be sure? How do you know?"

"Because you were in the car with your mother when she died, Molly. I thought you knew that."

BEAU WATCHED the blood drain from Molly's face as the bombshell his uncle had just dropped hit her. Damn, but he wished he'd asked Clay what he knew when he'd talked to him earlier that morning. Maybe he could have helped prepare her.

He met Clay's worried gaze over the top of Molly's head. "Why didn't I know that?" Beau demanded.

"I don't know, but I was one of the first officers on the scene, and I pulled Molly from the car myself."

Molly's hand trembled in his. Fear, shock and disbelief were mirrored in her eyes. "But how…" She broke off uncertainly, then tried again. "Why didn't my dad ever tell me that?"

Feeling utterly useless, Beau took her hand in his. "We may never understand his reasons, Molly, but I'm sure he did what he thought was best for you."

"No matter what problems he had with your mom at the end, your dad was a good man," Clay assured her. "We all knew he adored you."

She jerked her hand from Beau's and stood. "He adored me so much he spent the rest of his life lying to me?"

"He probably didn't want to hurt you," Beau said. "You'd lost your mother. Life at home hadn't been happy for quite a while. Maybe he thought you'd been through enough."

Molly's eyes grew cold and hard. "Are you defending him?"

"No." Beau stood to face her. He longed to take her in his arms and offer some comfort, but he could tell she wouldn't welcome anything from him right now. "I'm not defending him. I'm guessing. I'm trying to put myself in his place."

"So that's what *you'd* do?"

"No! Of course not. Dammit, Molly, I'm trying to help."

She turned away. "Well, don't. He lied to me for fifteen years! He let me think that he couldn't talk about Mom's accident because he was so destroyed by losing her. Now I find out that he wouldn't talk about it because he just didn't want me to know the truth."

"You don't know that, Molly."

"I don't?" She glared at him over her shoulder. "He let me grow up thinking that we were the happiest family in the world. He let me believe that he was grieving horribly for my mother. So much that I learned to keep my questions to myself so I wouldn't hurt him. Tell me, Beau, which part of that was the truth?''

He flinched under the fury in her eyes and shook his head. ''I can't. But I know what it's like to be a father, and I know that he must have had some reason for what he did—a reason he thought was a good one.''

Holding up both hands as if to ward off the words, she looked around the room and focused on the bag she'd left lying on the floor beside her chair. ''Don't say any more. I can't hear it right now.'' She snagged her bag and headed for the door, but halfway across the room, she turned back to Clay. ''Thank you,'' she said in a hoarse whisper. ''I…I'm sorry.'' And with that, she was gone.

Beau stood, frozen, until he heard the front door close. But when he would have gone after her, Clay caught his arm and stopped him.

''Leave her be, Beau.''

''I can't. She's too upset.''

''Yeah, she's upset, but she needs some space. Let her walk a bit. It'll give her a chance to burn off some of that energy.'' He turned toward the fridge again. ''Want another soda?''

Beau gaped at him in disbelief, but he realized that Molly would probably turn to Elaine or Jennifer for comfort, and maybe that was who she needed right now. But that didn't make him feel better. ''What I *want*,'' he snarled, ''is a few answers. Why didn't we ever know that Molly was in that accident?''

''I couldn't say.''

''You'd better say,'' Beau warned. ''If you know

anything else, you'd better come clean. About all of it. Right now.''

''I don't know anything else,'' Clay said evenly. ''We transported her to the hospital in Jackson. When they released her, Frank took Molly away. We figured it was so she could be near family, but we never knew for sure.''

''You should have found out.''

''Why? There was no evidence of foul play. We had no reason to question him, and he didn't want anything to do with any of us after that night.'' Clay pulled out two fresh cans and handed one to Beau. ''We're never going to know what happened between those two, Beau. The truth died with Frank, and Molly's going to have to accept that. He was so protective of her the chief didn't even tell Hannah down at the paper about Molly being in the car. He thought it was best.''

Beau shoved away from the table and paced in front of the window for a long time, trying to accept the story himself. But he couldn't swallow it, and he knew Molly never would. He wheeled back to face Clay once more. ''What did they argue about?''

''I don't know.''

''Bullshit! You were there. You heard them. Don't lie to me, Clay. This is too important.''

His uncle took his sweet time popping the top on his can and taking a seat at the kitchen table. Only habit and respect kept Beau from grabbing him by the collar and demanding the truth from him. When he couldn't stand it any longer, he planted his fists on the table and glared at Clay. ''*Tell* me.''

Clay looked him square in the eye. ''Frank and Ruby are both dead, Beau. Let 'em rest in peace.''

''And what about Molly?''

"You really think finding out what tore her parents apart is going to help her?"

"What right do you have to hide the truth from her?"

"Asking questions isn't going to help her, Beau. Trust me. You think she's torn up right now, just wait."

"So you *do* know." Beau raked his fingers through his hair, agitated and confused. "Tell me what it is so I can help her."

"I don't know anything for sure," Clay said. "I have bits and pieces of conversations and arguments, and I have a few suspicions I've never voiced aloud to another living soul. But if you think I'm going to tell you what they are, you're crazy." He gestured toward the door with his can. "You saw how she acted when she thought her mother had walked out on her. I'm not feeding any more maybes into that head of hers."

"Well, you can't just leave her like this. It's not fair." Beau paced to the far end of the kitchen, but his nerves felt as if they were on fire, and he'd just about reached the end of his patience. "You've always been fair, Clay. As fair as a man can be, anyway. So why are you doing this now?"

Clay let out a sigh and pushed his can away. "Why do you care so much, Beau? Why can't you just let it be?"

"Because this is eating her up alive. Can't you see that?"

"Sure I can, but speculating and making up stories, digging up things that are better left alone could be even worse. What I want to know is, what's she to you?"

"She's a friend. I told you that on the phone."

"I know you did." Clay hooked one arm over the back of his chair. "Can't say as I believe you, though. Seems to me you're smitten, and if you won't admit it, you're either lying to me or you're lying to yourself."

"What I feel or don't feel isn't the issue!" Beau shouted. "Dammit, Uncle Clay, quit trying to change the subject, and just tell me what you know about Frank and Ruby's divorce."

For a minute that felt like an hour, Clay sat perfectly still, considering Beau's demands. Beau had always admired the way his uncle never spoke without thinking, but today it made him want to hit something. "All I know," he said at last, "is that Frank found out something Ruby didn't want him to know. Whatever it was, he changed into a whole different person because of it. Like I said before, I didn't know him to socialize with, but he was one of those guys everybody likes. Lots of friends. Always smiling. I don't know what Ruby was hiding, but that friendly guy disappeared the day Frank found out about it."

"And they never said anything in front of you that would give you a clue?"

Clay ran a finger along the table's edge. "They said a few things in front of me, but nothing I could get a firm handle on. They might have been at each other's throats, but they were mighty careful about what they said once we got there. It's been a long time since then, Beau. Too much water under the bridge. Too many other things I've heard and forgotten. I wouldn't know how to separate what I heard from what I made up."

Everything inside Beau rebelled at his helplessness. "So nobody knows what really happened?"

"I didn't say that." Clay stood again and fixed him

with a look. "There's one person who does, and I reckon she'll remember when she's ready. If she doesn't, then maybe that's for the best, too."

A WEEK LATER, Beau drained the last of his soda from lunch at the Burger Shack, tossed a handful of uneaten fries onto the orange plastic tray on the table in front of him and checked his watch for the twentieth time in as many minutes.

"It's only two," Aaron said from across the table. "Would you relax? Harvey said he might be a few minutes late."

Relax? Beau had been on pins and needles since that day in Clay's kitchen, waiting for the other shoe to drop. One of these days, Molly was going to remember what happened between her parents, and he didn't know how she would react.

At least the two of them had reached a truce of sorts, but they still hadn't gone back to the easy way things had been between them in the beginning. He'd tried half a dozen times to talk to her alone, but she inevitably found some excuse to avoid him. Oh, she said things were fine between them, and she'd accepted his offer to stay in the cabin even though there was space at the motel now. She claimed to have forgotten why she was angry with him in the first place. But things weren't fine, and Beau cared a whole lot more than he should have.

To make matters worse, Mayor Biggs was still dragging his feet on finding a replacement for Beau on the WinterFest committee, and everyone—even his own mother—had an opinion about his efforts to resign.

When he realized Aaron was looking at him strangely, he tugged his sleeve down over his watch and leaned back in the booth. "I'm just wondering if we've missed Harvey, that's all. I could belt him for making us negotiate the use of that field for WinterFest parking. We've used it for ten years without trouble. What the hell is wrong with him?"

Aaron snorted a laugh and dumped sugar into his second cup of coffee. "Forget Harvey. What's wrong with *you?*"

"With me? Nothing." He could hear the harsh edge to his voice, so he tossed off a smile. "Really. I'm fine."

"Really." Aaron dabbed a finger into his coffee, checked the sugar content thoughtfully and tore open a package of creamer. "What is it? The kids? Work? Doris?" He stirred his coffee for a minute, then looked up at Beau with one raised eyebrow. "Molly?"

Beau tried to laugh off the question, but it was a useless effort. That annoying eyebrow of Aaron's winged a little higher, and he knew he'd never be able to pull off a convincing lie. "Okay, you're right. It's Molly. I'm worried about her."

Aaron's eyebrow dropped back into place and he took a noisy sip from his cup. "I saw her yesterday with Elaine at the Chicken Inn. She seemed all right to me."

Of course she did—to the casual observer. At least she wasn't pushing Elaine and Jennifer away. He was glad of that. He toyed with a paper jack-o'-lantern advertising pumpkin milk shakes and tried to decide how much to say. He didn't want to broadcast Molly's troubles all over town, but Aaron was his best friend. He'd been a sounding board for every tough issue Beau'd had to work through in his life, and he knew how to keep his mouth shut when the occasion demanded.

Pushing aside the pumpkin, Beau raked his fingers through his hair and glanced around to make sure nobody was listening. The Burger Shack was crowded, but nobody seemed to be paying attention to their conversation, so he decided to take a chance. "I guess you've heard that she's trying to find out about her mom's accident?"

"I have. What about it?"

"Somebody suggested that she talk to my uncle Clay. Apparently, Frank and Ruby Lane had some domestic trouble in the last few months before Ruby's accident. Clay responded to calls from the neighbors complaining about their loud fights."

"Molly didn't know that?"

"She can't remember anything about the last six months her mother was alive, and her dad would never talk about it. He died a few months ago, so when she got the invitation to Homecoming, she decided to come back to Serenity and find out for herself what happened. According to Clay, she was in the car with her mother when it went off the road."

Aaron whistled softly. "She doesn't remember that, either?"

Beau shook his head. "What I don't get is why her dad never told her that. Why would you keep that from your kid?"

Aaron shrugged. "Hell, I don't know. Maybe he didn't want to upset her."

"Well, if that's what he wanted, it didn't work. The man never spoke about the accident in fifteen years. Not one word, even though his daughter had lost her mother." He could feel Aaron getting ready to argue Frank's defense, but he cut him off. "I know, I know. She couldn't remember. No sense upsetting her and all that. But how did he know she wouldn't remember eventually? Why would you take a chance like that? Why just waltz through life and pretend it never happened?'' He looked his friend directly in the eye. ''Clay says that Ruby was keeping some secret and that Frank found out about it. But I'll tell you what *I* think. I think he was willing to take the chance he did with Molly because he was hiding something. Something big.''

Aaron stuck the stir stick between his teeth and leaned back in his seat. ''Like what?''

''I wish I knew.'' Beau crumpled a napkin and added it to the pile on his tray. ''It's driving me crazy. I can't even imagine how frustrated Molly must be.''

''How's she handling it?''

''I don't know. She's still here. Says she's staying until she knows the whole truth.'' Beau added a straw wrapper to the heap. ''I see her every day, and she seems fine on the surface, but she's pulled way back in on herself. The most serious conversation we've had in a week was when she asked to use my computer so she could look up something on the Internet.''

''And that bothers you?''

''It bothers me a lot.''

''Because…?''

''Because she's a friend. Because I hate to see anybody going through a rough time.''

Aaron laughed and slid down in his seat. ''Wow. What a saint. Now what's the real reason?''

Beau was beginning to wish he'd never started the conversation. He never expected to hide anything from Aaron, but he should have remembered that Aaron would never let Beau hide anything from himself, either. He drummed his fingers on the tabletop for a moment while he tried to argue himself out of the realization he'd been fighting all week.

"You care about her, don't you," Aaron said before Beau was ready. "You're falling for her."

"I care about her," Beau agreed. But that was where he drew the line. He had to. He'd been through hell in the past few years because he'd made decisions with his heart. It was time to let his head do what it had been created for. "She's a good friend," he said. "I hate to see her struggling through this alone."

"Doesn't sound like she's alone to me. But let's skip to the important question. What are you going to do?"

"Keep my ears open. Try to find the answers she's looking for."

"In your spare time?"

"Something like that."

Aaron arched that damn eyebrow again. "And the rest? You and Molly? What are you going to do about that?"

"Not a thing. There is no Molly and me. She's leaving as soon as she finds what she came for, and I'll still be here. End of story."

"Is that what you want?" The stir stick between Aaron's teeth bobbed up and down as he talked, and Beau fought the urge to snatch it out of his mouth.

"It's what *is*," he said with a casual shrug.

"Now. But things can change."

Beau let out a needle-sharp laugh, decided Harvey wasn't going to show and slid out of the booth. "That's where you're wrong, Aaron. What is, is. Things don't change. People don't change. And only a kid walks around with his head in the clouds, thinking he can make things work out the way he wants them to."

As far as Beau was concerned, he'd already been acting like a kid for too long. It was time to grow up.

CHAPTER THIRTEEN

"MOLLY! MOLLY! Come quick! Somebody's sent you something."

Startled out of the book she'd been reading, Molly sat up quickly and looked around to get her bearings. Clouds hung heavily in the sky, and the trees, which had still had their leaves when she arrived in Serenity just three weeks earlier, stood stark and bare.

The holidays were growing relentlessly closer, and even the thought of spending them with Cassandra didn't wipe the ache from her heart. She couldn't stay in Serenity forever. She knew that, but she couldn't make herself leave, either.

The first flakes of snow from a winterlike storm drifted past her window, and she could see Nicky, wearing just a sweatshirt and jeans, barreling across the lawn toward the cabin.

She hurried to the door, throwing it open just as the boy jumped onto the porch. His little chest heaved with excitement and his breath formed a cloud in front of him as he tried to stop panting. "You've...gotta... come." He bent at the waist and gripped his knees. "Right...now."

"I will, but what are you doing running around without your coat? It's freezing out there." Molly tried to draw him into the cabin, but he pulled back and shook his head.

"No! You have to come quick. Somebody sent you something. Boxes and boxes of stuff. It's all up at the house." He danced a little in his excitement and pointed across the lawn as if she might have forgotten where the house was.

Molly gave up and reached for her sweater. She'd spent far too much money ordering supplies over the Internet during the past week, and she'd been having second thoughts. She justified her decisions because she needed to stay busy while she was here, but she was really just creating false reasons to stay.

She had no business taking advantage of Beau's hospitality and no idea what made her think she could come close to recreating her mother's designs. She'd probably just thrown away a chunk of money from her dad's life insurance that could have gone for something more practical.

But now that the supplies were here, exhilaration bubbled up inside her again. It had been a long time since she'd felt excited about anything. It felt so good she almost didn't care whether she succeeded or failed.

She closed the cabin door and hurried down the steps. Nicky jumped to the ground, fell to his knees and got up running. Laughing, Molly put a little zip into her step and started across the lawn behind the boy, who could hardly contain himself.

Apparently he decided she still wasn't moving fast enough, because partway there he turned back and grabbed her hand. It was a completely spontaneous gesture, and Molly knew it meant nothing to Nicky, but her emotions had been raw since that day in Clay's sunny kitchen, and her eyes blurred with unshed tears.

She wasn't angry with Beau. She'd realized how over the top her reaction had been before she'd walked even just a couple of blocks that afternoon. But everything new she learned about her parents left her that much less certain of herself, and though she longed to find comfort in her friendship with Beau, she refused to let herself take refuge from the world. Not there. Not anywhere.

It was a completely logical decision, but it didn't do a thing to lessen the confusion in his eyes or still the whispers of her heart.

"Come on, Molly." Nicky dragged at her, making her move faster than she would have on her own.

She tried to laugh at the picture she knew they must make, but the sound caught in her throat. The cold air burned her cheeks and nose, and the scent of burning leaves reached her from somewhere nearby.

Her toe hit a bump in the lawn, and she nearly lost her balance. Tightening her grip on Nicky's hand, she managed to slow the determined little boy. "Hold on," she said, gasping for breath and laughing at the same time. "Let's get there without breaking my neck."

"But you gotta *see!* There's probably a hundred boxes."

"If there are a hundred, then someone's made a mistake." She regulated their pace a little more, and Nicky finally stopped fighting and fell into step beside her. "It's not really that exciting," she warned. "It's just some supplies I ordered for my new business." But just saying the words aloud made her fingers tingle and she felt as if a flurry of butterflies had been turned loose inside her.

"What kind of business?"

"I'm going to make jewelry like my mother did."

Some of the excitement in Nicky's blue eyes died away. "Jewelry? For *girls?*"

"I think so—at least most of it."

They reached the back of the house and Nicky released her hand to charge up the steps. "Well, that's dumb. Why don't you make something for boys?"

"Maybe I will someday." Molly followed him into the kitchen and closed the door to keep the cold out.

Brianne stood in front of a stack of brown cardboard boxes piled near the window. She turned one small box over in her hands and studied it carefully, but she jumped when the door opened, and set the box down with a guilty flush.

It was the first thing Molly had seen the girl show any real interest in, and she didn't want to scare her off, so she pretended not to notice. "Oh, this is great. They must have delivered everything at once. Who's that one from, Brianne?" She bobbed her head toward the box Brianne had been holding and picked up another to study the label.

The girl seemed to relax a little. "It's from someplace called JewelArt in California."

"Perfect. And this one's from Lisa's Jewelry Cottage. I can't wait to see whether the gemstones are as good as they looked on the computer." Molly glanced around and pretended to consider her options. "I'd like to get these boxes open and make sure everything's here. I don't suppose the two of you would be willing to help me get all this to the cabin, would you?"

Nicky jumped at the chance, but Brianne showed a little more restraint. "You want us to help you now?" she asked.

"If you don't mind. I don't want your dad to come home and find a mess."

Brianne actually laughed. "Yeah, that'd be *real* different."

"Things are getting better around here," Molly protested. "A little. And anyway, there's no reason I should add to the problem."

Nicky picked up two boxes at once and tucked one beneath his arm. "I'll help. I can carry lots. Brianne doesn't even have to help if she doesn't want."

To Molly's surprise, Brianne shushed him and planted her hands on her hips. "We don't have to carry all this stuff. Nicky has an old wagon somewhere. We can use that and take everything at the same time."

We. Molly liked the sound of that—maybe a little too much. "That's a great idea. Do you know where it is?"

"Probably in the shed—with all my mom's stuff."

No telling how the kids would react to seeing their mother's belongings, and Molly didn't want to ruin the moment by opening the door on painful memories. "Well, then, we probably should wait to ask your dad before we go rooting around and making a mess. How about a wheelbarrow? Does he have one of those?"

Nicky nodded solemnly. "In the shed."

"I see." Molly laughed and glanced out the window at the gathering darkness, then back at the stack of boxes. "Well... I guess there's not so much. We might have to make a couple of trips, but the boxes aren't heavy. What do you say? Should we waste time looking for the wagon or should we just load up and carry them?"

Nicky seemed oblivious to the hidden meaning behind the question, but Molly was sure that Brianne knew exactly what she was trying to do. The girl looked her up and down for an uncomfortably long time before she shrugged and picked up a box. "Let's carry them. There aren't *that* many."

Relieved, Molly helped the kids load up, grabbed as many boxes as she could and followed them out the door. She couldn't help thinking that she'd just scored a major victory, but victory in a war she wasn't going to be around to win seemed hollow.

These weren't her children. She barely knew them. But the thought of leaving when she'd finally started making progress with them made her sad.

Even more important, now that they'd started to respond to her, how would they react when she left?

She watched Brianne take a box that teetered dangerously on the stack Nicky was holding and told herself not to get carried away. Nicky liked her, but he was hardly attached, and one civil conversation with Brianne didn't exactly take their relationship to a whole new level. She was just longing for a family of her own, that's all. Wishing for things that could never be.

She shook off the slight melancholy and concentrated on recapturing her excitement, but it wasn't easy. She was tired of being alone, tired of hiding her true feelings, tired of living in the past. What she wanted more than anything, she realized suddenly, was to have a future.

IT TOOK ANOTHER two days after his conversation with Aaron for Beau to convince himself he needed to talk to Molly—and find the time to do it. The first night he'd arrived home late after a frustrating meeting with the mayor, and Molly had already been in bed—at least, her lights were out. The second day had passed in a blur of work, soccer practices, dance lessons and arguments with bullheaded people over the best way to conduct an ice-block carving competition during WinterFest.

Now it was Friday night, and he finally had a minute to call his own. He'd sent Nicky to invite Molly to dinner, and she'd come of course, but she'd kept him at arm's length with superficial conversation, just as she had for the past ten days.

Beau wondered if the kids could feel the difference in her. If anything, their relationship with her seemed stronger, while his seemed worse. There was something wrong with this picture.

He wasn't even sure what he wanted. He only knew that he didn't like this wall that had gone up between them, and he missed the time they'd once spent together laughing and talking. So he waited until the kids were in bed and asleep, then set off across the lawn to…do something. He'd figure it out when he got there.

He walked quickly, and as he drew near the cabin, he could see her through the window, sitting at the table, completely focused on something she held in her hands.

His heart turned over in his chest and he nearly lost his nerve, but he'd never been afraid of anything in his life before the divorce, and he wouldn't be able to look himself in the mirror if he ran scared now. Still, crossing the lawn and climbing those stairs with the memory of Heather's ugly words ringing in his ears was one of the hardest things he'd ever done.

Molly apparently heard him coming. Her head shot up with his first footstep on the porch, and she was at the door and holding it open before he could reach it. She'd removed her makeup and pulled her hair up with a clip, but soft curls fell around her face and made him long to touch them. She wore a pale-blue robe that looked about a million years old over a pair of pajamas covered with cartoon ducks, but Beau was quite sure he'd never seen a woman more alluring. Only uncertainty kept his imagination from racing off to places he shouldn't let it go.

The light inside the cabin formed a sort of halo around her, and that slow burn he'd almost given up hope of feeling again ignited deep inside him. He made himself smile. This was as easy as passing a football, he told himself. It took just a little determination, a little focus...

Smiling wasn't so hard. But making his mouth work to form words was a little harder. "Am I interrupting something?"

She shook her head and motioned toward the table. "I'm just sorting supplies. I thought I'd take your suggestion and try recreating some of my mom's designs."

She sounded normal, but he caught a glimpse of the pulse point just above her collarbone, and when he saw it jump, as if she was aware of him, too, he felt himself relaxing enough to carry on a conversation. "Well, you'll be great at it, I'm sure." He propped one hand against the door frame and leaned in just a little, needing to be where she was and wanting her to ask him to be. "Listen, Molly, we need to talk."

Her worried gaze shot to his face and he hurried to set her mind at ease. "There's nothing wrong. Not anything you've done, that is. But I don't like the way things have been between us since that day at Uncle Clay's, and I want to fix it."

She hesitated for a moment, then stepped away from the door and motioned him inside. "I've already told you that I'm not angry," she said when she'd closed the door behind him. "I know what you were trying to say. I just overreacted."

"Yeah, well, I said the last thing you wanted to hear right then. Have you found out anything more?"

"No, but I haven't really tried." She turned away, kneading her forehead with her fingertips. "I just can't figure it out, Beau. I've thought and thought, but none of it makes any sense. My dad was one of the gentlest people I've ever known. I can't imagine him fighting with my mother so fiercely that the police would need to interfere. But I also can't imagine him doing something so wrong that my mother would get that angry." She turned back to face him and her eyes swam with unshed tears. "The idea that they were heading into divorce court is so preposterous it just makes me crazy. There's more to the story. I just know it."

He needed to do something, so he closed the distance between them and pulled her into his arms. "Then we'll find it, Molly. I promise you we will."

She held herself stiffly for a moment, then relaxed against him, wrapping her arms around his waist and hanging on as if he held the key to her very survival. "I've been going through the days, ordering jewelry supplies and pretending that I can make it all better by stringing some beads on wire. I'm an expert at putting things out of my mind and forgetting what's too unpleasant to remember. But it's not going to go away this time. Some days that's what I want. Other days, I think I'll die if I don't remember."

He cradled her gently, brushing his lips across the top of her head and smoothing his hands along the soft fabric of her robe. "What are you saying? That you're choosing not to remember?"

She lifted her gaze to meet his. "I don't know. Maybe I am. Maybe I walked away from that accident and decided it was all too ugly to think about. Maybe

I was tired of hearing my parents argue. And maybe I decided to pretend it never happened.''

"Give yourself time, Molly. You can't undo fifteen years in a week or two."

She put a hand on his chest. She didn't push him away, but he could feel the agitation starting to take control of her again. "Meanwhile, I'm taking horrible advantage of you. I should at least go back to the motel.''

"Absolutely not. The cabin would just sit empty if you weren't here. And besides, the kids like having you around, and I feel better knowing they're not alone, even for only a couple of hours after school. So just relax and let yourself deal with this."

"I can't bear to think I'll have to go through years of this. I'd rather forget about it completely." She laughed harshly and stepped away. "And why don't I? Obviously my dad was good at forgetting about things *he* didn't want to remember. Maybe I should just go with the family tradition and avoid reality completely."

Beau hated what this was doing to her. "You're being too hard on yourself," he told her. "Strange things happen to people when they go through something traumatic, and they don't always get to choose their reactions."

"You don't get it, do you?" Her voice sounded frantic. "We talked to Clay ten days ago. I've known for over a week that I was in the car with my mom when she died. I've had all this time to dig into records, ask questions and find out the rest, but every day I find some excuse not to do it. I say I want to know the truth, but I sure don't act like it."

Beau sat on the arm of the couch. "I think you can cut yourself a little slack, Molly. You've been dealt a few surprises since you've been here. I'm sure it's not easy to take it all in.''

"It shouldn't take this long." She turned back to the table.

"I didn't realize there was a time limit," he said, trying to lighten the moment. When she didn't smile, he stood again and followed her. "I don't know how you can put a time limit on something like that. Look how long it's taken me to come to terms with the surprise Heather dropped on me. Are you saying I should have just dealt with it eight or nine months ago? Because if that's what you think happened, I've got news for you.''

Dropping into a chair, she began sorting tiny pieces of something shiny with quick, angry movements. "That's different," she said without looking up. "You haven't made avoiding reality the work of a lifetime. But you know what? This isn't getting us anywhere, so why don't we just drop it?''

She stopped working and met his gaze, and he could see that she'd already withdrawn. But he wasn't about to let her run him off.

He drew up a chair and straddled it, watching her intently as she kept sorting.

After a few seconds, her gaze returned to his face. "What?''

"Nothing. Just watching.''

"It's that interesting?''

"Riveting.''

She rolled her eyes and went back to work. "You're easily amused, aren't you.''

"So I've been told." He rocked the chair up on two legs and picked up a shiny pink stone. "This is pretty. What is it?''

"Rose quartz."

"What are you going to do with it?"

"I'll probably make a necklace." She reached out with an impatient hand and took the stone from him. "Maybe for Brianne, if you think she'd like it."

Beau nodded and pretended to give that some thought. "She probably would. It would look better on her than it would on Nicky or me."

Molly ignored his feeble attempt at humor, but when he didn't move for several minutes, she leaned back in her seat and met his gaze. *"What?"* she asked.

"You look good in this cabin," he said impulsively. "Like it was made just for you."

The sigh she released sounded exasperated, but her lips quirked and Beau could have sworn he saw a hint of a smile there. "I thought you said your grandparents built this place."

"I did."

"So you're saying I look old?"

Chuckling, he leaned over and captured her lips with his for the briefest kiss in history. Then he stood and turned the chair back around. "Yes, Molly, that's exactly what I'm saying." He bent and kissed her again, this time taking just a little more time and putting all the things he couldn't let himself say into the effort. She responded well enough to satisfy him, so he straightened, cupped her chin in his hand and lifted her face so he could see into her eyes. "Good night, Molly."

He heard her whispered "good night" as he stepped outside, a split second before he shut the door, but he carried the pleasure of it, and the look on her face, across the frozen lawn with him. He liked the fact Molly wasn't afraid to look at herself, even if she sometimes didn't like what she found. And though he still wasn't sure what he wanted from the future, he felt better about his ability to figure it out.

All he needed was time.

BEAU CAME AWAKE suddenly the next morning and bolted upright in bed. He blinked a few times to clear his eyes and realized that the sun was already streaming into the room. He rolled over and dragged the alarm clock around so he could see it. Eight o'clock! How in the hell had that happened?

Obviously he'd stayed awake too long thinking about Molly and wondering about the future. He wasn't thinking commitment, but the prospect of exploring possibilities made the days ahead look brighter.

He scrambled out of bed, tugged on a pair of sweat-pants and raced down the stairs to put coffee on. Thankfully, Gwen had canceled the kids' piano lessons this week so she could carve pumpkins with Riley's family, but he still had a million things to do, starting with an early meeting to discuss the city's Christmas decorations. At least this was one meeting he could get the kids involved in.

He felt a sharp pang of regret that Molly wouldn't be here for the holidays. He'd love to share WinterFest with her—the snowball toss, the sleigh rides, the snow-shoe races and even the snowman-building competi-tion. But he couldn't think about that now. He was already running so late he'd be lucky to finish every-thing before midnight.

Even with so much on his mind, he had a hard time not grinning as he put on the coffee. He pulled a load of clean towels from the dryer and left them sitting on the table while he dug through the fridge for breakfast makings. But his mind wasn't on laundry and bacon.

Whistling softly, he stuffed a load of sheets into the washer, then carried his mug of coffee back to the table and set to work. He even managed to keep himself from checking out the window for Molly between folding each towel.

He finished the task in record time and carried the towels upstairs to the linen closet, which he suddenly noticed was in desperate need of reorganization. Vowing to put them away neatly *next* week, he stuffed everything into the empty spots and hurried downstairs again to start breakfast.

He pulled bowls and pancake mix from the cupboards, eggs from the fridge and juice from the freezer. With a quick look out the window at the cabin, he tried sending a subliminal message to Molly that it was time to wake up. He couldn't wait to see her again.

Laughing at himself, he put the frozen juice and water in a pitcher, started to pour pancake mix into the bowl, then left the box on top of the washer while he dug through the cupboard for a measuring cup he could have sworn was there a few days earlier. When he couldn't find it at the front of the cupboard, he stretched high to check the back, craning to see over the jumble of bowls, plastic containers, ice-cube trays and other things he couldn't identify—but if the measuring cup was there, it was cleverly hidden.

He let out a growl of frustration and turned toward the next cupboard. His hand knocked over the pitcher, sending a shower of pale-pink water and half-melted juice concentrate to the floor before he could right it. At the same moment the washer clicked onto the spin cycle.

Cursing under his breath, Beau grabbed a dish towel and tossed it onto the floor. As he dropped to his knees and took one swipe at the mess, the washer let out an ungodly noise and began to shake as if something or someone was trapped inside. He shot to his feet again and lurched toward the machine, watching in horror as the five-pound package of pancake mix gyrated to the edge of the washer and plunged to the floor.

"No-o-o-o!" He dived after it, but the package split on contact and a cloud of pancake mix flew into the air, up his nostrils and into his eyes. He sneezed twice and swiped at his face with his shirttail. In frustration, he aimed a kick at the closest cupboard, forgetting that he wasn't wearing shoes until the pain shot through his foot and up his leg.

"Need some help?"

He glanced over to see Molly standing near the island, watching his disaster-in-the-making. Her eyes were clear and bright, her smile warm and friendly, and relief quickly overshadowed the humiliation of being caught covered in pancake flour and juice.

"Help? No." He scrambled to his feet and studied the mess on the floor with a wry expression. "Why do you ask?"

"No reason."

"That's what I thought. Obviously, I have everything under control." Molly's lips twitched, and Beau's heart soared with hope that they'd put the uneasiness behind them.

As she stepped around the counter, Beau drank in the sight of her. She wore jeans and a plain, long-sleeve white T-shirt tucked in at the waist. Her thumbs were hooked in her back pockets, causing her breasts to press against the thin white fabric, accentuating the lacy bra covering their soft swell. "I realize you don't need help from me, but out of curiosity, where's your broom?"

Beau jerked his gaze back up to her face. "Broom?"

"That thing with the handle on one end and bristles on the other? I'm sure you've seen one."

Her hair fell in lazy curls to her shoulders, and Beau had a sudden urge to forget about breakfast and remind himself why men and women had been created differently. He was having one helluva time concentrating on what she was saying. *Broom,* he reminded himself. "I've seen one. I just haven't decided whether or not to use it yet. I'm still pondering my options."

Her eyes sparkled with suppressed laughter and Beau added another entry to the list of things he was learning to love about her. "I'd suggest the broom first, then maybe a mop."

"A mop."

"Spongy thing. Long handle. Needs water." She glanced at the puddle on the floor. "I wish I'd gotten here sooner. I could have told you that juice doesn't work, as well."

He gave himself over to the game and narrowed his eyes in mock disbelief as he pulled the broom from the closet. "Are you sure? It's prettier than water. Pink."

"That's true," she said, somehow still managing not to smile, "but your floor isn't pink."

"Not yet."

She nodded, conceding the point, and turned away to pull the mop and bucket from the closet. "Did you *want* a pink floor?"

Beau swept a mound of pancake mix onto the dustpan and carried it to the garbage can. "I'm thinking about it. Brianne likes pink. It's a perfectly good color.

And it might even help me get in touch with my feminine side.''

Molly laughed, just once, before she sobered again. ''It might, but that's not really the thing to do anymore.''

''No?''

''I don't want to sound rude, but it's sort of... nineties.''

''Shows you what I know. And after I went to all this trouble, too.'' He stepped across a particularly noxious blob of pink dough and tackled another heap of dry mix. ''So what are men into these days?''

''I think it's all about 'being real.' Facing things squarely.'' She wagged a dismissive hand through the air. ''You know the drill. Dealing with life head-on. Taking it on the jaw. That sort of macho, manly, testosterone-y thing.''

''Head-on? Are you sure?''

''Well, not a hundred percent, but fairly sure. Honesty seems to be the thing these days for both sexes.'' She carried the bucket to the sink, found floor cleaner and mixed it with hot water. ''It's not a bad idea, actually. It comes highly recommended.''

''Honesty, huh?'' He scratched his chin thoughtfully. ''That sounds almost dangerous. Are you sure it works?''

''Well, I can't be positive, of course. It's a new idea and I've never been involved with anyone who actually did it...'' She shut off the water and turned back to him. ''But it sounds nice, and I think I'd like to try. If you're interested, we could work on it together. Maybe go back over the past few weeks and try again?''

Beau's throat closed and he could have sworn that his heart took up residence behind his ears. He couldn't hear anything but its incessant drumming for several seconds, and the blood in his veins felt as if someone had set it on fire. "What would you do differently?"

The humor fled her eyes and stark emotion replaced it. "Well, for one thing, I'd be more honest about my feelings for you."

He tried to smile. "Would those be *good* feelings?"

"That depends on your point of view, but I think so."

"That sounds promising." He left the broom and dustpan leaning against the fridge and moved closer to her. "I'd probably be forced to admit that I've missed this a whole lot more than I should."

She smiled and her eyes softened even further. "So have I."

Beau felt himself being drawn into their depths, and he suddenly wanted more than anything to spend however long it took to uncover all the mysteries there. "So we're friends again?"

She nodded without looking away. "I'd like that."

"*Only* friends?"

Her eyes widened slightly, but she shook her head and her lips curved into a slow, seductive smile. "I don't think so."

He slid his arms around her and pulled her close, sparing one brief thought for the kids and willing them to sleep just five minutes longer.

She snuggled into his arms and frowned up at him thoughtfully. "I guess if we're really going to get into this honesty thing, there's one more little tidbit I should share. I was madly in love with you back in high school. I would have given almost anything to take Heather's place."

The confession both stunned and delighted him, but

he wasn't about to waste time analyzing which feeling was stronger. The kids might wake up at any minute. He drew her closer and lowered his head until their lips were almost touching. "Maybe you should have told me back then."

"I was too shy."

"Yeah? But think of all the time we've wasted." And with that, he covered her mouth with his and put an end to the conversation. There'd be plenty of opportunity to talk later. Right now it was time to feed a starving man—and he didn't mean eggs and pancakes, either.

CHAPTER FOURTEEN

BEAU SQUINTED into the deceptive October sunshine and tugged the collar of his jacket up to protect his ears from the biting cold as he worked. A small pile of luggage sat on the tarmac a few feet from the Cessna, waiting for him to load up. His passengers, two guys who needed transportation back to Jackson after a successful elk hunt, had conceded to the cold and gone inside for stale coffee and doughnuts.

Perfect weather for Halloween. Perfect weather for a flight. In fact, everything had been pretty damn perfect for nearly a week. If he wasn't careful, he could get used to this.

Molly had been in Serenity for a month already, and there were times when Beau let himself forget that she wasn't going to be around forever. He liked coming home from work and finding her there with the kids. He got a kick out of cutting firewood for the cabin while she worked on her jewelry. No matter how many times he'd told her she didn't need to cook for them, it was a rare workday when he didn't walk through the door to the aroma of something in the oven or on the stove. But on his days off, he tried to pull his weight by fixing chili and biscuits or Brianne's favorite baked potato bar.

Yep, he could get used to this. And maybe Aaron was right. Maybe this *was* his chance.

He heard footsteps behind him and turned, expecting to find his passengers returning. But instead, he found Doris striding toward him, looking as if someone had just run off with her prize pickle recipe. He groaned silently and prayed for patience.

"Doris."

"We need to talk, Beau."

He decided not to assume the worst. "About what?"

"I think you know what."

"This isn't really a good time," he said, nodding toward the luggage in case she hadn't noticed it. "I have passengers inside, and I'm due for takeoff in just a couple of minutes."

"This can't wait. I'm worried about the kids."

"Did something happen?"

"*Yes*, something happened. It's been happening for a month, and I'm tired of hoping you'll wake up and be reasonable about this."

Would the woman never give up? Beau shook his head and hefted a duffel bag. He stuffed it into the Cessna's nose compartment and turned back for another. "I thought we'd agreed not to have this conversation again."

Doris tugged her cardigan sweater closer and folded her arms. The wind tousled her hair and the cold had already turned her nose and ears pink, but she looked ready to settle in for a long battle. "I don't approve of what you're doing over there with that woman. What will it take to get you to stop?"

Beau had to reach around her to get the rest of the bags. "I can't discuss this now, Doris. I'm scheduled to take off and my passengers are waiting."

"This doesn't have to take long. I just want you to promise me you'll be reasonable. That you'll start to care about Brianne and Nicky and the impression you're making on them, and that you'll send—'' she waved a hand as if she couldn't remember ''—Molly to stay somewhere else.''

Beau wedged the two small bags into the Cessna's nose and stepped back to latch it. ''In the first place, Doris, what I do isn't your concern. In the second, Molly and I aren't doing anything wrong.'' He stepped around her and stowed two leather briefcases behind the passenger seats. ''And third, I really don't want Molly to go anywhere.'' He turned back to face her. ''As a matter of fact, I'm hoping she'll decide to stay for a long, long time.''

''Oh, please, Beau. You don't know what you're talking about. You haven't been divorced that long, and you were in love with Heather since you were teenagers. Now someone comes back who knew you then and still sees you as the quarterback on the high-school football team, and you're going take a little flirtation with her seriously?''

Struggling to keep his temper, Beau moved past her again. Doris had been a constant presence in his marriage, a thorn in his side for fifteen long years. She'd controlled everything Heather had ever done, and through Heather, him. But he still wasn't willing to let down his guard and tell her everything in his mind. Call it respect, call it weakness, he wasn't sure which. But he bit his tongue as he always did.

And she came after him, as *she* always did. ''Don't you dare walk away from me. Everyone knew Molly had a thing for you in school, but Heather always stood in her way. Now Heather's gone, and who shows up? It's quite a coincidence, isn't it?''

''Don't be ridiculous. She's not here for me.''

"*Is* it ridiculous?" Doris's footsteps echoed on the tarmac behind him. "Why don't you go ask a few people, Beau? Eve knows. Heather always knew."

"I wouldn't trust Heather to tell me what time it is," Beau snapped. "And Eve's almost as bad."

"And Molly's just like her mother, sniffing around for any man who'd have her."

Suddenly furious, Beau whipped around and put himself at eye level with her. "You're a mean-spirited woman, Doris. You always have been. You drove Heather crazy with your constant nagging, and you're about to do the same thing to me."

Her mouth dropped open, but she snapped it shut again, and fire flashed in her eyes.

Beau didn't care. "For the kids' sake, I've put up with everything you've dished out, but you've gone too far this time. I'm going to tell you this just once. Leave Molly alone. And if I ever hear you say anything that vile about her mother again, it'll be the last time the kids go anywhere with you alone."

It was a rash threat, but he didn't let himself apologize. Doris had to realize how irrational she'd become, or the situation really would get out of hand, and the kids would be the ones who suffered.

Doris's pale eyes grew icy. "You don't mean that."

"Try me and find out."

"I'll take you to court. I'll petition for custody of those kids myself."

Perhaps he'd gone too far, Beau thought, especially with customers likely to come back at any moment. He also knew that if he kept arguing with her, things would go downhill—as if they could go any farther downhill than they already had. Clenching his fists as tightly as his teeth, he wheeled away from her and started across the tarmac toward his office.

"Don't you *dare* walk away from me," she shouted after him. "I mean it, Beau."

He kept walking, but only because he didn't completely trust himself not to do something he'd regret. Maybe he'd pushed her too far this time, but she had to understand that there were some lines folks didn't cross. Getting dealt a raw hand in life didn't justify becoming mean-spirited. And if she followed through on her threat and fought him for custody of the kids in court? Well, then he supposed Doris Preston would finally find out what he was made of.

"COME OUT WITH ME," he whispered to Molly that evening during a rare moment alone.

Scowling in concentration, she looked up from the lasagna she'd been layering into a pan. "Out?"

"For dinner. Let the kids have the lasagna. We'll go somewhere, just the two of us."

Molly's eyes grew wide. "On a date?"

"That's what I had in mind."

She tilted her head to one side and considered him for a moment. "Well, I do truly love my lasagna, but I guess leftovers would be just as good. Are you sure that's what you want?"

"Why wouldn't I?"

She lifted a shoulder casually, but a shadow crossed her eyes. "You know how people are. If we go out in public together—alone—people will talk. I'll be leaving sooner or later. You and the kids are the ones who'll have to live with it."

Leaving. He ignored the pang he felt and leaned into the corner, crossing his arms over his chest. "Don't worry about talk. We've gotten used to talk this year. Besides, I'm a big boy. I can handle it.''

Her gaze traveled the length of him and a slow smile curved her lips. She cleared her throat and looked at the lasagna noodle she held in her hands as if she didn't know what it was. ''It's not you I'm worried about,'' she said after she gathered her wits. ''Brianne seems to be doing a lot better lately. I don't want to do anything that might send her into a tailspin.''

''And you think that going on a date with me will do that?''

''I don't know.'' She met his gaze squarely. ''I think that her grandmother will cause trouble if you and I go out in public.''

''Doris is one of the reasons I want to talk to you— alone. She stopped by to see me today at the airstrip. I think you should know what she's saying.''

''About me?''

Beau nodded. The rest could keep until they were alone.

Molly's gaze faltered. ''You know she's not happy about me being here.''

''She made that pretty clear,'' he admitted, ''but how do you know?''

''She told me.''

Beau's good mood evaporated. ''She what?''

''She told me.''

''I got that part.'' He struggled not to let his anger with Doris spill over to Molly. ''When did she tell you?''

''The other day at the FoodWay. I was there picking up a few groceries and she made a point of... introducing herself.''

The anger he'd somehow managed to keep suppressed all day burst to life as if someone had tossed a lit match onto gas-soaked kindling. He'd had enough. More than enough. He turned away as he struggled to get it under control. "She's gone too far," he ground out when he could speak again. "I don't know what it's going to take to wake her up, but she can't keep doing this. I'm sorry, Molly."

"It's not your fault."

"Oh, but it is. She's been this way since Heather and I got married. Even earlier, if you want the truth. From the minute we told her Heather was pregnant, she started nosing her way into our lives, and I let her in because I was a kid and I felt so damn guilty about what we'd done. My parents were disappointed, but they took it in stride. Doris…" He paused and shook his head. "She's held every mistake I've ever made over my head, and she did the same with Heather. Miserable as she's been making me, I'll tell you who I'd hate to be right now, and that's Heather. She'll pay for leaving here for the rest of her life. Doris will make sure of it."

Molly touched his arm tentatively. "At least she's not alone. She has Dawn…and you."

He whirled back to face her. "Me?"

Molly went back to work, spooning great daubs of filling into the pan. "I know she hurt you, Beau. I understand you don't want to put your marriage back together, and I'm not suggesting you should." She set the bowl aside and looked into his eyes. "But regardless of what happened in the end, the two of you really have been friends forever. You've been through hell and back again. And you have children together. Wouldn't it be better for everyone if you could stop being angry with her and just be her friend? I know the kids would like it.''

"You're forgetting one thing. She isn't interested in seeing the kids.''

"I don't think you can be sure of that. If she *was* living a lie during her marriage to you, she must have been unhappy. Now you're hurt and angry, and her mother's...well, Doris. And let's face facts—Heather's obviously not strong enough to come back here and see the children she disappointed when there's not a soul in the world who'll back her. Dawn wouldn't be much help in that situation.''

Molly was wrong, and Beau wanted to tell her so, but deep down he knew that her argument made a certain kind of sense. He let out a brittle laugh and turned away, testing Molly's analysis in a dozen different ways and trying to find the flaws.

"If you shut her out,'' Molly said after a long moment, "then you're really doing the same thing my dad did with me.''

He whipped back toward her. "It's not the same thing at all. She left me.''

"And apparently my mom left Dad. She just didn't live long enough for anyone else to know about it.''

He dropped heavily into a chair and held his head with his hands, still trying to find faults in her logic and losing at every turn. "You're asking me to forgive her for lying to me? For hurting the kids? For ignoring them and putting herself first?''

"Yes. Because if you don't, you're putting your own hurt before the kids. You can't really believe that staying this angry with her is good for Brianne and Nicky. Whether or not she accepts your offer isn't the issue. For the kids' sake, you have to find a way to make it.''

A rush of affection swept through him for this woman who showed such concern for his children. He stood uncertainly and rounded the island. Some logical part of his brain warned him to think, but he was tired of thinking, and so very tired of fighting life's battles alone.

He cupped her face in his hands and leaned in close, half expecting her to pull away but praying she wouldn't. He brushed her lips once. Twice. Then covered them with his and poured everything he was feeling into the moment between them.

He could feel her heart beating against his chest, the rapid rise and fall and the unsteady breaths that spoke of her own emotions. He'd never been good at speaking his heart. He was much better at showing what he felt. But he could put everything he was feeling into one word, and he whispered it softly as he ended the kiss and pulled away slightly so he could look into her eyes.

"Stay."

Her eyes were closed, but they flew open at the sound of his voice and searched his for an explanation.

"Stay here for a while," he said hoarsely. And then, because she still looked confused, he added, "Stay, even if you find out what happened with your mom and dad tomorrow. Stay for Thanksgiving. Share Christmas with us. Spend New Year's Eve with me. Maybe with enough time, you and I can figure this thing out."

When she didn't immediately respond, he made himself be even more honest. "I never expected to feel something like this so soon after Heather. I don't want you to leave. Stay, and give us a chance to see where things go."

She put her hands on his chest, but instead of pushing him away, she splayed her fingers and studied them as if she wanted to memorize the way they looked there. Warmth spiraled through him from those places where her skin made contact with his, and he wished they were at the cabin, alone, instead of standing in his kitchen, about to be descended upon by the kids he could hear stirring overhead.

"It would also give us a chance to confuse your kids more than they already are," she argued reasonably. "And to hurt them all over again when I leave."

"There's no law that says you have to leave at all," Beau reminded her. "Serenity's a good place to live. Good people. Beautiful scenery.

"And zero opportunity," she said with a little shake of her head. "I haven't worked in nearly six weeks, and I can't count on Mom's jewelry to get me by."

"So get a job here."

She smiled softly, but there was a deep sadness in her eyes. She pulled her hands away and put some distance between them as the kids began to come down the stairs. "I don't want a job, Beau. I want a career."

"And you can't have one here?"

"Where? At the FoodWay? It's a nice town, and most of the people are wonderful, but it's not exactly a hub of industry. There's no call for a graphic-design artist here, and the market's so glutted I can't hope to get anywhere on my own. I need to be out there where the action is."

"Serenity's not the end of the world."

"I know that, but I'm just not interested in waiting tables or checking groceries."

He swallowed his disappointment and shoved aside the flicker of irritation at her attitude toward the town he loved. Much as he wanted to argue with her, she was right. Serenity was small and out of the way. Too far from anywhere to have any allure for someone like Molly.

"What about the jewelry?"

"It's a nice hobby. It might even add to my income a little. But it's never going to support me."

He turned away and tried to get his disappointment under control. Her argument was logical. It made perfect sense. But it didn't change the way he felt. He just had no idea how he'd ever convince her to stay when he had nothing to offer but himself.

A LITTLE AFTER noon the next day, Molly paced the foyer of the Chicken Inn as she waited for Elaine to arrive. She had a million things to share with her friend, beginning with the simple pair of earrings she'd made before she left the cabin and ending with Beau's unexpected request last night.

In spite of what she'd told him, she'd spent hours toying with the idea of staying. Beau's sense of humor delighted her. His obvious love for his children, his never-ending service to the city and that streak of self-doubt that she glimpsed occasionally all worked together to create an incredible man who captivated her at every turn.

Could she? Should she? The temptation was almost too strong to resist.

Elaine arrived just a few minutes later, and almost immediately the hostess led them to a table. There were a few other customers at tables scattered around the dining area, but no one sat at the neighboring tables, and Molly was glad for the chance to talk freely.

Elaine draped her napkin across her lap and

smoothed it thoughtfully, then, tilting her head, she studied Molly and said, "You look happy. Things are going well?"

"Very well." Molly pulled the small box holding the earrings from her purse and handed it over for Elaine's inspection. "What do you think? Not bad for a first effort, huh?"

After studying the earrings carefully for a moment, Elaine agreed. "Not bad at all. You made these?"

"I did." The waitress arrived with salads, and Molly unrolled the napkin holding her silverware. "Beau thinks I can make a living at this, but I'm still not sure. Still, it's a nice hobby, and I actually felt kind of connected to my mom when I was making those."

"Well, I'm glad," Elaine said, closing the box and passing it back to Molly. "It would be really nice if this worked into a little business for you. My mom always said that Ruby Lane made the best jewelry around." Elaine speared her salad with her fork, but didn't eat. "Have you found out anything more about her accident?"

"Just what I told you the other day on the phone. I know I need to keep digging, but Clay's news really rocked me. It's going to take a while to come to terms with it, I guess."

"So how long will you be staying?"

"I don't know. A while."

Elaine turned her attention to her salad. "And how are things with Beau?"

Molly grinned like a teenager. "Things with Beau are just fine. He's really great, isn't he?"

"He always has been." Elaine worked the salt and pepper grinders over her salad, then settled them back in place slowly and deliberately. "He was pretty torn up when Heather left, you know."

"I'm sure he was." Molly realized that sounded almost patronizing and checked herself. "I know he was. There are times even now when you can tell how much it hurt him." She wondered if Elaine knew the truth about why Heather left, but she wasn't going to betray Beau's confidence. "The kids have had a rough time, too, but I think Brianne is actually starting to like me, and Nicky's just a great kid."

"Yeah, he is." Elaine looked up at Molly. "He and Jacob play together sometimes." Her expression seemed almost cool, and Molly shifted with a sudden uneasiness.

"Is something wrong?"

Although Elaine smiled, there was no warmth in it. "Wrong? I don't know what you mean."

"You're angry with me, I can tell. Why? What did I do?"

"I wouldn't say I'm angry. Just cautious. Concerned." Elaine stabbed her fork aimlessly into her salad bowl several more times. "I don't know, Molly. This whole thing with Beau just seems wrong to me. I mean, it's kind of like you're over there playing house, isn't it?"

Molly froze. "No! It's not like that at all!"

"Isn't it? You're over there in Beau's cabin, making stuffed French toast for his kids, and lasagna for the family, but you don't have any intention of staying and making this thing between you real." She put her fork down. "What would *you* call it?"

Feeling a bit ill suddenly, Molly put her own fork on her plate and locked her hands in her lap. "That's not what I'm doing. Beau and I have become close, but he knows I'm not planning to stay. I told him so again last night.''

''And the kids? Have you told them?''

''Of course I have.'' But a pang of guilt zapped her when she realized how long it had been since she'd brought it up.

''Look,'' Elaine said. ''You're my friend and I want you to be happy. But Beau's a friend, too. A *good* friend. I know you want a family, Molly. I know you want children of your own. It's obvious every time somebody else talks about their kids. But if all you're doing is using Beau's kids to ease your longing, that's not right—for any of you.''

Molly recoiled as if Elaine had struck her. ''That's not what I'm doing.''

Elaine looked her straight in the eye. ''You know I love you. And if you were doing this with anybody else, I probably wouldn't say a word. But that family's been through enough. If you're not planning to stay, then all you're doing is playing with their feelings. If you're serious about Beau and the kids, then I won't say another word. But if you're not in this relationship for the long haul, I'm asking you—as your friend and Beau's—to walk away and let them heal.''

Molly's first response was to argue, but she knew in her heart that Elaine was right. She wasn't in this for the long haul. Even if she wanted to, she couldn't stay. There was nothing for her here, and much as she'd enjoyed pretending she could live this kind of life forever, she knew she'd never be happy if her days consisted only of laundry, dishes and dinners.

Elaine had circled the wagons to protect Serenity's Golden Boy, and there would be others. No one would want to see him hurt again—especially Molly. Much as she hated to admit it, Elaine had a point. She couldn't continue to pretend that Beau and his kids had any place in her life. Even more important, she couldn't continue to pretend that she had a place in theirs.

IT WAS A WHOLE LOT easier to make the decision than to act on it. When Molly woke up the next morning, Brianne was waiting in one of the porch chairs, ready to help sort supplies and interested—though she didn't want to admit it—in learning how to make jewelry. Even with her own arguments ringing in her ears, Molly hadn't been able to turn the girl away. Not that day. Nor the next day after school or any day of the following two weeks.

With Brianne at the cabin every afternoon, Nicky was never far away. When the weather was good, he'd ride his bike, play football with imaginary playmates or bring neighborhood friends by to show off in front of the windows. After dark or when the weather was too cold, he'd construct towers out of building blocks on the rug in front of the fireplace or sit beside Molly and chatter about things that happened in school. At the end of every day, Molly promised herself that she'd make the break first thing the next morning.

Beau spent long hours away from home, flying charters or working with the committees on Christmas and WinterFest plans. He took the kids with him when he could, and she could tell he felt worse than they did when he had to leave them.

By mid-November she and the kids had established a daily routine. While the kids were at school, Molly created sketches of the jewelry women around town had lent her, did research on the Internet and read everything she could get her hands on that dealt with starting a small business. In the afternoons she'd throw dinner together, do a load of laundry, dust, vacuum or tidy a corner while the kids did homework, then they'd all scurry across to the cabin, where they'd stay until Beau came home.

Whatever housework she did was a small price to pay for continued use of the cabin.

One weekend, she and Beau had had breakfast at the diner while the kids had their piano lessons with Gwen. Beau's mother, Vickie, had invited her for dinner on Sunday, and both she and Gwen had treated Molly like one of the family. Beau's dad, and even Beau's younger brother, Lucas, who was too busy dating to spend much time at home, had welcomed her without batting an eye.

Molly hadn't forgotten that she still had questions about her mother's accident, but every day she found a reason not to ask them. As long as she still had questions, she also had an excuse to stay.

The kids were only part of her reason for hanging around. Beau might not have many free moments, but she certainly got her fair share of the ones he did have. Long walks along the creekbed, dinners at the Chicken Inn, stolen kisses in the moonlight, evenings spent with the kids, rented movies and popcorn... Add the friendships she'd renewed in town, and it was heaven on earth. Molly went back and forth, one day convinced that she really could stay, the next irritated with herself for letting the situation continue.

On a cold Wednesday afternoon, she bundled herself into the coat she'd borrowed from Beau a few days earlier, stuffed her feet into the hiking boots she'd ordered online and trudged across the frozen lawn toward the house. Beau had flown a charter to Idaho Falls, but the kids would be home any minute, and she wanted to have cocoa ready when they arrived.

It was only a short walk from the cabin, but arctic air was blowing into the valley from the north, and the temperatures had dropped to nearly freezing overnight. Today, for the first time, she was having to face grim reality. The cabin was comfortable as long as she kept the fire burning, but it became uncomfortable quickly if she got distracted and didn't replenish the firewood soon enough. Much as she might like to, she wouldn't be able to stay in the cabin all winter unless Beau followed through on his plans to winterize it.

Inside the kitchen, she draped her coat over a chair and set to work. She filled the kettle with water and turned on the burner, then settled in with a paperback novel to wait for the kids. After only a page or two, the phone rang. Someone had left the cordless phone on the table, so she glanced idly at the caller ID screen. When she recognized Beau's cell-phone number, she lunged for the phone and punched the talk button, hoping she'd gotten to it before the call transferred to voice mail.

"I'm here," she said. "Don't hang up."

Beau laughed softly. "I was hoping you might be. What is it, laundry day?"

She'd been using his washer and dryer for weeks, and they'd fallen into a rhythm with laundry, as well. "Not today. Probably tomorrow." She glanced at her watch and frowned. "I thought you'd be in the air by now. Is everything all right?"

"Change of plans," he said. "There's a bad storm rolling in and there's no way I'll get out of here tonight."

She felt a pang of disappointment followed by shock at how much she'd grown used to being around him.

"I have another charter in the morning," he said, "so I probably won't be home until late tomorrow."

Molly got up to turn off the kettle. "Do you have someplace to stay?"

"I have a room at a motel near the airport. I'll make sure you have the number before I hang up. I hate to do this, Molly, but do you think you could stay with the kids for the night? They'd probably be okay there on their own, but I'd feel a whole lot better knowing they had an adult with them."

"Of course I'll stay. You don't even need to ask."

"Great. Use my room. There are clean sheets in the linen closet. Tell Brie I said for her to help you change them."

The thought of sleeping in Beau's bed lit a flicker of anticipation in her belly. "I'm capable of changing a set of sheets on my own," she said with a laugh. "If it's too difficult, I'll just make up a bed on the sofa." Which might be smart, but not nearly as much fun. "Is there anyone you need me to call? Don't you have a meeting with the planning committee tonight?"

"Canceled, but Rosetta Carlisle might drop off some information she's found about the snowball toss. If she does, just put it on my desk and I'll see it when I come home. And if you have a minute while you're online, could you check my e-mails?" He rattled off his screen name and password, and Molly scribbled them in the notebook he now kept near the phone. "The supplier we've always used for Wiffle balls went out of business during the summer, and I'm hoping bids from a couple of new companies will be there."

Molly folded the note and tucked it between the

pages of her novel. "You mean that people still walk off with the 'snowballs'?"

"It's worse than ever. We lose so many every year you'd think people needed them for food."

"What if the bids are there? What would you like me to do?"

"Accept the best one. We need three hundred balls by this time next month. I'll fill out the purchase order when I get back."

"You trust me with your Wiffle balls? I'm flattered."

"I trust you with a helluva lot more than that." His voice was low and intimate, and it sent the most delicious curls of anticipation through her. "I'm also trusting you not to drool on my pillow."

Molly laughed, and the rush of affection she felt for him nearly overwhelmed her. "I'll use my own. Then you don't have to worry."

"Oh, I'm not worried. Just a little annoyed by my rotten luck. I finally get you into my bed, and I can't even be there to enjoy it." A beep interrupted and he muttered something she didn't understand. "My battery's shot," he said. "I'll call later to talk to the kids."

The connection died suddenly and Molly hung up. Thanksgiving was in just two weeks, she realized as she returned the phone to the table. In a month, WinterFest would be in full swing. Two weeks after that it would be Christmas, then New Year's, and a whole new year would be under way.

She'd intended to leave Serenity eventually, but she'd been dragging out her visit with one excuse or another for weeks. Crossing to the window, she stared out at the yard, the frozen fields stretching away on one side, the roofs of neighbors' homes on the other.

Low clouds hugged the mountains rimming the valley, and she realized suddenly what she must always have known—she didn't want to leave.

Not now. Not in a few weeks. Not ever.

CHAPTER FIFTEEN

THE BIDS CAME through just before noon the next day. Molly had moved Beau's laptop to the kitchen table after the kids left for school so she could work without disturbing the notes and files spread all over his study. She considered both bids carefully, settled on the one that looked best to her, then sent the e-mail placing an order for three hundred Wiffle balls.

Hoping she'd made the right choice, she got up from her chair to make tea. As she reached for the kettle, she caught movement out the kitchen window. When she looked closer, she realized that Doris Preston was marching up the walk toward the door, wearing a look that meant business.

What was she doing here, and why now?

Determined not to let the woman intimidate her, Molly took a couple of deep breaths for courage and crossed to the door. She opened it just as Doris reached for the knob, and felt a flash of irritation that the woman didn't even have the courtesy to knock.

"Mrs. Preston. What a surprise." Molly didn't trust Doris not to look for something she could use against her later, so she kept a friendly smile in place. "Beau's away on a flight and the kids are at school. What can I do for you?"

"Not a thing, Molly. I'm just here to pick up a few things for the children." She brushed past Molly and into the kitchen, where she tugged off her gloves, one finger at a time.

Confused, Molly shut the door behind her and leaned against it. "For the children?"

"Brianne and Nicky. They'll be coming to stay with me after school."

"Oh. I didn't realize..." Molly pushed away from the door and glanced at the cordless phone sitting beside the laptop computer. "I must have been online when Beau called. I didn't know you were coming."

Doris spied one of Brianne's sweaters on a chair and practically swooped down on it. "Beau doesn't know I'm here," she said with a thin smile. "I heard that he was away and I decided to take matters into my own hands. There's no reason for you to be burdened with the kids. They're *my* grandchildren."

"You haven't talked this over with Beau?"

"Beau doesn't discuss the children with me these days." Doris ran a glance the length of Molly and turned away again. "I wonder why."

Her implication couldn't have been clearer, but it was so unfair Molly felt as if she'd been kicked. "You think it's my fault?"

"Well, someone's behind it. Things were fine around here until you came to town."

"That's not true," Molly protested. "Beau had already asked you to stay away before I arrived. I didn't get to town until later."

"That may be true—technically." Doris finished folding Brianne's sweater and held it close. "But if you hadn't come back when you did, I'm sure he and I would have patched up our differences a long time ago."

Was this some kind of joke? A bad dream? It certainly couldn't be real. Molly studied the older woman's face, trying to find some hint of a smile or a flicker of amusement in her eyes, but she saw only anger. "Surely you don't believe that. Why would I want to keep you and Beau from reconciling your differences?"

"That's the question, isn't it? I've asked myself the same thing a hundred times these past few weeks. I suppose some people are like that, always stirring up trouble…"

Molly couldn't believe what she was hearing. "I'm not here to stir up trouble," she said. "I'm just here to find out about my mother."

"*Still?* You mean nobody's told you the truth yet?"

Molly shook her head. She wasn't sure why, but she didn't want to talk about her mother with this angry, venomous woman.

"Well, that figures." Doris picked up one of Nicky's trucks from a corner of the room and moved it to another. "Really, Molly, this is pointless. I'm here to pick up a few things for the kids, not to argue with you. I wouldn't want the children to be a burden on you."

Molly's cheeks flamed with heat, but she managed to sound reasonable when she said, "In the first place, the kids aren't a burden. And in the second place, Beau asked me to stay with them. He's expecting to find them here when he comes home."

"That's easily fixed. I'll leave him a note and tell him where they are. I can have them back here five minutes after he calls."

Although she forced a smile, inside Molly was shaking like a leaf. Doris wasn't particularly frightening, so what was it about this that bothered her so? "It's not really a question of how soon you could bring them back," she said. Her voice still sounded almost normal, much to her surprise. "I told Beau I'd stay with the kids, and I really can't change plans without his consent."

Doris sighed and propped her hands on the table as if she meant business. "I don't think you understand, Molly. I'm not asking for permission. I'm *telling* you that I'm not letting my grandchildren back into this house until their father gets home."

Her voice was filled with such venom Molly had to fight not to recoil from it. "Is it just because Beau's gone, or are you saying that you have a problem with *me?*"

The expression on Doris's face left little to wonder about. "I really don't think we need to dig up all that old unpleasantness, do we?"

Molly stopped moving completely. "What old unpleasantness?"

"Oh, I think we both know the answer to that." Doris gave an airy wave of her hand. "You know what they say—the apple doesn't fall far from the tree."

"And I'm supposed to be the apple in your analogy?"

Doris looked at Molly over the tops of her glasses. "I don't blame you for what your mother did, Molly, but where children are concerned, you simply can't take chances. Everybody knew what your mother was up to back then—everybody but poor Frank, that is. But he found out eventually. The truth always comes out, no matter how hard people try to hide it."

The pounding of Molly's heart should have drowned out Doris's hateful words, but they came through loud and clear. A dozen questions rose to Molly's lips, but she wouldn't let herself ask them. Doris was too angry, too filled with whatever ugly emotion drove her, and Molly didn't want it to throw shadows on her mother's memory and make things worse.

She picked up Brianne's sweater, where Doris had dropped it, and very deliberately carried it to the washing machine. "I'm sorry, Doris, but I can't let you take the kids' things without Beau's permission. You're welcome to call him. If he's not flying, I'm sure he'll have his cell phone on. I just need to know that he's agreeable. I'm sure you understand."

"You don't have the right to tell me no. Those are my grandchildren."

"I understand that, but Beau is their father, and he asked *me* to stay with them." Something flashed in the back of her mind, but it was gone so quickly she couldn't identify it. Again, she tried appealing to Doris's better nature. "I know you're concerned about Brianne and Nicky. The past year has been rough on them—even an outsider can see that. It's also obvious that you love them and you want what's best for them."

"Don't patronize me," Doris snapped. "It's insulting."

Molly held up both hands to avoid the accusation. "I'm not trying to do either. I know how hard divorce can be, and I know that when one person makes a decision, it affects everyone around them. I know you love Heather, and this has been hard on you, too."

Doris didn't respond, which was enough to give Molly hope that maybe she'd listen. She'd never forgive herself if she made Beau's situation worse.

Motioning toward the table, she tried again. "Why don't you sit down? I was just about to make some tea, and I'm sure if we try, we can find a compromise."

"I don't need a compromise with *you*."

"But you do. It's not about me or about you. Brianne and Nicky are the ones who matter, and they'll be hurt if you and I can't at least be civil to one another as long as I'm here."

Doris's frown was grim, but she was obviously considering the suggestion.

Molly grabbed the kettle and headed for the sink, chattering as if Doris had uttered a gracious acceptance. "I've been meaning to talk to Beau about Brianne," she said as she filled the kettle. "She's nearly thirteen, and she seems very interested in hair and makeup and clothes and shoes." She stole a glance at Doris, who moved slowly toward a chair and gripped it with both hands. "I was going to suggest a shopping trip—maybe to Jackson? But I'm sure she'd rather go with you than me."

To Molly's surprise, Doris almost smiled. "I'm not so sure about that, but thank you. It's a nice gesture."

"The kids love you, Doris. You've been through something very upsetting together, and they need you to help them make sense of it. But I know from experience that it will only hurt them, to hide things from them or try to paint a pretty picture over the truth."

She found tea in the cupboard and smiled sadly. "I don't know exactly what happened between my parents before my mom died, but I *do* know it isn't even close to what my dad told me. I found out a couple of weeks ago that my parents were having problems in their marriage. I'm thirty-three, and I never knew that before I came back here. I'm so angry with him now, I can hardly stand to think about him—not because he and my mom were having trouble, but because he lied to me about it." She carried cups and saucers to the table.

"The truth is sometimes hard to take, but even when you're a kid, the truth is better than a lie."

"I don't believe that. I don't believe it would be better for those children to be told their mother isn't coming back."

"It would be better than being told she's coming back to live with their father when you know that's not going to happen."

"I don't *know* that," Doris insisted, but the sadness in her eyes told a different story. She shot to her feet again and turned her back on Molly. "It's a phase, that's all. A ridiculous, hurtful, selfish, indulgent phase."

The pain she was feeling grew more evident with every word, and Molly wondered if the poor woman had ever let herself discuss Heather's decision with anyone. Judging from the way she moved and the look on her face, Molly would bet she'd kept the hurt and anger locked away all this time.

The kettle began to whistle and Molly turned to get it. "I don't know Heather well enough to understand why she made the choices she made, but I don't think you should keep blaming yourself for what she did."

Doris whipped back around, and the grief on her face was so powerful Molly felt as if it might tear her in two. "I'm her *mother*. She is what she is because of me. I don't know what I did wrong. I don't know where I made my mistakes. I've gone over everything a million times since she came and told me what she was going to do. Maybe if I'd intervened more when she argued with her father. Maybe if I'd been stricter. If I'd taken her to church more often. Or less. Maybe I was *too* strict."

The older woman covered her face with her hands,

and her shoulders began to shake. "I've tried to make it up to those poor kids, but I can't. No matter how much I do, it's just never enough."

Molly abandoned the tea and moved closer to the woman, whose pain seemed to fill the entire room. "Oh, but, Mrs. Preston, don't you see? You don't have to make anything up to them. They don't blame you for what their mother did, and nobody expects you to 'fix' what their mother has done. You can't make Heather's choices for her. You're not personally responsible for the ones she makes. And if this isn't a choice, if she really can't change who she is, then doesn't she need you to just love her?"

"Do you have any idea what people will think if they find out?" The question came out in a rush of agony.

Molly's heart softened even more. "Some people might think the worst, but some won't. And surely Heather matters more to you than a bunch of neighbors. She's your own flesh and blood."

When Doris didn't say anything, Molly decided to leave that subject alone.

"What the kids need is for you to fill part of the gap Heather's left by going away. But that should be easy when you love somebody as much as you love them."

Doris dropped her hands and regarded Molly intently. "I guess I owe you an apology," she said after what felt like forever. "I misjudged you." She smiled ruefully and dug into her handbag, finally producing a tissue, which she put to work wiping away the remnants of her tears. "You really aren't anything like Ruby, are you?"

Molly's smile evaporated. "I don't understand." She wasn't sure she wanted to.

"It's a compliment, dear," Doris said, wagging the tissue in the space between them. "Your mother was a wonderful woman in a lot of ways, but she wasn't perfect, was she? And when you think about what she put your poor father through..."

Molly could hardly bear the thought of hearing the truth from Doris, but she forced herself to ask, "What did she put him through?"

"Well, I don't know all the details of course. But I do know that Ruby could be quite the flirt when we were younger. The men our age were just wild for her." Judging from the expression on Doris's face, a young man *she'd* cared about had probably been one of them. "All I know is that she lied to Frank about something. Whatever it was, it nearly destroyed him. I never could feel the same about her afterward."

"But you don't know what?"

"No, but I can guess."

Molly wasn't interested in Doris's speculations. She'd already endured enough of those.

"It's not good to speak ill of the dead," Doris said, "but I'm glad to see you're not like her, after all." She tucked the tissue away and glanced at the clock on the wall behind her. "I know you're making tea, but I really can't stay. I'll phone Beau in a day or two about taking Brianne shopping. You'll let him know?"

Molly nodded. She couldn't do anything else.

But as she watched Doris walk back to her car, she knew she'd just been pushed into making a decision she'd been putting off too long. Sooner or later, she was going to learn the truth about her parents' marriage. It was inevitable. The only real questions were how and when.

IT WAS WELL after dark before Beau finally finished up at the airstrip and headed home. His eyes burned and every muscle in his body felt as if someone had tied it in a knot, but he'd made a substantial amount of money for two days' work and wasn't about to complain. He just hoped that the kids hadn't been too much for Molly. She'd sounded fine when he talked to her that morning, but he hadn't had a spare minute since to check in with her.

The Halloween decorations along Front Street had given way to Thanksgiving, and Beau realized with a start that the holiday was just a couple of weeks away. His mom had invited them all for dinner, including Molly, but he hadn't discussed the invitation with her. Nor had he checked with Doris to make sure the kids would be included in Preston family celebrations.

Life was slowly becoming more organized. He still had a way to go, but the house wasn't a complete disaster anymore, and he had a lot to celebrate this year.

The idea of contacting Heather skittered across his mind, but he shoved it away again. Molly was probably right about him taking the initiative to invite her back into the kids' lives, and he might take her advice one of these days. He just wasn't ready to do so yet.

He pulled into the driveway and turned off the engine, yawning hard enough to make his eyes water. Lights burned in the windows, and the house looked more inviting than it had in months.

On the porch he stopped to watch his family through the window for a few minutes. He was captivated by the sight of Brianne's smile, the sound of Nicky's laughter and the joy on Molly's face. As if someone had opened a door, he felt warmth and something he couldn't identify rushing through him.

Long before Heather had told him the truth, he'd suspected that something was wrong, and his doubts and fears had been eating at him for a long, long time. It had been years since he'd felt anything but tightness and anger and suspicion in the deepest part of him, but those emotions were gone, and he had Molly to thank. And if he and Heather eventually made peace, he'd have Molly to thank for that, too.

He watched as she turned, laughing, and took a sparkly item out of a bag at her feet. Pulling Brianne's hair up on one side, she secured it with the jeweled clip. The delight on his daughter's face shocked him, and his reaction told him that it had been far longer than he'd realized since she'd been truly happy, as well.

Without even trying, Molly had worked miracles in all their lives, and in that moment Beau knew he couldn't let her leave Serenity.

Eager to join them, he reached for the doorknob, but the vibration of his cell phone in his pocket made him draw back his hand. He pulled the phone out, saw Doris's name on the screen and groaned softly. She was the last person he wanted to talk to right now, but maybe it was a good thing she'd called before he got inside where the kids could hear.

He stepped into the shadows and steeled himself for the usual argument, the same old discussion.

"I know you've been away for a couple of days," Doris said when he answered, "but I'd like to talk to you. Is this a good time?"

"Not really. I'm just getting home. I haven't even walked in the door yet."

"It'll only take a minute." She took a deep breath and let it out again slowly. "I'll get the hard part over with first. I owe you an apology. Heather leaving the way she did, announcing after thirty years that she's...not herself..." She laughed nervously. "Let's just say that I haven't dealt well with what's happened, and I've tried to place the burden for fixing everything on your shoulders. I shouldn't have done that, and I'm sorry."

Beau leaned against the porch railing and tried to take in what she'd just told him. "Okay, but... how...?"

Doris went on as if he hadn't spoken. "I'd like to stop being angry, the two of us. I thought maybe I could take each of the kids for a day—if that's okay with you. Molly suggested that Brianne might like a shopping trip, and I'm sure Nicky could use some new things, too. I promise there'll be no talk about reconciliations. I won't mention Heather unless the kids bring her up."

Letting out his own deep breath, Beau glanced toward the bay window. "That sounds fine, but..."

Doris laughed. "You're surprised."

"To put it mildly." He pulled out the gloves he'd stuffed into his pockets and put them on again. "Don't get me wrong—I don't have a problem with what you're suggesting, but I don't get it. What happened?"

"Can we just say that I came to my senses and leave it at that?"

"I guess so." He turned up his collar to protect his ears from the cold. "For what it's worth, Doris, I think this will be good for the kids."

"You won't mind if I keep hoping Heather comes to *her* senses one of these days?"

"Not a bit—as long as you understand that there's nothing but the kids left between us."

"I think I can finally accept that. At least, I'll do my best."

"Well, I can't ask for more than that." Beau pushed away from the railing and stretched to work the kinks out of his back. "When did you want to take the kids?"

"I was thinking maybe Brianne this Saturday, and Nicky the next?"

"That sounds fine to me." He still wasn't completely convinced he was talking to Doris—although this woman *did* bear a strong resemblance to the woman Doris had been a handful of years ago. He caught a glimpse of Molly near the sink and shifted the phone to his other ear. "You said something about Molly earlier. *She's* the one who suggested these shopping trips?"

"You're not angry with her, are you?"

"Of course not." He moved so he could see Molly better through the window—the curve of her cheek and the smile that was becoming so familiar. "I just wanted to make sure, that's all. I didn't realize you and Molly were friendly."

"Well, I don't know if you can say we're friendly, exactly." Doris laughed uneasily. "But she was kind enough to talk with me today, and she made sense." Doris paused. "I suppose you could do worse for yourself, Beau."

Her compliment was so backhanded, he almost laughed aloud. "Well, yes," he said. "I suppose I could."

In the house, Molly walked back to the table. She slid an arm around Brianne's shoulders and ruffled Nicky's hair with her free hand, then took her own seat and began to work, still chatting easily with the kids and creating a picture so homey it twisted Beau's heart.

Somehow she'd managed to create the home he'd been craving for years. The happy children. The home-cooked meals. The laundry under reasonable control and only a mild amount of clutter. Laughter and music and happiness. She'd created them all. She'd succeeded where he had failed—and once again, he was relying on someone else.

"I'll have Brianne call so you can set up the details," he said to Doris. "And we need to talk about Thanksgiving. I want to make sure you have time with the kids that day."

"Bless you, Beau. You're a good man."

With her endorsement ringing in his ears, he stuffed the phone back into his pocket and headed for the door again. But his heart sat heavily in his chest, and his future felt like a rock on his shoulder.

Did he love Molly? Or did he love what she'd done for him? The kids. The house. The renewed self-confidence. He just didn't know.

He leaned against the wall, the contentment he'd felt a few minutes ago slipping away from him. He thought he loved her, but what if he didn't? What if someday down the road, he had to look at her and confess that he'd mistaken gratitude for love? Too many people could get hurt if he was acting on feelings that weren't genuine, and he just couldn't do that to Molly or to the kids.

He was going to have to tell her the truth and ask for time. But he had the sick feeling that it was going to be the hardest thing he'd ever had to do.

CHAPTER SIXTEEN

TWO HOURS LATER, Beau walked slowly across the lawn beside Molly. The evening had dragged on endlessly, and he'd been dreading this moment ever since he'd walked in the door. Molly and the kids had looked so happy.

Looked? Hell, they *were* happy.

Brianne was herself again after far too long, and he was trying to remember if he'd ever seen Nicky so carefree. So what was wrong with him? Why couldn't he just relax and enjoy Molly's company? Why couldn't he let things keep going the way they were?

Because he knew how it felt to be lied to, that was why. Because he'd been through this once before, and he knew how he'd felt when Heather announced that she'd never really been in love with him. He couldn't let things keep going if there was any chance at all he'd ever say those words to Molly.

As if she could feel him thinking, Molly slid a curious glance at him. "You're awfully quiet tonight. Was there some trouble on the flight?"

He shook his head and resisted the urge to put an arm around her or hold her hand. The contact might make him feel better, but she'd hate him for it when she heard what he had to say. "The flight was fine."

Although he'd tried to sound normal, he must not have succeeded. The smile that had been hovering on her lips faded and her eyes filled with concern. "Is there some other problem?"

"I don't know if you'd call it a problem..." He glanced back at the house and asked himself one last time if he was doing the right thing. He stopped walking. "Yeah, I guess it is a problem."

She touched his arm gently. "What is it?"

Her concern nearly made him change his mind. It had been too long since anyone had looked at him like that, and he liked the way it made him feel. But that was just another part of the problem. He had to look away from her to get the words out. "I think we need to reconsider what's going on here."

He heard her soft, indrawn breath, then, "I'm not sure I understand."

Beau forced himself to look at her again. She deserved that much. "I came home tonight and saw you with the kids, the house smelling wonderful, dinner on the table, laundry done. Brianne's doing great, and Nicky adores you. Even Doris is acting like a new woman. You've worked miracles around here, Molly, and I'm grateful."

Her dark eyes roamed his face. "But?"

"But it also hit me that I haven't been fair to you—or to the kids. I swore I was going to take care of my kids on my own, without help. I swore I was going to get my house in order on my own. Well, the kids are doing great, and the house is in order, but I'm not the one responsible."

"Of course you are."

"No. I haven't learned how to balance. It's still all or nothing for me, and that's not good enough when you have a family. Having you here just makes it easier for me to compound that mistake. If there's anything good going on inside that house, it's your doing, Molly, not mine." She shook her head again, but he had to get the rest out. "You've turned the kids around. You've given me a new lease on life, and you have no idea how grateful I am."

"But now it's over? Is that what you're trying to say?"

"Not *over*." He wanted to reach for her, but he wouldn't let himself. "I feel things for you I never expected to feel again. But what if it's not real? What if it's a rebound thing, or just bone-deep relief that someone's come along to help me out of the mess that was my life?"

Pain flashed through her eyes an instant before they shuttered. "I see."

"I'm not explaining this well."

"I think you're explaining it perfectly."

"I don't want this thing between us to be over. I just need some time to figure out what it is."

"It's friendship, Beau. A few laughs. A kiss here and there. I don't recall ever asking you for a commitment or giving you one in return." The coldness in her eyes told him more than the words she spoke.

"But I'm not sure I *don't* want one," he said. "All I'm asking for is time and a little space. I just need a chance to get myself together and figure out what I'm feeling."

She took two steps backward, but her eyes never left his face. "You can have all the time you want, Beau. All the space in the world. I never meant to crowd you."

"But you haven't. That's not what I'm saying. I just…" He rubbed his face. "I care about you, Molly. You must know that."

Her lips formed a hurt smile. "You don't have to say that, Beau. I'm a big girl and I've been rejected before. I think I can survive one more time."

He closed the distance between them and took her hands in his. "I'm making a mash of this, obviously. I *care* about you, Molly. A lot. But I came home tonight and saw you and the kids together looking like a Norman Rockwell painting. And then I talked to Doris and found out that you'd even turned *her* around."

When he felt her getting ready to pull away again, he tightened his grip on her hands and locked eyes with her. "After Heather left, all I wanted was to prove that I could take care of the kids and the house on my own. That's it. And then you came, and I started falling in love with you. You were so beautiful, and I felt young and handsome and worth something again. It was wonderful and exciting and so good for my shattered ego."

Her gaze dropped to their joined hands. "And you think you were alone in that?" She looked back at him, and the raw emotion in her eyes sucked his breath away. "You think my rotten marriage didn't leave a huge hole in *my* self-esteem?"

"I know it did. That's another reason why we can't take this too fast. The kids are another. But honest to God, Molly, if things keep going the way they have been, I'll propose to you before the end of the week. The kids adore you, and I could be a happy man with you in my life and in my bed every night. But I'm not going to ask you for that until I'm absolutely sure of what I'm feeling."

She nodded, and for a split second he thought she truly understood. But then she stepped away from his embrace and looked at him with eyes so cold only a fool could fail to see that he'd lost her.

"Take all the time you need, Beau. I'm leaving Serenity." He tried to reach for her again, but she evaded him easily. "I understand that you're confused, and I understand why. I'm not angry. I knew the risks that came with falling in love with you. It certainly isn't the first time I've been down this road. I want someone who loves *me*, not someone who's trying to convince himself that he does. I love Brianne and Nicky, and it's going to be hell to leave them, but I won't stay just because they like this setup." She picked up her purse and slung it over her shoulder. "In the end, they'll only get hurt—and so will I."

MOLLY ZIPPED the last of her bags closed and told herself to pick them up, but she couldn't move. She stood there, blinking back tears and staring at the bed for probably the hundredth time that morning. She'd only been here six weeks, but already this cabin felt like more of a home than anything else she'd ever known.

She'd let herself get caught up in the fantasy. She'd allowed herself to believe that Beau and his kids could be family. That she could fill the empty places in her heart with someone else's life. And now she was paying the price.

A noise from outside caught her attention, and she flew to the window, foolishly hoping that Beau had changed his mind, that he'd realized he loved her and that he'd come to stop her from leaving. But the blond head she saw near the swing wasn't Beau's.

Nicky stood on the porch, hitting one of the chairs with a stick, and she could tell by the deep scowl on his face that Beau had told him she was leaving. She pulled back sharply and tried to think, but she already knew she wouldn't try to avoid him. No matter what happened between her and Beau, she wouldn't purposely hurt the kids.

She checked out the window again. Nicky had shifted to the edge of the porch, but the stick was still moving, and she knew it wasn't going to get better until she talked to him. Grabbing her sweater, she stepped out into the relatively mild morning. "Nicky? Are you all right?"

He whipped around at the sound of her voice and the eagerness on his little face pummeled her heart. "Are you leaving? Dad says you're leaving, but I think he's lying."

Molly would have given anything not to have this conversation. She sat on one of the chairs and leaned forward so she could look the boy in the eye. "He's not lying, Nicky. I am leaving. I've been here too long, already."

His eyes filled with tears before she stopped speaking. "But I thought you were going to stay. I thought you liked us."

Was it possible to die from heartache? Molly wondered. She drew Nicky onto her lap and kissed the top of his head, but his nearness only made the pain worse. "Oh, Nicky, I *do* like you. You have no idea how much. You're a wonderful boy, and it's not because of you that I'm leaving."

"Then why?"

It was on the tip of her tongue to make up a palatable reason, but she'd spent weeks insisting that children deserved the truth and she couldn't offer this child anything less. "I have to go, Nicky. For a while now, your dad and I have been kind of...playing house and having you and Brianne play along. But we finally realized that it's not fair to you two, and I need to go away before somebody's feelings get hurt.''

''Well, it's too late.'' Nicky swiped his eyes with a sleeve. ''Brianne locked herself in her room after breakfast, and Dad's in a really sad mood. You can't leave. They won't like it.''

She was hopeless. A lost cause. She wanted to be over there, deep in the thick of it, working through the problems with them. She wanted it all, the good and the not-so-good that went along with being part of a family. But she *wasn't* part of their family. Beau couldn't have made that any clearer if he'd written it out for her.

Resting her cheek against the top of Nicky's head, she struggled to speak. ''I'm so sorry that Brianne is unhappy, and I wish your dad wasn't sad. But your dad and I aren't in love, and we're not going to be a family. I don't want you and Brianne to think that we are.''

Nicky jerked away from her and slid to the ground. ''That's not fair!''

''I know it's not. It wasn't fair of us to let you and Brianne think things were different than they are.'' No fairer than it had been to let herself get swept up in that old dream. ''I'm so sorry, Nicky. I wish I could stay, but I just can't.''

''Well, that stinks!'' He jumped from the porch and swung back around to glare at her. ''You're just like my mom, and I don't like you anymore.''

With her heart shattered in a million pieces, Molly watched him run across the lawn as fast as his legs could move. She wanted desperately to go after him, to tell him she'd stay and to promise that everything would be okay, but she didn't let herself take a step.

She'd been foolish and foolhardy. She'd been reckless and irresponsible, and not just with her own heart. If she went through hell getting over this, it was no more than she deserved.

MOLLY WAS HALFWAY through town when she realized that, once again, she was running away from the one thing she had come for. She pulled to the side of the road and turned the car around, making her way through quiet neighborhoods toward Louise Duncan's house. After all, what did she have to lose? No matter what she learned about her parents at this point, the pain couldn't be worse than what she felt over losing Beau and the kids.

She parked in Louise's driveway a few minutes later and studied the house as she walked to the front door. Louise had always loved to decorate for the holidays, and that apparently hadn't changed over the years. Uncarved pumpkins perched on bales of hay, sheaves of dried cornstalks tied together with twine leaned against the house, and a garland of silk leaves in autumn colors rimmed the front door.

A shaft of pain lanced her, so deep she thought it might tear her in two. She hadn't let herself think about spending the holidays with Beau and the kids, but on some level she must have been planning to. Thanksgiving wouldn't be so hard, but knowing she wouldn't be with them for Christmas made her almost sick.

She pushed aside those thoughts and replaced them with memories of Ruby and Louise planning trips into Jackson to buy decorations and poring over mail-order catalogs together. She remembered the laughter they'd shared, the phone calls…the secrets? She could only hope.

When she rang the bell, a Thanksgiving tune she

remembered from schooldays began to play. Molly knew that if Ruby had been here still, she'd have used the same tune on her own doorbell. She closed her eyes and sent up a silent prayer that Louise would understand her need to know the truth, and that she'd somehow realize that talking to Molly would not betray her old friend. But after several minutes passed with no answer, she began to lose heart.

Just as she was' ready to give up, the door inched open and Louise's narrow face appeared in the opening. She didn't look at all surprised to see Molly standing there, and Molly guessed that she'd been watching from a window. The realization was disappointing but not surprising. After all, the woman had spent the past six weeks avoiding her.

Louise had grown thinner, deep wrinkles lined her brow and bracketed her mouth, and her eyes had lost some of their sparkle. Her once-dark hair was liberally streaked with gray, and a pair of thick glasses perched on her nose.

She looked Molly over without expression and sighed heavily. "So you're here."

Just like that. No shock. No surprise. No defiance. Just resigned acceptance of a moment she'd known was inevitable in spite of her efforts to avoid it. Molly should have realized it would be like this. She could have saved herself a lot of heartache.

"I'm here," she said, "and I need to talk to you."

Louise nodded and pushed open the screen door. "You may as well come in. I guess you're not going to go away until you get what you came for."

Molly stepped into the house, which was at once familiar and strange, and followed Louise into the carefully kept living room. Back when they were kids, this room had been a jumble of toys and books, of crayons and paper. Now, it was devoid of clutter and filled with furniture that looked as if it had never been used.

She perched uncomfortably on one end of a stiff white couch, while Louise settled into a chair covered in pale-cream brocade. "I know you don't want to talk about what happened between my mom and dad, but I hope you can understand why I need to know."

Louise's eyes clouded and she shook her head. "I wish I could, Molly, but I've never understood why your generation needs to look at everything so hard. Some things are better left alone."

"You wouldn't say that if you'd spent half your life wondering."

For a long moment Louise stared at her, then she shrugged and looked away. "Maybe not. We'll never know." She dragged her gaze back to Molly. "Well? Tell me what you want to know."

Molly sat back on the couch and tried to make herself comfortable. "I don't mean to be rude, but six weeks ago you left town to avoid talking to me. Today you're ready to just tell me anything? I don't get it. Why the change of heart?"

"It's not a change of heart, Molly. I still don't want to discuss your mother's tragedy. But all your questions have stirred up curiosity. It's just a matter of choosing the lesser evil. I can tell you what you want to know, or I can leave you out there asking questions and making other people wonder."

The answer disappointed Molly, but she wasn't going to quibble. She set her purse on the floor beside her feet and took a deep breath to steel herself for what was coming. She'd put together much of the puzzle, but there were still missing pieces, and she knew instinctively that finding them would cause more pain and heartache than anything she'd experienced yet.

"I've been told that Mom and Dad argued a lot before Mom's accident. Is that true?"

"You really don't remember?"

"I really don't."

Louise sat back in her chair and linked her hands on her knees. "Yes, it's true. They argued almost constantly."

"But why? That's so unlike what I *do* remember about life at home, I can hardly believe it."

"Oh, it's true, all right." Louise twisted her hands together slowly. "It was a horrible time for both of them—and for anyone who loved them."

"What happened? I thought they were happy."

"They were...until your father found out something he was never meant to know." Louise turned her head and stared out the window, as if she couldn't bear to look at Molly while she talked. "I suppose, in retrospect, it would have been a good thing for your mother to have told him when it happened, but it didn't seem like a good idea at the time. Of course, we were all so young, and what sounds brilliant at twenty doesn't always sound even a little smart at forty." She slid a thin smile toward Molly. "I was as much a part of this decision as your mother was. I regret it now, but I suppose that doesn't count for much."

Molly was ready to jump out of her skin, but she tried hard to remain patient. "What decision?"

After several moments Louise stood and walked to the window, sighing softly as she stared out at the yard. "We were just kids. I hope you can remember that. Your parents had only been married a couple of years, and things weren't going so well. They were young and foolish and selfish—as we all were, I guess.''

She trailed one finger along the windowsill, then studied it as if she'd never seen it before. ''During that time, your parents weren't happy together. Your mother…'' She flicked an uneasy glance at Molly. ''Ruby was disillusioned and miserable. Marriage to Frank wasn't what she thought it was going to be. Frank spent too much time indulging himself, playing pool with friends and doing all those things young men who aren't ready to be married do.''

''I'll have to take your word for it,'' Molly said. ''That doesn't sound like Dad at all.''

''The man you knew *wasn't* that man. He changed when your mother became pregnant. It was so dramatic, it was like someone had flipped a switch.'' Louise smiled sadly. ''If we'd had any idea becoming a father would have affected him that way, we'd have done things differently. We just never expected the marriage to last, and then, when Ruby realized that it could, there never seemed to be a good time to clear the air.'' She ran a hand along her collarbone and turned back to face Molly fully. ''We didn't know, Molly. We didn't think—that's what it boils down to. And by the time we realized what a difference it made in Frank, by the time we realized how much he'd changed…well, it was too late. Or so we thought.''

Cold dread filled Molly, but she couldn't let herself back down now. Voices from the past drifted in and out of her mind as wispy pieces of memory began to surface. So much anger, so much heartache, and all because of her. That was what she remembered most. *She* was the one they'd argued over. She was the one who'd killed their marriage.

She met Louise's gaze helplessly. "It was about me."

"No, dear. Not you. It wasn't your fault. Your mother and I... It was her secret, but I encouraged her. I told her it would be okay. I honestly believed it would be. How were we to know that Frank would turn into such a devoted father? He was so sweet with you, so utterly besotted, neither Ruby nor I had the heart to tell him that he wasn't really your father."

The ice turned to fire, and Molly closed her eyes to block out the pain. But the sudden, clear images of her father's face, hurt and angry, wouldn't go away. And the sounds of her mother's tearful pleas for forgiveness grew louder and louder.

A sob caught in her throat and hot tears spilled onto her cheeks even before she realized she was crying. She'd felt so responsible for the arguments that the accident must have been too much to bear. No wonder she'd locked the truth away for so long.

"I thought I'd killed her."

"That's what I was afraid of." Louise crossed to sit beside Molly and took both her hands lovingly. "I haven't been trying to protect Ruby, sweetheart. She's beyond needing that from me, but you're her daughter, and I couldn't hurt you." She blinked several times and sighed wearily. "Finding out the truth devastated Frank. There were only a few of us who knew about Ruby. Phyllis Graham, and me. Even...the other man never knew. But Frank was certain the story would come out if he stayed here, and he was terrified of losing you. He couldn't have borne that."

Molly almost asked who the other man was, but something stopped her. She didn't want to know. Not right now. Maybe later. She knew where to find the answers when she needed them. "So that's why Dad wanted to divorce Mom."

"He claimed he did, but it was just his hurt talking. He said it so much, though, she finally did something about it. But I don't think Frank would have let the divorce go through. He was hurt and angry, but he also had a heart of gold, and I think eventually they would have worked things out." She patted Molly's hand. "That's what I always tell myself, anyway."

Another wave of memories washed over Molly, and she closed her eyes. Sadness nearly overwhelmed her. She'd come to Serenity to discover the truth, and now she had. But she hadn't expected to lose her identity—and her heart—in the bargain.

CHAPTER SEVENTEEN

MOLLY HELD her breath as her stepmother dangled a pair of jade earrings from her fingers, turning them this way and that to catch the light from the small Christmas tree she'd thrown up at the last minute. Christmas was just a week away, but Molly's heart wasn't in it.

She kept imagining what Beau's house must look like decorated for the holidays. She kept picturing the fun at WinterFest and fantasizing about being there with Beau, Brianne and Nicky. This surprise visit from Cassandra helped distract her a little, and she'd be forever grateful.

Cassandra's eyes glittered with appreciation and she smiled as she lowered the earrings to the coffee table. "Oh, Molly, these are wonderful. I truly think these are my favorites." She glanced at the length of black velvet across the table, where Molly had displayed her most recent creations. "The setting looks almost like lace."

Even though she knew she was still a long way from matching her mother's skill, Molly flushed with pride. She tilted her head to one side and pretended to consider. With Cassandra's rich auburn hair and emerald eyes, the earrings were flattering—as she'd known they would be when she made them.

She picked up a small, red-velvet box, the trademark of Ruby Lane Creations, and put the jade earrings inside. "Take them," she said, holding out the box to her stepmother. "As a Christmas present."

Cassandra's eyes widened, then narrowed speculatively. "That's a lovely gift, Molly. But they're exquisite, and I feel a little selfish."

"Why? You're family. I made them for you." Molly refrained from stating the obvious, but the words echoed in the space between them. *You're the only family I have.* Besides, she hadn't been able to face shopping this year and was having enough trouble acknowledging the holiday at all.

Instead, she'd given up returning to graphic design and had thrown herself into turning Ruby Lane into a viable business. The reaction she'd had so far gave her hope that she'd be able to support herself in time. She'd used hard work, and lots of it, to keep thoughts about Christmas at bay.

The small tree in the window of her St. Louis apartment was her only concession to the holidays. She hadn't had the heart to decorate, to dust off her collection of Christmas CDs or to mail out holiday cards. Next year, she'd promised herself a hundred times. Next year, when her heart wasn't still so sore, when the pain of losing so much wasn't quite as raw.

She realized that Cassandra was watching her, so she forced a smile and held out the box again. "I want you to have them, Cassandra. Please take them."

Cassandra took the box, but Molly could see that she still wasn't convinced. She leaned forward to kiss Molly's cheek, and then cupped her face with one hand. "Oh, sweetheart, I wish there was something I could do to help you get through this."

"I'm fine," Molly insisted. She couldn't allow herself to be anything else. She stood and began straightening the books on her shelf as if there was nothing more important in the world.

"Maybe you should go back to Serenity, Molly. I'm pretty sure that's where your heart is. Besides, there are just too many unresolved issues there for you."

Molly shot a look at her stepmother over her shoulder. "Let's not talk about Serenity tonight, okay?"

"Why not?"

"Because it's nearly Christmas, and because that's a closed chapter in my life."

"Is it?" Cassandra stood and moved toward her. "Molly, honey, it can't be a closed chapter in your life. Not while you're still so angry with your dad. Not while you're still in love with Beau."

Molly pulled away sharply. "Don't, Cassandra. Please."

But her stepmother was relentless. "I know you're angry with me, but I have to say this. If I don't, I'll never be able to live with myself." She stepped in front of Molly and held her so she couldn't get away. "I know you think this is none of my business, but we *are* family. How we got this way doesn't matter, just like it doesn't matter how you and Frank became family. He *was* your father. He will always be your father."

Molly's heart twisted painfully. "He didn't *tell* me. And don't say he died too soon, because he had fifteen years to tell me the truth."

"He made a mistake. A *big* mistake, but still just a mistake. And it was because he loved you so much. Surely you know that."

Molly nodded. She would never deny it, no matter how much his deception hurt.

"I know you'd be happier if he'd never done anything wrong, but he was just a man, sweetheart. Just a man. No better and no worse than anyone else. And certainly not perfect.''

"I never expected him to be perfect," Molly protested.

"And yet you can't forgive him? For holding on as tightly as he could to the one person in the world he loved with all his soul? For making sure that he didn't lose his only daughter? He'd already lost your mother. Losing you would have destroyed him.''

"So instead, he chose to destroy *me?*''

Cassandra's eyes narrowed. "How did he do that? By loving you? Providing a home for you? Sharing holidays and special occasions with you? Really, Molly, how *did* he destroy you?''

"By lying to me. I don't even know who I am anymore.''

Her stepmother's eyes grew hard. "Shame on you. You're Frank and Ruby Lane's daughter, just as you've always been. That hasn't changed, and it won't change unless you want it to. If that other man had been any kind of a man at all, he would have known about you and he would have fought Frank for the right to be your father.''

She lowered her hand and turned back to the table. Her fingers lingered over the velvet box for a moment as if she couldn't decide whether to take the earrings or leave them. "This is no different from children who are adopted. The birth parents are in their lives just long enough to get them here. Their *real* parents search until they find them.''

Images of Brianne and Nicky flashed through Molly's head, but that only made her mood worse. "It's not the same," she argued. "But I'm not surprised you're taking his side. I wouldn't expect anything else."

"*His* side? Wanting you to stop hurting yourself is taking *his* side?" Cassandra laughed humorlessly. "It must be nice to think you've never made a decision that's hurt another person."

"That's not fair," Molly shot back.

"Isn't it? Do you think your decision to leave Brianne and Nicky is so very different from your dad's decision to stay with you? You did what you wanted, and you seem to feel your decision was justified."

Molly gasped in shock. "That's so unfair! I didn't do what I wanted to do. And I never meant to hurt the kids. I left because Beau didn't want me to stay."

"Really?" Cassandra trailed one finger along the top of the velvet box. "I thought you said he *asked* you to stay."

"Yes, while he tried to talk himself into loving me."

"Are you sure that's what he was doing?"

"You weren't there," Molly said flatly. "You don't know."

Cassandra forced a smile. "Well, you're right about that. And I don't want to argue with you. If you can't go back, you can't go back. I just hate to see you so unhappy. It's been far too long since I saw you smile."

Molly tried to rectify that, but her lips felt stiff and cold and she knew she failed miserably.

"Are you sure you won't come with me to Florida? We could spend Christmas with my mother and the rest of the week having fun."

Molly shook her head. "Thanks, but you need to spend time with your family, and I wouldn't be good company, anyway. Besides, I've already committed to spending Christmas Eve at the children's hospital. I can't leave them in the lurch.''

She tried again to smile, and this time thought she was a little more successful. ''I'll be okay, Cassandra. Just give me time.''

But Cassandra didn't look convinced, and Molly wasn't, either. Since she'd been back in St. Louis, she felt worse than she had when she left Serenity. She had an overwhelming longing for home, but she had no idea where that was.

''I AM SO TIRED of watching you mope,'' Gwen said as she handed Beau a wrench. He lay on his sister's kitchen floor with his head under the sink, dodging tiny pieces of hard-water deposit and other gunk that fell from the pipe seam over his face.

He closed his fist around the cold metal and tried to pretend she hadn't said anything.

But his sister wasn't one to let a little thing like being ignored stop her. ''When are you going to do something about it? That's what I want to know.''

Beau fought with the pipe fitting for a minute and sent another shower of dried calcium into his face. He brushed the worst of it away and leaned up just enough to see his sister's knees. ''What *I* want to know is why your damn sink had to act up three days before Christmas. And while we're at it, maybe you could explain again why your husband isn't the one down here getting a faceful of garbage every time he moves.''

Gwen nudged his foot with one of hers. ''You're lucky the sink didn't wait until Christmas morning,'' she said in that no-nonsense tone she used with the kids. ''And what do you want Riley to do? Close the store this close to Christmas? You know what kind of grief people would give him if he did that.''

Beau knew, but it didn't make him feel a whole lot better. He wriggled out from under the sink and stood, brushing dirt and debris from his hair. "This is going to be a bigger job than I expected. The fitting's shot, and the U-neck doesn't look much better. I can drive over to Hinkley's and pick up the supplies, but you're going to be without water for a couple hours more.''

"Great. I didn't want to cook dinner, anyway. So you and the kids want to join us at the Burger Shack? My treat. We'll stop by Hinkley's afterward.''

He laughed and reached for the sweater he'd left over the back of a chair. "Your treat? You'd better believe we're coming.''

"Well, it's the least I can do.'' She waved a hand toward a basket on the counter. "Grab that, would you? I promised Lisa Simms we'd look in on Hazel tonight, and I put together a little basket of goodies for her.''

Grabbing the basket with one hand, Beau swept the other through his hair once more. Hazel Simms had been Beau's fifth-grade teacher, and he'd always had a soft spot in his heart for her. "I haven't seen Hazel in a while. How's she doing?''

"She's fine. Just a little lonely. This is her first Christmas without Jonathan, and it's hard on her.'' Gwen snagged her keys from a hook by the door and leaned into the family room to tell the kids to get their things and come outside to the driveway. "I forgot to ask—did you and Aaron get the lights up at the Parkers okay?''

"With a lot of direction from Sheldon.'' Beau closed the cupboard doors, shut off the Christmas lights in the kitchen and followed Gwen to the garage. "He may have had a heart attack two months ago, but it sure hasn't slowed him down much.''

"That's good news, right?''

He grinned and opened the door for her. "Right. God willing, he'll be raring to go in time for next year's WinterFest, and maybe I'll finally be able to step down.''

Gwen looked at him. "Oh, puh-leeze. You don't want to step down. Don't even give me that load of horse manure. Why don't you just admit that you're like Dad and Grandpa and that you live for your committees?''

"I don't live for them," Beau argued. "I enjoy them, but there's a time and place for everything. This isn't my time to be involved in all that stuff.''

She shot him another look as she headed toward the door of her minivan. "Apparently this isn't the time in your life to be happy, either, is it?''

"Don't go there, Gwen. I don't want to talk about that in front of the kids.''

"Really? Why not?''

Because Brianne had become moody and sad since Molly left, and because Nicky asked about her every day. And because Beau himself had been fighting a horrible empty feeling for weeks. But he didn't want to admit that to his sister. "Because it's almost Christmas, and there's nothing to talk about.''

"Oh, there's plenty to talk about," Gwen said with a laugh. "You just don't like to hear what anybody else has to say.''

Beau put the basket on the floor of the van and climbed inside. "You know what, Gwen? You have a way of making a man wish he was under a sink with a faceful of gunk.''

She laughed as if he'd said something wonderful. "And you have a way of not hearing anything you don't want to hear. Face it, Beau, you blew it."

"You don't get it, do you?"

"I get that you freaked out because you realized you needed Molly in your life." Gwen stuck the key in the ignition, but she didn't turn it. "I get that you're still freaked out by the idea that the great Beau Julander might need a little help now and then. But you're right. I don't get why you'd let a wonderful woman like Molly, a woman who was perfect for you by the way, get away because you're too arrogant to accept a little help from time to time."

"Arrogant?" The word shot out of his mouth and echoed through the garage. "Are you kidding me?"

"Well, aren't you?"

"Hell, no!"

"I see." Wearing an annoyingly superior smile, Gwen pressed the remote to open the garage door and turned the key in the ignition. When a Christmas song came to life on the stereo, she turned down the volume so she could continue railing at him. "So it's perfectly all right for Sheldon Parker to need help, and for Hazel Simms to need help, and for me to need help from my big strong brother, but you're above all that. Is that how it is?"

He opened his mouth to protest, but he couldn't get the words out.

"You don't mind being needed, but God forbid you should ever need anything. If that's not arrogant," she said, putting the car in reverse and turning her attention to the rearview mirror, "I don't know what is."

Twinkling lights from neighboring houses cast a colorful glow on the snow. Gwen's kids bounced excitedly as they waited for her to back out of the garage, but Brianne and Nicky stood a little apart, and their body language sent a pang of guilt through him. He'd brought something wonderful into their lives and then he'd chased it away again.

Out of arrogance? Fear? Sheer stupidity?

He shifted uncomfortably in his seat and fumbled with his seat belt. "I did the right thing, Gwen. I wasn't sure how I felt, and I didn't let myself take advantage of her."

"And now?"

Now he was about as miserable as a man could get, but how could he go to Molly and ask her to forget what he'd said? The back door slid open and kids piled inside. Beau looked away from his sister, grateful that he didn't have to answer her. But he couldn't evade the answer in his heart.

He'd known for weeks that there was only one thing he wanted for Christmas. He didn't care if she never lifted a finger around the house. It wasn't what she'd done that had gotten under his skin, but who she was. The truth was, he loved everything about her. Her laugh. The way she listened. Her warm and generous spirit. He'd been the worst kind of fool. The very worst.

He had no idea if she'd be willing to forgive him, but what kind of chicken-livered nothing would he be if he didn't at least try? Not the kind he could live with, that was for damn sure.

He nudged Gwen with his elbow. "Do you think Mom would mind if we brought another person to dinner on Christmas?"

Gwen's lips curved into a pleased smile. "Mom?

Are you kidding? Besides, I thought Molly was an invited guest.''

Nicky lunged into the front seat with wide, excited eyes. ''Molly? Are we gonna go get Molly?''

Beau turned so he could see Brianne. ''I'd sure like to.''

Brianne rolled her eyes, but her smile spoke a lot louder. ''Well, duh! It's about time. I can't *believe* how long it takes you to figure things out.''

Laughing, Beau turned up the radio and sang along. He didn't even care that he couldn't carry a tune and only knew half the words. A guy couldn't be perfect, after all.

''YES. YES, OF COURSE I'm still planning to be there.'' Working automatically, Molly saved the changes she'd made to the Ruby Lane Creations Web site and glanced at the clock above her desk. ''I said I'd be there at four, and I'm planning to spend the evening in the oncology ward. Did you need me earlier?''

''Four o'clock is fine,'' the hospital's public-relations coordinator assured her. ''It's just that we always get a number of volunteers on a day like today, but too many of them 'forget' and never show up. I'm just following up to make sure you're still planning to be here.''

Molly rubbed her eyes and rotated her head to work the kinks out of her neck. ''I meant to ask when I called the first time. Is there anything special I need to bring with me?''

''Just yourself. We have plenty of books and games. The important thing is to be here. You can imagine how difficult a day like today is on kids who are stuck in the hospital.''

"I'm sure it is."

"If you want to bring a friend, feel free. The more the merrier, I always say."

Molly stood and stretched. "I'll keep that in mind." In case she stumbled across some poor soul with nowhere else to be.

"Just park in the back near the west entrance," the coordinator went on in a voice full of holiday cheer. "Come up to the fourth floor and introduce yourself at the nurses' station. They'll take you where you need to go from there. And thank you, Molly. You won't regret doing this."

"I'm sure I won't." When she hung up, she wondered what the nurse would say if she knew how badly *Molly* needed this. She turned back to the computer, but the sound of voices singing "I'll Be Home for Christmas" caught her attention and kept her from immersing herself back in her work.

She ignored the twinge of melancholy and decided to try for a little Christmas spirit. She was tired of feeling sorry for herself, and she didn't want to show up at the hospital wearing a long face. That wouldn't be fair to the kids.

Going over to the window, she glanced outside, but she couldn't see anyone at the building across the way or even down the road. The voices grew louder. Closer. Almost as if they were coming from her own front porch. A sign, maybe, that she needed to pull out of her funk and get her head on straight.

One of the singers, a man, went wildly off-key and the group broke off in a fit of laughter that sounded too much like Beau and the kids. She must be going crazy.

Settling back in her chair, she reopened the file she'd

been working on, but before it could load completely, the doorbell chimed and the singing began again. Still off-key. Still painfully familiar.

She stood again and realized she was trembling. *Get a grip,* she told herself sternly. It couldn't possibly be them. But as she hurried through her silent apartment her heart lodged in her throat as if it thought there was a chance.

Over and over she told herself not to hope for the impossible, but none of her warnings did a bit of good. Tears blurred her eyes before she could get to the door, and she knew that even if a miracle hadn't happened— even if she spent Christmas alone—she was going to find a way back to Serenity before the new year.

Hoping desperately, she threw open the door. The three most beautiful faces in the world swam into focus, but she still didn't let herself believe. She could just be wishing so hard that she was turning complete strangers into the family her heart ached for.

The singing came to an abrupt halt and Nicky threw himself at her, grabbing her legs so tightly she nearly lost her balance. Brianne didn't move, but the hope on her face filled Molly's heart with love and happiness.

And Beau...

She couldn't see him because her vision was too blurred with tears, but he was there. She could tell, even though she couldn't see his face. She just knew that she was lost. Or maybe she'd been found.

"Molly."

She couldn't breathe. She couldn't speak. She held Nicky's head against her and let the love she'd been hiding from for so long swell within her. She could hear Cassandra's words playing softly in the back of her mind. They were family. She knew it as certainly as she knew her name. It didn't matter how they got that way.

Dashing tears from her eyes, she blinked at Beau. She wanted to tell him…everything. All the things she'd realized about home and family and love. All the things she'd spent so many years running away from. All the things she was finally ready to turn around and embrace.

He came toward her and took her hand. His voice was gentle, but that sense of humor she loved so much was front and center. "Aw, shoot, kids. She's crying! And I was hoping she'd be *glad* to see us."

Molly laughed through her tears, but his little joke was just what she needed to pull herself together. "You're really here? I can't believe it. You're really and truly here? But how…? Did you drive? Fly? How did you manage this?"

"You're forgetting I have friends in high places. Of course, even *they* can't swing airline tickets on Christmas Eve, so we've been driving all night. But it all worked out. I called Heather and let her know we were coming. I offered to let her meet us here if she wanted to, and she agreed. I was hoping maybe you'd let me hang around while she and the kids spend a few hours together."

"She's coming here?"

"Well, not *here*. I'm meeting her at a motel in town. I'd have waited until we got home, but I thought neutral territory might be a good thing—and besides, I didn't know how long it would take to convince you to talk to me again."

"Apparently not long," Molly said with a laugh. She reached for Brianne and pulled her into a hug. The girl melted against her and wrapped her arms around her. Molly knew they'd bridged the final gap.

Beau leaned against one wall and crossed one foot over the other, whistling softly and looking around with exaggerated patience. After a minute he leaned up and tapped Brianne's shoulder. "You'll let me know when it's my turn?"

"Oh, Daddy." Brianne sniffed loudly and loosened her grip on Molly, but she grinned and the light in her eyes was so beautiful it was all Molly could do to keep from crying again. "He's got something he wants to ask you," she whispered to Molly.

"Oh?"

Beau straightened slowly. "So...what are your plans for the rest of the day?"

She laughed in disbelief. "Nothing set in stone, except that I promised to read to some kids at the children's hospital."

"Need some help?"

"That would be nice."

He put one hand in the pocket of his coat and took Molly's hand with the other. But there he stopped and sent a pointed look in Nicky's direction. The boy drew out a sprig of what must have been mistletoe and stood on his toes, trying to hold it over Molly's head.

Molly bit back a smile, but the joy surging through her was so complete it was almost impossible to maintain a serious expression. After his first question, she was prepared for almost anything.

He dropped to one knee and looked up at her. "And what are your plans for the rest of your life?"

"Nothing set in stone."

He grinned and her heart melted. "I've been a fool," he said. "Everybody I know has been telling me so since you left Serenity, but I knew it all the time. I don't have much to offer. Just one old farmhouse, a cabin to run your business out of, two great kids…and me." He held out a small black box and his eyes locked on hers. "I love you, Molly. The kids love you. We want you to come back."

Her heart was so full it hurt. "I love you, too. All of you."

Nicky nearly dropped his mistletoe. "Then you'll come home?"

Brianne elbowed him before Molly could answer. "Let Dad ask her, you dweeb."

Molly was afraid her heart would burst. "Yes, of course I'll come back."

Nicky let out a whoop and Brianne nudged Beau with her knee. "You're supposed to kiss her, Dad."

Casting a look of mock exasperation at his daughter, Beau got to his feet and drew her close. "All this help… Maybe I should have come alone, but I wanted to stack the deck in my favor." He kissed her, and the joy in Molly's heart filled her entire soul. His lips were warm and his breath slightly minty. He was familiar and exciting at the same time, and she hoped she'd never lose this feeling.

Too soon he drew away and gazed down at her, love in his eyes. "Marry me. Please. Come home where you belong."

"Yes," she whispered, and the last remaining empty space in her heart filled. "Let's go home."

Make your Christmas wish list – and check it twice!

Watch out for these very special holiday stories – all featuring the incomparable charm and romance of the Christmas season.

By Jasmine Cresswell, Tara Taylor
Quinn and Kate Hoffmann
On sale 21st October 2005

By Lynnette Kent and
Sherry Lewis
On sale 21st October 2005

By Lucy Monroe and
Louise Allen
On sale 4th November 2005

By Heather Graham,
Lindsay McKenna, Marilyn
Pappano and Annette Broadrick
On sale 18th November 2005

By Marion Lennox, Josie Metcalfe
and Kate Hardy
On sale 2nd December 2005

By Margaret Moore, Terri Brisbin
and Gail Ranstrom
On sale 2nd December 2005

By Lisa Jackson, Barbara Boswell
and Linda Turner
On sale 18th November 2005

Celebrate the charm of Christmases past in three new heartwarming holiday tales!

COMFORT AND JOY by Margaret Moore
1860 Llanwyllan, Wales

After a terrible accident, Griffin Branwynne gives up on the joys of Christmas—until the indomitable Gwendolyn Davies arrives on his doorstep and turns his world upside-down. Can the earl resist a woman who won't take no for an answer?

LOVE AT FIRST STEP by Terri Brisbin
1199 England

While visiting friends in England for the holidays, Lord Gavin MacLeod casts his eye upon the mysterious Elizabeth. She is more noble beauty than serving wench, and Gavin vows to uncover her past—at any cost!

A CHRISTMAS SECRET by Gail Ranstrom
1819 Oxfordshire, England

Miss Charity Wardlow expects a marriage proposal from her intended while attending a Christmas wedding. But when Sir Andrew MacGregor arrives at the manor, Charity realises that she prefers this Scotsman with the sensual smile…

On sale 2nd December 2005

1105/02 V2

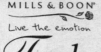

MILLS & BOON®

Live the emotion

Tender
romance™

A MOST SUITABLE WIFE *by Jessica Steele*

Taye Trafford needs someone to share her flat – and the bills
– fast! So, when Magnus Ashthorpe turns up, Taye offers him
the room, not knowing he actually has an entirely different
reason for living there: because he believes Taye is the mistress
who has caused his sister's heartbreak!

IN THE ARMS OF THE SHEIKH *by Sophie Weston*

Natasha Lambert is horrified by what she must wear as her
best friend's bridesmaid! Worse, the best man is Kazim al
Saraq – an infuriatingly charming sheikh with a dazzling wit
and an old-fashioned take on romance. He's determined to win
Natasha's heart – and she's terrified he might succeed…!

THE MARRIAGE MIRACLE *by Liz Fielding*

An accident three years ago has left Matilda Lang in a
wheelchair, and hotshot New York banker Sebastian Wolseley
is the man who can make – or break – her heart. It would
take a miracle for Matty to risk her heart after what she's been
through, but Sebastian knows he can help her…

ORDINARY GIRL, SOCIETY GROOM
by Natasha Oakley

Eloise Lawson has finally found the family she's never known.
But, cast adrift in their high society world, she can only depend
on one person: broodingly handsome Jeremy Norland. But
if she falls in love with him she could lose everything. Will
Eloise have the courage to risk all?

On sale 2nd December 2005

*Available at most branches of WHSmith, Tesco, ASDA,
Borders, Eason, Sainsbury's and most bookshops*

Visit www.millsandboon.co.uk

1105/03a V2

MILLS & BOON®

Live the emotion

Medical
romance™

GIFT OF A FAMILY by Sarah Morgan

A&E consultant Josh Sullivan is happily single – and despite many women's attempts he intends to stay that way! Single mum Kat O'Brien would usually be strictly off-limits – except he can't get the stunning doctor off his mind. But will Kat ever believe he can offer them a future?

The Cornish Consultants: Dedicated doctors by day... playboy lovers by night!

CHRISTMAS ON THE CHILDREN'S WARD
by Carol Marinelli

Nurse Eden Hadley hopes for two things this Christmas: that the little orphaned boy on the children's ward can have one real family Christmas, and that consultant Nick Watson will notice her again – and remember what they once had. It's up to Nick to make both her wishes come true...

THE LIFE SAVER by Lilian Darcy

Gorgeous Dr Ripley Taylor is a life saver – not just a doctor! He saved fellow GP Jo Middleton by helping her out of a king-size rut and revitalising her love-life! Now that Rip is single their attraction is snowballing into a passionate affair. Until Rip's ex-wife appears on the scene...!

On sale 2nd December 2005

Available at most branches of WHSmith, Tesco, ASDA, Borders, Eason, Sainsbury's and most bookshops

Visit www.millsandboon.co.uk

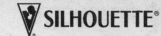

SILHOUETTE®

SPECIAL EDITION™

CARRERA'S BRIDE by Diana Palmer

Texan Lovers

While on a tropical island getaway Delia Mason was swept up in a tidal wave of trouble and owed her rescue to notorious casino tycoon Marcus Carrera. This mystery man moved in dangerous circles, but would he risk it all to take Delia as his beloved bride?

THE MD'S SURPRISE FAMILY
by Marie Ferrarella

The Bachelors of Blair Memorial

A handsome neurosurgeon comes highly recommended to a lonely woman looking for someone to save her little brother. Could he be a healer of bodies *and* of hearts?

A TYCOON IN TEXAS by Crystal Green

Fortune's Heirs: Reunion

Business whiz Christina Mendoza started a terrific new job and wasn't prepared for the ultimate distraction—her new boss. Where would one forbidden night of passion lead?

Don't miss out!
On sale from 18th November 2005

1105/23a V2

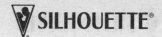 **SILHOUETTE**® 1105/23b V2

SPECIAL EDITION™

HIS FAMILY by Muriel Jensen

The Abbotts

China Grant and Campbell Abbott clashed like cat and dog, but once DNA tests proved they weren't relatives, they were fighting something else—an irresistible attraction!

NANNY IN HIDING by Patricia Kay

The Hathaways

Amy Jordan was making a new life for her daughter, so when the town's most eligible single father gave her a job as a live-in nanny to his two girls, she was thrilled; but her feelings for the sexy widower threatened to blow her cover.

THE AMBASSADOR'S VOW
by Barbara Gale

Ten years after a passionate affair, their child was in danger and the single mum needed help only the father of her child could provide. As passions rekindle and secrets are revealed, would they be tempted to try again?

Don't miss out!
On sale from 18th November 2005

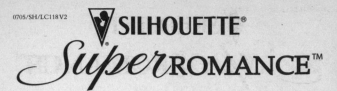

SILHOUETTE®
Super ROMANCE™

proudly presents
a brand-new series from talented new author

LINDA BARRETT

Pilgrim COVE

Sea View House in Pilgrim Cove offers its
residents the sea, the sun, the sound of the
surf and the call of the gulls.
But sometimes serenity is only an illusion…

THE HOUSE ON THE BEACH
July 2005

NO ORDINARY SUMMER
August 2005

RELUCTANT HOUSEMATES
December 2005

THE DAUGHTER HE NEVER KNEW
January 2006

SILHOUETTE®
Super ROMANCE™

A new six-book series from Silhouette Superromance

Enchantment, New Mexico, is home to The Birth Place, a maternity clinic run by the formidable Lydia Kane. The clinic was started years ago – to make sure the people of this secluded mountain town had a safe place to deliver their babies.

But some births are shrouded in secrecy. What happens when those secrets return to haunt The Birth Place?

August 2005
Enchanting Baby *by Darlene Graham*

September 2005
Sanctuary *by Brenda Novak*

October 2005
Christmas at Shadow Creek *by Roxanne Rustand*

November 2005
Leaving Enchantment *by CJ Carmichael*

December 2005
The Homecoming Baby *by Kathleen O'Brien*

January 2006
The Midwife and the Lawman *by Marisa Carroll*

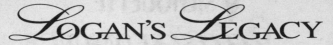

LOGAN'S LEGACY

*Because birthright has its privileges and
family ties run deep*

SILHOUETTE®
Sensation™

is proud to present
an exciting new trilogy from popular author

RaeAnne Thayne

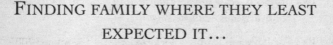

THE SEARCHERS

FINDING FAMILY WHERE THEY LEAST EXPECTED IT...

Nowhere To Hide
June 2005

Nothing To Lose
July 2005

Never Too late
January 2006

Visit our website at www.silhouette.co.uk